Wicked women and red-hot men...

Wild seduction leading to wild sex...

These women know what they want...

The

wicked

Collection

Three complete novels
from three sensational authors

**Joanne Rock, Heidi Betts
and Dorien Kelly**

Coming soon

The

innocence

Collection

Innocent virgins seduced by powerful men

D0488728

Joanne Rock writes sexy contemporary romances and medieval historicals that have been reprinted in twenty-two countries and translated into sixteen languages. A former teacher and public relations coordinator, she has a Master's in English from the University of Louisville and started writing when she became a stay-at-home mum, deceiving herself that she'd have more time. Twenty books and three kids later, she lives with her husband and sons in the Adirondacks, committed to mass chaos and happily-ever-afters.

Don't miss Joanne Rock's new novel,
*Up All Night***, available in January 2007,**
only from Mills & Boon® Blaze™.

Heidi Betts began her love affair with the romance genre in school and it didn't take long for her to decide that she wanted to write a few romances of her own. When she isn't writing, Heidi can often be found reading or watching television with a cat (or two) curled up on her lap. She lives in Central Pennsylvania with her family and pets.

Don't miss Heidi Betts' new novel,
*Seven-Year Seduction***, available with Katherine Garbera's** *Their Million-Dollar Night***, in February 2007, only from Silhouette® Desire™.**

Dorien Kelly wanted to be a writer from an early age. She has a degree in English and after attending law school was a successful lawyer for almost ten years. Her real love was romance novels and all of her spare time was spent reading them. But with a hectic schedule of a sixty-hour-a-week job and raising three children, she decided give up being a lawyer and start writing full time to pursue her passion.

The

Wicked
Collection

WILD AND WICKED

by
Joanne Rock

BLAME IT ON THE BLACKOUT

by
Heidi Betts

TEMPTING TROUBLE

by
Dorien Kelly

M&B

*M&B™ and M&B™ with the Rose Device
are trademarks of the publisher.*

*First published in Great Britain 2007
by Harlequin Mills & Boon Limited, Eton House,
18-24 Paradise Road, Richmond, Surrey TW9 1SR*

THE WICKED COLLECTION
© by Harlequin Books S.A. 2007

Wild and Wicked, Blame It On The Blackout and *Tempting Trouble*
were first published in Great Britain in separate, single volumes.

Wild and Wicked © Joanne Rock 2003
Blame It on the Blackout © Heidi Betts 2005
Tempting Trouble © Dorien Kelly 2005

*ISBN 13: 978 0 263 85544 9
ISBN 10: 0 263 85544 9*

10-0107

*Printed and bound in Spain
by Litografía Rosés S.A., Barcelona*

WILD AND WICKED

by
Joanne Rock

In loving memory of my friend and long-ago room-mate Rebecca Schaffer, who had only just begun to show the world how brightly she could shine. Her talent and energy inspire me still.

1

"KYRA!" JESSE CHANDLER shouted to his business partner as he strode into the barn housing the offices of Crooked Branch Horse Farms. He juggled purchases from the tack shop until he reached a sawhorse table where he could set them down. "I've got all the leather you wanted. Saddles and bridles, riding gloves and a dominatrix outfit—oh, wait. That last one wasn't a business purchase."

He sorted through the new supplies in the converted old building Kyra used strictly for storage and office space. The horses Kyra bred and trained lived in much more modern quarters behind this barn.

Removing price tags and testing the leather of the new stock, Jesse waited for his best friend and colleague to appear. He'd never made her blush in over ten years of trying, but hope sprang eternal. No matter that Kyra Stafford was the one woman in Citrus County he'd never hit on, he still loved to make her laugh.

"Perfect," came a feminine purr from over his left shoulder—far closer than he'd anticipated. "I think you need an assertive woman to keep you in line, Jesse Chandler."

For about two seconds, he reacted to the sultry promise he must have imagined behind the words.

Awareness fired through him, heated his insides despite the breeze drifting in the wide-open barn doors. The Gulf of Mexico rested a mere thousand acres away to border the northwest corner of the state-of-the-art Florida horse farm and training facility. Surely the gentle wind off the water should have helped him keep cool in February.

But then Kyra stepped around him to stand by his side and look over the new tack, her long blond hair grazing his arm. Smart, sensible Kyra Stafford who had never flirted with him for so much as five seconds.

What the hell was the matter with him?

Shaking off an absurd sense of attraction he'd never felt for his best friend before, Jesse attributed the *Twilight Zone* moment to too many nights alone. He definitely needed to remedy that situation this weekend.

"Funny, I don't see any dominatrix garb here." Kyra glanced up at him with her bright blue eyes. Innocent blue eyes, damn it. And smiled. "Be careful what you wish for, Jesse."

From any other woman, Jesse would have pegged that remark for blatant enticement. But he was obviously going through major sensual deprivation if he was hearing come-ons in Kyra's speech.

Hell yeah, he'd be more careful.

Clearing his throat, he decided maybe they were just both getting too old for the game of trying to make Kyra blush. "Guess I left the spiked collar at the store." He started hanging bridles on the wall, determined to make tracks between him and this ill-advised conversation. "That's okay. I don't go for the hardcore type anyway."

"Seems like you're not going for any type lately," Kyra observed, tossing her hair over her shoulder as she leaned a blue jean-clad hip into the sawhorse table. At twenty-four, she looked sort of like *Buffy the Vampire Slayer* meets *Bonanza*—a petite blonde in dusty cowboy boots with enough determination and drive to move mountains, or, more often, stubborn horses. "Is southern Florida's most notorious bad boy finally mellowing?"

Allowing a saddle created for one of their new ponies to slide back to the plywood with a thunk, Jesse turned to face the woman who knew him best. The woman whose question mirrored his own recent fear.

"You know I couldn't mellow if I tried." Not that he would try. He was too content with bachelorhood, even though his last girlfriend was sticking to him like glue despite his best efforts to move on. He needed to show Greta he wasn't the forever-after—or even a three-date—kind of guy.

"Why? Because there'd be ten women lined up in Victoria's Secret lingerie and armed with apple pies if they knew you were thinking about settling down?"

She tried on a pair of fawn-colored riding gloves and stared at her hand encased in suede.

Jesse grinned. "As if that would be such a hardship."

She cocked an eyebrow at him in one of Kyra's classic don't-bullshit-me looks.

He shrugged. "I don't know what's up. I've been putting in a lot of hours making final preparations around the Crooked Branch before I turn my attention to my custom homes business. Maybe I've just been working too hard lately."

He hated leaving Kyra to run the business all by herself, but that had been her stipulation from the moment they'd went in on the operation together. She'd vowed to buy back his substantial share of the farm once she'd made it a success.

And damned if she wasn't whooping butt on that promise already. As soon as she clinched one more horse sale, she'd own the controlling share of the business.

The farm had been great part-time work for Jesse in the years he'd played minor league baseball for kicks. But now that he was closing in on thirty, he was mentally ready to hang his own shingle for a custom home-building business and let Kyra go her own way with the Crooked Branch. His older brother had told Jesse last spring that he would never be able to still his wandering feet, but Jesse disagreed.

He might not be able to commit to any one woman, but he could commit to a place, damn it. Not only was he putting down roots in Citrus County, he was cementing his ties to the area by starting his own business here.

Still, he worried a little about leaving Kyra to her own devices at the training facility. Running a horse-boarding-and-breeding business wasn't exactly a cushy way of life and as the date for him to bow out approached, Jesse couldn't help thinking about all the tough jobs that Kyra would be left with to handle solo.

The physically demanding aspects of handling stubborn horses. The chauvinistic attitudes of some of the owners.

He hated the thought of anyone ever giving her a hard time.

She eyed him with quiet patience, reminding him why she was so damn good at working with antsy horses. "Are you sure you're working, Jesse, or are you maybe overcompensating for leaving in two weeks? No offense, but this is more tack than we'll need in two lifetimes." She studied him in that open, no-holds-barred manner that had made him trust her from the moment they met. "Are you just using the excuse of work to hide out from some overeager female of the week?"

Jesse shifted his weight from one foot to the other. Caught.

Why in the hell had he thought he might be able to hide anything from this woman? Kyra's eyes might be innocent, but they were wise.

Jesse shoved the stack of too many gloves to the back of the sawhorse table. "Honestly, I'm having a little trouble with Greta lately. She looks at me and sees picket fences no matter how much I avoid her."

He'd met the German model in Miami Beach last fall and they'd spent a crazy few days locked in her condo overlooking the water.

Between Greta's flashy lifestyle and jet-set friends, Jesse had assumed she wanted the same things from their time together as he did—simple, basic things like mind-blowing sex and a few hours to forget life wasn't as perfect as they pretended.

But ever since then, Greta had called him on and off, even going so far as to show up on his doorstep over the holidays to see if he wanted company.

"She thinks you're marriage material?" Kyra's skeptical tone suggested a woman could be committed for harboring those kinds of thoughts.

"Go figure. But she's damned persistent. And you know how I hate to hurt people." One of the foremost reasons he avoided relationships like the plague was to ensure he never hurt anybody. He'd learned that lesson early in life when his father had torn Jesse's whole family apart with infidelities until he walked out on his wife and kids for good.

Too bad Jesse's tact of keeping things light with Greta had bitten him in the ass this time.

"You need a different kind of woman." Kyra sidled closer.

Or was that his imagination?

"Damn straight I do." He folded his arms across his chest, unwilling to take any chances with his over-active libido today. The last thing he needed was any freaky twinge of attraction to Kyra again.

"A woman who wants the same things from a relationship you do." Her voice took on a husky quality, reminding him of what it was like to trade pillow confidences with floral-scented females in the dark.

Not females like Kyra, of course.

He cleared his throat.

"That's how I'm going to approach things from now on." Jesse turned back to the mountain of leather goods on the plywood table and mentally started dialing numbers from his address book. A night with Lolita Banker would satisfy every stray sexual urge he'd had today, and then some.

"Then why don't you let me help?" Kyra's hand snaked over to his, gently restraining him from shuffling around the new bridles. "I know exactly what you want."

Damnation. Her touch sizzled through him even as her words called to mind sensual visions. The arch of a woman's back, the pink flush of feminine skin, the sweet sighs of fulfillment as...

Jesse's gaze slid from Kyra to the mound of fresh hay that waited not ten yards away.

Holy freaking hell.

He withdrew his hand from her light touch as if burned. Then again, maybe he had been. At the very least, his brain circuits had obviously fried because there was no way in hell she'd meant anything remotely sexual.

Determined to escape that provocative vision forever, Jesse closed his eyes and clutched the new saddle in front of him like a shield. Maybe his mind was playing tricks on him because he wouldn't be seeing Kyra much once he started his new business.

"Great idea." He forced the words past dry lips, trying like hell to remember the color of Lolita's hair, the shape of her mouth, anything. "Let's grab a beer after work and you can help me figure out how to let Greta down easy. You know somebody to hook her up with?"

He backed toward the barn doors, clutching the saddle in a death grip. Perhaps it was a good thing he'd be leaving the Crooked Branch in two weeks after all. "Besides, Lolita Banker's waitressing at the bar on Indian Rocks Beach. Maybe I just need to meet someone else to help me—" *Forget all about seducing my best friend?* "Get my head on straight again."

Turning away from those vivid blue eyes and poured-into-denim body, Jesse shouted over his shoulder. "Happy hour starts at six."

HAPPY HOUR?

Why didn't they call it something more apt like frustrated-as-hell hour?

Kyra fumed as she watched Jesse's motorcycle kick up gravel on his way out of the driveway—as if he couldn't put enough distance between him and her lame attempt at seduction.

She'd had a thing for Jesse from the first time they'd met. His perpetually too-long hair, dark eyes and prominent cheekbones gave him a dangerous look that hinted of long-forgotten Seminole heritage. He wore one gold stud in his ear, which, according to high school legend, he'd had ever since his tenth-grade girlfriend convinced him they should pierce a body part together. Jesse had kept the stud long after the girl.

Kyra had met him right after the ear-piercing. She'd caught him sneaking out one of her father's horses at night to indulge in wild rides. Eventually, she'd discovered his midnight trips were more about escape than about raising hell. But that knowledge never altered her vision of Jesse Chandler as a danger-loving thrill seeker.

She'd been all of ten years old at the time and far too starry-eyed with Jesse to spill his secret to her manic-depressive dad. She'd started leaving Buster saddled for Jesse so he wouldn't break his neck riding bareback.

Every morning, Buster would be groomed and locked in his stall, his tack neatly hung on the wall.

Their friendship had cemented that summer, despite the five years difference between them. Their paths rarely crossed in the school system, but Kyra heard all the rumors about him and collected Jesse folklore the way some girls collected scrapbooks of their favorite rock stars. She'd outgrown that infatuation with him, but the man still had the power to dazzle her. To make her wonder…

Unwilling to put her heart on the line, she'd ignored the stray longings for her best friend over the years, even going so far as to convince herself they could operate a business together.

Crooked Branch Farms was now one of the most

prestigious breeding and training facilities in southern Florida, but all of Kyra's hard work and new success still hadn't fulfilled the ache within her that had started one sultry summer night fourteen years ago. In fact, now her workplace was tainted with longing for Jesse, ensuring she could never fully escape from thoughts of him.

Ever the practical thinker, Kyra had devised a two-prong plan to solve the problem. First, she was working her way toward taking over the controlling half of the business. If she could sell one more horse this year, that goal would be attainable and she'd be able to run the Crooked Branch independently.

Part two of her plan was much more fun. She wanted to seduce Jesse and experience the mythical sexual prowess of a man who'd long inhabited her dreams.

She knew he would never settle down. Yet that didn't make her want him any less. In some ways, it made him a safe—temporary—choice for her wary heart.

If he ever noticed she wasn't sporting pigtails anymore.

Sighing, Kyra stalked back to her office and flung herself onto the futon across from her bookshelves. As she idly sifted through a stack of paperwork, she admitted to herself today's attempt to make Jesse see her as a woman had been an unmitigated flop. It's not like she wanted picket fences either. She simply wanted a night to act out her longtime fantasy before he left their business for good.

So there wasn't a chance she'd facilitate his seduction of Lolita Banker at the Indian Rocks Beach bar. For all Kyra cared, he could just twist in the wind while Greta the German Wonder-bod made him feel guilty about not playing house with her.

And in the meantime, Kyra would turn up the heat on her own seductive plans—just as soon as she figured out what they were. Heaven knew suggestive talk wasn't the key according to her experience with him today.

How could a man be so blind?

She needed a more fast-acting approach, a surefire way to get his attention.

Just then a flyer caught her eye from her pile of paperwork. A pamphlet advertising Tampa Bay's annual Gasparilla festival. This year the mock pirate invasion of the city was sponsored by a company Jesse's older brother owned.

Her eyes scanned the paper, slowing over a phrase that suggested the festival was hiring a handful of actors to stage strictly-in-fun kidnappings of partygoers. Jesse's brother Seth had hand-scrawled a note across the paper asking Jesse to consider playing one of the buccaneers himself, in fact.

Kyra knew he had nixed the request pleading that he needed to indulge in some R & R and just enjoy the festival before his home-building gig kicked into high gear in another two weeks. She also knew that probably meant he would be searching for a flavor-of-the-week woman at Gasparilla. Especially since his usual method of telling a woman they were through was insinuating himself in a new five-day relationship.

All of which put Jesse at the festival while leaving one buccaneer slot still vacant.

She'd wanted a way to make Jesse Chandler see her as a woman hadn't she? She had the feeling an old-fashioned corset and fishnet stockings would do the trick. So what if pirates were usually peg-legged men dressed in rags with bad teeth?

Kyra would improvise.

And abduct the hottest man in Tampa Bay for a night he wouldn't forget.

THREE DAYS LATER, Kyra stood on the deck of the famed *Jose Gaspar* pirate boat. As the warm February breeze lifted her hair from her neck, she tugged the strings on her black leather corset a little tighter and more breasts magically appeared.

The modern day push-up bra didn't have anything on eighteenth-century technology.

Studying her reflection in the blunted steel of a costume dagger given to her by an overzealous event stylist on board the boat, Kyra thought she looked as close to a sexpot as she was possibly capable. Sure she'd never have the perfect figure of Greta the German Wonder-bod, but by a miracle of her black leather getup, she had more curves than ever before.

No matter that any spare ounce of flesh on her rib cage had been squeezed northward in order to achieve the effect. For today at least, she looked downright voluptuous.

Kyra shoved her dagger into a loop on her black cargo miniskirt. Her leather corset just reached the waist of the skirt while a gauzy, low-cut blouse skimmed her breasts underneath the leather. She hadn't bothered to wear a bra for the event given the old-fashioned lace-up garment currently holding her breathless.

She wouldn't lack for support, but if the February Gulf breeze turned cold, she'd probably be showing a little more than she'd like through the white cotton blouse. Who'd have thought the wardrobe they'd given her would be so treacherously thin?

Still, Kyra was pleased she'd taken the plunge and committed herself to today's cause. After years of near invisibility around Jesse, she needed something dramatic to make him notice her as a woman.

How hard could it be to sway him once he noticed her in *that* way?

As the bellow of mock cannons echoed in her ears, Kyra peered across the ship deck filled to overflowing with local luminaries dressed as pirates and waved to Jesse's scowling older brother, Seth. A self-made millionaire, Seth Chandler had always enjoyed a more low-profile approach to life than Jesse. Yet Seth had been forced to don an eye patch today when the lead buccaneer had quit an hour before the *Jose Gaspar* set sail.

A role he didn't seem to be enjoying if his surly expression was any indication.

The dull roar of the crowd standing onshore near Tampa Bay's convention center jerked her thoughts from Seth back to the present. Leaning on the rail surrounding the main deck, Kyra squinted out across the water in the hope of finding her quarry.

A swirl of purple, yellow and green gleamed back at her. The Gasparilla event shared several things in common with New Orleans's Mardi Gras—its signature colors, a parade organized by Krewes that tossed beads and other souvenirs to attendees and a serious party attitude.

But the resemblance ended there. Gasparilla celebrated a distinctly Floridian heritage with its nod to a famous pirate and the events on the water. As the 165-foot boat sailed toward shore, a flotilla of over two hundred smaller watercraft followed in its wake.

And of course, Mardi Gras didn't present the opportunities for a friendly kidnapping that Gasparilla offered for the first time this year. Anticipation tingled through Kyra as her chance to open Jesse's eyes drew near.

Just as they dropped anchor, she spotted him.

All six foot two of rangy muscle and masculine grace talking animatedly with friends. Or maybe some new conquest. Kyra couldn't fully see who he was speaking to through the crush. Funny how her feminine radar had been able to track *him* without any problem, though.

She'd known he would be here because Seth had asked him to drop off his boat at the festival today. Jesse had mentioned that he was looking forward to spending most of the day in downtown Tampa—after the invasion of the city there was a parade, followed by a street festival into the night.

A night Kyra intended to claim for her own.

Before she could secure a solid plan for making her way through the throng to reach Jesse, Seth swung out over the mass of partygoers, signaling the start of the pirate invasion. Chaos ensued on the boat and off as buccaneers leaped, swung or ran off the *Jose Gaspar* to greet attendees and abduct a few innocent bystanders.

Born athletic and toned from days on horseback, Kyra didn't flinch at the idea of climbing a rope and flinging herself out into the mob. She was a little surprised at the substantial chorus of male appreciation as she did so, however. Apparently her fishnet stockings and brand-new cleavage invited attention because she was seriously ogled—and groped—for the first time in her life.

"Take me, honey!" a partygoer shouted as he stumbled into her path. Wearing a crooked three-cornered hat emblazoned with a Jolly Roger and a Metallica T-shirt, the guy sloshed beer over the rim of his plastic cup onto the toe of her lace-up black boots.

Kyra righted his precarious cup and sidled past him, her gaze scanning the crowd for Jesse. She wasn't so desperate for attention that she'd settle for the lecherous stare of a drunken stranger.

Unfortunately, her corset attracted plenty of the wrong kind of attention.

She smacked away a hand that brushed along her thigh, wishing she'd brought along a riding crop for crowd control. Who'd have thought a glorified push-up bra could turn so many heads?

Desperate to find the only man whose attention she really cared about, Kyra caught sight of him leaning into the shade of a palm tree planted in between the concrete slabs of sidewalk some fifteen yards away. Focused on her muscle-bound goal, she stepped around a strolling hot-pretzel vendor and a mother clutching the hands of toddler twins wearing eye patches.

Only then did she spy Jesse's companion. Greta the German Wonder-bod giggled relentlessly at every word out of his mouth, her perfect figure looking svelte and toned in yellow shorts that barely covered her ridiculously tiny butt. A white T-shirt spelled out Monaco in matching sunny yellow letters.

Kyra knew damn well Greta didn't need the aid of a corset to give her those amazing curves. The German model had an effortless beauty that wouldn't desert her when the festival was over. Even if she made a living slinging hay in blue jeans.

The ache of second-guessing tightened in Kyra's chest. Would it be cruel to pull Jesse away if he would honestly rather patch things up with Greta? God knows, it looked like he was enjoying himself, his dark eyes alight with good humor and his lone dimple flashing in his left cheek.

But then again, Jesse had a way of making any woman feel like she was the center of his universe even as he plotted how to dance around any sort of commitment. His elusiveness was part of his charm.

And hadn't he just confided to Kyra three days ago that Greta wanted much more than he could provide?

Refusing to allow a little feminine insecurity to thwart her plan, Kyra charged toward the couple. No way would Jesse have invited Greta here today if he was worried that she was taking things too seriously. Greta was probably just chasing him the same way so many women did.

She pulled herself up short.

The way Kyra was chasing him for the first time in her life.

But at least Kyra knew what would come out of a relationship with her best friend. A few nights of amazing pleasure so she could get over her age-old crush on him and they would go back to being strictly friends.

Committed to her plan, Kyra withdrew a silk scarf from the pocket of her cargo skirt and wrapped one end of the filmy material around each of her hands.

She didn't have the option of carrying off Jesse over one shoulder the way a guy pirate might kidnap his wench of choice. Therefore, she had to resort to more underhanded means of abduction.

Edging up behind Jesse, she was neatly hidden from Greta's view by his broad back. A white tank shirt bearing the name of a horse show she'd competed in long ago exposed his tanned shoulders and strong arms. Low slung black shorts hugged his hips and a very fine…back view.

A shiver of excitement jolted through her as she neared him, along with a slight tremor of nerves.

Before she could change her mind, Kyra looped her pink silk scarf over his head to cover his eyes. In a flash, she pressed herself to his warm back to whisper in his ear.

''Don't fight it, hotshot. Consider yourself a pirate prisoner.'' The words tripped off her tongue in a breathy rush as her body reacted to his with spontaneous heat. ''For today, you're all mine.''

2

JESSE RECOGNIZED the silky voice whispering into his ear. Yet he couldn't merge his image of practical Kyra Stafford with the decidedly feminine curves pressed against his back. Or the exotically scented scarf blindfolding him into a world of pure sensation.

A world where it was getting mighty damn difficult to remember why he and Kyra had always maintained a strictly platonic relationship.

For a moment, the roar of the overcrowded street faded from his hearing. The only sound penetrating his brain was the soft huff of breath in his ear as his captor demanded compliance.

Before his hormones recovered enough to reply, he could hear Greta start squawking a few feet in front of him.

"Excuse me?" Her words dripped sarcasm like a Popsicle in July. "I came here with this man. You can't just—"

"Well it looks like you won't be leaving with him," Kyra retorted from behind him, her voice all the more familiar now that it was lifted in normal conversation. "A Gasparilla pirate doesn't exactly need to ask your permission."

Maybe Kyra was only trying to rescue him from Greta today. A welcome intervention given that Jesse hadn't brought Greta with him and had been trying his best to avoid her. Still, she'd managed to track him down in a crowd of a hundred thousand people with unerring instincts.

She'd have him chained to her side on the first boat back to Berlin if he wasn't careful.

He held both hands up, resigned to whatever scheme Kyra had in the works. He just hoped she eased away from him soon, before his body started reacting publicly to those breasts against his spine. "Sounds like I have no choice but to surrender."

Greta's spluttered indignation took a back seat to Kyra's seductive whisper.

"Excellent decision," she breathed in his ear, steering him through the crowd and away from Greta with slow steps. "You are wise to come along quietly."

Each stride brushed her body against his, making him keenly aware she wore a blouse with no bra to speak of underneath. Those awesome C-cups couldn't belong to Kyra. Could they?

She was holding him captive wearing some kind of laced leather outfit that bit into his back even while it thrust her breasts forward in luscious offering, sort of like a—

Holy freaking hell. Maybe after all his lip about buying a dominatrix outfit, she'd decided to call his bluff.

Raw lust ripped through him with a vengeance. He

stopped dead in his tracks and twisted around to face her, whipping off the scarf with an impatient hand. The sight that greeted his eyes was better than a dominatrix outfit.

No, make that worse. He wasn't supposed to be licking his chops over his best friend, of all people.

She was dressed as a pirate. Not any normal pirate with a bandanna and a blackened tooth, though. More like the kind of lush X-rated lady pirate you'd expect to find in some half-baked adult film called *Blow the Man Down.*

His eyes did a slow ride over her barely there blouse partially covered by the leather corset he'd felt earlier. The garment pushed her breasts up and out and straight into any man's view, the tops of that creamy white flesh exposed while the rest was only marginally hidden beneath thin cotton.

Where had those amazing breasts come from? Was he that blind that he'd never noticed them underneath the men's T-shirts she normally favored? And he'd definitely never noticed her legs before. At least not like this, he hadn't. Somehow he had overlooked her lightly muscled thighs and long, lean calves in the jeans she always wore when she worked with the horses.

But her abbrieviated black skirt and fishnet stockings practically put a neon sign on those gams and screamed, Look At Me!

And was he ever looking.

Jesse was carefully scrutinizing every inch of her right down to her high-heeled lace-up boots when she cupped one hand under his chin and forced his gaze back up to her face.

Too bad he couldn't make visual contact with her. He'd obviously popped an eyeball along the way.

"What's the verdict, matey? You like what you see?" She cocked one hand on her hip and did a little shimmy that left him gasping for a breath.

An appreciative whistle emanated from somewhere nearby. Although they'd moved out of the densest part of the crowd, they were still surrounded by enthusiastic festival attendees draped in colorful beads and drinking beer from plastic cups in the shape of old-fashioned steins.

And if Jesse found out who the hell was whistling at Kyra he'd sew the guy's lips together.

Jamming her silk scarf into the pocket of his shorts, he tucked Kyra under one arm and hauled her even farther from the masses. "Are you insane?" he hissed, wishing he could have thought of another way to get her out of there besides touching her. His hand burned where it rested on one slim but perfectly curved hip. "There are a bunch of guys halfway to drunk and slobbering in that crowd. You're a walking target for trouble in that outfit."

She shoved away from him as they rounded the corner of the Tampa Convention Center away from the water and the excitement of the pirate invasion. "The only one who seems to be targeting me for trouble is you, Chandler. Are you halfway to drunk and slobbering?"

Drunk—no. The jury was still out on the slobbering

issue. There was definitely some drooling going on right now.

He took a deep breath and made a stab at sounding reasonable. "You're just a bit—" He searched for the right words as his gaze roamed her outrageous costume. Her sexy-as-hell body. "Naked to be out in public, don't you think?"

"You call this naked?" She planted one fist on her hip, the breeze from the bay blowing in to ruffle her hair and mold her blouse to her body.

Jesse swallowed—twice—but still couldn't find his voice in a throat gone dry.

"Your German playing is showing off half her butt cheeks in those little shorts of hers today while I remain decently covered." Kyra tugged her skirt hem for emphasis.

Jesse wasn't sure he even remembered their thread of conversation anymore since the wind had conspired to show him the shadowy outline of Kyra's naked body beneath her clothes. "The skirt half of you isn't what needs covering."

He never thought he'd hear himself beg a woman to put her clothes back on. But this was Kyra, the one woman he'd always made it a point to treat honorably. The one long-term, enduring relationship he'd ever managed with any woman save his sister.

And damn it, he couldn't seem to stop staring at her breasts.

She flashed him a wicked smile as she trailed her hand along her shoulder where bare skin met the edge of her blouse. "Oh. You mean this half."

Transfixed, he watched her fingers skim over her own flesh. He couldn't have turned away if there'd been a hurricane blowing in off the bay.

Her finger paused just before she reached the top of one breast, then hooked into the loop of a single strand of gold plastic beads she wore in deference to the day. "Guess it is a bit much, isn't it? Maybe the costumer decided to go flashy because of the good media coverage Gasparilla is receiving this year. Although we're far removed from the spotlight way back here."

She looked around meaningfully at their relatively quiet position at the back of the crowd.

Not that Jesse had any intention of returning to the heart of the festival with Kyra dressed like this. She'd be fending off too many wolf whistles to have fun.

Scavenging for control, Jesse swiped a hand across his forehead. Had it ever been this hot in February before? "I think the coast is clear. I appreciate you saving me from Greta back there." That had to be the reason for Kyra's abduction scenario, right? "I don't know how she found me in a such a big crowd, but she's been glued to me all day. I appreciate you showing up when you did."

He hoped he sounded marginally normal and unaffected.

She shrugged. "Guess you lucked out then. You got what you wanted by me getting what I wanted."

"How do you figure?" Even if he hadn't been choking on his own damn arousal, he had the feeling he wouldn't have followed her thinking.

"You gave Greta the slip, which is what you wanted. I got you for the night, which is what I wanted."

Her Cheshire-cat smile fanned the flames of his already molten imagination.

Jesse refused to screw up this friendship by allowing his libido to translate for him. Surely she didn't mean what he thought she meant.

"We're friends from way back," he reminded himself as much as her. "If you need me, all you have to do is let me know."

She laid both of her palms on his chest. "But I've never needed you quite like this before."

The cool strength of her small hands permeated his shirt. No doubt she had to feel the slam of his heart, the furnace heat of his body.

"No?"

"No. Tonight isn't going to be about friendship." Her blue eyes locked on his. "Tonight is going to be about you and me, man to woman." She leaned in closer, her incredible breasts almost brushing his chest. "And since you're still technically my captive, I'm going to demand that you treat me like the woman you've never been able to see in me."

That sounded dangerous as hell. But before he could protest, her voice turned to a whisper, forcing him to listen all the more carefully.

"That means we're going to be sipping champagne instead of swilling beers. That means I expect you to feed me from your fingers. Dance with me hip to hip." She sidled closer for emphasis, her hip grazing his. "In general, Jesse, now that I've got my very own bad boy at my fingertips, I'm going to wield every trick of seduction I've ever seen you use on other women and apply them to you. Slowly."

Jesse didn't remember when his jaw hit the ground, but he definitely recalled when the heart failure started to set in. It had been right about the time the word "seduction" had rolled off of Kyra's tongue like a promise of erotic torment.

Finally, he knew exactly what she was asking.

Too bad he didn't know if he'd survive it.

KYRA WATCHED Jesse clutch his chest as if she'd just shot him in the heart with her proposition.

Did he have to be so melodramatic about this?

Finally, he raised both hands in surrender. "Okay. You win. You'd better quit right now or I'm the one who'll damn well be blushing. And I'll never make another crack about dominatrix outfits."

"I assure you this is no joke." Could she be any more obvious in her approach? "I mean it, Jess."

"No." His response was delayed, but from the stern set to his jaw, he sure looked like he meant it.

"What do you mean *no?* You can't defy a pirate." What had happened to the playful man she'd known for over a decade? Didn't he know how to indulge in a few games anymore? "I could make you walk the plank. Or I could tie you to the mast and give you fifty lashes."

In fact, the thought inspired a few other ideas....

"What are you smiling about?" He studied her through narrowed eyes.

"I was just thinking fifty lashes might be more effective if I wielded my scarf." She made a dive for the pocket of his shorts. "Where did you hide that anyway?"

He caught her wrists in a steely grip. "No. No. And hell no."

She hadn't seen such a serious expression on his face in more years than she could count. Probably not since he'd had a big blowout with his older brother about who was in charge of Jesse's finances before he left Florida to start his baseball career. Jesse had won that argument along with his financial independence from Seth.

Now, his adamant rejection stung just a little. He'd gone out with every woman in her graduating class but her at one time or another. Was she so much of a turnoff that he couldn't even conceive of one romantic evening with her?

Thankfully, her stubbornness wouldn't allow her to be daunted. She was only asking for a night, not a happily ever after. In two more weeks he would start his own business and sever their long partnership anyway. Would it kill him to indulge this final request?

She took a calming breath, inhaling the salty scent of the bay along with the jumble of culinary aromas from food stands lining today's pirate parade route. "Hell no I can't have my scarf back?"

"Hell no you can't corral me into this misadventure with you today. Have you really thought about what you're asking me?'' He loosened his grip on her wrists, lowering her hands to her sides until he finally released her.

She allowed her gaze to slide down the length of his body. ''Oh, I've definitely thought about it.''

Was it just her imagination or had steam started hissing from his ears?

Sure he was angry with her. But what if just a little of that overheating was rooted in sexual excitement?

''Damn it, Kyra, you usually make more sensible decisions than this. You know better than anyone how badly I suck at relationships. Which is why I don't even *have* relationships.'' He paced the sidewalk in front of her like a nervous father on prom night. ''Did I ever tell you about that documentary I got roped into last spring in Miami Beach—*Dangerous Men and the Women Who Love Them?* They put my interview in the 'commitment phobic' section like I was some damn psychology experiment.'' He paused to frown. To scowl. Then he turned the full force of his glare on her. ''But that ought to tell you something.''

''That documentary is the very reason I picked you. Nobody's looking for a relationship here, least of all me. My life's crazy enough right now. Being with you, I can be certain there will be no risk, no commitment.'' She allowed her gaze to linger on his body. ''And proven expertise.''

''You're looking for sex?'' He said it so loud pseudo-pirates from fifty yards away turned to stare.

''After food, clothes and shelter, it's a pretty basic human need.'' She wasn't about to feel guilty about it. She'd been saving it up for twenty-four years after all. No one would ever accuse her of being promiscuous. Or even moderately wild.

Lowering his voice, he leaned closer. "You're thinking of love. Love is what people need after food, clothes and shelter."

"Sex seems to be serving *you* well. I'm a healthy woman with natural appetites. And since I'm not looking for a relationship, who better to scratch the itch than my best bud?" She leaned closer. "Especially since local legend says you're the most skilled lay in town."

"We are *not* having this conversation." Tucking her hand in his, he stalked back toward the crowd and the dozens of tents set up to temporarily house food-service stands and other vendors.

"Damn. Just when the conversation was getting really interesting." Kyra followed him, content to let him vent his outrage until he was ready to listen to her side. She had been patient for half a lifetime for this man. She could wait another hour or two if need be. "Can I at least ask where we're going?"

"We'll find champagne to sip if it kills me. And then you can never say I didn't put forth an effort today."

Score.

Kyra allowed herself a small smile of victory since Jesse was too busy plowing through dozens of bead-clad festivalgoers to notice.

JESSE KNEW if he turned around right now Kyra would be wearing a hint of a grin—the same exact

one she wore in the training arena when she'd coerced
a stubborn horse into doing exactly what she wished.
She'd have him leaping hurdles in no time if he
wasn't careful.

Lucky for him, he had a plan.

As he guided Kyra through the mass of pirate rev-
elers, Jesse glared at anyone who stared at his captor
while he thought through his strategy. He damned
well didn't want her deciding to scratch that itch with
one of these leering morons.

All he needed to do was appear semiagreeable.
He'd have drinks with Kyra and make polite conversation instead of talking horses. He'd spin her around
the dance floor a few times—or parking lot, given
their locale—in front of one of the many bands playing at the festival.

And in the meantime, he'd try not to take it too
personally that she only wanted him for sex. He liked
sex as much as the next guy. Probably even more.

But he'd thought Kyra was the one female in his
life who saw more in him than that.

Damn.

Refusing to get sidetracked, Jesse told himself he'd
fulfill her requests on his terms and then tomorrow
everything could go back to normal. And if she continued to look even mildly interested in something
beyond the scope of friendship, he'd flirt wildly with
any woman within winking distance to remind Kyra
he was an ass when it came to the fair sex.

Simple.

Assuming he could peel his eyes off Kyra's body long enough to remember how to flirt wildly with another woman. He didn't know how much more of this kind of provocation he could take. He'd never had much in the way of immunity when it came to females.

And this wasn't just any female. This was his best friend. No matter that she was tying him in knots today, he owed her more respect than to engage in a one-night stand. She might think she could handle a no-strings affair, but that was probably because she'd never engaged in a meaningless relationship before.

At least not that he knew of.

Damn.

Maybe as long as he kept their conversation on neutral terrain and his thoughts out of her corset, he'd survive this day. He wouldn't bend his personal code of honor—limited though it might be—to give Kyra what she thought she wanted. He'd end up hurting her, and she'd end up resenting him—end of story. And he wouldn't risk losing the best friend he'd ever had for sex.

No matter how heady the temptation.

He turned around to hurry her along and found her lingering around a makeshift vendor's booth consisting of a few overturned wooden boxes half-veiled with a black velvet cloth and covered in silver jewelry. No way the overgrown beach bum in a Hawaiian shirt and shades behind the melon crates had a city license to sell anything.

Worse, the guy was staring over the top of his sunglasses to get a better look at Kyra's...blouse.

Gritting his teeth, Jesse tore through a group of cigar-smoking partyers cheering in Spanish and a kid's makeshift hopscotch game to reach Kyra.

He gave the so-called jewelry clerk the evil eye and wrapped a possessive arm around Kyra's waist. It hadn't been part of his plan to touch her, but he would damn well do whatever was necessary to keep the wolves at bay while she was dressed in her pirate garb.

So what if he was being hypocritical not wanting her to be ogled by ten thousand strangers while he played the field? *He* was a player. *She'd* barely left the Crooked Branch in the past five years, and now she wanted to go manhunting in fishnets?

Over his dead body.

She smiled up at him while he tried not to notice the smooth glide of her leather corset under his hand, the wildflower scent of her that he'd scarcely ever noticed before but knew he'd never forget now.

"You ready?" He edged the words out over a throat gone dry and a tension in his body so taut he thought he'd snap with it. He needed to get this day in motion and over with.

No dawdling allowed.

"In a minute." She grinned up at him with a siren's smile, a tiny piece of jewelry in her hand. Holding it up to the light, she squinted to see a pattern on the silver loop. "I was just contemplating a nipple ring."

3

KYRA WONDERED if Jesse Chandler normally gawked at women who slid the names of erotic body parts into casual conversation.

He was definitely gawking right now as he stared at her with his perfect mouth hanging wide open. Or at least he was until he edged out a strained, "The hell you will."

Plucking the tiny ornament out of her hand, Jesse slapped it back on the velvet-covered melon crate.

"Excuse me?" Kyra stared him down, more than ready for a serious face-off with this man.

It had required major effort to edge the word "nipple" from her mouth. Kyra could discuss the particulars of animal husbandry at the drop of a hat, but somehow a nipple reference in regard to her own body struck her as rather risqué. Nevertheless, the effort had been well worth it considering she had Jesse's full attention now.

Or else the body part in question had his full attention. He stared at her blouse as if he could envision the tiny silver loop locked around the peak of her breast.

"This isn't working," he growled in one ear as he

propelled her away from the jewelry vendor's display and back into the swell of the crowd. "We're getting out of here."

"Fine by me." Kyra shot back over her shoulder as they edged past a Gasparilla reveler wearing a skull mask and a cape decorated in shiny white bones. She backed up a step to avoid the man, effectively plastering herself against Jesse's chest. The hard strength of his body taunted her with sensual visions of their limbs intertwined, taut muscle to smooth skin. "That's all the sooner I can take you home and have my way with you, ye scurvy knave."

She felt his body stir behind her a split second before he nudged her forward again. "We'll see who's having their way with whom."

The strangled rasp of his voice weakened the power of his threat. Kyra smiled her satisfaction as they wound their way past a man on stilts selling eye patches and bandannas.

"Whatever would you want from me if you could have your way, Jesse Chandler?" She glanced over her shoulder to find herself eye-level with a rock solid jaw and forbidding frown.

"Friendship of the platonic variety. And a promise never to wear leather again."

"The corset is working, isn't it?" She mentally applauded the Gasparilla costumer for hooking her up with the sex-goddess pirate outfit.

As they hit the next crossroad to Bayshore Boulevard, Jesse steered her away from the festival toward the city. In the background, Kyra could hear the marching bands in the distance as the pirate parade charged toward the convention center.

"Is it working to turn every bug-eyed male head within a five-mile radius? Yes. Is it working for the preposterous purpose of sacrificing our friendship for a few hours of great sex? Not a chance in hell." He guided her through gridlocked downtown traffic toward his motorcycle parked sideways on the street between two pickup trucks.

She'd ridden into Tampa with a neighbor, so it wasn't like she minded being given a ride home. Still, she didn't appreciate being hauled around by a man who wasn't willing to bend an inch.

Jerking to a stop by his Harley, she tried not to be discouraged as he handed her a helmet—the spare he always carried in case some brazen female talked her way into a ride. Or more.

Why couldn't *she* be that woman today?

"You think I'd forfeit our solid working relationship for amazing sex? Come on, Jesse. You know me better than that." She strapped the helmet under her chin. She didn't mind leaving Gasparilla if it meant time alone with Jesse to persuade him of her cause.

Besides, the idea of straddling his bike—and him—while clad in fishnets and a miniskirt was making her seriously hot and bothered.

Swinging one leg over the bike, Kyra gave Jesse a clear view of inner thigh, stopping just short of flashing him. A girl needed to keep some sense of mystery intact. "And you seem to be forgetting that you're not in charge here today. Leaving the festival grounds doesn't mean you stop being my prisoner, and as long as I'm calling the shots, you're going to have to please me.''

She patted the leather seat in front of her. ''Now why don't you give me that ride I've been wanting?''

THE SEXUAL IMPLICATION of Kyra's words echoed through Jesse's mind as he maneuvered the motorcycle around a tight turn just before the sign for Crooked Branch Farm. He was sweating bullets after the hour-long ride back to the ranch, which spread along the Crystal River in Citrus County.

Kyra's thighs hugged his hips while her sweet, sunny scent teased his nose. Her arms wrapped around his waist, pressing her breasts into his back. And he couldn't even think about that *other* part of her that grazed his jeans. Her short skirt provided intimate exposure for the pink lace panties he'd spied when she first straddled his bike.

Now all he could think about were those ultrafeminine undergarments and what it might be like to peel them from Kyra's body.

Her invitation to take her for a ride had paralyzed him for a heart-pounding five seconds. Jesse had zero experience turning down those kinds of invitations. Having realized at an early age that he was too restless to settle down, too much like his old man to tie himself to any one woman, Jesse had carefully constructed a reputation for himself as a player. With that legend-in-his-own-time aura preceding him, no woman would ever be surprised by his lack of commitment.

And in turn, he'd never disappoint anyone.

But the strategy that had worked like a charm for ten years was unraveling in a big way. First, Greta staunchly ignored all the hype about him and—according to what she'd told him earlier this afternoon—she'd sold her Miami Beach condo for an apartment in Tampa.

Now Kyra was suggesting a fling he couldn't afford to take any part in.

No matter how much his body screamed at him otherwise.

Bringing the bike to a stop a few feet from Kyra's long, low-slung ranch house, Jesse willed away all provocative thoughts as he disengaged himself from her. He needed a cool head to talk her out of the big mistake she seemed determined to make.

She slid from the bike with the fluid movements of a woman who'd ridden horses all her life. Odd that he'd never noticed the quiet grace and strength about her before.

"Come on inside and I'll get you a drink," she offered, slipping her helmet from her head to place it gently on the seat.

Jesse stared in her wake as she sauntered up the flagstone path toward the front door, her lace-up boots clicking a follow-me tempo. He'd been too caught up in her new subtle politeness to ride off into the sunset on his bike while he had the chance.

Shit.

How could he just leave without even saying good-bye? He found his feet trailing after her before his mind consciously made the decision to go inside the house.

She'd left the door open wide into the cool, sprawling home he'd helped her build on a patch of the Crooked Branch property five years ago. The mish-mash of Spanish influenced stucco archways, miniature Italian courtyards and contemporary architecture had been the first house he'd ever custom-designed from scratch and he continued to be proud of it in the years since his skills had improved tenfold. The house was so uniquely suited to Kyra he couldn't picture anyone else ever living here.

He'd always felt at home here before. Today he had the impression of a fly venturing farther into a silken, sweetly scented web.

One quick goodbye and he was out of here.

''Kyra?'' He didn't see her right away as his eyes adjusted to the dimmer lighting indoors. The sound of the refrigerator door thudding shut called him toward the kitchen.

She stood at the triangular island in the center of the room, tipping a longneck bottle of Mexican beer to her lips. A few damp tendrils of blond hair clung to her neck from the warmth of the day.

He'd worked side-by-side with her for years and not once had the sight of perspiration on her forehead turned him on. Was he so freaking shallow that all she had to do was slide into fishnet hose to make him start salivating?

Before he could fully form and analyze a response to that question—let alone say goodbye—Kyra set her beer on the kitchen counter with a clang.

Foam rose up in the throat of the bottle to bubble over onto the granite surface around her sink, but Jesse was too mesmerized by the sight of her strutting into the hallway to do anything about it.

Something about the take-no-shit attitude of her walk told him she meant business. He'd seen that determined stride of hers before when she was dealing with shifty horse sellers or uncooperative studs.

And he had the feeling he wasn't going to fare any better against the will of this woman than the men who'd been forced to give her a good price on her horses or the studs who procreated when and where she wanted them to.

As a matter of fact, he felt his own desire to play stud rising to the surface in a hurry.

"Kyra, I don't think—" was as much as he managed before she came toe-to-toe with him in the hall lit with flickering electric sconces intended to look like candles along both walls.

Jesse didn't realize he was backing up until his butt connected with the stucco wall behind him. Her hands materialized on his chest as if to hold him in place.

He could see the rapid rise and fall of her chest half-exposed by her low-cut white blouse. His gaze seemed stuck on that creamy white flesh no matter how desperately his brain sought to unglue his eyes.

But then his brain had a full-time job simply willing his hands to ignore the overwhelming temptation to touch Kyra.

When her lips touched his, he lost the battle.

Sensation exploded through him at the brush of her soft mouth. There was a sweet taste to her that even the beer couldn't hide, and he drank her in like water, swirling his tongue with hers in an effort to savor every nuance.

His hand moved to her shoulder, powerless to remain immobile any longer. He molded the delicate skin of her collarbone, his thumb dipping down to the gentle swell of her breast above the neckline of her blouse.

And then it was as if someone had tossed gasoline on the fire of his want for her. Heat exploded inside him in time with that touch, burning through him with a fierce desire to scoop her up and walk her into the bedroom he knew was at the back of the house.

He could only think about laying her down and unfastening the laces that held the leather garment together. About seeing the perfect breasts she'd been hiding from him her whole life.

She moaned low in her throat as she edged her way closer to him, settling those delectable breasts against the insubstantial cotton of his tank shirt. The beaded peaks rasping over his chest tantalized him to touch.

To taste.

It's just a kiss. He repeated the lie over and over again in his mind, needing to give himself permission to hold her, to indulge this fantasy come to life for just a few minutes.

Her sunny scent wrapped around him with renewed strength as their body temperatures soared. The stucco wall scraped into his back, a discomfort he barely acknowledged while in counterpoint to the lush softness of Kyra plastered to his front.

Soft blond hair tickled his arm where it wrapped around her back, teased his nose when he bent to kiss her neck and taste her warm skin.

"Jesse," she sighed as she tipped her head back, granting him free reign over her body.

He smoothed a hand down her arm and over her hip as he kissed her neck down to one shoulder. The feel of the leather corset in his hand called him back to the place where a neat bow held her outfit together.

If this was just a kiss, he wouldn't go there.

If this was just a kiss, he'd sure as hell never untie those ribbon-thin leather straps and free the breasts he wanted so damn badly.

But with the encouragement of her hips wriggling against his own, Jesse tugged one end of the bow until the laces slid free. He told himself he would be content just to look. One glimpse of those breasts and he was out of here.

Then his gaze connected with Kyra's in the moody, flickering hallway light. Perhaps his intentions were written in some small facet of his expression because she grabbed one of his hands and laid it to rest on her breast, catapulting him into major meltdown mode. The peaked nipple lined up perfectly between his thumb and forefinger as if to beg for his touch.

"Come with me," she whispered, never releasing his hand as she backed up a step.

Oh, how he wanted to.

He wanted nothing better than to come with her about ten times before morning. To make her hot, wet and mindless for him.

But to take advantage of Kyra's momentary lapse of judgment would be the equivalent of hurting her, sooner or later. Besides, he could somehow still believe himself redeemable if he didn't seduce his own best friend.

Hissing a sigh between his teeth, he had to face up to that fact. "I can't do this."

Of all the rules he'd broken in his life, Kyra Stafford was one line he had promised himself he would never, ever cross.

THE FINISH LINE loomed ten feet away in the form of her bedroom, but Kyra sensed she wouldn't be clearing that threshold soon enough.

Jesse obviously possessed powers of restraint foreign to her if he could stop himself in the midst of the conflagration that had been going on between them. Either that or those kisses hadn't affected him nearly as much as they were affecting her.

The thought daunted her in spite of the molten heat churning through her veins and the tingly alertness of every square inch of her skin. But damn it, if she didn't press her case now, she knew she'd never have another chance. Once Jesse quit helping her out around the Crooked Branch two weeks from now, she wouldn't even see him as much let alone have an excuse to indulge in sexy captive scenarios with him.

If she was ever going to live out her fantasy with him—or have an opportunity to get over his sexy self for good—Kyra needed to act now.

"You can't?" Kyra forced her breathing to some semblance of normal and scavenged for a teasing smile as she hoisted her corset back into place. "You say that as if you had some choice in the matter."

Jesse scrubbed a hand through his too-long dark hair, his gaze straying encouragingly often to Kyra's leather outfit. "It's the right choice and you know it."

"I know no such thing. I left the festival with you because I thought you understood what I expected." Had she been so wrong to think maybe they'd end up together after he'd hauled her out of Gasparilla for mentioning nipple rings? She tugged the laces tighter on her pirate garb. "You can't just quit the game now that we're out of Tampa."

"The hell I can't." He turned his back on her while she tied the leather straps into a bow. Squeezing his temples with the thumb and forefinger of one hand, he stepped out of the hallway and into the wide-open courtyard behind the living room.

"Spoilsport," she called after him, removing her boots as she followed him out into the late-afternoon sunshine spilling across the terracotta tiles. He sat on top of a teakwood table facing a simple marble bird-bath fountain in the center of the courtyard. "Maybe you ought to take me back to the festival so I can find someone more willing."

She leaned against the table he sat on, giving her a rare opportunity to be nearly eye-to-eye with a man half a foot taller than her.

"You're going nowhere today even if I have to lock you in the house to make sure of that."

She smoothed one of the leather straps to her corset between two fingers. "Why not just tie me to my bedpost instead?"

He opened his mouth to speak and snapped it shut again. He swallowed. Flexed his jaw as if grinding his teeth. Then pointed a finger in her face. "You don't know what you're asking for."

"So show me." He'd been with more women than she could count. Would it kill him to indulge her for a day? Maybe two? She edged her way closer to stand between his knees. "Especially since you robbed me of the chance to abduct a more fun captive."

Trailing a hand over his thigh, Kyra absorbed the heat of him through her fingers. The bristly hair of his leg lightly scratched over her palm.

"You've temporarily lost your mind, woman." Jesse imprisoned her wandering hand just as she reached his shorts. "What else would you have me do?"

As he held her there, immobile but far from powerless, Kyra could see the quick pulse in his neck, feel the tension in his body.

She insinuated herself farther into the vee of his thighs, their bodies a scant inch from touching. Leaning close, she whispered in his ear.

"I think I'd have you barter sexual favors for your freedom."

4

IF KYRA HAD BEEN any other woman, Jesse would be well on his way to making her forget her own name by now.

As he held her slender wrist with one hand, it occurred to him he'd never restrained a woman's touch before. Hell, he'd never restrained his own desire to touch for that matter.

Women had always given him the green light, and he'd always accepted it with pleasure. To hold back was an all-new experience. One which he hoped fervently he'd never have to repeat.

"Sexual favors have no place between friends. You know that." He tried not to notice the satiny texture of the skin on the inside of her wrist.

"Since when?" Her other hand slid over his chest in a provocative swirl.

Before he imprisoned that one, too. "Since always. What kind of friend would I be if I let you sleep with a low-down two-timer like me?"

She lifted a sunny blond eyebrow and met his gaze dead-on. "What kind of friend would you be if you denied me the best orgasms in Citrus County?"

So much of his blood surged south, she might as

well have set up a damn IV to his Johnson. Damned if he didn't feel light-headed.

"My reputation has definitely been overstated," he managed to croak in between gulps of much-needed air.

She leaned closer, her breasts brushing his chest. "I don't think so."

Somewhere between the brush of her breasts and her whispered words, Jesse must have let go of her hands. All of the sudden, they were everywhere, on his shoulders, spilling down onto his back, drawing him closer.

Such soft, silky palms. He'd seen her riding and working with gloves on a million times over the years. Never once had he suspected she'd been protecting such smooth skin underneath that dusty leather.

He reached for her—thinking he'd insert some space between them—but instead he pulled her closer when his fingers met the cotton of her skirt. Her hips were narrow along with the rest of her body, but they curved gently from her waist, providing an inviting niche for a man's touch.

For *his* touch.

A soft moan escaped her lips, a cry both earthy and feminine. The note of hungry longing pushed him over the edge. He might have been able to resist his own sexual urges. But how could he continue to refuse hers when he'd never been able to deny her anything in over a decade of friendship?

Assuring himself he would find a way to keep

things under control, Jesse slid off the table and onto his feet, never letting go of Kyra's hips. He took one look at her flushed cheeks, her half-closed eyelids, and knew he wasn't going to be able to walk away anytime soon.

She raised both palms to his chest and pressed him gently backward. Not that he moved anywhere.

"Where do you think you're going?" she whispered, sultry as Eve before the fig leaves.

"I'm going to barter for my freedom." He tugged her toward the bedroom, a room he'd built with his own two hands long before he ever suspected he'd spend any time within those four walls. "And I've got a sexual favor in mind that will curl your toes, melt your insides and make you forget all about playing pirate for the day."

OH. MY.

Kyra's footsteps followed in the wake of Jesse's as he pulled her into the bedroom. She'd dreamed about this moment more times than she could count, yet a niggling fear gave her pause. Was he acting on seductive autopilot in giving her what she wanted, or did he feel a small measure of the same sensual hunger she did?

Or what if—God forbid—he was acting out of some sense of pity?

As much as she wanted whatever toe-curling, inside-melting experience Jesse Chandler had to offer, first she needed to be certain his erotic overtures were fueled by a little passion and not some misguided sense of duty as her friend.

And she could only think of one way to find out as Jesse drew her down onto the simple white linens of her king-size four-poster bed.

She dove for his shorts.

The move wasn't exactly subtle, but until she touched him, she couldn't be entirely sure how she affected him. Granted, she would have to be blind not to notice the man wasn't turned on at the moment. But for all she knew, men automatically responded to leather corsets and a few throaty sighs.

Kyra had always been a practical, salt-of-the-earth type of girl, and she felt more comfortable getting her own handle on the situation, so to speak. She needed to see how he reacted to her touch.

"Holy—" Jesse's swallowed oath and wide eyes weren't exactly the reactions she'd hoped for.

"What?" She smoothed her fingers over the altogether pleasing shape of him beneath his clothes. She had little enough experience in this arena, but she possessed enough to be impressed.

Jesse's eyelids fell to half-mast before he caught both her hands in his. "Have you always been this much of a pistol and I just missed it?"

Their gazes connected in the dim light filtering through closed wooden blinds and sheer lace curtains. Between the setting sun and the muted colors of the room, Kyra couldn't even see where the dark brown of his eyes stopped and the black center of his pupils began.

She sat perfectly still, transfixed by the rapid beat of her heart, the steady warmth of Jesse's stare. "You ought to know I only do things all or nothing. Starting the Crooked Branch. Helping you build this house. Going for broke at the horse shows. If I want something, I am very willing to work for it."

In fact, she was quite willing to do whatever it took to make sure Jesse noticed her, to make sure he stayed tonight. But he was making it a bit of a challenge by restraining her hands at every turn.

Working on instinct, she settled for leaning back into the Battenburg lace pillows to recline the rest of the way on the bed.

Like an indomitable force of nature, her breasts remained standing even when she lay down. Corsets rocked.

"You're a wild woman." Jesse's eyes burned a path down the leather laces holding her outfit together.

Kyra rather liked the idea of unveiling a whole new side of herself that only Jesse would see. Because she felt safe with him, she could be more adventurous than she would be with any other man. More daring.

"Wild and wicked." She ran the top of her bare foot up the inside of his calf. "That's me."

Jesse dodged the path of her marauding toes and followed her down to the mattress, pinning her hands over her head. "Not for long you're not."

His nearness cooked up a thick heat in her veins and sent a rush of liquid warmth through her body.

His tanned muscles flexed on either side of her cheeks as he held her in place on the bed.

"I'm not?" She sure felt certifiably wicked at the moment.

"No." He released her hands to trail his fingers up her bare arms to her collarbone, then down her sides to rest on her hips. "In a few minutes you're going to be sated and tame."

"Promises, promises." Her limbs went heavy and liquid at the thought of what he might have in mind. "Are you sure you can deliver on such a bold pledge, Jesse Chandler?"

He surveyed her body with the slow thoroughness of a world-class artist sizing up a new project. His brown eyes flicked over her stocking-clad thighs, her zshort skirt and the peekaboo laces holding her corset in place. "Your pleasure is guaranteed."

Her heart jumped, skipped and pumped double time.

She walked her fingers up one sinewy bicep. "If I'm not completely satisfied, can I ask for a repeat performance until you get it just right?"

He tugged one of the laces free from its knot to loosen the corset, leaving the leather garment in place while exposing a deep vee of cleavage. The movement shifted her cotton blouse to tease over her sensitive nipples and send a rush of heat between her thighs.

"I take great pride in my work, Kyra. I would never stop until I got it just right." He skimmed his hand over the flesh he'd exposed, carefully avoiding her breasts and making her all the more urgent to be touched.

She just barely resisted the urge to fan herself. No wonder the man had captivated feminine imaginations from one end of the Sunshine State to the other. Every inch of her felt languid and restless, heavy and hungry at the same time.

Opening her mouth to speak, she was surprised to discover words failed her at the moment. She could only think about indulging her every fantasy about Jesse. Could only envision tying him to her just this once to realize the sexy dreams that had plagued her nights and prevented her from being able to appreciate any other man.

Although as Jesse stared deep into her eyes and trailed his fingers lightly down the valley between her breasts, Kyra wondered if she'd ever be able to pry this man from her fantasies.

His voice growled husky and deep in her ear. "Are we agreed then?"

She blinked, fought for a rational thought even as the magic of his hands lured her deeper into a world of pure sensation. "Agreed on what?"

"My freedom for your pleasure?" His touch hovered close to one scarcely covered nipple. So close. His breath huffed warm against her shoulder as he staked his terms for sensual negotiation.

And she couldn't have bargained for a better deal to save her life. Insistent hormones and liquid joy crept through her veins and made her amenable to anything—everything—he wanted.

"Deal."

The moment the word left her lips, her unspoken wish was granted. Jesse's fingertips smoothed over the aching tips of her breasts through the thin cotton, then plucked the sensitive crests until she shivered with wanting.

Hungry for more, she wriggled closer to him on the bed, desperate to experience the press of his chest against her bared skin. With eager, clumsy fingers, she tugged his shirt up to the middle of his chest and laid claim to his heated skin with her palms. Greedily, she absorbed the nuances of his body with her hands, mentally reconciling the muscles she'd stared at for years with the ridges and angles underneath her touch.

He felt hot and hard and better than she'd ever imagined. But if she wasn't careful, Kyra knew she'd find pleasure with him far too soon, long before she'd had a chance to tease and tantalize him.

Forcing herself to slow down, she stilled her fingers and looked up at him to find his eyes glittering with the same heat that fired through her.

But before she could celebrate that small victory, Jesse covered her with his body, cradled her cheek in his hand and caressed her mouth with his own.

SHE TASTED LIKE honeysuckle—warm, sweet and heady. Jesse was drowning in her already and he'd only just barely touched his lips to hers.

Everything about this encounter had "mistake" written all over it, but he couldn't have stopped himself now if he tried. The hell of it was, even if he could have scavenged some last remnant of control, his sensible best friend had turned into an exotic temptress and she urged him on at every turn.

Her hands fluttered restlessly at his shoulders, delicately steering him where she wanted him. Her calf wrapped around the back of his to mold him more tightly to her, demonstrating a strength he hadn't suspected in her slight form.

He deepened the kiss, claiming her mouth for his own even as he reminded himself to be gentle. He didn't have a clue how he'd walk away from her, as if she was any other woman, tonight after he showered her with earthly delights.

But he would. He *had* to.

He'd never allowed any woman to get under his skin before and Kyra was more dangerous than most because he cared about her.

Already he was taken by surprise to realize how much her satisfaction meant to him. Maybe he hadn't wanted to be roped into this ill-advised escapade, but now that they lay so close to one another in her monstrous four-poster bed, Jesse wanted nothing so much as to make tonight one she'd never forget.

Breaking the kiss, Jesse brushed his lips across her silky soft skin, over her cheek and down to the throbbing hollow of her neck. He'd known her for half a lifetime, yet everything about her was new and different tonight.

He'd noted in the past that Kyra was passionate about anything and everything she'd ever done—a quality he'd always admired because it was so foreign from his own love 'em and leave 'em approach. But now, having all that passion turned on him scared him to the roots of his too-long hair. Her fingers had found their way under his shirt, crawled across his chest and clutched him to her until he had no choice but to feel every square inch of her perfect breasts pressed up against him, the thin layer of cotton between proving no barrier at all. Still, he couldn't resist plunging both hands into the loosened remains of her leather corset and unbuttoning the tiny fastenings on that blouse.

Gently, he nudged the fabric aside. Exposed her all the more to his gaze.

The sensation of seeing her breasts bared to him seemed incredibly decadent, yet forbidden because Kyra was his friend. But it was all so damned awesome he wanted to kneel before her gorgeous body and worship her in ways no other man had ever dreamed of.

"Kyra." Whispering her name in the darkness, Jesse wondered if he'd ever be able to speak it again without getting turned on. "Lay still for me so I can look at you."

Her blue eyes glittered back at him in the near darkness that had settled over her bedroom. Her restless hands slid away from his chest to fist at her sides. "I'm not good at being still."

She wriggled against the simple lace bedspread as if to prove the point. Fleetingly, Jesse remembered how difficult it had been for her growing up with her father when he was in a depressive state. A high-energy teenager and a tired old man who only wanted to retreat from life had been a challenging combination on both sides.

"But I've never gotten to see you this way before." He pinned her wrists on either side of her head, levering himself above her in a half-hearted push-up. "And who knows when I'll ever get another shot at seeing you naked. I plan to look my fill."

A slight breeze slid through the blinds at the window, rustling the starched curtains alongside her bed and stirring a lock of her hair to blow against his arm. She'd wrapped herself around all his senses just as thoroughly as those long blond strands conformed to his bicep.

Tonight she looked so soft and fragile. Intellectually, he knew her petite body concealed kick-butt strength and behind her delicate features lurked a sharp wit and clever mind.

Still, Jesse couldn't resist tracing her perfectly crafted cheekbones with his lips. Couldn't stop himself from skimming the smooth skin at her temple with the edge of his jaw.

"I don't think it's fair you get a sneak preview while I'm still left wondering what's in store for me." Her gaze dipped downward to linger on his…shorts. "Don't you think I ought to be entitled to a little show-and-tell here too?"

As if in a quest to be seen, his Johnson reacted of its own accord. She was killing him already and she hadn't even touched him yet.

He swallowed. Gulped. Sought for an even delivery of his words but still ended up sounding as strangled and hoarse as the Godfather in his old age. "I think you ought to behave before I have to get rough with you."

Even in the dim light he could see the answering spark in her eyes. The definite interest.

"I'd like to see you try." Her dare whispered past his better judgment and straight to his libido stuck in overdrive.

Ah, damn.

He had no business playing kinky sex games with Kyra Stafford. Why then did he find himself slipping his finger into one looped end of the loosened leather laces that had held together her corset?

"Don't bait me, woman." He tugged the slender ribbon of leather free from one eyelet after another until at last he held the long black strap in his hand. "I'm armed."

A wicked smile crossed her lips. "Do your worst, Chandler. I'm ready for you."

His mouth watered with the hunger to test the truth of that statement. Was she really ready for him right now? So soon? Before he'd even slid off her tiny skirt?

The notion teased, taunted, tempted the hell out of him. He wanted to slide his hand up under the hem of her outfit and touch every hidden nuance of her body, every intimate feminine curve that he'd never allowed himself to contemplate before.

But he didn't.

Not yet.

Instead, Jesse called upon his considerable experience in pleasing women and forced himself to choose the slower path, the one that would drive both of them more wild in the long run.

"Never say I didn't warn you." He breathed the words into her ear, grazing his body gently over hers.

Doubling up the skinny leather corset strap in his hand, Jesse pulled the end of the loop taut to make the two sides slap together with a sharp *snap*.

5

THE THIN *CRACK* of leather echoed in the sultry air, inspiring alternate waves of shivers and sizzles through Kyra. Breathless, she stared up at Jesse with his wild long hair and his broad, square shoulders and wondered what he had in mind.

He still held the long, looped strap in his hand as he grazed it lightly over her thigh. "You sure you don't want to run?"

"And lose my chance to experience Jesse Chandler's legendary prowess firsthand?" She flung the remains of her corset onto the floor and settled more deeply into the pillows. "I don't think so."

He dangled the leather tie like a pendulum over her hip, than up to her bare waist. The insubstantial little touches heightened her senses, made her crave more of his touch.

Her attention focused on the contrast of black leather against her pale skin, just in time to see him move his teasing instrument down her stocking-clad leg.

With clever hands, he walked his fingers under the edge of her skirt to tug down her thigh-high fishnets, careful never to touch her where she wanted to be touched the most. While her thighs tingled and ached, he soothed them with the soft stroke of leather and an occasional hot swipe of his tongue as he kissed her all along the hem of her skirt.

Desire trembled through her with a force she hadn't fully expected. She'd wanted Jesse forever—had fantasized about sexy interludes with him since she was barely sixteen—but in all that time, her imagination had never hinted it could be this hot between them. This wild.

She couldn't stifle the throaty whimpers, the sighs of pleasure his mouth wrought. Liquid heat seared her insides, pooled between her thighs. She ached for him in the most elemental way, and none of his skilled, seductive torments would satisfy it.

She needed *him.*

All of him.

Now.

"Jesse, please." Her hands scratched lightly across his back, tugging his shirt up and over his head.

In silent answer, he slid her skirt down her hips and pressed a kiss to her pink lace panties, just beneath the rose. Tension coiled even more tightly inside her, making her twitch restlessly beneath his touch.

But Jesse couldn't be rushed as he smoothed his hands over her hips, palmed her thighs, cupped the center of all her heat. Instead, he seemed to study every inch of her, bared completely to his gaze but for the tiny pink panties, and whispered, "How the hell did I not notice you were this gorgeous?" He licked a path from her belly button to her lacy waist-band while he traced the outline of her curves with the loop of leather still wrapped about his hand. "This hot?"

Maybe because she was usually covered with dust from working with the horses. Maybe because he'd never been able to get past his early vision of her in pigtails. Or maybe because he normally had German bikini models on his arm to compare her to.

But she wasn't about to offer up her thoughts on the subject. Let him see her as steaming and sexy just for tonight.

Heaven knew, she felt pretty close to smoldering right now anyway. Especially when he slid a hand down the curve of her hip and under the scrap of pink lace.

"You can bet I won't forget now," he muttered as he inched her panties down her legs, over her knees and sent them sailing across her room to land on an antique wingback along with the leather strap from her corset. "How the hell am I ever going to look at you again Kyra, and not see…" His gaze wandered up and down the length of her naked body, sending tremors right through her. "…the nip of your waist?" He kissed the curve in question. "Or the little birth-mark on your hip that I never knew was there?"

His tongue smoothed the pale patch of flesh to one side of her belly button and Kyra thought she'd lose her mind.

"Maybe you shouldn't bother trying to fight it." She smoothed her hand over the tanned muscles of his chest, down to the warm heat of his belly. She followed the thin line of dark hair down the middle of his abs to the waist of his shorts. "Besides, your fascination with any woman lasts all of what—a week maybe?" She trailed her fingers along the seam of his fly until he groaned. "You can undress me all you want over the next seven days."

JESSE STRUGGLED to hang on to his control in a way he hadn't needed to since high school. The woman was pushing him to the brink with her siren's body and her erotic suggestions.

Her invitation to undress her anytime wasn't exactly going to put the lid on his lascivious thoughts down the road. Hell, knowing that enticement was out there—free for the taking—he'd be envisioning her naked twice as often.

And it didn't help that his mind was already inventing ways to justify spending the night with her. He wanted so much more from her than he could possibly take.

He needed to focus on his goal and get out of here before he lost all control.

With an effort, he leaned back out of her reach. Keeping his damn shorts on was critical to his success in this mission. If Kyra started flicking buttons free, he was a goner.

Lucky for him, she was hanging by a thread too, despite the fact that she could talk a good game. He'd seen what she wanted, knew what she needed as soon as he'd laid that first kiss on her thigh.

And it would most definitely be his pleasure to give it to her.

Stretching out alongside her on the bed, he looked deep in her blue eyes before brushing his lips over her mouth. The honeysuckle taste of her invited him to linger, to lavish her with attention.

Her soft moan encouraged him, aroused the hell out of him, sent his hand wandering over her sweet curves to the silky inside of her thigh.

He broke his kiss to watch her face as he dropped his touch lower to the white-hot center of her. Her cheeks flushed, her mouth opened with a silent cry.

He wanted to be inside her now, hips fused until he slaked his thirst for this woman. Normally, he was a patient man. Normally, he had endurance for every sexual trick in the book.

With Kyra, he transformed into a sixteen-year-old on a car date—pure lust and no caution.

Knowing he'd never restrain himself while their hips rested so close together, Jesse edged his way down the bed, down her body, licking every inch of her creamy skin on the way.

The scent of her body—something wild and heady, jasmine maybe—permeated his senses to implant itself in his memory. Her hips shifted, wriggled as he kissed his way past them and over the pale blond triangle that hid her from him.

He couldn't slow his progress if he tried.

The moment he touched his tongue to her sex, her back arched off the bed. Her out-of-control reaction drove him as crazy as the taste of her, the feel of her on his lips.

The knowledge that sensible Kyra Stafford was underneath him, wild and untamed as any of the fiercest horses ever sent to the Crooked Branch, nearly drove him over the edge.

He couldn't get enough of her like this, would never get enough. Dipping one finger inside her, he tried like hell not to imagine penetrating her with so much more....

But then her sex clenched all around him and he forgot about everything but enjoying every second of her pleasure. She screamed a throaty note before crying out a litany of his name, over and over and over.

And even though he knew their bargain was fulfilled and he ought to make tracks from this woman's bed, Jesse felt more connected to her than any woman he'd ever had full-blown sex with for days on end.

This was Kyra, after all. His best friend.

So despite the driving need for her he couldn't ever possibly indulge, Jesse tucked her blankets around her still trembling body and held her in his arms. He could stay with her a little longer, couldn't he?

Just until he got his body back under control. Just until Kyra fell asleep.

Or until he let her talk him into taking this encounter a little further. He was so damn hot for her he didn't think he could move without losing it. Maybe he'd underestimated the merits of a sexual relationship.

Trailing one finger down her arm, he knew he

shouldn't make decisions when he was hanging by a thread, but he couldn't resist seeing what Kyra would do next. He was dying for her touch, but she was lying utterly motionless.

He indulged a moment of pure male satisfaction to think he'd knocked her for such a loop she was still recovering from the orgasm. But then, as he listened to the long, even breaths stealing across his chest, Jesse realized he'd *really* knocked her for a loop.

She was fast asleep in his arms.

WELL, DIDN'T THAT just make a lovely picture?

Greta Ingram stared through Kyra Stafford's bedroom window at Jesse Chandler gently covering his naked *business* partner with a lace duvet. Greta couldn't remember him ever treating *her* with such tender concern.

Since when did a man turn away a European model with internationally celebrated breasts for a skinny horse trainer who probably had leather hands and dusty hair?

Sighing, Greta slipped away from the window, no longer wishing to make a scene. At least not tonight.

She'd hitchhiked from the Gasparilla festival to the Crooked Branch after Kyra had lured Jesse away with a leather corset and a lot of attitude. Confident in her own allure, Greta had hoped to entice him back with a little topless strolling around the ranch or maybe some naked moon-bathing outside his office window. But obviously the man was already engaged for the night.

Damn.

Tiptoeing across the lawn in her high heels, Greta looked longingly at Jesse's bike, wishing she could just straddle the big Harley and wait for him to join her. But after seeing the way he snuggled his partner into her linens, Greta feared he probably didn't run out of Kyra's bed the way he usually ran from Greta's after sex.

A minor obstacle.

Greta had left the hectic world of modeling and perpetual jet lag to live a more simple existence. Her home life sucked in Germany and she'd refused to look back at her verbally abusive father once she'd dug her way out of that particular hellhole.

She'd been paying her own way as a model since she'd lied about her age at fourteen. The sophisticated world of catwalks and globe-trotting that had seemed so glamorous to her then didn't glitter quite so brightly at twenty-three, however. She wanted out and Jesse Chandler had made her realize it.

What woman didn't secretly crave the kind of gallant attention and sexual bliss he lavished all over his partners? She was definitely ready to trade her stilettos for bare feet and picket fences. A man like Jesse Chandler would understand how to make her happy, how to indulge her idiosyncrasies.

He also possessed a certain charm and emotional distance that suited her wary heart. Her father had used his temper and his strength to intimidate her at every turn, making her fearful of too much in-your-face male strength.

And, truth be told, Jesse definitely made for great arm candy. A girl had to be able to hold up her head at the spring shows in Paris, after all. She'd have a lot more fun attending as a celebrity member of the audience rather than actually having to participate. This way, she could have Jesse by her side and she wouldn't have to starve herself for four days prior.

Halting at the edge of the county route that wound past the Crooked Branch and Kyra's home, Greta recalled the half-eaten fried dough she'd stuffed in her bag at the festival. Scrounging through her oversized purse while she waited for a car on the quiet road, she tugged out the napkin she'd wrapped the treat in and tore off a corner with her teeth.

After years of counting every calorie and weighing her skimpy nonfat, unsweetened, boring-as-hell portions at mealtimes, she enjoyed the taste of real food. All kinds of food.

Funny how cold fried dough still managed to bring her so much pleasure even when the man of her dreams had just boinked another woman fifty yards away.

Maybe that was because she knew Jesse would fall in line. She hadn't met a man she couldn't manipulate since she'd left Frankfurt and her father's rages nine years ago. Surely Jesse would see the light soon and come running back to her.

But to facilitate the process, Greta realized she needed to be sure Kyra the lascivious pirate woman understood Jesse was no longer a free man.

Seeing headlights in the distance, Greta tossed the

fried dough back in her bag and set one foot on the blacktop to expose one long, bare thigh. Flicking out her thumb, she brought a white Cadillac screeching to a halt beside her.

While an elderly gentleman pried open the passenger side door for her, Greta made plans to return to the Crooked Branch for a visit with Jesse's bimbo buccaneer first thing in the morning.

Someone had to let the woman know—Greta Ingram always got her man.

6

So this is what morning-after regret felt like.

Jesse squinted at the clock next to Kyra's bed just before dawn, his eyes dry and his thoughts scrambled.

Of course, he wasn't entirely sure which he regretted more—giving into Kyra's crazy scheme last night, or having to pry himself away from the soft warmth of her sleeping form this morning.

How could any woman look so confoundedly perfect at 5:00 a.m.? Her shoulder-length blond hair swirled across the white pillow, still smooth and silky even after all their nocturnal maneuverings. Eyes closed, inky black lashes fanning her cheeks…

And her body…

Jesse didn't even dare to let his gaze wander lower or he'd never get out of her house this morning.

Limiting his visual inventory to her face, Jesse stared at her and waited for some revelation as to why the hell he'd never seen Kyra as remotely sexy over the course of their long friendship.

Had he simply refused to acknowledge what was right before his eyes all this time? Or had he been so damn shallow that he could only see the blatant external beauty in showy women like Greta Ingram?

Didn't that say a hell of a lot about his character?

All the more certain he didn't deserve to be in Kyra's bed, Jesse shoved off the crisp white linens and searched around in the dark for his shirt.

He spied it strewn across the walnut bureau, sandwiched between a simple wooden jewelry box and a framed photo of Kyra's parents on their wedding day.

Scooping up the wrinkled tank top, he couldn't help but notice a baseball card tucked into the framed mirror above the dresser. He didn't need to read the fine print to know whose card it had to be.

Jesse Chandler—rookie shortstop in the triple-A minor league.

Kyra was surely the only person on earth to have collected such a rare and simultaneously worthless item. But then, she'd always been a friend—a fan— no matter whether he was hitting the cover off the ball or falling into a major batting slump. He'd never asked her to attend any of his home games, but she'd always been there to hurl insults at any umpire who ever dared to call him out.

How could he screw up a friendship with a woman like that? Kyra could ride motorcycles, horses and— should someone happen to dare her—just about anything else that moved on wheels, wind or water. She could shoot pool, throw darts and she genuinely liked domestic beer. A guy just didn't mess with a friendship like that.

Jamming the baseball card back into the mirror frame, Jesse tugged his shirt over his head and promised himself not to let last night ruin what he had with

Kyra. It's not like they had crossed that sexual line of consummation, after all.

He'd simply pretend the heated encounter never happened and hope like hell she did, too. He'd never been the kind of guy to be plagued by morning-after regrets, and today shouldn't be any different.

No matter that—for the first time ever—he was having a hard time walking away from a woman's bed.

At least he would be checking out of his position at the Crooked Branch in less than two weeks. That meant he could avoid Kyra—avoid this attraction—and concentrate on getting his business up and running. Every house he built would prove to himself a little more that he could stay in one place, that he could commit to something.

His night with Kyra didn't do anything to change that.

And if he occasionally looked at her body and remembered the erotic-as-hell events of last night…that would just have to remain his secret.

INSISTENT RAPPING on her front door interrupted a very sexy dream Kyra had been having. She'd been envisioning a night with Jesse that had involved full-blown consummation, multiple orgasms and lots of leather.

In fact, Jesse had been just about to nudge her over that amazing sensual ledge again when the rapping at her front door pounded through her fuzzy consciousness to awaken her completely.

Blinking against the pale sunlight already streaming through her blinds, she realized it was later than she usually slept and that Jesse was no longer beside her.

He'd given her enough intense pleasure to send her into sated slumber until nearly dawn and she hadn't given him so much as a second of satisfaction.

He'd done his friend a good deed, apparently, and then left.

She'd expected him to leave while she was sleeping, but the reality of seeing his side of the bed empty still stung. Thanks to her practically passing out in his arms, Jesse had slipped away without actually relieving her of her virginity or providing her with the complete sexual experience she craved. That stung even more. Sighing, she levered herself up on one arm and moved to investigate the loud rapping at her front door.

On the off chance that Jesse had somehow locked himself out and wanted to get back inside the house, Kyra pulled on a buff-colored cotton robe and jogged to the foyer.

"I'm coming," she shouted, half-smiling to herself as she remembered the events of last night when she really *had* been coming.

She felt the flush of arousal in her cheeks and throughout the rest of her body as she yanked open the front door and hoped she'd find the man who could fulfill the sensual longing still pulsing through her this morning.

Instead, her gaze fell upon a bonafide cowboy, a

breed that had grown more rare in southern Florida over the last decade.

A tall, rangy body took up her whole doorframe. Well-worn denim encased his thighs while an honest-to-God western shirt with a snap front covered an impressive chest.

He had a craggy face worthy of any Marlboro man, complete with hat. He was the scarred, dark antithesis of Jesse Chandler's dazzling good looks and sunny charm, but Kyra would bet this man had still turned a few female heads in his day.

In fact, she was pretty sure if she weren't nursing a major crush on her best friend, her head would be turning right now. That is, if she wasn't also just a little bit nervous about what the Marlboro man wanted with her at 7:00 a.m. on a Sunday.

"Umm?" She tightened the sash on her skimpy robe and tried to rein in her scattered thoughts. Between the leftover effects of her steamy dream and the nerve-racking ability of a dangerous man on her doorstep, she felt a far cry from her normally sensible self this morning. "Can I help you?"

"I damn well hope so. I'm Clint—"

She gasped, remembering exactly who he was. "Mr. Bowman. The horse psychologist. I'm so sorry I forgot about our meeting."

She'd called his Alabama ranch last week to request some help with Sam's Pride. The horse had been raised at the Crooked Branch, and although the gelding had the sweetest disposition with Kyra, the temperamental three-year-old wanted nothing to do with anyone else. She couldn't sell a horse that balked at responding to anyone but her. Although Kyra had always been a solid horse trainer, the case of Sam's Pride stumped her.

But once Kyra had come up with the scheme to catch Jesse's attention last week, she'd forgotten all about today's appointment with the equine specialist. A horse whisperer of sorts.

Clint frowned, crossed his arms. "I waited around down by the barns, but everything is all locked up tight at the office and stable." Frank gray eyes sized up her outfit as he took a step back. "You want me to head back down there while you—dress?"

"Good idea." She appreciated a practical man. God knows she'd never run across many in her life. Between her manic-depressive father and her committed-to-pleasure best friend however, Kyra's experience with males had probably been skewed. "I'll be five minutes if you're ready to face Sam's Pride without the benefit of coffee, ten minutes if you'd rather fuel up first."

Clint Bowman smiled and touched the brim of his hat like a character out of an old Western movie. "Coffee it is."

He turned on one booted heel and made his way across her driveway, headed for the barn.

Kyra gave herself a long moment to watch him and wonder what her life might be like if she could get over Jesse Chandler and pursue a guy like Clint.

Unfortunately, her night with Jesse hadn't come close to curing her crush. Maybe her method hadn't worked because she hadn't been able to convince him to carry out her original plan to its full extent.

She needed the complete Jesse Chandler experience, beginning to end. The whole shebang.

For years, she'd had a vision in her head of having her first time with Jesse. Perhaps she just needed to fulfill that longtime fanciful vision in order to shake her attraction to him.

Only then would she be able to pursue someone more appropriate for her.

Someone like Clint Bowman.

She turned away from the intriguing picture of a real cowboy in her driveway to make the coffee. Putting clothes on had never taken her more than sixty seconds anyway.

No sooner had she dumped the coffee grounds into the filter than she heard raised voices outside.

Or rather, a lone, raised female voice.

"...I've walked across every red carpet in Europe on these heels, I'll have you know." The tone was a mixture of feminine indignation and catty pride. A woman on a roll.

Intrigued, Kyra set down the coffee scoop to peer out her kitchen window.

Greta the German Wonder-bod stood toe-to-toe with the Great American cowboy, one French manicured finger leveled at his chest. What on earth was Greta doing at the ranch on a Sunday morning?

"For that matter," the model continued, shifting her weight from one practically nonexistent hip to the other, "ask anyone who owns the runways from

Milan to Paris, sweetheart, and they'll all point to me. I earned that reputation with four-and-a-half-inch heels strapped to these very same feet." Greta tilted her chin at Clint, a gesture which only drew attention to the fact that despite the four-and-a-half-inch heels in question, the horse whisperer still had an inch or two on her.

"If I can manage all that on my own, I'm fairly certain I can negotiate a little gravel by myself."

Kyra couldn't hear Clint's reply, but she saw his mouth move, saw him apply one hand to his hat in the same courteous gesture he'd shown to Kyra and then she saw Greta's cheeks turn a huffy shade of pink before she stormed away from Clint and toward the house.

This was getting more interesting by the moment.

Kyra finished pouring water into the coffeepot, slopping a little onto the ceramic tile countertop in her haste.

A fierce rapping on her front door prevented her from cleaning up the mess.

Tempted to ignore the summons, Kyra tugged open the door again anyhow, too curious to simply go get dressed.

Greta barged inside, oblivious to common good manners. Dressed in a slinky purple silk skirt and a gold bikini top that looked like something *I Dream of Jeannie* might have worn, Greta cocked one slight hip. "Who the hell is that guy?"

"Nice to see you, too, Greta." Kyra searched her brain for a way to avoid answering the question directly. She'd never been the type to lie, but she hardly wished to discuss her horses or Clint Bowman with Greta. "If you're looking for Jesse, I'm afraid you're going to be disappointed. He's not here."

Greta smiled as she dug through a brown leather satchel she carried on one shoulder. "He rarely wakes up in the same bed he goes to sleep in. Hadn't you noticed?"

Kyra took a deep, cleansing breath and struggled not to grind her teeth. "Is there a reason you're here?"

"I came to warn you away from Jesse." Her German accent had softened to mild, clipped tones— a more Americanized Marlene Dietrich. She pulled a silver cigarette case from her bag and flicked it open to reveal a handful of long, skinny smokes with a foreign label stamped across the butts. "He's very much taken."

Kyra reached over and flipped the case closed again, unwilling to fill her house with smoke fumes. "And you think I'd be interested in this because…?"

She'd be damned if she showed Greta Ingram how much she cared about Jesse. She'd protected her friendship with him from envious girlfriend-wanna-bes for plenty of years. She sure as hell wouldn't get sucked into a catfight with a woman who was bound to be disappointed in the nonexistent commitment a consummate bad boy could offer.

Greta shoved the case back into her purse with a frown. "Just trying to save your heart a little wear and tear. I'd hate for you to get all hot and bothered over Jesse only to find out later that he's the un-equivocal property of a woman you have no chance of displacing.''

With a jaunty little shake of her perfect blond mane, Greta smiled at Kyra as if to soften the blow.

Not that Kyra was exactly reeling from the threat.

She backed into the low rock wall outlining a small fountain and miniature garden planted in the center of the foyer. Tucking her short cotton robe around her thighs, she eyed Greta as the German model paced the smooth stone floor with the restless grace of a hungry feline.

''Correct me if I'm wrong, but did you just refer to Jesse Chandler as someone's unequivocal prop-erty?''

Greta paused her pacing to fold her arms and shoot Kyra the evil eye. ''Yes. Mine.''

Despite the woman's hideous lack of manners, Kyra couldn't help but feel a twinge of sympathy for any female who so completely misunderstood a guy like Jesse.

''Don't you realize you're consigning yourself to an abysmal case of heartbreak if you try to tie your-self to a man who's more proud of his bachelorhood than his record-breaking minor league batting aver-age?''

''His what?'' Greta blinked, furrowing her per-fectly shaped brows.

Kyra suspected it wouldn't be the last time this woman's quarry confused the hell out of her.

Sighing, she started again. "Jesse won't ever commit himself to any one woman."

Well aware of this fact, Kyra guessed that her best friend's propensity to roam was probably half the reason she'd pursued him in the first place.

Okay, rampant lust might have something to do with it, too. But beyond that, Kyra knew she would be safe trying out her long-unused feminine wiles on Jesse.

He'd never try to tie her down any more than she'd tie him. After her mom had died long ago, leaving her father in the grips of manic depression that made him emotionally off-limits, Kyra preferred not to trust other people with her heart.

But she and Jesse *both* valued their independence. She wouldn't need to worry that he'd ever get the wrong idea about potential romance between them. Yet Jesse was supremely capable of supplying her with the multiple Os she'd dreamed of, the sensual heights she'd hoped for but had never experienced until last night.

For a moment, Kyra wondered what things might have been like between her and Jesse if she hadn't been a bit wounded and Jesse hadn't been so wary. How cool would it be to hang out with her best guy friend forever and luxuriate in the great sex without worrying about getting her heart stomped?

Too bad that would never happen.

Greta hissed a long breath between pursed lips, almost as if she was exhaling the smoke Kyra had denied her. She cast Kyra a look of exaggerated patience. "The only reason Jesse hasn't committed fully yet is because I haven't made it apparent that I want exclusive rights. Once we sit down and discuss this, he'll be thrilled to be mutually monogamous."

The no-nonsense, I'm-doing-you-a-favor expression assured Kyra that Greta believed every word she was saying.

Two weeks ago, Kyra might have felt sorry for her naiveté. But now she found herself experiencing boatloads of jealousy at the thought Greta might be able to sway Jesse into a relationship Kyra would never be able to manage.

And even if he dodged Greta, what about the next slinky runway goddess who came along? Would Kyra ever be able to look at those women and not feel twinges of envy for the time they got to spend with Jesse?

But she'd be damned if she'd show any weakness to Greta. As far as the rest of the world knew, Kyra Stafford had never been—and would never be—hung up on Jesse Chandler.

"Fine." Nothing she said at this point would save Greta from believing what she wanted anyway. No sense arguing her morning away when she needed to join Clint in the barn and get down to business about Sam's Pride. "Thanks for the heads-up on your relationship with Jesse. Believe me, I'll be the first one to run in the other direction if he starts spouting the merits of monogamy."

A little voice from the deep recesses of her brain called her a liar. Kyra staunchly ignored it.

Nodding, Greta hitched her bag up higher on one shoulder. "I'll let you get back to your coffee." She stared rather pointedly at the empty mug Kyra had been flinging around throughout their conversation. "And your cowboy." She rolled her eyes at the mention of Clint and sniffed.

Before Kyra could explain that Clint wasn't "her" cowboy, Greta charged through the front door and stomped down the front walk as if her four-and-a-half-inch spikes were as durable as high-top sneakers.

Kyra couldn't imagine where the woman was headed as there wasn't a car or other mode of transportation in sight.

Obviously, Jesse was in over his head with the persistent German beauty. Not that it mattered to Kyra. He was a grown man and he could extricate himself from his own problems.

Her only concern was finding an opportunity to wrest a whole night of pleasure from him—complete with the deed that would save her from her unwanted virginity. She could be with Jesse without falling victim to his heartbreaker ways, damn it. Surely all the years she had known him—all the occasions she'd had to see the man behind the myth—would help her remain immune.

Although, after the twinges of jealousy her visit with Greta had inspired, Kyra had to admit she liked the idea of him moving to offices across town in two weeks to start his house-building business.

That left her plenty of time to enjoy Jesse Chandler on a brand-new level.

Happily ever after and monogamy be damned.

JESSE CHECKED his watch as he stood outside the private stables at the Crooked Branch. He'd been able to stay away from Kyra, for what? Three whole hours?

So maybe he hadn't done a great job of putting space between them. But he'd recalled the house-call appointment for Sam's Pride and he was more than a little curious about the horse whisperer Kyra had hired.

Besides, this was his last window of opportunity to oversee strangers' activities at the training facility. For years he'd taken it upon himself to be around when new staff members started their work or when new vendors showed up. Kyra was extremely keen about her business, but Jesse sometimes worried that her isolation on the ranch allowed her to be slightly naive about human nature.

For that matter, she often cut herself off from people on purpose, preferring equine company to the two-legged variety. Maybe it had something to do with growing up responsible for a manic-depressive father who had abdicated his authority along with his capacity to love.

Whatever the reason for Kyra's loner tendency, she hadn't developed the same abilities to read people that Jesse possessed. So he'd made it his personal mission in life to make sure no one ever cheated, deceived or swindled her.

God knows she seemed so self-sufficient in every

other area of her life and work. Jesse had to contribute where he could.

Convinced he was hovering around the Crooked Branch for completely altruistic reasons and not because he simply wanted to see Kyra today, Jesse charged through the stable doors and into the high-tech horse environment Kyra had designed herself.

Wide masonry alleyways and spacious stalls lined both walls. Year-round wash stalls were housed inside the barn, providing the horses with more showerheads and better water pressure than the bathroom in Jesse's apartment.

The stables bustled with noise and activity as Crooked Branch staffers led the horses to the turnout pastures for some morning exercise. But the door to Sam's Pride's stall—the one at the very end of the long corridor—remained shut.

Picking up his pace, Jesse's boots clanked down the clean barn floor toward the closed door. He'd bet his motorcycle that there wasn't a million-dollar thoroughbred housed in a more state-of-the-art facility than the one Kyra Stafford managed. The only scent that hinted the place was a barn emanated from the pile of sweet-smelling hay tucked inside an open supply room.

Slowing his steps as he neared the closed stall door where Sam's Pride normally resided, Jesse's ear tuned to the soft throaty laughter inside the enclosure.

Soft, sexy-as-hell laughter.

Followed by a man's low whisper.

An icy cold, clammy sort of fear trickled through

his veins as he realized the feminine voice belonged to Kyra. Only it wasn't quite fear that he felt.

More like mild dread. A little anger.

Jesus-freaking-Christ, he was *jealous*.

The realization rolled over him with surprising clarity considering Jesse had never been jealous of anyone for anything before.

But he was pretty damn positive that this unhappy feeling in his gut could only be attributed to the fact that another man was making Kyra laugh right now. God forbid the guy made her blush, too, or Jesse would have to kill him.

He hadn't realized until just this second how badly he wanted to be the man to make her cheeks turn pink some day.

Gritting his teeth, Jesse burst through the stall door, determined to make sure everyone inside Sam's Pride's private retreat knew exactly how pissed he was. And the sight that greeted his eyes did zero to soothe him.

Kyra stood beside her favorite horse, stroking his nose and cooing to the beast while a way-too-touchy stranger stood beside her, his hands placed friendly-like over her hips.

In just the same spot Jesse had touched her last night.

Leveling a finger at them both, he didn't think about what to say. He merely blurted out the first thing that came into his mind.

"Care to tell me what in the hell happened to monogamy?"

7

KYRA WAS THE FIRST to move, the first to break her physical connection with the Don Juan in a Stetson.

Too bad she didn't look nearly as contrite as she should. In fact, her expression struck him as downright furious as she turned a snapping blue gaze on him.

"Care to tell me what happened to basic good manners?" she shot back.

Sam's Pride sidestepped in his stall, impatiently stomping his hooves in reaction to Kyra's displeasure. The Romeo cowboy merely crossed his arms and shuffled back to watch Kyra.

Damn the man.

Jesse had never noticed other guys ogling her before yesterday. Now, he felt male eyes on her generous breasts everywhere he went. "Good manners are low priority in the midst of my best friend being debauched."

The cowboy in the corner lifted an eyebrow. "Your best friend?"

"Damn straight." Jesse was only too happy for an excuse to glare at the letch. His day would be complete if only this joker would take a swing at him.

But Kyra's gropey companion simply nodded and did a piss-poor job of hiding an amused smile.

Kyra shouldered her way in between them. "There was no debauchery involved here, Jesse, and I seriously resent the implication. You just interrupted an important moment between me and Sam's Pride and I won't be forgiving you anytime soon if you've set back his treatment because of this morning's melodrama."

She patted her horse on the nose before plowing out of the roomy stall.

Jesse spun on his heel to follow her and her swinging ponytail down the wide alleyway between stalls. She was back to her old self today—no leather corset in sight.

Clad in blue jeans and a man's T-shirt, Kyra wore the same clothes she always had around the ranch, but she didn't look remotely the same to Jesse. Now, instead of seeing her loose shirt that hid her phenomenal breasts, Jesse could only notice how low the V-neck dipped and how tiny her waist was where the shirttail disappeared into her jeans.

"No way are you making me out to be the bad guy, Kyra, when it was clearly *you* who was submitting to another man's touch three hours after I rolled out of your bed."

Her ponytail stilled along with her steps. Slowly, she turned to face him just inside the stable's main doors. "Submitting to another man's touch?" Her nose wrinkled. "How can you call that—" Her jaw fell open, unwrinkling her nose. "Oh my God, Jesse. Don't tell me you're jealous of the horse whisperer."

Jesse had never experienced a migraine before, but he suspected the blinding pain in the back of his head had to be sort of similar. "Of course I'm not..."

He couldn't even say the damn word. How could he possibly *be* jealous when he couldn't even edge the term out of his mouth?

"You're jealous!" Kyra squeezed her hands together in delight, drawing his attention to the incredibly soft fingers that had traveled all over his body last night.

"Jesus, Kyra, that has nothing to do with it."

"Since when have you developed a possessive streak for your one-night stands?"

That did it.

Jesse shoved open the stable doors and dragged her out into the morning sunlight, hoping they'd be able to avoid being overheard. "Last night was *not* a one-night stand."

"Does that mean I'll get a repeat performance tonight?" She blinked up at him with such a wicked gleam in her blue eyes Jesse wondered how he'd ever viewed her as an innocent.

"No." He took deep breaths to steel his body against the eager response to her suggestion of spending another night together. "That means you can't call it a one-night stand when we didn't..."

How to put this delicately?

"Go all the way?" she supplied helpfully, snagging the attention of one of the college kids Kyra hired to help exercise the horses. "Actually, I've been meaning to talk to you about that."

Sighing, he caught her by the elbow to tug her around the back of the stables. The last thing he needed was some college kid eyeing Kyra, too. He hadn't ever cared if the whole world stared at Greta in her lingerie on a Milan runway, but somehow his eyeballs felt ready to explode at the mere thought of a male eye straying too long on Kyra.

He definitely needed to get over whatever the hell was the matter with him.

"This might not be a good time with so many people around." Maybe if he just appealed to her ever-practical nature, he could extricate himself from this mess.

"It may not be a good time, but you made it the *right* time when you charged in on Sam's Pride's first session with the equine psychologist. You know how important it is to me to sell that horse, Jesse. I won't even be able to *give* him away if he keeps up the bad temper with everyone who looks at him." She propped one foot on the three rail fence outlining the turnout pasture behind the stable and stared out at the horses who weren't being exercised at the moment.

In trainer language, the horses were enjoying "leisure time."

"And you're sure in an all-fired hurry to sell him, aren't you?" Jesse prodded, surprised to realize how much her haste annoyed him.

She flicked a curious glance in his direction before turning her attention back to the assortment of jumpers and racking horses grazing in the field before them. "He's my ticket to buying the controlling percentage of this place. If I can't unload him, I don't have any sale prospects that will be profitable enough to allow me to do that until next year."

"And I'm such a tyrant that you can't stand having me in charge here for that much longer?" They both knew Jesse was the silent partner. He'd been wandering the U.S., either as a minor league baseball player or as a student of life for most of the years they'd known one another. So it wasn't like he hung around southern Florida very often telling her how to run their business. He'd earned enough of his own money over the past ten years to ever worry about how much profit the ranch turned.

"You know that's not it." She pivoted around to face him. Tucking one boot heel onto the lowest wooden bar, she propped her elbows back on the top rail.

The stance couldn't help but draw his eyes to her incredible curves. The lush body he'd been able to touch and taste just last night....

Even though he was definitely concentrating on their conversation.

"...but I really need to claim some independence," she was saying while Jesse prayed he didn't miss much.

He focused solely on her eyes.

"You're the most independent woman I've ever met and you're all of twenty-four," he countered. "How much more self-sufficient can a person be?"

"I'm unwilling to rely on other people to supply my happiness or my security."

The alive-and-well bad boy within him couldn't resist teasing her. He leaned back against the fence beside her. "Aw, come on, Kyra. You have to admit I managed to supply a little happiness for you last night."

Why did he remind her of it when he'd been so hell-bent on forgetting all about it? Obviously, seeing her so close and personal with the horse shrink this morning was still screwing with his head.

"I'm not saying other people can't provide me with pleasure."

Was it his imagination or was there a tiny hint of pink in those cheeks of hers?

She cleared her throat and lifted her chin. "I just don't want to ever *rely* on someone else for…my most basic…needs."

A momentary vision of Kyra erotically taunting him with her ability to provide her own pleasure acted like a carrot dangled in front of his sex-starved body. Every inch of his flesh tightened. Hardened. Hurt for her.

Leaning into the fence, he turned away from her to look out over the horses and get himself under control.

"But it's only me helping you out here." His voice sounded strangled. "Surely you can trust me as the controlling partner for another year to give Sam's Pride time to work through his behavior issues on his own."

She stared out at some distant point on the horizon and said nothing.

"You can't trust me for another year?"

"It's not so much a matter of not trusting you, Jesse. It's more a case of me wanting to prove something to myself. I spent my whole childhood at the whim of my father's moods and I feel like I can't spend another day catering to someone else or living by anyone else's rules. I want to work for me."

"Since when do I expect to be catered to?" Where the hell was this conversation going? And how had he moved from erotic visions of Kyra to semiscary realizations about her isolated upbringing?

"You don't." She shook her head so emphatically her ponytail undulated with the backlash. "But again, this is about me. I've got a goal in my mind to be independent and self-sufficient by the time I'm twenty-five, and no bout of horse stubbornness is going to keep me from realizing that goal. I've got a buyer lined up for Sam's Pride, and with Clint's help, he'll be ready by the time the sale goes through."

The look of clear determination in her eyes reminded him of his brother's gritty resolve to support their family when Jesse's father had walked out. He'd never realized how much Kyra resembled Seth in her staunch drive to be independent, her steely will never to rely on anyone else.

Jesse, on the other hand, had never felt called to prove himself the way Kyra and his older brother did. It was enough for him to charm his way through life and without shouldering ten other people's burdens along the way.

He never ran the risk of disappointing anyone because he never offered more than what he was certain he could give.

Did it matter that what he could give was usually simple, sexual and fleeting? At least he was honest about it. No woman could ever say he'd deceived her into thinking otherwise.

He held up his hands in surrender. "Fine. Sam's Pride is your business. I just can't help but empathize with any creature who gets a shrink tossed in his direction."

A BITING ANGER lurked behind Jesse's words. So much so that Kyra couldn't help but wonder who had tried to crawl inside Jesse Chandler's head to leave him with such a wealth of resentment.

But then—almost as if she'd imagined the moment—shades of Jesse's teasing smile returned. A hint of flirtation colored his words. "Or maybe I just don't like the idea of a horse shrink who thinks he can put his hands on you."

Kyra had the distinct impression the man used his sexual charm as a replacement for deeper emotions. But she barely had time to mull over that bit of new insight before he stepped closer and made her forget all about *how* he wielded that major magnetism.

She was too busy getting caught right up in it.

"When I saw his fingers on your hips, all I could think was that I'd just touched you there." His gaze dipped down to her jeans, lingered. "And that you'd felt so damn good."

Heat coursed through her with the force of a thoroughbred in the homestretch. Yesterday she'd had to chase him down and practically hog-tie him to get him to notice her.

It was pretty heady to have Jesse Chandler pursue *her*. If not with his actions, at least with his words. Especially after he'd slipped out of her bed last night without ever reaching the pleasure pinnacle she'd found so quickly.

"Sam's Pride was sort of edgy having somebody new in there with him this morning. He gave me a nudge that was a little more forceful than usual and Clint was just helping me stay on my feet."

"Clint?" He made it sound like an infectious disease.

"The equine psychologist. His name is Clint Bowman."

"Ah." Jesse's shoulders relaxed just a little.

He looked like he belonged at the Crooked Branch today. He'd traded his shorts for jeans and a gray T-shirt with the Racking Horse Breeder's Association logo on the front. Kyra didn't need to see the back to know it read, "You're not riding unless you're racking." She had one just like it in her drawer.

Jesse stepped back from her, a clear visual cue he was retreating from any flirtation.

But Kyra wasn't about to let him off the hook that easily. After last night's encounter, she was all the more hungry for him, damn it, and no closer to getting over her ancient crush.

They needed to finish what they'd started and she planned to make some headway in the department. Pronto.

"So Clint obviously made no claims on my body." She pushed away from the fence and sidled closer. "Frankly, I'm still waiting for you to take up where we left off last night."

He was shaking his head before she even completed the thought. "I don't know—"

"Unless you're too scared?"

She could practically see the hackles rise on the back of his neck. Good. She needed to do *something* to convince him to give her another shot.

"It's hardly a matter of fear."

"Then come see me next weekend." She backed him into the fence rail, giving him no room to run. If he wanted out of this, he'd have to tell her as much.

"I've got to be in Tampa next weekend on business and then—"

She cut off whatever other excuses he might throw her way. "So stop by the week after that. The buyer for Sam's Pride is going to be here that Thursday. You can come bid your farewells to my horse and then have dinner with me."

"I want to, Kyra." A flash of heat in his brown eyes made her believe him. "But this thing between us…it's complicated."

"I think we could figure it out if we had a little time together." She hadn't meant that to come out quite as suggestive as it sounded. Chasing Jesse had turned her into a hoyden in the course of twenty-four hours.

To her surprise, he nodded. "We definitely need to think through what this means for us down the road, anyway. I'll swing by that day and we'll…"

"Think?"

"Exactly. Besides, if you're hell-bent on selling Sam's Pride for the sake of shifting the scales of ownership this spring, I want to at least be around for his big send-off." He edged around her, and she backed up enough to let him pass.

She could afford to be gracious now that she'd won this small victory. As she watched Jesse retreat across the driveway toward the barn where he normally parked his motorcycle, Kyra was satisfied just knowing she'd see him again. In fact, it surprised her how much she looked forward to seeing him again. She would miss his recurring presence at the ranch. No matter how sporadic his appearances had been in the past when he'd been on the road, she'd always known he'd show up on her doorstep sooner or later to help her, tease her, force her not to work so hard all the time.…

Refusing to worry about an uncertain future, Kyra stifled the thought. Assuming the sale of her temperamental horse went off without a hitch, she and Jesse would at least have one more evening together—alone—before he walked away from the Crooked Branch for good.

And no way in hell would they spend it thinking.

GRETA SCRAMBLED to stub out her cigarette as she spied Jesse walking toward the barn.

Finally.

She'd seen him drive in an hour ago just as she'd been leaving the training facility after her talk with Kyra. Greta had delayed hitchhiking home and headed right back to the Crooked Branch, unwilling to leave Jesse in the hands of her biggest competition for his affection.

After he'd parked his Harley in the barn and disappeared into one of the outlying buildings, Greta had staked out his bike and settled in to wait. No way would she track him down amidst a slew of smelly barnyard animals.

Draping herself over the seat of the motorcycle, she managed to strike a sultry pose just as he yanked open the door to the barn. Crossing her hands behind her head, she knew her breasts would be cranked to an appealing height.

And one of the benefits of eating all the fried dough she wanted was that the mammary twins had put on a little weight over the past few weeks.

"Going my way?" she called out across the well-lit expanse of concrete, hanging tools and small tractors. She considered flexing her legs up and over the handlebars, but she wasn't certain how well she could execute that kind of maneuver.

Besides, the disadvantage to all the fried dough was that her body wasn't always totally well balanced.

His step slowed as he neared her. "Do I even want to know what you're doing here?"

"I'm paving the way for us to be together, of course." She lowered her arms and held them out to him. "Feel free to start showing me your gratitude anytime."

And Jesse was so deliciously capable of adoring a woman. Greta hadn't fallen into all that many beds, but she'd been with enough guys to know Jesse was different. He had a way of making her feel special. Important.

Too bad he didn't seem to recognize an invitation when he heard one.

"What's the matter?" she prodded, her arms falling to her side—empty—as she sat up on his motorcycle. "Afraid your *business partner* will see us?"

She couldn't help the sarcasm that dripped from her words.

"She's my best friend," Jesse snapped, with none of his usual trademark charisma. Perhaps he realized as much because he let out a deep sigh. "Could we keep Kyra out of this?"

"My thought exactly." Greta would gladly let Kyra eat her dust as she sped off into the sunset on the back of Prince Charming's bike. "Why don't you come with me to Miami this weekend? We can go jet-skiing and I'll take you to the international swimwear show that all my friends will be in."

Most men salivated at the prospect of leggy models in bathing suits. Jesse looked like she'd just consigned him to Dante's third circle of hell.

"Sorry, Greta. I'm not on vacation anymore—can't do those spur-of-the-moment trips." He made a big production of peering at his watch. "In fact, I'm late for a meeting right now."

Greta scrambled to straddle the bike, ready to follow Jesse wherever he might be headed. She'd come to Tampa for white picket fences and happily ever after, damn it. She wasn't leaving this town without a man in tow.

"That's great." Greta smiled, batted eyelashes and tapped the most basic weaponry in the female arsenal. "Why not drop me off wherever you're going?"

"A vacant lot in the middle of nowhere?" Jesse leaned down and scooped her up in his arms. "I don't think so."

Before she could fully appreciate the titillation of being wrapped in those big, strong arms, Greta was plunked unceremoniously to her feet in between an all-terrain vehicle and a horse trailer.

"Wait!" She stormed back toward the bike, but her shout was lost in the throaty roar of the Harley kicking to life.

And much to her dismay, Jesse Chandler hauled ass out of the barn, leaving *her* in the dust.

This was her Prince Charming?

If it wasn't for the serious pleasure the man could bring a woman, Greta might have had to rethink her choice for significant other.

As it stood, she merely shouted a string of epithets in his wake as she barreled out of the barn under the power of her own two feet. She may have been living a privileged life the past few years, but Greta still remembered how to work for the things she wanted.

By the time her feet hit the smooth pavement of the winding main road, Greta had reapplied her lipstick, fluffed her hair and adjusted her attitude.

For Jesse—the perfect man for her—she was willing to put forth a little effort. Once he realized they were meant to be together, he'd come around. And then he could apply himself to the task of making up for his wretched behavior toward her today.

A blue pickup truck rolled out onto the county route from an unmarked dirt road a few hundred yards away. Lucky for her, the vehicle was headed in her direction, back toward Tampa.

Promising herself she would learn to drive and buy herself a car very soon, Greta flicked out her thumb to hail the oncoming truck. She'd met some interesting people while hitchhiking, but she knew every time she hopped in a car with a stranger she was taking a ridiculous risk.

And jet-set, international models might take risks, but settled women who lived in houses with picket fences did not.

The truck slowed to a stop beside her. The passenger door swung out, pushed from inside. Greta stepped on the running board to pull herself up into the shiny, midnight-blue vehicle, wishing she could have had a better visual of the truck's driver before she committed to getting in.

She recognized the scratchy southern drawl at almost the same moment she came face-to-face with the tall, weathered cowboy in the driver's seat.

''Doesn't a city girl like you know better than to take a ride with a stranger?''

8

HORSE BREEDER Clint Bowman had always been a gentleman. Treating women with courtesy and respect had been a cornerstone of his strict, Alabama backwoods upbringing and he'd implemented those teachings with every woman he'd ever met.

So it made no sense to him that he would be sitting in his truck cab stifling a chuckle at seeing Greta Ingram's million-dollar cover-girl smile morph into a red-cheeked huffy pout today.

But then, nothing about Greta Ingram made him feel much like a gentleman.

"Do you have any idea who I am?" she asked, nose tilted in the air as she settled into his passenger seat and fastened her seat belt.

Clearly, she didn't consider him a threat to an unsuspecting hitchhiker.

Reaching across her world-famous legs, he yanked her door shut. "Two *Sports Illustrated* swimsuit covers in a row sort of makes you a household name doesn't it?"

All of America had seen her face on countless magazines over the past five years. Her perfect features, dominated by her generous, trademark lips. The woman was a walking sexual fantasy.

At the mention of her well-known status, she preened with a vengeance. Greta sat up straighter, angled her shoulders, tossed her head…Clint lost track of her flurry of movements, all no doubt designed to make a man drool.

"Good." The hair fluff thing she did was pure diva. "Then perhaps you won't mind dropping me off downtown. Preferably near the Gasparilla events." She didn't ask. She issued orders.

"And do you find that trading on your famous face makes people more inclined to forgive the bad manners?" Shifting the truck into gear, he pulled out onto the main road.

He expected her to get all puffed-up and indignant again, but this time she only rolled her eyes and started digging through her mammoth purse. "My manners surely aren't any worse than yours. But then, the world rather expects me to be haughty. I'm rich and pampered and I find that conceit makes a damn good weapon in a cutthroat business. What's your excuse?"

He wasn't about to share his excuse. Lust—pure and simple—didn't seem like a wise thing to own up to right now.

"Nothing nearly so rational as yours, I guarantee you." He watched her wave a silver cigarette case in one hand while she excavated shiny compacts and lipstick tubes from her handbag with the other. "Need a light?"

"Would you mind?" She dropped her handful of lipsticks back in the purse. The look of gratitude she flashed his way hit him like a thunderbolt. He caught a nanosecond glimpse of what it might be like to be on the receiving end of other, more sensual gratitudes....

Scavenging through a pile of roadmaps in his truck console, Clint refused to let his mind wander impossible paths. He found a long unused lighter and flicked up a flame after two dry runs.

She leaned close to catch the fire, holding his hand steady with her own. A spark jumped from her flesh to his that had nothing do with the combustible vial of fluid he clutched.

When she glanced up at him with shock scrawled in her bright green eyes, Clint flattered himself to think maybe she felt that bit of electricity, too. Although, judging by how fast she scrambled back into the far recesses of the passenger side, it was pretty damned obvious she didn't appreciate the connection.

"You want one?" she extended the case across the cab, her hand a little unsteady.

Did he make her nervous? Hard to believe the woman who thought nothing of hitchhiking on an isolated Florida back road would be unnerved by old-fashioned sexual chemistry.

Still, he didn't see the need to say as much. At least not yet.

"No thanks. I quit." Across the spectrum of his bad habits, smoking had been the easiest to kick.

"Really?" She rolled down her window halfway

and exhaled into the sultry Florida air. "I find recovered smokers to be the most sanctimonious."

She seemed to relax a little behind the weapon of her sharp tongue.

"Not this one." He tossed the lighter back in his console and half wished he hadn't discovered touching Greta was even more explosive than talking to her. "I'm a firm believer in 'to each his own.'"

She cast him a cynical look over one shoulder before staring out the truck window again. Engaged in constant, jittery movement, Greta was either nervous as hell around him or severely caffeine addicted.

Either way, Clint couldn't help wondering if there was any way to slow her down for a few minutes.

Or for a few days. Nights.

"I'm Clint Bowman," he offered, remembering the manners she'd suggested he didn't have as they sped by local produce stands advertising oranges and boiled peanuts. "Want to have dinner with me tonight and I'll behave at my non-sanctimonious best?"

He probably shouldn't have subjected his ego to looking across the cab at her, but he'd never been a man to take the easy way out. Sure enough, her eyes widened in surprise—at least he hoped it was surprise and not mild horror—her jaw dropped open, and her cigarette fell from her hand, straight out the truck window.

Not exactly good signs for his suit.

"I don't think so." Shaking her head with more vehemence than was strictly necessary, she folded her arms across her body and shouted her refusal with every facet of her body language.

"You have better things to do with your time than hang out with an Alabama cowboy?" Normally, he wouldn't needle a woman about that sort of thing. But Clint's psychology degree and every instinct about human nature told him Greta Ingram felt more comfortable conversing under the shield of verbal sparring.

"I'll be with Jesse Chandler. I assume you know him if you're familiar with the Crooked Branch?"

He was familiar all right. "We met this morning when he was having a conniption over me getting too close to Kyra Stafford. Guess I assumed they were a couple."

Steam practically hissed from Greta's ears as they rolled through a construction site near the interstate.

"Hardly. Jesse and I have been an item for months." Her mutinous look dared him to contradict her.

"Then it strikes me as damned funny I saw him roaring away from the ranch on a Harley not ten minutes before I found you hitchhiking on the side of the road." Clint would stake his horse-breeding business on the fact that Jesse Chandler was tied up in knots over Kyra.

Which, to Clint's way of thinking, left Greta very much available to a man with a little bit of patience.

Or ingenuity.

"He must not have known I was at the ranch then,

I suppose.'' She sniffed. Tilted her perfect nose high in the air.

"Dinner with me might make him jealous as hell.'' So he was ten kinds of no-good for tossing that out there to serve his own ends. But it was definitely in keeping with today's lack of manners.

The notion caught her attention.

She arched a curious brow in his direction. "You think so?''

"Nothing like a little competition for a woman to make a man get his head out of the sand.''

She pursed her perfect lips. Clint stared at her mouth, so mesmerized by the sight he nearly took out a few orange construction cones on the side of the road.

"Okay,'' she finally agreed. "But we're only going through with it if we can find a time Jesse will be around to notice. And you need to behave like an attentive gentleman.'' She flashed him a narrow look as if still debating whether or not he could pull off such a thing. "If we're going to do this, we do it on *my* terms.''

Yes.

"Honey, I'm all yours.'' Clint swallowed the smile that tickled his mouth.

He'd just talked himself into an evening with a walking, talking spitfire who also just happened to be one of the world's hottest women.

Which only proved that sometimes it didn't pay to be a gentleman.

NEARLY TWO WEEKS LATER, Jesse put the finishing touches on a custom-made strip of crown molding with his jigsaw and realized he couldn't remember the last time he'd been able to think of another woman.

God knows, he'd been trying—hard—for days now.

Switching off the saw, Jesse brushed a fine layer of sawdust from the elaborately carved piece of wood before leaving his workshop for the day. Ten days had passed since he last tore out of the private driveway that led to the Crooked Branch, kicking up gravel in his wake. Yet for long, torturous days on end, the only woman he'd been able to conjure seminaked in his mind had been Kyra Stafford.

Not good.

Out of desperation, he'd finally hightailed it out of town over the weekend. His older brother Seth had asked him to deliver his boat to the sleepy Gulf coast town of Twin Palms and Jesse had jumped at the chance for temporary escape.

Too bad the trip hadn't helped him take his mind off Kyra. If anything, seeing his brother's newfound happiness with artist Mia Quentin had only hammered home the fact that Jesse didn't have a clue how to make a relationship work.

As he checked his watch, he realized he needed to haul ass if he wanted to make it over to the ranch in time to say goodbye to Sam's Pride.

And to Kyra.

He couldn't put off seeing her any longer. And he

couldn't delay a serious conversation in which he un-wound the complications of their relationship and put them back on firm ''just friends'' footing.

Shoving a helmet on his head, he straddled his Har-ley and headed north, grateful for the long ride to the Crooked Branch so he could get his head in order. For days he'd made excuses not to think about the ramifications of his night with Kyra, telling himself they hadn't really done anything anyway.

Of course, in some long-buried portion of his con-science, he knew that was a lie.

They had done something monumental that night. Had touched each other in ways that scared the hell out of him if he let himself think about it for too long.

That's why tonight had to be a quick, efficient case of get in, get out.

And *not* in a sexual way, damn his freaking libido.

He'd say goodbye to Sam's Pride because the three-year-old was a damn good horse. Jesse and Kyra had been at the ranch together the night Sam's Pride had been born. And for some reason, the horse had always followed Kyra around like a shadow, had even rescued her from the river one night when another horse had thrown her.

Jesse sort of owed it to that animal to at least be there when he got booted off the Crooked Branch so Kyra could make enough profit for her controlling partnership.

Damn, but that bothered him.

Half an hour later, as he pulled into the drive lead-ing to the Crooked Branch, Jesse wasn't any happier with the situation, but at least he had a plan for his approach. Balancing his helmet on his bike's seat, he coached himself on the basic principles he needed to remember. As he walked toward the exercise arena, he could already see Sam's Pride trotting in circles and he ran through the mission in his mind.

Give Kyra her controlling percentage and say his own goodbyes. To the horse, to the ranch and—much as it didn't feel right—to her.

Get in. Get out.

Figuratively, damn it.

And—above all things—try not to think of Kyra naked.

Rounding the corner of the private stables, Jesse caught a better view of the exercise area and the fence surrounding it. Two figures leaned up against the rails, much as he and Kyra had earlier last week.

He didn't need to see the tall guy's face under the Stetson to know Kyra's companion was Clint Bowman—Sam's Pride's personal psychologist and Kyra's obvious admirer. The guy wasn't touching her right this second, but give him two minutes and he probably would be.

The oddly foreign sense of jealousy that he'd experienced the last time he saw them together roared back with a vengeance. All his "get in, get out" mental coaching was lost in a firestorm of "get your hands off Kyra and get the hell out of my way."

Clint noticed him then and nudged Kyra to let her know they had company. Jesse might have bristled more at the physical contact of that nudge, but then Clint took an obvious step back away from Kyra.

Smart man.

"Hey, Jesse," Kyra called, her faded jeans skimming gently curved hips and covering a pair of worn red cowboy boots she'd had since high school. Her red tank top was new, however. At least to his eyes. It bore little resemblance to the men's T-shirts she usually favored for working and it definitely showcased the amazing body he'd only just recently discovered she possessed. "Sam's Pride is in great form tonight."

Sam's Pride wasn't the only one. Kyra looked so good it hurt.

As Jesse neared, he could see the animation in her blue eyes, the restless energy of her movements. She was genuinely excited about starting a new chapter in her life. One that didn't involve him, or the horse they'd helped deliver.

Not that he intended to care all that much. She was entitled to be independent, to kick up her heels a little, right?

"He looks good," Jesse agreed, forcing his eyes to move over the sleek black three-year-old instead of the thin sliver of bared skin between Kyra's jeans and the hem of her tank top.

"Clint says he's been responding really well all week, so I'm pretty optimistic about tonight." Her gaze settled on him. Lingered. "You okay?"

He was walking away from the one steady friendship he'd managed to form in his life tonight and he hadn't been able to work up desire for any woman but her in over ten days.

Hell yeah, he was just peachy.

"Never been better."

She eyed him critically while Clint called to Sam's Pride behind her.

Thankfully, the sound of tires crunching on gravel and the squeak of a trailer in tow saved Jesse from further questioning.

"Looks like your customer has arrived." Jesse steeled himself for the easier of the two goodbyes he planned to make tonight.

A shiny black pickup truck with two cherry-red racing flames down the side slowed to a stop on the other side of the stables. Kyra strode forward to shake hands with the newcomer—a crusty rancher with a mountain-man beard and a black-and-red jacket to match his truck.

She looked utterly at ease with the horse buyer. Jesse watched her nod in response to something he said. She smiled. Laughed.

Her anticipation for the sale was palpable and not because she was a fan of a healthy profit margin. No, Kyra wanted to sell Sam's Pride to cut a few more ties with Jesse and claim the controlling partnership in the Crooked Branch as her own.

When had she developed such a thirst for independence?

Of course, maybe it had always been there and he'd just never been in town long enough to see it.

Now, Kyra waved to Clint, spurring the cowboy

into action. She stared at her horse, the horse who
was never far from her side while she was at the
ranch, and seemed to send him a silent message with
her eyes. *Behave.*

Funny that Jesse could hear it some thirty yards
away.

Clint steered the horse toward the driveway and the
waiting trailer. The glossy black three-year-old had
been washed and brushed and adorned with his best
bridle. He looked like a candidate for a horse magazine cover—until he neared the trailer ramp.

The horse danced sideways and stopped.

Jesse launched into motion, ready to help. He might
not agree with Kyra's decision to sell the horse, but
he knew how important this was to her and he'd do
whatever he could to make sure Sam's Pride went up
that trailer ramp.

He stood on the other side of the horse so he and
Clint were flanking him. Sam's Pride balked, stepped
backward, snorted.

"Maybe if you lead him?" Clint called out to Kyra
even as the horse started tossing its head and stomping his hooves.

"I don't think so." Jesse took the reins from Clint,
unwilling to let Kyra come between nine hundred
pounds of willful horse and the trailer. Already,
Sam's Pride was twitchy and nervous.

Kyra sidled closer anyway, reaching for the bridle
as she cooed to the animal. "I can take him, Jess,"
she whispered, maintaining eye contact with Sam's
Pride as she reached to help.

Jesse tugged the horse to one side to keep Kyra out of harm's way. "He's too unpredictable, damn it."

As if to prove his words, Sam's Pride bucked and jumped, yanking his reins from Jesse's hands so hard the leather burned and sliced both his palms.

While Sam's Pride pawed the air and then galloped into the woods, Kyra's customer let a string of curses fly and Clint whistled low under his breath.

Jesse, on the other hand, could totally identify with the three-year-old. He couldn't help thinking the horse didn't want a noose around his neck any more than Jesse ever had.

"Deal's off," the bearded customer huffed, clomping back to his fancy truck. "I don't have time to kowtow to a temperamental horse."

"Wait!" Kyra called, hastening to catch him.

But the pickup truck's engine drowned her out as the old guy shifted into reverse and sped away from the Crooked Branch.

"He's not temperamental!" Kyra shouted in the man's wake in a rare display of anger. "He's just…"

She trailed off, shoulders sagging.

"He just wants to be near you," Clint offered, stroking his jaw as he stared out into the field.

Jesse and Kyra followed his gaze only to find Sam's Pride quietly munching grass and swatting flies with his tail. Almost as if he hadn't just pitched the fit of a lifetime.

Kyra made a strangled sound that probably only reflected a tiny fraction of her exasperation. She looked deceptively fragile and alone as she wrapped her arms about her own shoulders and stared back at the animal that had let her down today.

How long had she been handling all her problems on her own?

Clueless how to comfort her given that she only wanted to buy independence from him anyway, Jesse itched to touch her but kept his hands to himself.

Clint whistled for the horse and Sam's Pride trotted over like an eager puppy. "I think he's just really protective of Kyra." He patted the animal's neck and spoke to Jesse when Kyra didn't seem ready to talk yet. "Does he have any reason to have a special attachment to her?"

"He shouldn't, but he does. He saved her once after another horse threw her down by the river." God knows no one else had noticed her missing. Jesse had been on the road with his baseball team. Her father was too depressed to check on his daughter.

"But I've raised and trained hundreds of horses," Kyra argued, finally giving Sam's Pride a begrudging pat on the nose. "I don't understand why this one would grow so attached to me."

Clint shrugged. "I'm not sure either, but I think he considers himself your self-appointed guardian."

Jesse couldn't help but think he didn't have so much in common with Sam's Pride after all. Instead of running from the noose the way Jesse had all these years, Sam's Pride kept running straight for it. The crazy animal wanted to be near Kyra and he wanted to take care of her.

Great. Even a horse was a more loyal friend than Jesse.

Not that Kyra didn't mean a lot to him. She always had. He'd just been so busy running in the other direction that maybe he'd never really seen it before.

He'd spent almost two weeks trying to deny the obvious. Just because he hadn't been "in and out" with Kyra didn't make what they'd done together any less intimate. And damned if he wasn't about to explode with the need to see her unravel all over again. And again.

A better man might have turned away. He wasn't a better man. Jesse already knew that about himself. And so did Kyra, yet she seemed to want him anyway.

He was through fighting what they both wanted.

As his gaze fell upon Kyra again, Jesse absorbed every nuance of the only woman he'd ever wanted to be with day after day. The only woman who'd kept his interest even after he'd seen her naked.

She laughed and jumped back as Sam's Pride nudged her bare shoulder with his nose. A twinge of longing curled through Jesse, a hunger so strong he didn't know how he'd keep himself from devouring her right then and there.

Slipping a hand around her arm, he drew her away from the horse and the Alabama cowboy who had gotten to spend more than his share of time with Kyra this week.

The ends of her long blond hair slid invitingly against his hand. Her skin felt smooth and cool beneath Jesse's touch. Vaguely he wondered how long it would take to spike her body temperature by a few degrees.

He promised himself he would find out.

Tonight.

She glanced up at him, blue eyes wide. Perhaps she was startled that he would initiate physical contact between them after how much he'd fought this. He swore he could feel the rush of adrenaline through her veins underneath the pads of his fingers.

Or was that only his own?

As they neared the side of the stables, he leaned closer, narrowing their world to just one another.

"Was it my imagination or didn't we decide that once your customer left we were going to explore this thing between us much more thoroughly?"

9

KYRA STARED into Jesse's magnetic brown eyes and knew she would get sucked in all over again. They'd left Clint far behind in the training yard, along with any other potential prying eyes. That left little distractions for her to take her mind off what she really wanted.

She'd half managed to convince herself she was insane to pursue any sort of physical relationship with him. He'd broken hearts too numerous to count, after all. And he'd been able to walk away from her for nearly two weeks after a night that had practically set her on fire inside and out. Obviously, the man was well versed in separating himself from the erotic draw of sensual experience.

Kyra, on the other hand, was not.

She'd been thinking and fantasizing about Jesse's hands on her body nonstop for days on end. As much as she wanted one more night with him—one *real* night where they saw their attraction through to its natural...climax—she had grown a tad more leery about the potential risks to her heart and their friendship.

"Did we say that?" she asked finally, wondering

if he felt the nervous pump of her heart right through her skin. ''I got the impression that you weren't ready to explore things quite as…thoroughly as I'd wanted to.''

''Maybe I changed my mind.'' His wide shoulders shielded her from any view of the exercise ring, Clint or her traitorous horse.

She had no choice but to focus solely on him.

And the words that signaled a provocative new twist to their friendship.

''Meaning you're ready to finish what we started?'' An electric jolt of sexual energy fired right through her. Still, she wanted to make absolutely certain they were discussing the same thing.

She needed to sleep with him and get over her crush on him. Dispel the myth, the local legend that was Jesse Chandler.

Even as she thought as much, a little twinge of worry wondered what would happen to them afterward, but Kyra shoved it firmly aside.

He stared down at her with that dark, suggestive gaze of his. ''Meaning it's taken me this long to realize we already did finish what we started, and I'm kidding myself to pretend otherwise.''

''I don't follow.''

He looked around the grounds for a moment, and then led her inside the stables through a back door. He didn't stop there. Guiding her through a maze of the training facility's back corridors, Jesse brought them through a side door into his old office in the converted old barn that housed the Crooked Branch's lobby and business offices.

She hadn't been in here in ages—partly because all their files were electronic and she could access any of his paperwork via computer, but also because being around his things was such a guilty pleasure.

High-gloss hardwood floors gave the office warmth and an aged appeal all the high-tech computer equipment couldn't negate. Because Jesse's office was at the back of the building ensconced in one of the two turrets of the old-fashioned structure, the walls were rounded with only a few high windows. He'd added a skylight over his desk to flood the room with natural illumination.

Now, he led her past his hammock installed between two ceiling support beams and gestured toward the curved sectional sofa that lined part of the wall. He'd bought it along with a television wall unit so he could keep tabs on the Devil Rays score while he worked. His Work Hard, Play Hard ethic would no doubt raise a few eyebrows in the corporate world, but Jesse was one of the most fiercely productive people Kyra knew.

When he wanted to be.

Sinking into the bright blue sectional, Kyra watched him pace the hardwood floor.

He scrubbed a hand through his dark hair. "It's taken me this long to realize it, but I'm not as virtuous in all this as I thought."

She blinked. Twice.

He stopped pacing. "I figured I was being so damn

noble by not committing the final act that night we
spent together. But the more I thought about it—and
believe me, I've thought about it *a lot*—I realized that
we've already committed the acts that really matter.''
He dropped down to sit on a sanded crate that served
as a coffee table directly in front of her. ''I mean, it's
sort of splitting hairs to say nothing happened between us just because we didn't…finish. When it
comes down to it, something big *did* happen between
us and there's no sense running from that fact.''

Nodding slowly, Kyra absorbed what he said but
couldn't possibly fathom where he might be going
with it. ''So you figure now you're off the hook with
me because you've already crossed the sexual line?''

''No. I figure now that I've crossed the sexual line,
I'm an ass if I don't go for broke before you wise up
and boot me out of your bed.''

''Oh.''

''The question is, are you still game?'' He crowded
her. Stole the air.

The ramifications washed over her with enticing
sensual possibility. She became acutely aware of
Jesse's knees brushing hers, two layers of denim between them not even coming close to stifling the
sparks they generated.

''That depends.'' Her practical nature demanded
they hammer this out right now, despite the rising
temperature in the room. She refused to worry and
wonder for another week about where things stood
between them. ''Let's say for a moment that I am

game. I wouldn't want to be treated like a best friend once we hit the sheets.''

"Who said anything about sheets? I was thinking of much more imaginative scenarios.''

Her breath caught. Refused to come back for a long, pulse-pounding moment. "A figure of speech. Regardless of where we conduct our liaison, I just want to be certain there's no attack of conscience midstream.''

He crossed his heart with the tip of one finger. "Luckily, I left my conscience back at my apartment. I'm morally free to have my wicked way with you.''

Gulp. She was having a devil of a time staying on track here. "Which brings me to another point.''

"I have to say, Kyra, I've never been with any woman who ironed out the details quite so thoroughly as you.''

"If we are going to indulge one another in this way, I want the full tutorial in wickedness.''

A smile hitched at his sinfully beautiful mouth. "You're not asking what I think you're asking.''

Damn straight I am.

"You've got all the experience in this arena, Jesse. Teach me a few things from that seductive arsenal of yours.'' This way, when he left her—and he *would* leave her—she would at least have a little more confidence about physical relationships.

Not that she could currently envision using provocative wiles on any man except Jesse, but she refused to dwell on that fact. She had to believe that a night with Jesse would shatter his mystique just a little—at least enough so that she could look at other men and maybe find someone more suitable, someone more practical down the road.

"How could I unleash you on an unsuspecting male population then? Wildly beautiful *and* an expert in titillation? I think that would be giving you too much of an advantage."

"Wildly beautiful?" Kyra suspected Jesse had earned his bad-boy reputation with sweet-talking lines like that one. "We both know you're exaggerating. Wildly. I think a little more provocative advantage would be a good thing for me."

Jesse studied her. Frowned. "This is against my better judgment."

She folded her arms, growing more confident with every moment he sat across from her that he wouldn't—couldn't—walk away from this. The attraction between them was like the force field between magnets just barely out of reach from one another. She had all she could do to stay in her seat and not give in to that pull. "It'll be a deal-breaker."

"You drive a hard bargain, woman."

"I'm thinking it's easier to deal with you in a businesslike fashion than as a pirate hussy."

He pointed a finger at her. "Don't you dare knock the pirate hussy. I'm going to have a lifelong fascination with leather corsets thanks to you."

"So do we have a deal or not?" she pressed, more than ready to put the business part of the night behind them so she could cash in on all that Jesse magnetism.

"Deal. But I have a condition of my own."

She had a good idea what sort of conditions *he* might come up with. "Forget it. I already sent the corset to a leather cleaner."

He leaned closer to plant his arms on either side of her against the couch, effectively cranking up her pulse with every inch he closed between them. "I mean it. If I'm going to be in an instructor position, I want you to agree to be a dutiful student."

She caught a hint of his scent—motorcycle exhaust, leather and male. His knees edged more firmly between hers. Licking her lips, she met his gaze. "Trust me, I'm pretty eager to learn."

"That means you'll do whatever I say?"

She couldn't wait. "Within reason."

"This could be a deal-breaker." He tossed her own words back at her, but she sensed he was bluffing when he slid one of his hands into the back of her hair to tease sensual touches down the curve of her neck.

Shivers of anticipation coursed through her. "So keep your requests reasonable and we won't have any problems."

He stroked his way over her shoulder and right down into the vee of her tank top. The palm of his hand skimmed the curve of her breast and practically made her flesh sing.

"Tonight's not going to have a damn thing to do with reason." He nudged the edge of his hand into her shirt until he reached the barely-there red bra she'd bought to go with her new top. "Or practicality." Plunging deeper, he smoothed the pad of his finger over her nipple. "It's going to be all about sensation."

Sensation poured over her in time with his words as he teased the pebbled flesh between his thumb and forefinger.

The man certainly knew how to get his point across.

"Yesss." The word hissed out on a sigh of pure pleasure.

And just like that, she found herself agreeing to anything—everything—Jesse had in store for her.

"EXCELLENT." Jesse bent to kiss a path between Kyra's breasts, mesmerized by the accelerated rise and fall of her chest. "I think we can safely say that lesson one is Jesse knows best."

Her back arched as he drew on her flesh, her hips wriggled with a delightfully restless twitch.

Most tellingly, she didn't argue.

"Ready for lesson two?" He released her long enough to murmur over her skin.

"Hopefully it's less talk, more kissing."

His hand strayed over her hip and toward the snap of her jeans. "Actually, it's less denim, more skirts. Preferably without panties. There's a good reason why men find dresses sexy, you know."

"Duly noted." She flicked open the snap herself to help him. "I can appreciate practicality."

He dragged her zipper down a few notches to discover a swath of shimmery red silk beneath the stiff fabric of her jeans. His practical business partner was full of surprises. "Although when the panties look like this, I can definitely see the appeal."

He smoothed his hand over her abdomen, teased the edge of the silk with one finger. Her skin felt so creamy perfect to his touch it was difficult to tell where the silk left off and her skin began.

Her breathing hitched as the heel of his hand nudged farther south.

"I'm ready for more," she whispered against his ear. "More lessons. More touches."

"Keep in mind lesson one."

She pried an eyelid open to stare at him with a mixture of confusion and pure lust.

"Jesse knows best," he reminded her, leveraging his position of power to the fullest.

Instead of conceding his superior sexual wisdom, however, Kyra merely reached for his belt buckle.

"Hey!" He nearly choked on the word as her fumbling struggle brushed a straining erection. God, she was going to be the death of him. "What are you doing?"

The look she gave him was pure menace. "Fighting fire with fire."

Heat flashed through him. No other woman had ever given him so much hell in bed. Or out of it for that matter. Still, he couldn't help but admire her for not letting him get away with anything.

And truth be told, her touch felt like heaven as she slipped questing fingers beneath the denim to curve around him.

With an effort, he stopped her. Tugging those adventurous hands away, he stretched her arms up over her head as he dragged their bodies down to lie on the couch. "The most important lesson of all is patience."

She squirmed against him. "Not my forte. Especially not when I feel so…edgy."

Jesse was right there with her in the edgy department. If her hips brushed over his one more time he'd be lurching *over* the edge pathetically premature, in fact. He needed to take charge here if he wanted a fighting chance of maintaining his status as Kyra Stafford's private sex tutor.

"I can take the edge off," Jesse assured her, already sliding off the couch to help her find a release or two of her own before allowing himself the full pleasure her body had to offer him.

She grabbed his hand as he reached for jeans. "No, wait. You need to show *me* how to take the edge off for *you*. The lessons are to teach me, remember?"

Jesse felt his eyes bulge from his head like a damn cartoon character.

And that wasn't the only thing bulging.

"No." The protest croaked out a mouth gone dust-dry.

"Yes." Kyra sat upon her knees, already sizing up the situation. "And don't look so worried. I'm sure I can do this."

His blood pounded through his head so damn loud he wasn't sure he'd heard her correctly. "Are you telling me you've never done this…I mean, *that*…before?"

He'd suspected that Kyra didn't have a huge amount of sexual experience. She'd never indicated any of the guys she dated were superserious. But then again, she'd definitely had her fair share of dates. Obviously, none of those guys had been all that adventurous in the bedroom.

"Unless you want me to ask a bunch of nosy questions about *your* sexual past, I don't think it's very polite to quiz me about mine." She whipped his leather belt from the loops, doubled it up and then slapped the sides together with a snap. "Now, get comfortable and tell me what I should be doing to drive you wild."

This had gone far enough. And if Jesse had been able to breathe past his raging lust, he might have explained as much to her.

As it stood, he settled for roping her with his arms and hauling her back down to the couch alongside him.

He muted all potential protests by clamping his mouth to hers in a kiss designed to make her forget anything and everything but him. He slid the leather belt from her hands and flung it across the office. Then he dragged her jeans down her hips, over her soft thighs and past her feet.

The patience he had touted a few minutes ago was gone, but he was determined to get it back.

Not until Kyra was naked, however.

He slid her tank top up over her arms and tugged her bra off her shoulders until both garments were somewhere in the middle of the hardwood floor. She was left clad in nothing but a scrap of shimmering red silk, a scrap which he hooked with one finger to shift and maneuver against her skin in a teasing caress.

Only when she upgraded from incoherent sighs to breathy pleas for fulfillment did he pull the panties down her legs.

"Apparently you're having a problem with the whole patience concept in all of this." He confided the words into her left ear, the one that was closest to his mouth. He nipped her earlobe for good measure, still struggling with his own desire to explore their attraction at full speed ahead.

It galled him that he, of all people, had to be the responsible one in this.

"It's never been my strong suit," she admitted, arching her neck to give him better access.

"Since it doesn't seem to impress you when I *tell* you that patience pays, I think I'd be better off proving it to you firsthand."

KYRA HEARD Jesse's words somewhere in the back of her passion-fogged brain and knew she was headed for the equivalent of sensual torture. How could the man be so cruel to make her wait?

As for her lessons—forget it! She didn't have a chance of retaining any good provocative moves when she was so thoroughly engrossed by them. All in all, the man turned her on far too much to be of any use in her sexual education.

Then again, he turned her on far too much for her to ever consider stopping him.

Next time she'd pay closer attention. Next time she'd retain more of the nuances of his technique. For now, his fingers were finally creeping up her thigh and she thought she might come totally unglued.

She'd waited and waited for him to touch her and now—finally—he eased his hand around the wet heat of her, slid one finger deep inside of her.

And ohmigod. All the waiting had made her ready.

Her body clenched involuntarily around him, just one quick spasm she knew would be a precursor to so much more.

He must have felt it as plainly as she did because he released a stifled groan and lowered his mouth to her breast. His tongue laved her swollen flesh and nipped at the peaked center of her.

Heat radiated from the places he kissed to the most intimate places he touched as if the two were on an electric current traveling in both directions. Kyra ground her hips against his hand, but he withdrew his finger, teasing her slick folds until she thought she'd die of pleasure.

Once, she crested so high she could barely catch her breath and then he slid two fingers inside her, heavy and deep. The pressure inside her burst, exploding out in an orgasm that rocked her whole body. She dug her heels in the couch and pressed herself against him, greedy for every silken sensation Jesse could provide.

When the sensations finally slowed and then

stopped, Kyra could barely scavenge a thought other than that she wanted Jesse even more than she had two hours ago and ten times more than she wanted him last week.

She experienced a twinge of fear that her plan to get over him by indulging in him completely was going to crash and burn in a big way. The man was seriously—frighteningly—addictive.

He walked his fingertips up her bare belly. "You ready to see why patience pays?"

"Very ready." Her whole body burned with the truth of the sentiment.

Unfolding himself from his place on the couch, Jesse rose to pull his T-shirt over his head. He cast a molten glance in her direction before he retrieved a condom from his pocket and shoved his way out of his jeans.

Kyra practically purred at the sight of him as he sheathed himself for her. He was all bronze skin and hard muscle—emphasis on the word "hard." The man should have been statuary in a world-class museum. Jesse was male perfection at its most devastating.

Any lingering strains of satisfaction from the orgasm he'd given her faded in a new surge of desire. Any nervousness she might have experienced about her first time had deserted her as soon as Jesse touched her. She couldn't be in more experienced, or more talented, hands.

She glanced up at his eyes to gauge his expression. The answering heat she found there reassured her.

Despite his qualms about sex complicating their friendship, he wanted this every bit as much as she did.

He lowered himself over her. Her legs inched farther apart seemingly of their own will.

The sleek male power of him gave her a secret thrill, a feminine rush of delight.

And then he was nudging his way inside her, slowly and carefully in spite of his bad-boy reputation. She was grateful for his gentleness as her body stretched to accommodate him. Muscles she'd never known she possessed protested the invasion.

A little spark of fear flared to life inside her. Not that she didn't want this, but what if her body's resistance tipped him off about her virginal status? Or worse yet—turned him off?

But as she met his gaze in the dimming illumination from the skylight from over his desk, Jesse's eyes held no reproach, just a little concern and a lot of restraint.

Then he reached between their bodies to touch her and the rush of desire returned. Her body gave way to his, opening itself to a delight even better than all the other pleasure he had given her so far.

He continued to touch and tease until he could move inside her without hurting her. Until every move of his body added fuel to the fire that raged inside her all over again.

And once again, his patience paid.

Kyra felt the sensual tide rising up, lifting her beyond the couch and into the realm of sublimely erotic.

Only this time, when she thought she would explode with the sweet joy he gave her, Jesse found his release, too, and shouted his satisfaction to the rafters.

Afterward, as they lay quiet and still together on the curving sectional couch, Kyra wondered if he'd say anything to her about her lack of experience. Could men really tell? And if they could, would Jesse be upset with her for not telling him in advance?

She rather hoped he had no idea. Dealing with the fallout from tonight would be fraught with enough land mines without having the virgin issue thrown in the mix.

He'd touched places deep inside her on so many levels. Physically, he seemed to take over her whole body. Emotionally, she couldn't begin to contemplate the effects of this new connection with him, but she knew she'd never walk away from tonight without some kind of indelible stamp on her heart.

10

JESSE AWOKE to a cold, empty couch and an even colder attack of conscience the next morning. Stretching the crick out of his neck, he wondered how he could have gotten such a good night's sleep while twisted pretzel-like around Kyra on his office sectional. He'd held her while she fell asleep and it bugged him he wasn't holding her now.

Somehow, she'd slipped out of his grasp early this morning before he could discuss a few things with her. He'd done a hell of a job staving off those irritating scruples last night while he'd been losing himself in Kyra. But this morning he couldn't escape the bare facts.

He'd somehow managed not only to sleep with his best friend, but a virgin to boot. Firsts for him on both counts.

The crick in his neck throbbed back to life with a vengeance as he scrubbed a hand through his hair and tried to figure out how to handle this latest development in his shifting relationship with Kyra. He'd slept with more women than he cared to admit to, yet in all those encounters he'd never been with a virgin.

The fact that Kyra had never been with anyone else

scared him. The fact that she'd deliberately chosen him for her first time demonstrated a level of trust she had no business bestowing upon him.

What if he'd messed up her first time?

A guy ought to be informed of those preexisting conditions, damn it.

Scooping his jeans off a purple Tampa Devil Rays hassock, Jesse decided to tell Kyra as much. And more. Just as soon as he located her, he would demand to know what it meant that she'd squandered her first time on someone like him.

Unless of course, she *hadn't* squandered it in her mind.

What if her choice of an experienced stud had been very deliberate? A possibility which seemed all the more likely given how damn practical the woman had been her whole life.

He was surprised how much the idea stung. She wouldn't have used him like that, would she?

Jesse jammed his arms through the sleeves of his T-shirt and shoved on his boots, determined to get some answers—and, God help him, a commitment— from his wild and wicked best friend.

KYRA HAD HALF-HOPED Jesse would find her and demand she come back to bed this morning. As she hung the grooming tools she'd used to brush out Sam's Pride on the stable wall, she thought about how amazing her night with Jesse had been.

So amazing, in fact, she wondered if sex could be addictive. She couldn't even ride her horse around the exercise arena without getting totally turned on by the rhythmic movement between her thighs, for crying out loud.

Obviously, she was a woman in need of a little extra sexual attention. And, in her defense, she had put off sex long enough in life where she felt like she deserved some making up for lost time anyhow.

But as she led Sam's Pride into his paddock, Kyra heard the determined clomp of Jesse's boots across the gravel driveway out front. The purposeful stride of a normally laid-back man gave her the sinking feeling *he* wasn't daydreaming about making up for lost time today.

As he rounded the corner of the stables, Kyra noticed he still wore his jeans and T-shirt from yesterday. He was a little rumpled, but if anything, the tousled dark hair and wrinkled shirt only added to his sexy, bad-boy appeal.

Of course, Kyra had always known there was a lot more to Jesse Chandler than a charismatic aura and bedroom eyes. It was just tough not to get distracted by them. Especially when she had sex on the brain.

He closed the gate to the paddock behind Kyra with a bit more clang than usual. Turning to face her, he met her gaze head-on. "Leaving in the middle of the night is *my* M.O., you know."

Unsure where he was headed with his comment, Kyra merely smiled. "Good morning to you, too."

"So if you're trying to send me a reminder that our relationship has definite boundaries, you're singing to the choir.'' He jerked a thumb toward his chest. ''I wrote the book on boundaries.''

''Trust me, I wasn't trying to send any message, I just woke up with a major cramp in my calf.'' Sex in Kama Sutra positions was awesome, but falling asleep in those positions was definitely not relaxing. Kyra had been too enraptured after her second off-the-charts orgasm to move, however. ''I figured I'd walk it off and check on Sam's Pride before Clint arrived to work with him this morning.''

A little of the stiffness slid out of Jesse's shoulders. Had he really been worried about her?

The notion caught her off guard.

''I shouldn't be offended you fled the scene?'' He reached to stroke Sam's Pride's nose as the horse moved toward the gate and involved himself in their conversation.

It surely soothed a woman's ego to have a man be so concerned about her pleasure. Kyra couldn't help the warmth unfurling in her chest as she carried a fallen bale of hay over to a neatly stacked pile that had been delivered to the ranch the day before. ''Definitely not.''

''Good.'' Giving the horse a final pat, Jesse turned the full force of his attention on her. ''Then we can check that off my list and move right along to why you didn't tell me ahead of time that you were a virgin.''

The bale of hay slipped from her fingers and fell to the ground with a thud.

"Excuse me?" The small voice that tripped along the morning air seemed to belong to someone else.

Jesse tossed the hay bale near the pile then maneuvered a few of the other rectangular packs into a makeshift seating area. He guided Kyra onto one stack of hay and then dropped down onto a similar heap in front of her.

"I want to know why you didn't say one word about—" he peered around the yard one more time as if scouting for potential eavesdroppers "—last night being your first experience."

Kyra sighed. Apparently men could tell about these things. "The first time thing doesn't matter."

"It matters to me." The stubborn tilt of his chin suggested he probably wouldn't let the matter rest anytime in the foreseeable future.

Embarrassment flustered her. Made her snappish. "Is this typical morning-after protocol?"

"I've never had a morning-after with a virgin before so I guess I don't know. Honestly, Kyra, my mind is so freaking blown from last night I couldn't think straight right now if my life depended on it."

The warm swell of happiness she felt at his words unsettled her. When had it become important to her that she hold a special place in his memory? "You've never been with another first-timer? Ever?"

"Not even one."

A small sense of satisfaction chased away some of her lingering embarrassment. Besides, she was outside among her horses, sitting right in a big pile of hay with a guy who'd taught her how to drive and still changed her oil. She ought to at least feel safe enough to tell him the truth about last night. Unfortunately, sharing her first time with Jesse had tangled her emotions in ways she'd never anticipated. "I couldn't tell you because I was afraid you'd change your mind about going through with it if you knew."

"Of course I would have changed my mind. You can't just give a gift like that to a guy like me." He plucked out a single blade of straw from the bundle and tucked it behind one ear.

"Don't be ridiculous. I trusted you enough to go into business with you. Why wouldn't I trust you with my body?"

He shook his head as he pulled another strand of hay from the bale and proceeded to tie it around her wrist. "That's the most twisted bottom line I've ever heard."

"But utterly practical." Her eyes roved over his sexy male body sprawled back against a hay bale. "And now that I've answered your question, do you want to come back to my house and see if I can improve upon last night's performance?" She fingered the collar of her white V-neck T-shirt, her wrist adorned with the bracelet made of hay. "I'd like to get a good grade from my teacher."

She watched Jesse's eyes dart to her fingertips and lower. He licked his lips…almost allowed her to divert him…and then cursed.

"Hell no, Kyra. I'm trying to have a meaningful conversation here. You can't use sexual distraction to throw me off the course."

"Don't tell me—you wrote the book on sexual distraction too?"

"You damn well bet I did." He reached for her hands, stopped them from fiddling with her neckline. "But I'm not going to lose sight of what I came here to get this morning."

She waited.

And waited.

Until finally he nudged the words past his lips. "A commitment."

She couldn't have been more surprised if he'd announced a desire to take up croquet. "You're kidding."

"I'm completely serious." His steady brown eyes attested to the truth of that statement. Too bad he also looked like he'd just taken a bite of an exotic dish he was already regretting.

"You don't have to do this, Jesse." Hurt welled up inside her that he would think he needed to offer something after last night. "Moreover, I don't want you to."

His mouth dropped wide open. "You wanted me enough to sleep with me but not enough for anything else?"

"Of course not. But—"

"Then it's all settled." His jaw muscles flexed—a surefire sign of stress. "We are going to date. You and me. Exclusively."

And he looked about as happy about it as lancing a boil on a horse's butt. As if following up last night with a dating invitation was a necessary evil to be dispensed with as quickly as possible.

Anger, far more comforting than the hurt, broke free. "The hell we are! Jesse it was one night. You've had a zillion and one nights with other women and you've never grilled them about dates afterward."

"Last night was different and you know it." He glared at her in the warm February sunlight, his dark eyes illuminated to three different shades of brown by the Florida sun. "Last night was special."

She felt some of her anger melting away at his words. Part of her wanted to believe him. But damn it, the man was known countywide for sweet-talking his way into just about anything. How could she really trust him on this?

"So special you're going to force yourself to endure my repeated company?" She wouldn't allow herself to get sucked in by all that charm. The hell of it was she would have been more than a little tempted by his invitation if it had been sincere. "Come on, Jesse. I'm sorry I didn't own up to being a virgin."

He shook his head as if her apology solved nothing. "If last night was special enough to you that you saved yourself for it, then it must have been special enough where you can be my girlfriend for a few weeks."

That was his idea of commitment?

Kyra couldn't believe he called a few weeks a commitment. She vowed to open her phonebook first thing this afternoon and find the man a Bad Boys Anonymous.

"Fine," she agreed, relieved to have sidestepped a bigger obstacle with Jesse but just a little stung that he had already carved out a distinct time frame for their *commitment.* "But you're being ridiculous."

He nodded. Harrumphed. "We're still doing a real date."

"Great." She stood, shuffled her bale of hay back into place, and wished she were back in bed with Jesse instead of agreeing to something he didn't want. Back in bed where things were less complicated, where she didn't have to face all the churning emotions over what should have been a simple, sensual encounter.

"You and me. Alone. Very romantic." He shoved to his feet and tossed the bales of hay back onto the pile with so much force there was dried grass flying out of the stack in every direction.

"You're terrified, aren't you?"

His jaw flexed again. "I can't wait."

Yeah, right. She struggled not to roll her eyes as he walked back toward the barn where he parked his motorcycle. She struggled even harder not to feel the hurt welling up inside her.

As he reached the barn door he shouted the final instructions in this morning's list of commitment demands. "I'll pick you up tonight at seven."

"SEVEN O'CLOCK TONIGHT?" Greta parroted back Clint Bowman's dinner request as the tall, attractive-for-no-good-reason cowboy lounged against her doorjamb. She hadn't seen him since he'd given her a ride and tried to coerce her into a date.

And although she hadn't been expecting him this afternoon, she'd known even before she opened the front door who would be on the other side. The man had major chemistry even though he wasn't classically handsome like Jesse. She could *feel* Clint Bowman even before she laid eyes on him and she didn't like it one bit.

How could she be attracted to someone so rough around the edges?

Clint smoothed the brim of his hat with one hand while he held the Stetson in the other. "That's the time I heard Jesse and Kyra agree on for dinner. I was pulling in with my truck just as Jesse jumped on his bike to leave."

"And that was at nine o'clock this morning?" she prodded, hating to think Jesse had spent another night with his too-cute business partner and that she'd somehow misunderstood Clint's story.

Then again, Greta was having more and more trouble even coming up with a mental image of Jesse lately so she had to question how much the news truly bothered her. The only man she ever seemed to see in her mind's eye these days was the rugged male wrapped in muscles who stood on her doorstep.

Nodding, he stared at her hastily tied bathing suit cover-up as if he had a good idea what she was wearing underneath it.

Nothing.

"I get to the Crooked Branch right around nine

every day to work with Kyra's horse." His knowing gray eyes fairly crackled with heat by the time he met her gaze again. "But what do you think about dinner? You still in the market to make Jesse sit up and take notice?"

Clint's hot stare made her knees weak. Her breasts tightened beneath her cotton beach robe. Her body definitely wanted this man.

Fortunately her brain knew better. She'd always avoided men she couldn't control. And she especially avoided men with whom she couldn't control herself.

Greta had the feeling Clint Bowman fell neatly into both those categories.

"I'm in." Maybe all she needed was to see Jesse again and remind herself how perfectly he fit her vision of high-class suburban lifestyle. Besides, Jesse possessed an innate chivalry toward women that assured her he would never turn into the verbally abusive sort her father had been. "But how will we know where to have dinner?"

"Why don't we meet at the ranch right about seven, too? We can always follow them to whatever restaurant they hit. Shouldn't be too much of a coincidence in a town this size." His gaze dropped south again. "Did I catch you sleeping?"

And just like that, Greta was certain Clint knew she was naked underneath the yellow knit cover-up.

Her skin tingled from her ankles to her elbows, but it downright burned in all the best places in between. "Hardly."

"Sunbathing?"

"No, I—"

"Not that a woman ever needs an excuse to run around the house naked as far as I'm concerned." He flashed her a sexy, unrepentant grin as he replaced his hat on his head and backed toward his shiny blue pickup truck. "See you at seven?"

She had a good mind to say no. In fact, the sooner she put some distance between her and the cowboy badass who made her blood simmer, the better off she'd be.

But then how would she ever make Jesse notice her or rescue her from boorish guys like Clint Bowman?

"I'll be there." She draped herself in a little extra hauteur for good measure—and to help maintain some definite boundaries with Clint. "I just hope you can control yourself because my outfit tonight will make nakedness seem positively tame."

"I'll be the epitome of restraint." He levered open his truck door. "But if lover boy doesn't take notice by the time our last course rolls around, all bets are off."

"Meaning you're only going to be able to restrain yourself for so long?" Surely she was a sick woman that his wolfish look sent a little thrill through her when she was planning to seduce…her gaze gobbled up the curve of Clint's oh-so-fine ass.

Wait. Jesse. She was planning to seduce Jesse.

"Meaning that if you're still sitting with me at eight o'clock, I'm considering you fair game for dessert."

He angled himself inside the truck cab and shifted into reverse before she could think of a retort.

Damn the man.

But Greta had no intention of allowing Clint Bowman and his sexy-as-sin body tempt her away from her Great American Dream. The trick would be to intercept her quarry *before* seven o'clock tonight.

She hadn't managed to survive on her own since she was fourteen without accumulating a fair amount of goal-setting skills.

And right now, she had one goal in mind to complete her mental vision of where she wanted to be in life, one man who would be the perfect counterpart to her suburban lifestyle complete with a rose garden and filled with voices raised only in laughter.

The most charming man she'd ever met.

Jesse Chandler.

A BLACK CLOUD seemed determined to follow Jesse around ever since he'd uttered the damning word *commitment* to Kyra.

That same day his jigsaw broke, spinning a piece of nearly completed crown molding into the blade sideways before it conked out completely. He'd ruined a detailed piece that would take hours to reconstruct.

Then his customer's financing had fallen through for the first custom home he was supposed to have started on Monday, leaving him scrambling all afternoon to shuffle his spring schedule and fill the void.

Now as he sped up the rural county route toward the Crooked Branch on his Harley, it started to rain.

And then pour.

By the time he reached the ranch his khakis molded to his thighs like a wetsuit. Even worse, the rain hadn't let up a bit so he wouldn't be able to take them to dinner on the motorcycle.

If they wanted to go out for his first date as part of a couple in his entire lifetime, he'd have to ride shotgun in Kyra's pickup.

The joys of commitment.

Jesse sensed the black cloud stalking him as he parked his bike in the barn and swiped the worst of the raindrops off the seat. No, wait.

That wasn't just a dark mood stalking him.

Footsteps sounded behind him. Too close.

A black cloud in stilettos and not much else stood behind him. Greta Ingram appeared every inch the world-renowned cover model as she struck a pose in a tissue-thin scarf she'd knotted at her navel as if it was a dress.

Objectively speaking, Jesse knew she must look gorgeous, but all he could think in his current frame of mind was that she had to be damn near freezing.

He couldn't afford the complication of her tonight. He barely knew what role he was supposed to be playing in Kyra's life anyway. And he'd already spent enough time trying to send Greta a message she refused to hear. "We've got to stop meeting like this."

Her trademark full lips turned even more pouty. "Tell me about it. A barn is hardly my idea of mood-setting ambiance. What do you say we go back to my place for a few hours and I'll show you some more of my yoga moves? I've been working on limbering up my neck muscles and you'll never believe what I can reach with my tongue.''

She hovered closer, almost as if she was going to start teasing him with yoga tricks right here in the equipment storage barn.

''Greta, I can't see you anymore. Ever.'' He hated having to spell it out in such stark terms for her but her following him around had gotten way out of control. At one time her over-the-top antics might have swayed him, but he didn't feel even remotely interested tonight.

Oddly, he could still only think of one woman naked today. Even after a night in Kyra's arms Jesse could only think about her. Despite the hellish day he'd been having and the fact that he'd gone and devoted himself to some kind of relationship with her, he had thought about being with her nonstop.

Still, Greta looked at him like he'd lost his marbles. She put her fists on her hips and stood toe-to-toe with him. ''Excuse me?''

''I'm seeing Kyra now,'' he told her, amazed to discover the words didn't feel as awkward as he'd feared they might. In fact, the declaration felt damn good. ''And I know for a fact she's not going to appreciate you following me around. Now, if you'll excuse me, I've got to go meet her for dinner.''

Jesse saw the steam start to hiss from her ears, but he couldn't find it in his heart to care anymore. He was still too caught up in the revelation that it hadn't really hurt to talk about Kyra as his girlfriend.

What if he could pull through on this commitment thing after all?

He nudged around Greta, making his way toward the door. The rain had slowed, but it hadn't stopped. Clint's truck was pulling into the driveway, an odd occurrence for seven o'clock in the evening.

Or so he hoped.

The horse whisperer hadn't seriously thought he could make time with Kyra behind Jesse's back, had he? Before Jesse could think through what to do about Kyra's admirer, Greta hustled around him to plant herself in his tracks all over again.

"What are you doing?" He held his hands up but he didn't intend to surrender to this woman.

He was a committed man, damn it.

The rain pounded down on them. Jesse didn't care much since he was already soaked. But Greta's scarf turned X-rated within seconds. Not that he noticed.

She shouted at him through the rumble of thunder, her eyes lit by a fire within. "What does it look like I'm doing? I'm putting up a fight!"

He hadn't fully processed the comment when she grabbed him by the arms, plastered her wet body to his and fused their mouths in a no-holds-barred kiss.

11

KYRA SWIPED a brush through her hair and peered out the window just as the thunder started. The driveway was empty but she could have sworn she'd heard Jesse's Harley rumble past a few minutes ago.

Would he be late for their first date?

Judging by how pained he'd looked as he issued the invitation earlier today, Kyra half wondered if he'd show up at all. But then, he had always kept his word to her, even while he was standing up his so-called girlfriends left and right. Would their new committed status relegate her to his ''B'' list of personal priorities?

She resented his attitude even while she wished he felt differently about her. He had no right to make her feel as if she'd somehow twisted his arm into a relationship. Sure she hadn't shaken her age-old crush on him as easily as she'd once hoped, but she knew better than to ever hope for him to be a one-woman man.

Didn't she?

Simmering with restless energy and more than a little frustration, Kyra marched out into the foyer and prepared to face her personal demon.

Aka her best friend-turned-lover.

She knew damn well she'd heard his motorcycle a few minutes ago. Was he dragging his feet in the barn because he couldn't face his new ball and chain?

Throwing open the front door, Kyra didn't move so much as an inch into the blistering rain before she saw him.

Or rather *them*—Greta and Jesse in a lip lock as fierce as the storm pelting their shoulders with rain-drops.

Of all the two-timing lowdown tricks…

What more proof did she need that he'd never be a one-woman man? He hadn't even bothered to be sly about his indiscretion, opting instead to practically de-vour Greta whole while standing no more than two feet from Kyra's front porch. And it didn't really soothe Kyra a bit that the woman stuck to him was an internationally recognized sex symbol clad in an outfit that left her as good as naked.

"It's a new commitment record for you," Kyra shouted through the rainstorm, doing her level best to keep her voice calm. Practical. "I think you lasted almost six hours this time."

So maybe sarcasm wasn't exactly practical.

She was entitled to be a little peeved, curse his two-timing hide.

Jesse pried himself loose from Greta's arms, but not without a struggle. The Wonder-bod nearly lost her outfit in the process—an outfit comprised of one artfully tied purple scarf.

But instead of appealing to Kyra by laying on the

charm or spinning ridiculous tales to cover his hide, Jesse glared at Greta. "You'd damn well better come clean about this."

Out of the corner of her eye, Kyra noticed Clint climb down out of his truck cab and stalk toward them. Impervious to the water, Clint's Stetson shielded him from the driving downpour.

Greta shot Jesse the evil eye. "You're *not* the man I met last fall. And I don't have a thing to come clean about." As Clint neared, she sniffed and straightened. "Now, if you'll excuse me, I have plans for dinner."

Jesse looked ready to argue the point, but Clint stepped in like a hero right out of an old Western. Offering Greta his arm as if she wore hoopskirts and a bustle instead of a silk scarf masquerading as a dress, Clint was every inch the gentleman.

And it was obvious from a lone protective hand around Greta's waist that Jesse didn't have a chance in hell of grilling her about the kiss that had just taken place.

Leaving him very much on his own to explain himself.

Not that Kyra needed whatever explanation he concocted for her benefit.

Determined to cut him off before he could suggest some lame reasoning for what just happened, Kyra folded her arms across her chest and stared him down. "I'd just like to point out that I thought we had enough of a solid friendship where we didn't need to play games like this."

Spinning on her heel, she ducked back onto her porch and inside the house.

"Oh, no you don't." Jesse followed her, dripping rainwater from khakis that clearly outlined his thighs. Outlined *him*. "Cowboy Clint might have spirited witchy Greta away so she didn't have to deal with this, but you don't have any choice but to talk to me."

"I most definitely have a choice," she argued, seeking refuge from those wet male thighs in the kitchen. She was not succumbing to anything charming, sexy or otherwise appealing about Jesse Chandler tonight.

The man was a first-rate cad. A cad with fire-engine red lipstick smeared across his damned face.

He stomped his way into the kitchen, his wet socks squishing along the tiles. "On the contrary, we have a date tonight so I've already reserved this time with you. You can at least hear me out."

"Well, guess what, Romeo? Necking with another woman on my front doorstep pretty much nullifies our date." Kyra pulled a prepackaged dinner out of the freezer and attacked the shrink-wrap with a vengeance.

"That wasn't necking. That was the attack of the wicked wedding-bell woman. She was making some sort of last-ditch play for me with the kiss and the crazy outfit—"

"What outfit?" Shredding the last piece of plastic from an ancient TV dinner box, Kyra yanked open the microwave. "And since when is a woman who values marriage some kind of villain anyway? You make her sound like a comic book foe when maybe she's just calling you to the carpet on your fast lifestyle.''

Jesse intercepted her meal before she could chuck it in the microwave. ''How can you defend her after she practically suffocated me? In front of you, no less? She's been following me around for months, Kyra. And you know I've told her the deal more than once.''

Kyra hesitated. Considering. She was being unreasonable and she knew it. But damn it, seeing Jesse kissing another woman had hurt her more than she could admit.

''I don't think you can call it suffocation when you were standing there with your arms at your sides making no attempt to push her away.''

''She surprised me!''

Kyra tugged the Chicken Kiev with both hands, tossed it in the microwave and stabbed the keys to start heating her meal.

She needed to insert some space between them and move on. Even if the kiss wasn't his fault, she was quickly realizing how much it was going to hurt when she had to let him go. Something she'd never really considered before. ''Fine. I believe you. But please excuse me if I don't feel like having dinner with you or being any part of a bogus committed relationship.''

''You *are* having dinner with me.'' Jesse stopped the microwave, and inserted himself between Kyra and her chicken. ''It's not going to be out of a box from the freezer. And the commitment I made to you is hardly bogus.''

Kyra forced herself to quit grinding her teeth. But how could he say that to her when he'd already tangled himself up with another woman? Jesse's whole life had been one entanglement after another. He probably didn't know how to live any other way.

''It was a commitment based on sex.'' Surely that wasn't the premise for most healthy relationships.

''First of all, let's not knock sex.'' He stared at her with steady brown eyes that had a way of making her heart beat faster even though she was definitely still angry at him. ''And second, there was more to it than sex and we both know it.''

Admitting there was more than sex at stake here would be like admitting…too much. And damn it, she wasn't foolish enough to fall for Jesse.

''There couldn't have been more than sex involved, Jesse, because you went out of here more hangdog than I've ever seen you aside from when your team lost the pennant race that second season you played baseball.'' She opened a drawer near the sink, fished out a towel and threw it at him. ''Obviously you hated the whole idea of a relationship from the get-go. I don't know why you ever brought it up.''

He mopped off his face with the towel and then scrubbed his too-long hair to dry it out. Kyra's gaze tracked his muscles in action as he stretched his arms above his head, twisted his shoulders.

''You've got it all wrong.'' Jesse folded the towel over the back of a barstool that sat at her kitchen counter. "I would have been overjoyed if this had been all about sex. It's precisely because there's more at stake here that I'm scared as hell to mess it up. Sorry if I acted like an ass about the whole thing, but I don't have a clue what I'm doing when it comes to dating."

His honesty deflated her anger. She'd never thought of him as a sort of dating-virgin. Maybe they were on more even ground after all.

She had wanted Jesse so badly, but this morning she'd realized that sleeping with him had made things more complicated than she'd ever dreamed. Her irrational behavior over the whole Greta incident only proved she couldn't keep an emotional distance from the man.

She definitely needed to drag this conversation back on firmer terrain before she fell as head-over-heels for him as every other woman he'd ever met.

Kyra leveled a finger at his chest. "Well for starters, you can't kiss women outside the main relationship. That's a standard taboo."

"No kissing other women. Duly noted." Jesse edged closer, his every muscle defined and highlighted by his wet clothes. "As long as you present plenty of kissing opportunities for me, I don't think I'll find that a problem."

JESSE WATCHED the swirl of emotions parade across Kyra's face—the unguarded sensual response to his words, the confusion and finally the lip-pursing resistance that told him he was getting nowhere with that approach tonight.

Damn.

He hated that he caused so much uncertainty for her. She deserved a hell of a lot better than what he could ever offer her. Yet for the first time in his life he found himself genuinely wishing he was capable of giving a woman more.

Much more.

But he didn't trust himself not to hurt her. And that was no way to start a relationship.

Kyra slid out of her seat to move back toward the microwave and her very practical dinner. "Sorry, Jesse. I think we both know better than to offer each other any further sensual opportunities. Maybe you were right all along when you said we'd only screw up our friendship."

Panic chugged through him. It would hurt enough just knowing he'd never see Kyra naked again. He couldn't stand the thought of not being able to hang out at the ranch and sneak out one of her horses or try to make her blush. "You don't think we've really messed that up too, do you?"

"I think we're pretty damn close." She pressed the buttons that would start the oven all over again. "Honestly, I'm having a hard time figuring out how to relate to you in the wake of last night. Guess I sort of underestimated how sex could screw with things— pardon the pun—but chalk it up to a first-timer mis- calculation. I'm sorry I didn't listen to you that day at Gasparilla when you said this wouldn't work."

She blinked too fast. A definite indication she was upset and refusing to let it show.

But ruining their friendship?

His brain refused to hear this message. He'd jumped from one woman to another without even blinking his whole life and Kyra had remained his one constant. The Crooked Branch had been his home base when he'd been on the road with his baseball team—the one place where no one expected him to be charming or successful or to pretend he had the world by the tail.

Here, with Kyra, he'd always been able to just *be*.

"But you believe me that I never intended anything to happen with Greta, at least." How could that pushy woman's one impulsive act cost him his best friend?

Of course, as soon as he thought as much, he knew. If he lost Kyra's friendship, it wouldn't be Greta's fault. It would be his own damn doing because he'd approached the commitment thing all wrong.

"This doesn't have anything to do with her. Or the kiss." She tucked a blond strand of hair behind one ear, her quiet, unassuming air so totally at odds with every other woman he'd ever dated. He'd probably never noticed she was beautiful because she never flaunted herself in front of him.

At least not until that eye-opening day at Gasparilla.

"It doesn't?" He found it hard to believe she wasn't pissed about the kiss. Greta had put a squeeze-hold on him like an anaconda. If he'd ever seen Kyra in another man's grasp like that, he would have lost his damn mind.

"No. It has more to do with you acting like you've sentenced yourself to a prison term by going out with me. I'll admit I've always had a little bit of a thing for you, Jesse."

He nearly hit the floor with the shock of that particular news. She'd had a *thing* for him?

The automatic warmth he'd felt in reaction to the statement quickly turned to panic as he realized the fallout from this could be worse than he'd expected.

Shit.

He never wanted to hurt her.

Perhaps sensing his shock, Kyra rushed to reassure him. "But I'm over it now. You don't need to sacrifice yourself to me just because we're friends." She shrugged her shoulder in a gesture that seemed too precise to be totally careless.

Or was that wishful thinking on his part?

"I don't think I ever tried to sound like I was making a sacrifice."

"But you didn't exactly behave like a man overjoyed to ask me out."

Maybe she had a point there. "But that wasn't because of *you*."

"That was just because you're a commitment-phobe." As the microwave timer began to beep, Kyra tugged an Aztec-printed potholder from a drawer near the sink. "I realize that. That doesn't make your resistance any more flattering."

Jesse made a mental note never to ask a woman

out before he had fully resolved any internal conflict on the subject. Obviously he sucked at masking his emotions. "What can I do to make you give me a second chance?"

She bit her lip. Furrowed her brow. Obviously wrestled with the whole notion of second chances. It scared him to realize just how important that second chance had become for him.

"I don't think I can. I'm over you, remember?"

How could she be over him when he hadn't even applied himself to the task of winning her in the first place? "Come on, Kyra. Have you ever considered getting involved with someone just because? Just for the fun of it? Just because you felt like it? Couldn't I ever potentially warrant a date like that again?"

She sighed. "I'm not saying yes."

Then again, she wasn't saying no. Jesse counted that as progress. "Understood."

"First of all, if we ever decided to date again, you couldn't bullshit me." She juggled the steaming cardboard tray on the potholder and dumped them both on a lone placemat at the kitchen counter.

"Done."

"Second, if you ever want to ask me out again make sure you do it with some sincerity." She rummaged through another drawer and came out with a fork. Waving it at him like a weapon, she expounded her point. "No woman wants to think she's being courted out of some misguided sense of responsibility. I'd like to think a man asks me out because he really wants to be with me and *only me*."

He could do that. Because damn it, he really did want to be with Kyra. He'd been thinking about her nonstop for two weeks running.

It was just the *only Kyra* part that caused him to think twice. He'd never been a one-woman man in his life. Could he pull it off now?

Just as he was thinking *hell yes* he could, Kyra sighed and stabbed at her Chicken Kiev. The woman who'd been so intent on cooking dinner now seemed to do little more than mangle her meal.

Tired of waiting for him, no doubt.

"You'd better go, Jesse. I need to get on the phone tonight to see if it's too late to offer up Sam's Pride at the horse auction in Tampa this weekend." She shoved some broccoli around her cardboard plate. "I'm thinking with all the action going on at an event like that, I might be able to trick him into loading onto another horse trailer and closing a sale on him."

"Wait a minute." He didn't want to talk about that damn horse or how badly Kyra wanted to boot him out of the business all together. Not yet anyway. "I can do this, Kyra. You and me."

She looked up from her dinner to meet his gaze, and a tear perched on the outer corner of one blue eye. "This isn't the same as you talking me into riding with you at night while my father was sleeping, or convincing me to compete in the jumper class instead of the show ring. There's a lot more at stake here for me."

Shit.

He'd already screwed this up and he hadn't even

managed to get to the date part yet. The lone tear Kyra blinked away wrenched his insides more than the practiced pouts of a whole legion of femmes fatales.

Still, he backed away, knowing he'd been at fault for putting that tear there, if only for a moment. And instead of defending his actions or getting upset about what he and Kyra might have had together, Jesse found himself pleading on behalf of her horse.

"Don't sell Sam's Pride tomorrow. He deserves another chance." His wet socks trailed footprints across the ceramic tiles as he made his way toward the door. "Don't force us both out of your life yet."

Kyra scrubbed her wrist over her eyes and stabbed another bite of chicken with her fork. "He's just a horse, Jesse. Half our business has been built on raising them and selling them. I need that extra money."

Yeah, so she could wall him out of every area of her life.

"I'm starting work on the houses full-time on Monday. I don't stand a chance of being in your way here." Already the thought of spending that much time away from the ranch didn't set well with him. Who would he regale with stories about his first day as an honest-to-goodness working stiff?

"I have to put the business first, Jesse."

I have to be practical, Jesse. She didn't voice the sentiment, but Jesse heard it between the lines.

Why the hell didn't he have the right words to convince her otherwise?

Then again, she'd probably made up her mind al-

ready and Jesse had never been able to compete with
her tough-as-nails resolve once she decided what she
wanted.

Her voice scratched just a little, however, as she
tossed out one final, ''Goodbye.''

''IT WAS A HELL of a performance.'' Clicking on the
overhead light in his truck cab, Clint finally broke the
silence that had fallen thick and heavy in the course
of the last twenty miles.

He hadn't known what exactly to say in the wake
of Greta's last desperate play for Jesse Chandler, but
seeing how much passion she'd thrown into the effort
had humbled him just a little. Obviously, she liked
the guy more than he'd given her credit for.

Not that he was one bit sorry how the evening had
turned out.

Jesse didn't deserve a spitfire like Greta. Hell, that
guy could barely keep pace with Kyra Stafford,
who—from Clint's observation—seemed to be the
sanest woman on earth. No way could Jesse ever
wade through the complex tangle of over-the-top behavior that characterized Greta Ingram.

Now, she sat in her corner of his truck, her wet
purple scarf clinging to totally outrageous curves
while she stared out the window at the gray blur of
rain.

''What was a great performance?'' She swiveled in
her seat to face him. With the help of the overhead
light, Clint could see her green eyes were all the more
bright for the tears she hadn't shed. ''You riding in

to the rescue on a damn white horse? Excuse me if I don't applaud, I'm just a little choked up over that really warm reception I received from the so-called man of my dreams.''

Clint had to admire her spunk in the wake of disaster. ''I wasn't referring to me. You're the one who put your heart on the line and had the nerve to go for what you wanted. And when Chandler was too blind to see what was right before his eyes, you bucked up and shipped out of there just as cool as you please.''

She shoved a wet hank of hair off her forehead. The small stretch combined with her transparent outfit made him recall exactly why she'd graced two *Sports Illustrated* covers in a row. Greta Ingram might be a little down on her luck, but she was a feast for the male eye.

Not that he was interested in her because of that.

Pretty women were a dime a dozen in Alabama, but none of them had ever affected Clint the way Greta did. Despite her perfect exterior, Greta had the guts of a prizefighter and a wilder spirit than any horse Clint had ever tried to tame.

She met his gaze with a level look of her own. ''Sometimes we don't have any choice but to walk away.''

Clint heard the message. Knew Jesse Chandler wasn't the first person Greta had needed to leave behind. One day soon he'd find out who else had been foolish enough to let this woman go.

''Damn straight. No sense sticking around someone who doesn't recognize your worth.'' Clint thought he noticed her shiver out of the corner of his eye. "You cold?"

She rolled her eyes.

"Hell yes, you're freezing." He reached a hand back behind the bench seat and pulled out a blue cotton blanket that had seen better days. "It's clean, I swear. You want me to pick you up something to eat?"

Greta spread the blanket over herself and shot him a surly look that was halfhearted at best. "Why are you being so nice to me today? You've been borderline hideous every other time we've ever spoken."

He steered the truck over the back roads toward the suburbs of Tampa. The roads were peppered with palm trees and a few houses, but for the most part, they passed little traffic. The rain had slowed to a mist. "Didn't I tell you I was going to break out the refined manners tonight if you let me take you out? I'm not some hick from a Mississippi backwater town, you know. We Alabama guys have class."

"Mississippi. Alabama. There's a difference?"

"I'm going to let that slide because you're not a U.S. native." Even though he was pretty sure she was trying to yank his chain. "And yes, there's a huge difference."

He saw her gaze stop on a McDonald's sign and stay there. He wouldn't have pegged Miss Supermodel for fast food, but he had to at least offer.

"You want me to stop—"

"Bacon double cheeseburger, please. And a strawberry shake."

He slowed down but didn't put on his signal light. What woman wanted carry-out burgers on a date? "I could take you somewhere—"

"No! This is perfect."

Clint turned into the drive-thru lane. "You like burgers that much?"

"I've been waiting half my life to finally eat them again. I lived on coffee and cigarettes the whole time I was modeling. I feel as if I've been given a new lease on life." She poked him in the side as he was calling his order into the drive-thru speaker. "Can you get fries with that?"

He ordered enough food for a small army and then edged the truck out onto the main road. "You mind eating while we're on the road?"

"Actually, this is perfect because I can watch you drive."

Or at least that's what Clint assumed she said. It was damn hard to tell when the woman's mouth was full.

"Did you just say you wanted to watch me?" Because he was going to be very turned on if that was really the case.

"I want to learn how to drive and buy a car. It's good for me to pick up the shifting rhythm, so I'll just observe while I eat." She popped another fry in her mouth and furrowed her brow as he hit fourth gear. "Where are we going?"

Personally, he was really hoping for third base.

"I thought I'd show you a great American tradition."

She licked the sauce oozing out one side of her burger with a sensualist's delight. "I've lived in the States on and off for years. I'll bet I've already seen it."

He rather hoped not. "I don't know. You might not have since you don't drive." He couldn't help but smile. "Are you familiar with the age-old pastime called parking?"

12

GRETA SMOTHERED a laugh. Clint Bowman was nothing if not entertaining but she wasn't entirely certain she should allow herself to relax with him yet. Behind tonight's affable manner lurked a man with lots of dark corners and hidden depths.

Translation—Clint could still prove dangerous to a woman wary of men she couldn't control or at very least, understand.

Jesse had been every bit as dark and enticing as Clint with his bad-boy ways, but at least Greta had the peace of mind that he channeled them into games of seduction. While she'd never stood a chance at controlling him, she'd understood him. And she'd never been fearful of sex and all the erotic delights that went along with it.

But after the tense atmosphere of her childhood, Greta refused to get tangled up with any man who possessed a scary temper or who liked to power trip. And while Greta hadn't pegged Clint for that type, she still hadn't managed to peg him for any type. Period.

Deeper emotions frightened her far more than a guy sporting a set of handcuffs or a wicked grin.

"I know exactly what parking refers to, Clint Bowman. And I may be a cheap date, but I've given you no indication that I'd be easy."

"Amen to that." He turned off the main road onto a quiet stretch of highway lined with towering Georgia pines and banyan trees. "You're talking to the guy who kicked off our first date by watching you tangle tongues with another man. I didn't think for a second you'd be easy."

Clint *had* stayed awfully calm in the wake of her throwing herself at Jesse. Some guys might have been jealous or picked a fight. Or worse. But Clint hadn't been ruffled in the least.

A man like that must surely possess great stores of patience. Which, if Greta decided she might be interested in him, would definitely be a good thing.

Now, she watched the play of his muscles beneath his white polo shirt as he shifted gears. She'd totally forgotten to look for pointers on driving in her quest to simply watch Clint. He might not have the sculpted perfection of Jesse, but his rough-hewn features and solid, muscular build had definite appeal.

Her body was warming up beneath the blue cotton throw blanket Clint had given her. And it wasn't just because her dress was drying out.

"I guess I needed to see if things were really dead between Jesse and me," she said finally, crumpling up the remains of her dinner and stuffing them in the paper bag on Clint's truck floor.

"And?"

"You saw with your own eyes how he turned me down cold. Obviously, he's not carrying a torch."

"But what about on your end? Still some sparks there?"

"Surprisingly, no." Ever since she'd stumbled over Clint at the Crooked Branch, she'd had a hard time finding much enthusiasm for her pursuit of Jesse Chandler. "I think my feelings for him died a while back, but he's just so damn perfect for the vision I have of my life that I couldn't let go of the dream. Is that totally ridiculous or what?"

"I think you're smart as hell for moving on once you figured out he wasn't right for you. Too many people settle for relationships that don't really work or that died a long time ago." Something in his voice made Greta think his thoughts had jumped far beyond the confines of the truck cab.

"Speaking from experience?"

Clint stared out the window, but she could tell his expression changed. Hardened. "Put it this way—I'd sure as hell never want anyone to feel like they were settling with me."

Again.

He didn't say the word, but Greta heard it just the same. She studied the hard angles of his face as he slowed the truck and pulled into a paved turnoff on one side of the road.

"That begs the question what on earth are you doing asking me out when you knew I was chasing Jesse?" She thought they were turning around until Clint parked the truck and clicked off the ignition.

The rain had stopped completely and they stared out at a clump of trees still dripping from the downpour.

Turning to face her, Clint stared at her with intent gray eyes. "Call it gut instinct, but I couldn't see you with a guy who doesn't recognize what's in his own backyard." Rolling his window down, he tossed the crumpled up fast-food sack into a trash can some ten feet away. They sat at some roadside pull-off with zero scenery in sight. A few trees loomed in the shadowed distance. No houses lined the road. "Besides, a girl as pretty as you ought to hook up with a less-than-perfect guy. Sort of even out the gene pool a little."

She had a mind to quiz him on who he might deem appropriately less-than-perfect, but she was too curious about what they were doing out in the middle of nowhere.

"Not that I'm suspicious or anything, Clint, but I couldn't help but notice your truck is now parked." She squinted out her window, but there were no streetlights here to illuminate their surroundings. In the distance, through a scant line of fat trees, she spied little blue lights on the ground.

"So it is." He smiled, unconcerned.

"We wouldn't be parking by any chance, would we?" Okay, maybe the idea intrigued her just a little bit. All that gear shifting and flexing of male muscle had revved her engines a bit.

And for reasons she still couldn't fully fathom, she and Clint had some major chemistry going.

His mouth hung open as if he couldn't be more

offended. "You wound me, Greta. Didn't you specifically nix the parking idea? I just thought an international jet-setter like you would appreciate the slow pace of Saturday night entertainment where I come from."

She waited for the other shoe to drop. "Watching the windshield fog up?"

"Watching planes take off. We're on the outskirts of Tampa International Airport. See the runway lights over there?" He pointed to the strip of blue she'd seen before. "Although if you decide you want to work on fogging up that windshield, I'll be more than happy to help."

"Because you're such a gentleman?"

"Exactly."

Too bad the fire in his gray eyes didn't look the least bit gentlemanly. Greta was experiencing hot flashes over the idea of wrestling around the truck with Clint Bowman and all those unrefined muscles of his.

She'd picked Jesse as a potential husband candidate because he seemed so perfect for her on the outside and what a total disaster that had been. What if this time, she ignored her damned preconceived notions of what kind of man she ought to be with and dated a guy who just plain made her feel good?

And Clint had only been armed with a bacon double cheeseburger and his wit. Imagine how he could make her feel if she allowed him to use those big, broad hands of his?

The mere thought sent shivers through her that didn't have a thing to do with her limited attire.

Greta stared out the truck window for at least twenty seconds. "If this is your idea of fun, Clint Bowman, it's no damn wonder you're still single."

Making up her mind to follow her instincts instead of her old, immature notions of perfection, Greta levered open the passenger side door and tossed off the blanket she'd been hiding under.

"What are you doing?" He reached for his hat, shoulders tense. "This is *not* a good place to hitchhike, Greta."

The flash of concern in his eyes sent a little thrill through her. When was the last time anyone had expended energy worrying about *her?*

She was definitely making the right decision tonight.

Even if it was just a little over-the-top.

"No?" She slid out of the truck and down to the pavement. Glancing back toward the main road, she didn't see a car anywhere so she hooked one finger in the lone knot that held her dress together. "Is it a good area to get naked?"

SHE WOULDN'T.

Clint stared at Greta's right index finger curved into the loop of purple fabric at her navel. He'd been the freaking epitome of control and restraint all night long.

Even when Greta had wrapped herself around another man for a kiss that *he* wanted to taste.

Even when she'd wriggled her way into his truck with a wet scarf plastered to her body and highlighting every sinfully sweet nuance.

But he couldn't handle seeing her whipping off that scarf for his eyes only. Not when anybody could happen by their deserted stretch of runway.

He found his voice. Barely. "Outside the truck is probably *not* a great place to get naked." His vocal cords hit a new depth of bass. The rest of his body seemed to be striving to reach new heights. "Inside the truck is perfectly safe, however." He stretched across the front seat to offer her his hand. "So why don't you climb in and we'll pitch off all the clothes you want?"

Preferably starting with that fluttering piece of silk she was trying to pass off as a dress.

But dress or no, Clint just couldn't wait to put his hands on her. Any part of her. Surely even a PC kind of guy could interpret the suggestion of getting naked as a bit of an invitation?

An airplane screamed down the runway while she stood out in the Florida night air, making up her fickle woman's mind. Greta turned to watch it.

Faster.

Faster.

Before it shot like a bullet straight into the inky sky.

She laughed with the heady delight of a woman heeding the call of the wild. And with a snap of her wrist, she unleashed the scarf and banished it to the cool night wind.

That was *definitely* an invitation.

Clint didn't see nearly enough skin in his scramble to get out of the truck. He followed her out the passenger side door, unwilling to lose track of her for even an instant.

She was already sprinting—barefoot and laughing—toward the shelter of the banyan trees at the edge of the fenced runway. Her luscious pale body caught the hints of moonbeam even in the dark, making her an easy target for a man on a mission.

He'd never been so motivated in his life.

Less than ten steps and he caught her around the waist from behind. Drew the back of her to the front of him and nearly lost his mind at the onslaught of sensual impressions.

The creamy smooth skin of her belly beneath his palm. The exotic scent at her neck that didn't originate in any dime-store perfume bottle. The perfect dip at the small of her back that gave way to hips other men could only dream about.

But mostly he felt the soft curve of her rump snuggled tightly to an erection that wouldn't quit.

At least not any time tonight.

He might have tried carrying her back to his truck. That would have been the safest, most sensible thing to do with a naked woman.

But then Greta turned in his arms to pin him with hungry eyes and a wordless sigh, and robbed him of that option.

Her breasts pressed into his chest, making him very much aware of her arousal even through his polo shirt. The tight peaks teased and tormented him, called to his mouth.

He was already bending to kiss them when she ground her hips against his and caused a white flash through his head that could only be sensory explosion. Never had any man been inundated with so much delectable woman at one time.

The dull hum of a car engine flitted through his consciousness, but Clint couldn't seem to make his feet move back toward the truck. Not now, when his lips were closing over Greta's tight pink nipple.

He nudged her back into the protective cover of the scant trees and ignored everything else but the sweet taste of her rain-washed skin. She moaned and the sound vibrated right through him. Vaguely, he wondered if he'd drawn her too far into his mouth, but he couldn't seem to let go of her enough to ask, and she kept squeezing him harder and harder.

God, she was incredible.

The car sped by the parking area, the flash of headlights behind them barely a blip on Clint's mental radar. He normally played things so safe. He was normally a gentleman, damn it. But this woman got under his skin.

And right now, she'd gotten into his khakis in record time.

Her soft hands curved around him through his boxers and he knew he was so done for. A stone encrusted bangle of some sort scraped against his abs, a welcome momentary sting to balance the pleasure that was robbing him of logic and reason.

"Greta, you deserve better." He wanted to worship this woman. Lick every inch of her and stir her senses all the way to multiple orgasms.

Instead, he was halfway to taking her naked in the woods. Against a banyan tree of all the freaking things.

She bit his shoulder. Kissed his neck. "I don't want better. I want more. Now."

Running her hand up and down the length of him to prove her point, Greta presented arguments too persuasive to ignore. This time.

Clint promised himself next time would be different. Next time he'd be the one taking off her clothes. And she wouldn't have a prayer of rushing him.

But for now, he was more than willing to get caught up in her wild ways.

She was in the middle of freeing him when she pulled back with a start. "Do you have anything with you? Um. Protection-wise?"

He reached for his wallet and pulled out a plastic packet. "Good thing one of us kept our clothes on."

She stared at him accusingly even as she tore open the condom. "You *did* think I'd be easy."

"Are you kidding? Hope springs eternal for every man. I carry one when I go to church, too, if it makes you feel any better."

"Really?" She flashed him a conspiratorial smile, her blue eyes glowing with a feral light as she nudged his boxers down and rolled the prophylactic over him. "That sounds very wicked of you."

He forgot how to breathe. She stroked him with

urgent fingers while she wrapped one calf around his thigh.

When he found his voice again, he steadied her hips, not ready for her to fast-forward through this. "I prefer to think of it as optimistic."

Staring down at her bared body in the moonlight, so perfect and totally uncivilized, Clint had to admit he would have never been this optimistic, however.

To have *her*.

Tonight.

The more he thought about it, the less capable he was of slowing things down. Her peeling her scarf off had been his personal breaking point—a total explosion that left them both burning out of control. And if this time was fast and furious, he could tell himself he'd only been looking out for her best interests.

He couldn't allow a world-famous cover model to be discovered running around the outskirts of Tampa International while buck naked, could he?

Yeah, right. Just call him Mr. Unselfish.

"Please, Clint." She whispered it over and over like a seductive mantra while she rubbed herself against him.

The sultry night air whispered across his senses, but mostly he could only see, feel or hear Greta. Her little moans worked him to a fever pitch while her hands smoothed their way under his shirt and her short nails scraped lightly against his back.

She was too fast for him, but he didn't stand a chance of slowing her down. He settled for sliding one hand around the back of her neck and tilting her head to receive his kiss. She tasted like sex—hot, wet and mind-blowingly sweet.

So he indulged himself. Thoroughly.

And all the while he kissed her he sought the other source of her heat. The silky wet essence of her that had brushed ever so lightly against his cock and made him insane to be inside her.

His fingers brushed over the damp curls that sheltered her from him, tunneled through the soft blond fuzz she'd shaved into some precise pattern or another. He'd look later.

In detail.

Right now, he bypassed that pleasure for later, needing to feel the pulsing—

Ah, yes.

She was slick and ready for him. Swollen and every bit as eager as he was. He would have slid his finger inside her, but she was lifting herself into his arms and wrapping those long, perfect legs around his waist before he had the chance.

Her position placed her snugly against him, opened her to him with an invitation he couldn't hold off any longer. He had to be inside her.

He hoped like hell she didn't regret this later. In his gentleman mode tonight, he'd planned to come clean about his work and his special interest in psychology. For some reason, he had the feeling Greta, and all her intriguing depths, was going to have a problem with his fascination with neurosis—human and equine alike. But bottom-line, he was a horse breeder. She couldn't take issue with that.

And if she was a little incensed about his other work, he'd deal with that later.

When he wasn't on the verge of the best sex of his life.

Forgetting all about anything but claiming the woman in his arms, Clint hoisted her a few inches higher. Slowly, he resettled her, positioning her above him.

And then he was inside her and she was squeezing him all around. Greta's ankles clamped together behind his back as if she'd keep him right there forever. Her breasts brushed his cheek, filled his nostrils with her soft woman's scent.

Another motor rumbled in the distance and Clint made sure they were hidden from view of the road. But as the growl of an engine grew louder, headlights hit them—not from the street behind them, but from the runway dead ahead.

For a moment, they were caught in the bright light and Clint saw every facet of Greta with piercing clarity. Head thrown back, teeth sunk into her full lower lip, cheeks flushed with the night air and the sex.

And right there, in the middle of that white hot spotlight, she unraveled.

Her cry all but lost in the whine of the airplane engine, Greta went taut against him, her back arching with her pleasure. Clint might have gone over the edge just looking at her like that. But her body pulsing around his in quick little throbs stole all his control within seconds.

He flew right up there with her for a long, breath-stealing moment while the plane turned to accelerate up the runway. They clung together, damp with sweat and sex and Clint had never felt so fulfilled.

They were so damn right together in the big scheme of things. So balanced.

Cast in darkness once again, the image of Greta in the bright light burned itself on the backs of his eyelids.

And he knew from that one blinding moment he wouldn't be letting this woman go anytime soon.

If ever.

He'd find a way to reach past that haughty attitude she wore like armor. And once he did that, convincing a sophisticated globe-trotter to trade in her frequent flyer miles for a life on an Alabama horse ranch would seem like a walk in the park.

13

THE AUCTIONEER'S hyper-speed monologue rang out over the county fairgrounds on the outskirts of Tampa Sunday morning. Kyra scanned the crowds for Clint as she led Sam's Pride away from the unloading zone and toward his assigned stall for the day.

The glossy black three-year-old snorted and stayed close to her in the unfamiliar terrain, but after hearing Clint's thoughts on why the horse acted the way he did, Kyra suspected that was more for her protection than out of any fear of his own.

Patting the horse's broad neck, she ignored the twinge of guilt that had been niggling at her all morning. She could almost see Jesse frowning his disapproval at her in her mind's eye.

Jesse.

The pang she felt when she thought about him hurt even more than her guilt over the horse. She'd purposely found errands to do away from the ranch over the past few days just in case he dropped by.

Of course, her long absences were the reason she'd never been able to make connections with Clint about meeting her at the auction today. She'd called his cell phone several times since Thursday night but never got an answer. She'd finally left a voice-mail message for him last night with the details about the auction on the off chance he could help her out this one last time.

Technically, his work with Sam's Pride was complete and Kyra knew he had his own breeding farm to attend to in Alabama. From what she'd gathered about him from other trainers, Kyra understood Clint's first priority was his own ranch. He simply had a fascination with unusual horse behavior and enjoyed the diversion of working with those cases.

But she really would have liked the extra hands today to help her with the nine-hundred-pound Tennessee walking horse in case Sam's Pride turned nervous when she sold him. The fairgrounds were already brimming with noise and activity as the auctioneer's energetic delivery blasted over an old public address system and horses changed hands in every direction.

In the past, Jesse had always helped her with things like this. The last auction they'd attended together, Jesse had bought a few ponies despite Kyra's adamant objections. Providing pony rides and training for children wasn't their focus.

But he and his controlling percentage had won the argument. Much to her surprise, the ponies had established a veritable gold mine for the Crooked Branch, as tourists and locals alike turned out in droves to indulge their kids.

Jesse's whim was actually the business coup of the year. And now that she remembered how much she had protested that day at the auction, Kyra wondered if she'd ever remembered to tell Jesse how right he had been about the ponies.

Another pang of guilt pinched her as she tried to discern one Stetson from another in the crowd, still hoping for a glimpse of Clint.

But not half as much as she hoped in vain for a glimpse of Jesse. Sure she'd told him she wanted to take Sam's Pride to auction today. That didn't mean he'd show up at the last minute the way he sometimes had in the past. She hadn't realized how much having his support had meant to her over the years. How much his roguish smile would bolster her.

The sound of footsteps running across the gravel behind her made her heart leap nevertheless. She turned, cursing the hopeful jump of her heart.

Clint skidded to a stop next to her, Stetson nowhere to be found as he huffed out a greeting sporting running shorts and a T-shirt that was…inside out? "I just got your message this morning while I was making coffee."

"Good morning to you too. Long night?" She nodded at his T-shirt, curious what sort of woman caught this practical man's eye. And even more curious what sort of woman caught it so thoroughly he hadn't even noticed his own shirt was wrong side out.

He frowned down at the seams on his shoulder. "A pleasantly long night. But I hauled ass over here this morning as soon as I heard your voice mail. You can't sell him, Kyra. Not after the way he acted the other night."

"You think it will upset him too much?" She didn't want to traumatize her horse, but damn it, this was business. She'd really counted on the income from his sale this year. Not just to win a controlling percentage of the business, but to uphold her end of the partnership and show real progress toward buying Jesse out. She'd agreed to going into business together five years ago because she couldn't have afforded to do it by herself. But damn it, she'd always intended to pay him back.

"Maybe." He stroked the horse's nose and shook his head. "Honestly, I don't know. But I do think he has something unique to offer with his protective instincts. We ought to give him a chance to show us what he can do with those skills before you sell him off as your everyday average three-year-old."

Hadn't Jesse told her the same thing three days ago? *He deserves another chance.*

She'd ignored him then, just like she would have ignored him about the ponies if he hadn't forced her to listen. Was she dead wrong about this, too?

Still, Kyra had trusted her own instincts all her life. Unable to count on her father's guidance between his medications and his battle with manic depression, she had learned to rely solely upon herself. And old habits died hard.

"Do you really think there's something rational behind this behavior, Clint? I wouldn't want to spoil a horse who's just demonstrating routine negative behavior."

Clint shoved his fingers through his hair, making it

stand up even straighter. ''Call me crazy, but I would swear that horse thinks he's on a mission to look out for you.''

His words resonated through her, struck a nerve and a long-ago memory. Her father had visited the stables shortly after Sam's Pride was born. He'd been having one of his lucid days and he'd been fond of the horse at first sight, going so far as to christen the animal after himself—the original Sam. Her dad boasted he gave Sam's Pride a mission that day—to watch over Kyra, his other pride and joy.

She'd been touched, but she'd also been worried that her father's sensitivity would morph to sadness and she proceeded to drive him back home for the night. She'd forgotten all about the remark until Clint's words revived the memory. ''You think he's on a mission?''

''It's the damnedest thing. I make no claim to horse telepathy, believe you me. But that's the sense I get from this animal every time I'm near him. He's on a mission.''

Kyra wouldn't, *couldn't* give any credence to that line of thinking. Still, a part of her longed for Jesse's input. What would he think of her crazy memory of her dad giving Sam's Pride a mission, let alone Clint assuring her the horse was acting it out?

Would he howl with laughter? Or would he actually consider the possibility?

His advice seemed all the more important to her now that she knew she couldn't seek it. Although bottom-line she'd always made her own decisions, Kyra had been counting on her partner's advice more than she ever realized.

Either way, she was certain Jesse didn't think she should sell the horse.

Clint had bent to tie his running shoes while she was thinking. Now, he stood, his gaze connecting with hers again. "Don't sell him, Kyra. Or if you're really hell-bent to get rid of him, sell him to me."

Taken aback, she peered up at him. "Why would you ever want to buy Sam's Pride with all his…emotional baggage?" In the back of her mind she could hear a bidding war break out on the auction floor and the auctioneer's frenzy to up the bids. Sam's Pride wasn't listed to go up on the block until almost noon, however, so Kyra didn't need to rush to get him to his stall.

Either that, or she was procrastinating.

"I think Sam's Pride has a lot of potential if he can ever transfer his protective streak from you to…someone else." Clint folded the pamphlet with all the horses' names listed on the day's auction roster and shoved the paper in his pocket.

Kyra frowned. Was he just offering to buy the horse to be nice? "You seem pretty self-sufficient to me, Clint. I can't picture you needing this guy following you around like a shadow." She patted Sam's Pride's neck. "And he'd probably get upset when you went out of town to visit other troubled horses—"

"He wouldn't be for me. I'd buy him to keep an eye on Greta." Clint exchanged a quick hello with one of the auction attendees shouldering their way past them. The equine world was small enough that events like this were guaranteed to bring together at least a few familiar faces.

"Not Greta Ingram?" Kyra would have fallen over if she hadn't had a hand on Sam's Pride to keep her up. She couldn't picture the Marlboro Man and his boots with the German Wonder-bod and her stilettos.

"One and the same. If she'll have me, that is."

Kyra immediately regretted her obvious surprise. His inside-out shirt took on a whole new level of meaning. "I take it the two of you hit it off the other night after the incident in my driveway?"

"You could say that. I don't know how she'll take to life in Alabama, though. And I wouldn't mind having some help looking out for her while she makes the transition." He made a soft sound to Sam's Pride and the horse whickered back at him. "I wish I could convince Sam's Pride to watch over Greta the way he watches over you."

An interesting proposition. And it certainly revealed how much Greta meant to Clint if he was so concerned about her. How would it feel to have a man watch your back that way?

Dismissing the thought before she wandered down wishful paths she had no business traveling, Kyra turned her attention to Clint's idea. She'd already been questioning her decision to sell her horse today. Maybe Clint's offer would give her a few more days to weigh the consequences. "If you're going to stick around Citrus County a little longer, maybe you could bring Greta over to the Crooked Branch and introduce her to Sam's Pride. See how they get along to sort of test the waters.''

''I'll get my checkbook out of the truck. How much were you hoping to get for him?''

Tempting as the offer sounded, now that she was faced with the do-or-die moment to commit to the sale, Kyra couldn't follow through. She couldn't sell Clint a horse until she was certain the animal would behave for him. Which meant she also wouldn't be selling the horse to anyone else today, either.

Especially not after what she'd learned about Sam's Pride this morning. She shook her head. ''Wait to see how he does with Greta. I'll gladly sell him to you if the two of them hit it off.''

Smiling, Clint stuck out his hand to seal the bargain. ''You've got yourself a deal.''

After making arrangements to drop by during the week, Clint and his running shoes made tracks for the parking lot, leaving Kyra to wonder what had happened to her ability to make a decision, let alone to be practical.

Her sound business sense seemed to have waltzed out the door when Jesse had left her kitchen Thursday.

Was she being stubborn where he was concerned for no good reason? From the outside looking in, Clint Bowman and Greta Ingram probably had even less in common than her and Jesse. Yet Clint obviously had every intention of making things work between them.

If a grounded, intelligent guy like Clint could set

his sights on someone as over-the-top as Greta, why couldn't she at least try a relationship with Jesse? In all fairness, she'd given up before they'd even gotten started.

Maybe, with a few practical ground rules in place, she could at least give it—give *them*—a chance.

JESSE JOGGED through the fairgrounds with his auction placard in hand, searching for any sign of horse #54, Sam's Pride, who wasn't in his temporary stall for public viewing. He'd arrived first thing in the morning to glance over the day's lineup, and when he'd assured himself Kyra wouldn't be auctioning off her horse for another few hours, he'd headed back to his workshop to put the finishing touches on the crown molding for his first home—the house that *had* to be a showplace.

It had taken him this long in life to figure out what he would enjoy doing outside the ranch, but now that he had a focus on building custom homes, he planned to do it right. First and foremost, he wanted Chandler Homes to succeed for himself. But maybe—just a little—he wanted to be able to show Kyra his success, too.

He hadn't bothered to force his ideas on her at the Crooked Branch, his need to give her something that was just for *her* outweighing any selfish need to be right. But now that she'd made it clear she wanted complete independence from him—professionally *and* personally—Jesse couldn't help the desire to prove she'd overlooked his contributions.

He might like to work on the books while watching the Devil Rays on TV. And he might look like he was having a good time doing it, but that didn't make his efforts any less important, damn it.

Kyra just didn't seem to realize work and fun could go hand in hand.

Finally, he spotted her. A blond waif in blue jeans crooning to her horse amid a crowd of cowboys in boots and cigar-smoking businessmen. And he cracked a smile to see her among the rest of the horse-crazy auction-goers. Maybe she'd developed some of her all-business attitude from hanging out with the good old boy network for too many years.

She *had* to be tough or she would have been steam-rolled right out of business five years ago.

Jesse approached her slowly, waiting for her to notice him but she was too wrapped up in silent communication with the ornery three-year-old gelding who only listened to her. As he neared them, Jesse waved his red auction placard under her nose.

She snapped out of it then, her gaze connecting with his in a moment of electric awareness.

A vivid picture of her underneath him on his office sectional invaded his brain, scattered his thoughts.

"Jesse." Her voice held a tiny note of relief. Or so he chose to think. "What are you doing here to-day?"

I came to claim you for my own.

He would have said it in another day and age. And he would have scooped her right off her feet and walked out of there with her. Cursed modern sensibilities.

"I came to see a woman about a horse." He allowed his gaze to linger on her. To wander over her. He wanted her to know what he *meant* to say, even if he hadn't really spoken the words.

Kyra stared back at him for a moment, and damned if the slightest hint of pink didn't color her cheeks.

Obviously, she'd gotten the message.

For the first time in fourteen years, he'd succeeded in making her blush.

Before he could revel in that bit of news, Kyra plowed forward. Perhaps in an effort to distract him. "I'm not selling him. Not yet anyway."

"You're not?" Relief sighed through him.

She shook her head, her blond hair brushing the tops of her shoulders. "Clint convinced me to wait a little longer. He thinks the horse is on a mission. And you know what?"

Jesse fought past the jealousy that Kyra was listening to Clint Bowman's advice in a way she never seemed to listen to his. "What?"

He took Sam's Pride's bridle out of her hands and led the horse toward the parking lot where he'd seen Kyra's truck earlier this morning.

"You'll think I'm insane, but I swear to you I had a crazy memory when he said that. The moment he mentioned it, I remembered my dad telling me he gave Sam's Pride a mission a few days after he was born."

Jesse stopped in the center of the unused midway

area, right in front of the merry-go-round. "I remember that day. I was on the road in Houston and I didn't go out that night because you were worried about Sam. You thought he was getting a little morose or something, and you drove him home so he could take his meds."

"You remember all that?" She looked like she didn't believe him.

"Geez, Kyra, you've allowed yourself to be upset in front of me something like two other times in your whole life." How could she not know she was freaking important to him? He'd always thought at least their friendship had been rock solid, and now he wasn't even so sure if she'd ever fully trusted in that. "Yeah, I can remember them."

She looked toward the parking lot, ever eager to move forward. Jesse dug his boots in the gravel a little deeper. She could take five minutes to talk to him face-to-face.

She folded her arms and pivoted toward him. "It just gave me the heebie-jeebies listening to Clint say he thought my horse was on a mission and me remembering that day with my dad telling me he gave Sam's Pride a mission to watch over me. I don't believe in any kind of supernatural stuff, but it spooked me."

Jesse let the horse's bridle fall, trusting him not to stray far from Kyra. He put his hands on her shoulders and assured himself he only wanted to comfort her.

Not to feel her incredibly silky skin. Her warmth

of spirit and natural vibrancy that had pulled him to her from the first day they'd met.

"It shouldn't spook you. It should lift you up to think that even in his later years, Sam had such moments of clarity he could commune with an animal as clearly as Clint Bowman does. Hell, maybe your old man should have been the Citrus County horse whisperer."

The shadow of a smile passed across her lips. "Somehow I doubt my dad would have been able to take his animal act on the road."

Jesse tilted her chin up with one hand, drawing her gaze to his to let her know he was completely serious. "Maybe not, but it might be a sign that he'd reached a peace of sorts with his disease and where he was at in life. He might not have been able to be the father to you he would have liked, but maybe he made sure you had a stalwart guardian in the form of a four-legged protector. It's a lot more than some totally healthy parents manage to give their kids."

Kyra's blue eyes widened. Flickered with just a little spark of hope. "You really believe what Clint says about the horse, don't you?"

He rubbed his hands over her arms, needing to reassure her that she wasn't the only one looking out for her in the world. Didn't she know how much he wanted to be there for her? Even when they were just friends, he would have sprinted to her side if she ever gave him the least indication she might need him.

"I definitely believe it. Clint's theory explains every weird action that horse has ever taken. And I think it makes total sense that your old man would try to find a way to watch out for you even when he couldn't be there for you himself.'' He paused, letting her absorb his words. Giving her time to get used to the idea that her dad had wanted so much more for her than she ever realized. ''If you want, I could take you by his grave this week. Give you time to talk to him or—''

She was already shaking her head, her hardheaded practicality back in full force. ''I can't ask you to do that.''

His hands fell away from her.

Frustration fired through him, an emotion that— along with jealousy—he wasn't accustomed to feeling. At least he hadn't been until he'd gotten all tied up in knots about Kyra. ''Since when did you ask? Damn it, Kyra, you can't shut out anyone and everyone who wants to be there for you. I'm not going away just because you don't *need* me.''

Her brow furrowed. Confused.

Didn't she realize it would be okay to need him sometimes? And why couldn't she understand that it was okay just to want him—need be damned.

''For that matter, I'm not going away until you agree to see me again. Talk to me. Hell, we never even had our date. I felt too guilty to press the issue the other night, but I don't have a damn reason to back down. You know I never asked Greta to—''

''Okay.''

''—ever kiss me like that and—'' He couldn't have heard what he thought she'd said. ''What?''

"Okay. We'll do the date. I was upset the other night, but I know there's nothing going on between you and Greta."

Jesse felt a burden sliding right off his shoulders. "Damn straight there's not." He reached for Kyra, his hand curving around the delicate face that hid such a strong, proud woman. "I was upset, too, in the wake of the whole kiss thing and I was distracted when you asked me if I could handle just seeing *you.*" He stroked a strand of hair behind her ear, then followed the silky lock all the way to the end as it curved about the top of her shoulder. "But I can handle it. And I want it more than anything."

Her lips parted in surprise. Beckoned him to assure her of his words with the persuasive power of his mouth.

But he wouldn't. Not until he'd sewed up the matter of the date in the most businesslike fashion for Kyra's benefit. He couldn't afford to leave any loopholes this time.

Somehow, one freaking date had become more important to him than a whole baseball season had been. More important than anything he could think of.

She licked her lips as if she missed tasting their kisses almost as much as he did. "Maybe we should set a few ground rules before we—"

"Not a chance. I'm not going to let you ground rule yourself into some sort of safe zone where I can't touch you. This time, I want to handle things my way."

He braced himself for an argument.

But maybe Kyra read his commitment to his own plan in his eyes because she huffed out a breath and nodded. ''Name the place, Jesse. I'll try it your way. At least for one night.''

One night.

The words were music to his ears. She had given him one night and he planned to make sure one night would never be enough for her.

14

GRETA PADDED her way into the kitchenette area of Clint's hotel suite, bleary-eyed and in desperate need of caffeine. For the last two mornings, Clint had served her coffee in bed, but he'd needed to run an errand this morning, forcing her to fend for herself.

Funny that in the course of a mere three days she already craved Clint more than her morning java.

She was addicted to the man.

Mindlessly, she tore open the single-serving packet of grounds wrapped in a filter and jammed the bag into the coffeepot. After spending eight years on the road with her modeling career, she had the art of hotel coffeemakers down to a science.

As she went through the motions, she thought about how much Clint Bowman had come to mean to her in just a few days' time. And even though she knew Clint was an amazing man worthy of total feminine adoration, it scared her just a little to think she had gone from sighing over Jesse Chandler to swooning over Clint in such a short amount of time.

What if she was wrong about Clint, too?

Her relationship with Jesse had started off with a bang—she snorted at that choice of images—as well.

And she'd ended up being dead wrong about his affection for her. What if she had no better judgment now when it came to Clint?

Dumping the water into the machine, Greta closed the lid and flicked on the switch to wait for her brew.

Of course, with Clint this time, everything had felt more real. They'd talked in a way she and Jesse had never bothered to. She'd learned that Clint ran a horse-breeding farm in Alabama and that he took extended trips related to his business. She knew he had two hell-raising brothers whose goal in life was to never settle down.

But mostly, Clint had asked about *her*. Not her life in front of the spotlight, but her life behind it. If she was lonely on the road. What she did in strange cities to entertain herself. What her favorite airport snacks were.

Things no one ever thought to ask her before.

But she hadn't managed to share any stories about her family—her father who'd always used his strength and his temper to intimidate her. She was totally over her old man.

She just didn't happen to like to talk about him.

Other than that, she and Clint had shared just about everything. Surely all those conversations they'd had proved they were connecting on more levels than just the physical plane. And as an added bonus, she hadn't smoked a single cigarette in the three days they'd been together.

A wicked smile curled her lips as she thought about

all the ways she'd traded one oral fixation for another infinitely more fulfilling one.

While Greta assured herself she couldn't be wrong about what she felt for Clint, she slid into the chair at the tiny kitchenette table while the coffeepot steamed and burbled.

The peach and blue silk flower arrangement had been cleared off to one side of the table to make way for a massive tome with tiny print open to a page about narcissism. Curious, Greta kept her finger on the open page and flipped the book closed to check out the title. *Advanced Studies in Clinical Psychology*.

A warning bell went off in her head in time with the beeping coffeepot letting her know her coffee was ready. Too engrossed in her new find, Greta ignored it and flipped the book back to the passage on narcissism.

A passage circled with a hand-scrawled note in the margin that read—*check her for signs of this.*

Her?

Greta's eyes cruised over the page to glean that the neurosis was a manifestation of self-obsession. A sickness that placed too much emphasis on outward appearances. And which often resulted from deep-seated loneliness.

Does it get lonely out on the road?

Okay, Clint had asked her that, but that didn't mean he thought she was narcissistic. Then again, why the hell did a horse breeder from Alabama need to lug around advanced psych texts?

Unless he thought he was dating a woman who was totally crazy.

Greta fumed, unwilling to wait around for Clint's explanation. No doubt he would only think she was narcissistic for thinking the damn book related to her.

Fine. Let him tack on paranoid, too. She wasn't sticking around to hear about it. Slamming the book closed on the table, Greta started hunting for her clothes.

She was so busy muttering to herself, she didn't even hear the door to the suite open. But all of a sudden, Clint was standing there in his T-shirt and running shoes looking utterly mouthwatering.

And like a total dead man.

He grinned. Stalked closer as if he would drag her into bed again only to psychoanalyze her while she was sleeping. "Hey, honey. I'm home."

A TEN-POUND MISSILE sailed past Clint's head, narrowly missing his temple and landing with a thud in the open closet behind him. Before he could turn to see what Greta had just thrown at him, his Stetson was winging his way like a Frisbee turned deadly boomerang.

She couldn't mess with his hat, damn it.

"Now wait just a minute." He caught the Stetson in midair and slammed it on his head for safekeeping. Storming across the room, he caught her in a bear hug from behind just as she was picking up a vase of silk flowers. "That's stainless steel, woman. Are you out of your mind?"

Prying the vase from her fingers, he set it back down on the kitchen table, the peach and blue flowers dangling sadly from one side.

"Obviously *you* think so, Mr. Junior Psychologist." She glared back at him over one shoulder. "Or are you going to try and pretend that you were thinking *another* woman in your life was narcissistic and not the internationally known model you're dating? Or rather the model you *were* dating."

As she spoke, Clint realized what the ten-pound missile had been that she'd sent winging past his ear. Evidently, she hadn't enjoyed the notes he'd been making in his psych book.

"Greta, you're so damn far off base you're going to laugh when I explain this to you." He had wrestled cranky horses that were less determined to get away from him than Greta. She was all elbows and knees.

"Ha! You're so damn screwed you'd probably make up anything to explain this away." Unable to break her way free, she settled for pinching him in the forearm.

Clint stifled a curse and vise-locked her hands with his own. If she flipped out over his psych background, how would he ever get her to agree to throw away her sophisticated lifestyle for an Alabama ranch? "I probably *would* make up just about anything if I had been truly trying to psychoanalyze you and I got caught in the act. But no matter how far-fetched of a story I might come up with under pressure, do you think I could ever dream up something as crazy as that I read the book to psychoanalyze horses?"

She stilled in his arms.

Obviously, he'd caught her attention.

But since he had no idea how long he'd be able to retain it, he forced out his story in a condensed version. "I should have told you earlier that I treat troubled horses on the side. Sort of a special interest job that I fell into after I worked with some abused animals confiscated from a foreclosed farm near where I grew up."

Greta hadn't moved as he spoke, so he released her. When she didn't reach for the steel vase again, he figured it was safe to continue.

"I had so much success with those horses that I developed a local reputation and a couple of ranchers came to me with questions about different behavioral problems they were seeing among their stock. Soon, word of my sideline spread all over the country and now I find myself getting all sorts of bizarre calls about troubled animals." He paused, tried to gauge Greta's expression. He knew he should have told her about this before, but he'd been afraid of her reaction. Being a shrink of any kind—even to horses—had a way of scaring people off.

"So you're the Dr. Doolittle of the equine world. Great. What does that have to do with narcissism and the note in your textbook to check somebody—a female somebody—for signs of it? Don't tell me you're dealing with vain four-legged creatures." She folded her arms across her chest, wrinkling the shirt she'd worn to sleep in last night.

His shirt.

God, he wanted to work things out with this woman. Wanted to find more than just amazing sex with her.

She was so smart. So full of contradictions with her high-profile strut and her down-home love of cheeseburgers. Greta Ingram would keep him on his toes forever.

If only he could convince her she wasn't a guinea pig for his psychoanalytic work.

"Actually, I keep the book around to jog my memory about different symptoms. You'd be surprised how many parallels there are between how horses behave and how we behave. They have as much potential to succumb to fears as we do."

She lifted a speculative brow as if trying to decide whether or not to believe him.

He forged ahead. "I make a lot of notes in the book while I work. That particular comment is over a decade old from my college days. We did a practicum each month to try our diagnosing skills on students who would fake a disorder. Must be I thought somebody was playing narcissist."

Greta sniffed. "You didn't think I was?"

Sensing a chink in the armor, he smiled. "Narcissists are totally self-absorbed. And look at you. You're wolfing down more cheeseburgers in a month than the Hamburgler because you're so happy to break out of an industry that required you to be just a little self-absorbed."

Called by the scent of brewed coffee, Clint gave Greta some breathing room and a moment to think about that while he poured two steaming mugs. Spending the last few nights with her—and consequently, a few mornings—he'd learned she was infinitely happier postjava in the a.m.

He made a mental note to purchase himself a coffeemaker with a timer feature. She'd be able to go straight from horizontal to sipping position.

Greta accepted the cup and drank gratefully. ''But now that I launched into a tirade over the narcissism thing, doesn't that just prove I think the world revolves around me in a sort of 'the lady doth protest too much' logic?''

Clint shrugged. ''Doesn't prove a damn thing to me. Besides, I'm the one running around playing Dr. Doolittle to horses with my college psych book in hand. I'm the last person to cast stones in the mental health department.''

She tipped her head back and laughed. The warm, rich sound flowed over him, soothed and excited him at the same time. He could get lost for days in that throaty laughter of hers.

But he was running out of time to linger with her. He'd already extended his trip to Florida, first because Sam's Pride had made for such an intriguing case, and second because of Greta. He didn't regret a moment of their time together, but he knew it couldn't last.

At least, not here.

''Come to Alabama with me, Greta.'' He found himself saying the words before he'd given himself a chance to think about them.

And judging by Greta's semihorrified expression, he knew the moment he said them he damn well should have thought about them.

A lot.

"Go where?" She twisted a finger through her breezy blond hair, a gesture smacking of nervousness that he'd never seen in her before.

Damn.

"Alabama. Home of the Crimson Tide. Home of—" Bear Bryant, football coach with the most Division I victories in history. Like she'd give a rat's ass about that. "Home of some great state parks."

She didn't look swayed.

"Rich southern history?" he prodded.

In fact, she looked downright ill.

"Come on, Greta. Take a week and at least check it out. We've got the best damn barbecue sandwiches in the U.S. of A. You'll never go back to hamburgers. Besides, you international women like to travel, right?"

"Preferably to places with more than one cosmetic counter in town. And preferably to cities with international flight connections so that we can haul our butts out of there if necessary."

"Birmingham International is just a hop, skip and a jump away. Atlanta's only a few hours. But if you need to come back here, I'll loan you my pickup." Hell, he'd buy her a damn pickup of her own. "And I'll teach you how to drive it, to boot."

"Clint, I'm sorry." She was shaking her head, that

silky blond hair of hers sweeping the tops of her shoulders. "But I don't think—"

"Don't say it." God, he didn't want to hear it. Couldn't stand to think he'd found the only woman who would ever be right for him only to lose her over something as superficial as where they were in the world. "Not yet."

"It's not just Alabama."

His heart damn near dropped to his ankles. "It's not?"

"It's the horses, too. And all the animals in general. And just the whole—farm thing." She wrinkled her nose as if to underscore her words, but it was obvious there was more to her reluctance than that. Shadows of insecurity clouded her eyes, and Clint didn't have a clue how to interpret them.

Something was holding her back. Something bigger than her desire for a more cosmopolitan lifestyle. But if she wasn't ready to share it with him, there wasn't a damn thing he could do about it.

Yet.

Until he could figure out what worries she hid from him, he would give her some space, respect her boundaries. In his work with troubled animals, he'd learned the value of patience.

"I think we could work around your issues with rural life, Greta. If you're not ready, I understand. But I've got to go back this week." His brothers were good about taking over for a few days. A week, maybe. By now he was really stretching it. "I don't have a choice."

She fluffed her hair. Shrugged her shoulders as if him leaving wasn't a big deal. But her hands trembled just a little.

"I want you to go with me. Stay with me. Move right in and never leave." He stared into her eyes until he was certain she knew he meant it. "If you're not ready for Alabama—or for me—I can come back here next weekend. And the one after that. However long it takes to convince you to come with me, or until you tell me not to bother anymore. But it's my home, Greta. Eventually, I'll always have to go back."

"Home is where your heart is, cowboy." She set her coffee mug on the table and stared up at him, eyes flashing a challenge. "Maybe you're just not enticed enough to try living somewhere different."

She didn't understand. Couldn't understand if she'd never been close to her family.

"It's not that. You could entice me to do just about anything, woman. And you have." After the experience near the airport runway, there'd been the time on his hotel balcony. Then the hotel elevator. "I just can't walk away from what's so much a part of who I am."

The tiny frown that crossed her face was almost imperceptible, but Clint had studied every nuance of her expression for the past three days and he saw it. Knew the idea of being apart hurt her almost as much as it hurt him.

But she wasn't ready, didn't have the advantage of

knowing with every fiber of her being that they were
right together the way he did.

"I don't know if I can do a relationship of half-
measures, Clint. I wasted too much time and emotional energy on Jesse when that didn't have a chance
in hell of working out. I can't commit myself to a
man who won't even live in the same state with me
now."

There was more to it than that. And Clint intended
to figure out exactly what was holding her back.

"Give me at least next weekend. Let me think
about how to change your mind this week, and if you
want to, you can go ahead and think about how to
change mine, too. But at least give it until next weekend before you make that decision."

She stared into the bottom of her empty coffee cup
for a long moment while Clint held his breath.

Finally, she met his gaze. "One more weekend.
But I have to be honest with you, Clint. I can't picture
me ever wanting to spend any time with one horse,
let alone a whole ranch full of them." She blinked
fast, as if to keep her emotions at bay. As if to make
sure Clint didn't realize she was scared of a whole
lot more than the horses. "And you'll have to show
me a hell of a lot more than great state parks to get
me to set foot in Alabama."

"I'M NOT SETTING FOOT on that yacht without you,"
Kyra warned Jesse as she stared up at the boat where
tonight's date was to take place.

When she'd agreed to go out with him last weekend, she hadn't realized he already had a very specific event in mind—his brother Seth's engagement party.

Now, she leaned against Jesse's Jeep beside pier eleven in the sleepy beach town of Twin Palms and tried not to panic. "Why don't I go to the liquor store with you?"

"I'll only be a minute. I just forgot to pick up the champagne for the party." He slid his hands around her waist to ease her away from the Jeep. "I was too busy thinking about other aspects of tonight."

A shivery sensation shot through her at his touch, his words. The sun winked on the waves as it dipped low over the horizon, illuminating a string of surfside shops and restaurants culminating in a cedar-sided gift store called the Beachcomber, and finally, a small marina where the yacht was docked.

Twin Palms should have been the perfect date destination. Their cruise on the water tonight was a romantic's dream. But Kyra couldn't help the nagging fear that she wouldn't be able to live up to Jesse's expectations.

She'd wanted this kind of night with him forever, but now that it had arrived she only wanted to run back to the Crooked Branch and return to their friendship—an association that seemed so much safer than the edgy, scary new feelings this relationship inspired.

Her mouth went dry in response to his touch, his suggestive words. But only one response came to her nervous brain. "You'd better go search for the champagne. Your family will be arriving any minute."

Jesse's hands lingered on her waist, his warm fingers brushing the bare skin at her back that her dress exposed. He smiled even as he shook his head. "Ever the practical one. When am I going to get you to take a few chances, Kyra Stafford?"

Taking chances gave her heart palpitations, thank you very much. Of course, Jesse's touch might have contributed to that racing pulse a little bit, too. "The date is my risk for today." A pretty big one.

"You're wrong there. I'm watching over you better than Sam's Pride. You couldn't be any safer than when you're with me." Jesse picked up her hand and kissed the palm.

Slowly. Languidly.

He kissed his way up her wrist, up the inside of her arm the way Gomez had done to Morticia a thousand times. Only Jesse's technique left her breathless and weak in the knees.

"You'd better get the champagne." Before she did something crazy, like jump him in the middle of the marina parking lot. The scent of the sea had an aphrodisiac effect along with the warm breeze and lazy beachside town. Something about visiting a strange place made her feel adventurous.

Or maybe that was just because she was with Jesse.

"We have time." His kisses trailed across her shoulder to her neck. He drew her closer, broad calloused palms catching on the silky thin fabric of her navy dress. "And we still have that little matter of getting you to take some risks to address."

She might have protested, but he chose that moment to steer her hips to his. The feel of his hard length against her made her voice catch, sputter and die out in her throat.

"Are you ready to take a risk tonight, Kyra?" His words were rough, tinged with the same desire that churned through her. His hands smoothed their way up her waist to her ribs, his thumbs just barely grazing her aching breasts.

She didn't have to ask what kind of risk he had in mind. He was proposing a clandestine encounter, something hot and fierce and totally out of control.

And she wanted to share that experience with him so badly she could hardly see straight.

"This is an awfully public place." She glanced over her shoulder and noted the scant pedestrians peopling the sidewalks.

"I'll find us someplace more private." He skimmed his thumbs discreetly across the undersides of her breasts.

Her eyes fluttered closed for a long moment as the provocative ripple effect of one small touch vibrated through her. The man had probably forgotten more about seduction than she would ever learn in two lifetimes. "Are you trying to get even with me for abducting you and making you my sexual prisoner at Gasparilla?"

"Revenge is best when it's sweet." He kept his words a soft whisper in deference to an elderly couple walking by in matching running suits holding hands. After shooting conspiratorial winks in their direction, the couple passed and Jesse cupped her chin. Ran his finger over her lower lip. "And it *will* be sweet."

Oh.

A melting sensation started at that combustible point where his finger touched her and then dripped all the way through her.

"Yes." The word jumped out before she consciously decided it.

But if she was going to have this last date with Jesse, she didn't have any intention of playing games about what she wanted. She wanted *him*.

Tonight.

Now.

Even if that meant taking a few chances.

"YES WHAT?" His eyes pinned her down, wouldn't let her go until he'd wrested all the words from her. Or maybe until he made sure she knew exactly what he had in mind for them.

Their window of time before the party was narrow, but it existed. He knew Seth's boat was back in the harbor because he'd driven it to Twin Palms again just yesterday. And it just so happened the keys were still in his pocket.

But no matter how eager he was to get Kyra alone in the intimacy of a boat's cabin, he had all the time in the world to hear her say that she wanted this as much as him.

Then again, given how hot he was to have her beneath him right now, he'd probably settle for having her want this *half* as badly as he did. "Are you sure you know what you're agreeing to?"

"Does it involve a sexual encounter in the next five

minutes?'' She tilted her head to one side and eyed him with a smoky stare.

Gulping for air, he sought a response.

And found his throat dried up to desert standards.

He settled for nodding.

Kyra leaned just close enough to brush her breasts against his chest. And practically brought him to his knees in the process. "Then consider me well informed of what I'm agreeing to. I still say yes.''

If he opened his mouth to tell her how great he thought that was, he'd only end up devouring her then and there in the middle of the Twin Palms marina parking lot. He had no choice but to let his actions do the talking.

Pulling her forward across the tarmac, he made double time to get them to the pier where Seth's boat was docked. Jesse might have lingered to hear her say that she wanted to be with him, but now that he knew where they were headed, he wasn't wasting a single second.

Never in his life had he felt this kind of urgency to have a woman. Hell, had there ever been any urgency about sex before? He'd developed a legendary reputation among women because he'd always been able to take his time. Play games. Enjoy the seduction.

But right now when he should be applying every skill he'd ever learned to wooing and winning Kyra, finesse eluded him.

He held her hand to try and help her onto the 32-foot cabin cruiser, but one look at her long leg stretched forward through a slit in her conservative navy dress had him hauling her into the boat and into his arms.

She stumbled against him, propelling them backward toward the stairs leading to the cabin door. He drew her down the steps with him, praying he could hold out another thirty seconds while he found them some privacy. He kissed her while he fished for the key in his pocket, devouring her now the way he'd wanted to onshore.

And she kissed him right back. No holds barred. Like she meant it.

He forgot about the key. Had to touch her.

But some hint of her practicality must have surfaced just enough to make her reach in his pocket. As she did so, her fingers grazed his thigh—and a hell of a lot more—an act which sent him beyond urgent and straight into desperate terrain.

Control was nowhere to be found.

He couldn't wait. Ate up the silky fabric of her dress with his hands, sought for a way to get beneath it to touch more.

When he reached for her hem, she smiled triumphantly and dangled the key in front of his nose with one hand. In her other hand, she waved another prize—a condom.

With a growl, he yanked the key back, jammed it into the lock, and pulled her down into the cabin with him.

Maybe Jesse closed the door behind them. Maybe he didn't. It scared the hell out of him to think he wasn't paying attention to the details, or that maybe he wasn't taking care of Kyra the way she really deserved to be taken care of.

But her hands were all over him, her one palm still clutching the condom wrapper. And the need to have her consumed him. Drove him out of his freaking mind. Turned him into someone else completely, someone who...

Unable to finish a train of thought, Jesse focused on the only thing he could finish. This. Incredible. Freaking. Encounter.

The bedroom was too far away. But Jesse's calf bumped into a cushion for the built-in couch. The living area.

Close enough.

Sultry heat melded them together. The scent of the sea breeze permeated the cabin area, mingled with the light floral note of Kyra's skin. Her skin was hot and silky beneath his hands and somehow—thank you, God—a fraction of his bedroom prowess from another time, another life, must have helped him to unzip her dress and make the navy fabric vanish.

She stood before him in navy high heels and black lace panties.

Totally impractical.

And the thought that Kyra had indulged in something so frivolous and so decadent—possibly with him in mind—turned him on even more than the black lace.

He wanted to linger over every inch of her, taste

the way her skin felt through black lace, but he couldn't wait. Not this time.

His hands found her hips and tugged her to him as he drew them down to the couch cushions. Kyra's weight on top of him a delicious restraint, he let her undo his shirt buttons, unfasten his belt.

Her hair slithered down across his shoulder and over his chest. He wound the length around his hand, allowed the silky strands to tease his palms.

Then he made the mistake of looking down. Caught a glimpse of her black lace panties up against his open fly.

And promptly lost his mind.

Releasing her hair, he rolled their bodies to swap positions. He shed his clothes faster than a virgin on his honeymoon. Two seconds later he had Kyra beneath him and her panties in his hand.

Kyra blinked up at him in the semidarkness, her eyes soft with desire and little amazement as she offered him the condom she'd been holding. "How did you do that?"

He slapped the condom on the coffee table and flung her panties away, concerned only with what they'd concealed. Reaching between their bodies, he trailed a hand over her hip to her belly, to the soft heat between her legs. "I had excellent motivation."

Eyes fluttering closed she leaned into the pillows. A sensual acquiescence. Her back arched, and with the movement, her breasts seemed to command attention.

Bending to kiss a peaked nipple, Jesse nudged a

finger deep inside her to the place she liked to be touched best of all.

The heat of her closed around him as her soft sighs turned to breathy moans. When her breath caught, held, told him she was on the verge of release, he let go.

Her eyes opened wide until he settled himself between her thighs and rolled the condom on. Her short fingernails dug into his shoulders as she urged him inside.

As if he needed urging.

The boat rocked beneath them, and Jesse wasn't sure if it was from the waves in the marina or the waves they were making. But he knew for damn sure he'd never felt this good, this right, this complete in his life.

No wonder being with Kyra made him feel a sense of urgency today. There was something about *this* that was pretty damn important.

Before he could think through all the ramifications of what *this* meant, however, another wave crashed over him—a tide of sizzling sensation that drew him right back into a purely physical realm.

Kyra's body clenched around him, under him, as she hit the pinnacle high note. She yelled his name, locked her ankles around his hips.

And he was done for.

He found his release a scant few seconds behind her, drowning in a flood of sensations that were familiar and yet new all over again.

Maybe because there were a hell of a lot of un-identified emotions attached to those sensations.

But for now, he simply closed his eyes and pulled Kyra more tightly to him. He savored the rightness of being together and knew he'd finally hit on something good. Something essential.

And he had no intention of letting her go.

"THAT WAS AMAZING." Kyra finally spoke the words aloud that had been circling in her head nonstop for the last five minutes.

"Incredible." Jesse's voice held the same note of wonder she imagined must be in her own.

Was it possible he'd been as blown away by the sex as she had been?

Jesse ran warm fingers over the cool skin of her arm. "Incredible enough to make me skip Seth's engagement party if you want to hang out here."

"Oh my God." How could she have forgotten? She shoved him off her and started a frantic search for her panties. "You'll never have time to get the champagne."

He levered himself up to a sitting position. Gorgeous and naked. "Are you sure you want to go?"

She tugged her dress over her head and prepared to write off the black lace underwear until she spied them dangling from a lampshade. "Of course we are going. Seth is your *brother*."

Tossing clothes at him, she shoved her toes into her shoes.

"They might already be on the yacht. Will you

mind going on board without me?'' He pulled his clothes on with almost as much quick efficiency as he'd taken them off.

Almost.

''I don't want to face everyone without you.'' Not when she had no clue what her relationship was to Jesse anymore. Not when she didn't even know what she wanted that relationship to be. Hadn't she always been too independent to feel this attached to someone?

Especially someone with so much power to hurt her.

It was just as well their date would play out around an audience tonight. After a close encounter of the most intimate kind, Kyra sensed a need to rebuild boundaries and reinforce defenses, thank you very much.

They bolted out of the cabin and down the gangplank, still tucking and fastening. And even though she knew she needed to scavenge some distance from Jesse tonight, Kyra couldn't help but smile that she'd done all her risk-taking in life with him at her side, urging her on.

''I'll run down to the boardwalk and see if I can scrounge up some champagne.'' Jesse skidded to a stop at the end of the pier and straightened the shoulders of her dress, carefully tucking in an errant strap. ''Hell, I'd settle for wine coolers if I can find some. If Seth goes by, just let him know we're here.''

Kyra nodded, watching him until he disappeared

on the Twin Palms boardwalk among a small throng of tourists arriving by bus.

If she wanted to track his progress, all she would have had to do was watch for the trail of turning feminine heads. But in the shadow of the big yacht docked along the pier for Seth's engagement party, Kyra was suddenly too busy warding off last-minute doubts to enjoy the stir Jesse always managed to create.

Funny how the man had so much presence, so much vitality, that watching him walk away invariably filled her with a sense of loss. And made the air seem too still, too quiet all around her.

Why couldn't she just enjoy what they'd shared and leave it at that? Why worry it to death the moment he left her side?

She trusted him. Had realized he would never look at another woman as long as they were together. But strangely, instead of comforting her, the notion had only made her all the more wary. If she believed Jesse could commit himself to her—and by now, she did—then it was only another short leap to think that maybe their relationship could be bigger, more important than she'd ever dared to dream.

And frankly, that terrified her.

It was one thing to trust in Jesse. But it would take a lot more effort to believe in herself. Would she be able to commit herself to him for more than just a friendship, more than just a weekend of great sex?

Assuming, that is, he wanted something more?

She'd been so busy giving him a hard time about

the whole commitment factor that she hadn't really stopped to consider if *she* was ready to take such a big step. Ever since her father's illness, Kyra had grown accustomed to being independent, to making her own decisions and running things her way. How could she ever share that role with someone else?

Tonight's date took on all the more importance in light of those fears. She had no idea if she could live up to Jesse's expectations, and now she'd have to find out in the public setting of the engagement party—in front of Jesse's family.

She'd always liked Jesse's older brother Seth, but how would Seth react now that she and Jesse had taken their relationship to the next level? And Kyra had never met their uncle, who would also be in attendance tonight. Would they sense in five minutes that she and Jesse had no business together?

She didn't exactly have experience with healthy family dynamics.

Not that she cared, she assured herself. It just seemed like tonight's family setting and joyous occasion upped the stakes for what should have been a simple date for her and Jesse.

Kyra smoothed the skirt of her navy dress and willed her nerves to settle, distracting herself with thoughts of what Seth Chandler's new fiancée might be like. Jesse had told her on their drive over tonight that the couple met for the first time at Gasparilla after Seth carried off Mia pirate-style. And after that, they just *knew*.

The story made Kyra question her relationship with

Jesse all the more. How could Seth be head over heels and ready to tie the knot after a couple of weeks, whereas she and Jesse had known each other half their lives and still had no clue if they were right for one another?

The sound of feminine laughter caught her ear before she could worry about it anymore. As Kyra turned toward the sound, she spied two women walking out of the Beachcomber store several yards away. One of them flipped the sign on the door to read Closed before they headed in her direction juggling loaded straw platters full of food covered in plastic wrap.

She tried not to stare, but there wasn't exactly a lot of action in Twin Palms on a late Saturday afternoon. And besides, they were definitely the kind of women who caught your eye. Not in an overtly gorgeous Greta way, but simply because of the carefree, happy air about them, an easy manner that seemed inherent to people who lived by the water.

The women could have been twins—except for the maybe fifteen years between them. Long dark hair spilled over their shoulders while they balanced the jumbo trays. Still laughing, they nudged each other with an occasional shoulder on their way toward the marina in halfhearted attempts to dislodge the other's burden.

Kyra's interest in them evaporated, however, when she saw them turn down pier eleven toward the biggest yacht docked in the tiny marina. If these women were part of the crowd attending Seth Chandler's en-

gagement party, she needed to make herself scarce
before she was—

Noticed.

No sooner had she thought as much than the
younger woman glanced back over her shoulder and
paused.

Stared.

It was too late to hide in Jesse's Jeep so Kyra
smiled and willed the woman to move along.

Kyra didn't consider herself socially inept or anything, but she did spend far more of her time with
horses than people. Small talk and charm was Jesse's
strength, not hers.

And he was so dead for leaving her here to fend
for herself while he searched for champagne.

Damn.

The younger brunette shouted over her platter, the
breeze fluttering the petals of a red flower tucked behind her right ear. "Kyra Stafford?"

"That's me. Are you going to the engagement
party too?" Kyra managed a smile and tucked her
purse under one arm. Apparently she wouldn't be able
to hide any longer. She just hoped she could remain
in the background of this shindig before Jesse arrived.

"I'm Mia Quentin and I'm the lucky bride-to-be."
Grinning, she nodded toward the pier, her hands full.
"Come on aboard. I've been dying to meet the lady
pirate who had the nerve to kidnap Tampa's most
notorious bad boy."

15

GRETA SNAKED AN ARM behind Clint's neck while he drove the pickup truck across long, dusty acres of dirt road behind the Crooked Branch. She hadn't been able to pry her hands off him since he rolled into her driveway late the night before after their week apart.

Just for fun, she rested her other hand on his thigh.

"If you don't watch what you're doing there, I'll never get to show you the surprise," he growled, downshifting as he navigated a dried-out irrigation ditch.

"There's only one surprise I want you to give me right now," she whispered back, licking a path alongside his ear.

The week without him had been hell. She still didn't want to go to Alabama. And although she seemed to have him partially convinced it was because she didn't want to live next to a barn full of horses, deep down Greta knew her fears had more to do with giving a powerful man so much say in her life.

She hadn't consciously thought about growing up in her father's house in years. No, she stayed as removed from those scary memories as possible. Yet the fears of being emotionally betrayed by a man she loved still lingered.

But she'd definitely gotten a taste of how much it would hurt to walk away from Clint over the past few long, lonely nights.

As she sidled closer to sit hip to hip with him, Greta fully recognized that she was probably trying to tie him to her with the promise of awesome sex. On some level she felt like if he would come to her, take up residence in Florida to be by her side, then she still had some control in their relationship.

If she went there, on his terms, she was giving him everything. Her heart, her soul—and an even bigger potential to hurt her.

Clint peeled her hand away and kissed each of her knuckles with slow precision. The patience—endurance—of this man had proven a continual source of delight. "Trust me, you're going to like this surprise."

She could think of one other present she would really like. "You've bought a house in Florida?"

Slowing the truck just before the dirt road took a sharp turn, Clint stopped and swiveled in his seat to face her. "No. But this definitely has to do with getting us closer together."

She fought the pang in her chest. Of course he wasn't moving here. He'd as good as told her he would be trying to come up with ways to get her to move there, not the other way around. "On your terms."

"On mutual terms." He brushed his hands up her

arms to her shoulders, his fingers brushing over her collarbones. "I want you to be happy, too. So answer this for me. If I can get you to like horses, would you at least give Alabama a try?"

Again with the damn horses. Of course, what could she expect when she hadn't been able to share with him her deepest fears. "I can't see me liking anything with four legs. They're too—"

Big. Powerful. Frightening.

Greta would always be intimidated by animals—or people—she couldn't control.

Clint was staring at her oddly and Greta realized she'd never finished her thought. "They're too hairy. Too messy. Too much work."

"But that doesn't answer my question. If you *did* like horses, would you come to Alabama?"

Greta had to smile. The man was incredibly focused. Would he be as determined to ease her real fears if she were ever brave enough to share them with him? "On the off chance I was ever able to get within five feet of a nine-hundred-pound animal, I might be swayed to cross the state line."

"Excellent." Clint slipped a hand around the back of her neck and tugged her forward for a kiss. A slow, deep, full-of-approval kiss. When he finally pulled away, he put the truck in drive while her eyelids pried themselves open.

Rounding the turn, Greta grew suspicious about the whole horse conversation. "Just where exactly are we going?"

Even as she asked, the scent of the surf filtered in

through the truck window. The air had turned damp somewhere along the way and the breeze carried the sound of seagulls.

"I'm taking you to the favorite place of every Florida sunseeker. The beach."

Sure enough, as they rounded the last curve, the dirt road ended in front of a tiny patch of ungroomed sand and gently rolling waves from the Gulf.

But the beach wasn't what snagged Greta's eye.

It was the big black horse standing in the middle of the shore.

"Oh, no." Had she mentioned she wasn't a horse lover? The beast on the beach could probably trample her five different ways without even trying. "Clint?"

He was already out of the truck and coming around to the passenger side to help her out. "You can't knock it until you've at least said hello."

Actually, Greta was pretty certain she could do a terrific job of knocking it without getting anywhere near the huge horse, but she took Clint's hand and stepped out of the truck. She'd always been able to count on her sense of adventure to pull her through almost anything, but her usual pluck seemed a bit sapped where Clint and his horses were concerned.

She'd taken a risk just by allowing herself to be with him—a guy so different from any man she'd ever known. But Clint was settling for a superficial relationship from her and she knew that on a deep, instinctive level without him having to spell it out for her in so many words.

Maybe she'd chosen Jesse first because he'd appeared as outwardly superficial as Greta liked to be. She could appreciate a man who just wanted to have fun for fun's sake. But Clint wanted—expected—so much more from her. Jesse hadn't ever made her question what was really important to her in life the way Clint did.

As if sensing her thoughts, Clint turned toward her as they neared the animal. "You nervous?"

Greta eyed the horse as it stomped the ground and shuffled its feet, swinging its head around to shake off a fly. She squeezed Clint's hand. "Not at all," she lied. "I'm just hoping you've got a Plan B in mind once we leave here and I don't like this...creature any better."

Her heart hammered in her throat where it had lodged the moment she'd realized she needed to face her fear. Perhaps even from the moment she'd considered saying goodbye to Clint.

He reached out to the horse and patted its nose. Snout? Greta had no clue.

"Greta, meet Sam's Pride." Clint lifted her hand to touch the side of the horse's face.

Her fingers barely grazed its fur—hair?—when the thing bucked his head and made a snickering sound halfway between laughing and snoring.

She jumped back. "You see?"

Clint arched an eyebrow, and by the sympathetic look in his eye, Greta had the feeling he did see. All too well, and right through her.

He knew there was more to this than a fear of

horses. But patient, gentle Clint seemed willing to let her work through it her own way.

"I see a tentative streak I never expected to find in gutsy Greta Ingram. How can a woman who's traveled the world alone and hitchhiked on deserted stretches of rural highway be so intimidated by a lone horse?"

Greta felt her feathers start to ruffle in spite of her fear. "I am not intimidated. And it doesn't exactly indicate bravery to hitchhike on a deserted road. I think most people would take it as a sign of sheer stupidity, but since I never learned how to drive, I get around as best as I can."

Clint moved around her and patted the horse's side. "I'm going to help you fix that today." He pulled himself up onto the animal's back. No easy feat considering this horse didn't come with any convenient running boards or other step-stool device. "Ready to learn how to drive?"

"You've got to be kidding." She didn't know much about horses, but she was pretty sure they were supposed to have a little more equipment than this one, who looked naked, as far as she was concerned.

"Come on up here." He reached a hand down to her. As if she would take it and suddenly be transported on top of the humungous animal beneath him. "Those mile-long legs of yours surely have a few more uses than making men drool."

Okay, call her shallow, but flattery did have a way of distracting her from her fears just a little. Frowning, she stared down at her bare legs and short skirt. "I'm wearing a dress."

His voice lowered a few notches. "Then that'll just make your first time all the more fun."

Before she could follow that line of thinking, Clint slid his hands beneath her arms and lifted her through the air. She squealed, but she didn't flail, unwilling to risk his balance on the horse. A little thrill shot through her as it occurred to her how strong his thighs had to be to stay on that horse while pulling her aboard.

Settling her before him, Clint seated her with her back to his front, her bottom settled neatly against his hips. The backs of her bare thighs molded to the jean-clad fronts of his.

Having her legs spread across the back of the horse was a naughty thrill sort of like riding a motorcycle. Only her thighs were forced apart a bit more widely.

Just as Greta started to fully appreciate the provocative power of the position, Clint's hand clamped to her rib cage, the rough texture of his broad palm apparent through the thin cotton of her insubstantial little sundress. The top of his thumb grazed the bottom of her breast and rubbed the soft flesh in a slow arc.

Clint's voice rumbled behind her, through her. "Good thing you remembered to wear panties."

"Is it?" She heated up beneath those panties. Longed for him to move his hand lower. And lower still.

He chuckled. "Didn't you tell me animals were too messy? Too hairy? Too much work?" His hand slid lower over her belly. To the top of her thigh. "I figure it's a good thing you have a little something between you and him."

His fingers brushed up the hem of her dress to slip between her and the horse. She was already damp with arousal. And overwhelmed that Clint would take so much time and care to make her feel at ease when she was scared.

Clint's voice was thick with the same hunger she felt. "Are you ready?"

Leaning her head back on his shoulder, she looked up into his eyes. And in that moment, she saw something in his horse whisperer eyes that calmed her fears even as he stirred her heart and her body. A subtle communication that told her she could trust him to love her no matter how over-the-top her antics. No matter how many times she dragged him to Paris during the spring show season.

Yet, just then, Greta had the feeling she would grow deep roots in Alabama beside this man who seemed to understand her better than she understood herself.

She leaned forward to press against his palm all the more deeply. Thrusting her hips into his touch and giving herself into his care. She knew, now more than ever, that a man like Clint would never try to control her. Even now he was finding new ways to make her feel in command of her own fears, her reservations. "I think you know I'm ready."

But instead of reaching inside her panties and teasing her to the climax she wanted, Clint moved his hand back to her waist and nudged the horse forward with his heels.

Greta tried to voice her protest, but then the horse's shoulders moved underneath her as the animal walked, and then kicked up the speed even faster to run along the beach. Her protest came out as a moan, the rhythm between her thighs too obvious to ignore.

Clint held her to him, his hand locking around her breast to tease and caress even as he kept her steady. The nudge of his arousal against her bottom was made all the more erotic by the bump and grind effect of the horse beneath them.

And then the heated center of her gyrated in slow motion, keeping time with the horse's gallop. Dizzy with need, she couldn't help but throw her head back to the wind and the water the horse kicked up as it pounded through the surf. Faster.

Faster.

Until she soared right into the horizon on a wave of pure fulfillment.

Laughing and happy, there was no way Greta could ever pretend she hadn't liked this. Hadn't liked the horse. Hadn't appreciated Clint's efforts to let her face her fears.

Turning in Clint's lap to face him, she locked her legs around his hips and pressed herself to what she really wanted.

Him.

Not just now, but forever.

"I think I just got my first glimpse of the Crimson Tide," she whispered, her blood still surging through her veins in a flood of heated fulfillment. She allowed her forehead to fall against his, ready to give herself over to this man in every way possible. "When do we leave for Alabama?"

JESSE SQUINTED to see the shoreline in the last purple rays of the setting sun. Half an hour into the engagement party cruise he had commandeered Kyra to stand at the rail with him and watch for the small patch of beach that belonged to the Crooked Branch.

He'd ridden that narrow stretch of coastline enough times over the past few years that he ought to recognize it from the water.

"There it is." He pointed over the water and used the opportunity to drape an arm around Kyra's shoulders. She was nervous and edgy about tonight. He could feel it in her every gesture and movement. More than anything, he wanted to reassure her. Distract her. Help her to have fun for a change. "Who's on our beach?"

Kyra squinted right along with him. Leaning forward over the rail just a little.

She smiled. "It's Clint and Greta."

Jesse could barely make out the couple in the last rays of daylight, but he definitely caught a glimpse of feminine bare thigh wrapped around a man's waist.

And he was probably just imagining it, but he could swear he saw the guy in the Stetson grinning like a son of a gun.

Clint Bowman had obviously figured out how to make a relationship work. Would Jesse be so lucky?

Pulling Kyra closer, he hoped like hell he could offer her the kind of relationship she deserved. But if his vision served him and that horse Clint and Greta had been riding was the same three-year-old Jesse had asked Kyra not to sell, he had the feeling they were in for a long haul toward understanding one another. "I think it's great they found each other. But I can't help but think that was Sam's Pride they were riding. You didn't—"

"I didn't. I just loaned the horse to Clint so he could help Greta with him and see how they do." She didn't pull out of his embrace. Hadn't ignored his input to do what she wanted with her horse.

Damn but that felt good for a change.

He'd always tread carefully with her because she was so independent. But if she was willing to bend occasionally...the possibilities for a future together seemed a little more within reach.

Jesse definitely liked that. Liked holding her. They could rejoin his family in a minute. Right now, he just wanted to savor a few more minutes with Kyra. "Good. I'm betting Sam's Pride will go to Clint without so much as a whicker once that horse knows you're happy."

Kyra laughed, a soft musical sound that carried on the Gulf breeze and wrapped right around him. "So I spent all that money on a horse whisperer to figure out Sam's Pride's problems when all I had to do was ask you? I'm already happy. Why don't you just tell Sam's Pride as much for me, and that will solve a lot of problems?"

Jesse considered the matter and how to explain the esoterics of horse intuition to a woman who was as practical as she was beautiful. "I think you need to show Sam's Pride you're happy for good. That you're—"

All mine.

The thought was as plain as day. But where the hell had it come from?

Jesse blinked. He hadn't had a thought like that about any woman. Ever. His father had walked out on his mother and three kids at a vulnerable time in all their lives. Seth had pulled man-of-the-house duty for most of his life and had done a damn good job of it, but Jesse had always resented how much his old man had hurt his mother. While Seth worked his butt off to help support them, Jesse had been at home enough to see a lot of his mother's tears.

He knew how much it hurt when someone was unfaithful.

And he'd always had so much fun playing the field, that he told himself it was okay as long as he didn't ever hurt anyone in the process. As long as any woman he dated understood what to expect—and not to expect—from him.

"Jesse?" Kyra stared up at him, waiting for him to finish.

But he had no idea what he'd been talking about.

He could only wonder why he thought he'd never be able to make a commitment to a woman when Kyra had been showing him by example what commitment was all about for fourteen years running.

She'd taken over her father's ranching business at an early age when he'd succumbed to bouts of depression. And she'd made the ranch work by sheer force of will, eventually taking all that she'd learned and funneling it into a business of her very own. Her single-minded determination had inspired Jesse in more ways than he could count.

He'd ignored a college scholarship to play professional baseball because she told him it was okay to follow a dream. For nearly eight years he'd lived a fantasy and paid his bills to boot, earning him a place in the minor league record books.

And when he'd achieved all he wanted to there, he'd built his own business. Slapped his name on a shingle, for crying out loud.

He was all about freaking commitment.

"Jesse?" Kyra tugged his arm, calling him from his thoughts.

Focusing on her big blue eyes, Jesse nearly drowned in them. So wise and innocent at the same time. So driven and determined to achieve her dreams. Even if she had to wear a corset in public.

He loved this woman. No question.

And he could commit himself to her forever without a single fear.

"They're getting ready to toast the happy couple." She dragged him toward the center of the main deck. "And you might want to come up with a speech. I think Seth wants you to say a little something."

Jesse smiled. He'd gladly allow this practical woman to keep him on task his whole life.

Assuming he could distract her from those damn tasks every now and then.

He brushed a kiss along the top of her head and slowed her brusque pace across the deck. "Don't worry, Kyra. I've got plenty of things to say tonight."

16

KYRA TOOK A DEEP BREATH. Exhaled. Absorbed the warmth of Jesse's hands on her shoulders, the heat of his chest at her back.

Sometimes being with him excited her to a feverish pitch, but other times he grounded her in a way no else could. She'd always been so driven. Determined nothing would slip past her or be overlooked in her quest to build a profitable business she would enjoy all of her life.

No question, her relentless approach had served her well in many ways. But something about spending time with Jesse made her relax. Catch her breath.

She couldn't stand the thought of losing that connection. Of tonight being her last chance with Jesse.

They approached the throng of Jesse's family in the middle of the main deck. Since his sister was in California working on her internship in landscape design, the party consisted of his older brother Seth and his fiancée, Mia Quentin. Jesse's Uncle Brock and his lady love—Noelle Quentin, who also happened to be Mia's mother—rounded out the small group.

The four of them sprawled on blankets while the hired captain of the yacht took care of navigation in his secluded cabin above them. Three torches positioned around the deck made the party bright and festive even in the twilight. The breeze was starting to cool down now that the sun had dipped below the horizon, but that only gave Kyra an excuse to indulge a slight shiver at Jesse's warm touch.

Noelle thumped the empty space on the deck next to her. "Have a seat, Kyra. We can enjoy the speech together."

Jesse's Uncle Brock reached behind him into the cooler, then handed her a longneck from the case of beer Jesse had brought aboard when his last-minute search for champagne had been a bust. There wasn't a liquor store on the Twin Palms boardwalk, but at least there had been a convenience store.

Complete with cold beer.

"A little something for the toast." Brock eyed the label critically. "Nice vintage, Jess. Malt hops at its best."

"Hey, at least I got the imported stuff in deference to Seth's expensive taste." He snagged a bottle of his own while Kyra settled next to Noelle.

Jesse sat down beside her, exchanging verbal guy jabs with his brother and their uncle while Kyra soaked up the atmosphere of the night.

The happiness in the air.

At least, for two of the couples on board.

Seth and Mia were obviously head over heels about one another. Even while Seth good-naturedly raked his brother over the coals for his plebian beverage choice, he kept one hand draped over Mia's shoulder, his hand tracing tiny circles on her upper arm with his thumb.

Mia glowed beside her fiancé, and not just because of the torchlight reflected on her face. She smiled with the warm contentment of a woman who knows she'll be waking up beside the man of her dreams for the rest of her life.

Brock and Noelle radiated every bit as much bliss as the engaged couple. While Brock leaned back against the cooler, Noelle sat between his thighs to rest against his chest.

And of course, the image of Greta and Clint on the horse had remained in Kyra's mind to taunt her with the kind of love that meant happily ever after.

She couldn't pretend that she didn't want that for herself.

And, if she were honest with herself, she wanted it for her and Jesse.

As she stared up at him in the flickering light, Kyra knew she would never be content to simply return to their old relationship. Neither their business partnership nor their friendship would be enough for her anymore.

Now that she'd had a taste of what they could be like together, she didn't want to go back. She wanted to sleep by his side. She wanted to go to baseball games with him and listen to his one-of-a-kind color commentary on the sport he'd always loved. She wanted to drive by the houses he was building to see his progress in his new business.

But most of all, she wanted her happily ever after with him—the only man she'd ever fantasized about.

If only he felt the same way.

Her heart ached with wishing for impossible things as Jesse whistled for attention. He settled on his knees—a fitting height to toast a party sprawled on a yacht deck—and raised his beer bottle.

Clearing his throat with ceremony, he gave her one last wink before addressing the group. "I may have committed a small faux pas with the beer masquerading as champagne tonight, but trust me Seth, I put more time into the sentiment than the beverage."

Brock and Noelle clapped and cheered.

Kyra smiled to watch Jesse's innate charm in action. In their partnership at the Crooked Branch she didn't usually get to see him in his "work the crowd" mode, but she missed seeing that charisma of his flex its muscle. She had always loved going to the press conferences after his baseball games and seeing him send all the reporters home laughing.

Jesse pitched a crumpled-up cocktail napkin at his uncle. "So without further ado, please join me in toasting Seth and Mia."

Kyra gladly lifted her bottle. She might envy the kind of love the new couple had found, but she didn't begrudge them a minute of their happiness together.

"I wish you a lifetime full of shared joys. And in between all those good times, I wish you the comfort of being able to share your sorrows. I wish you the kind of partnership that comes with knowing one another year after year." As he looked around the members of his audience, his gaze stalled on Kyra, his sentiment meant for her as much as the words were directed toward his brother and Mia.

Kyra's heart caught in her throat.

"May you appreciate one another's strengths while bolstering each other's weaknesses. But most of all, may you remember to celebrate your love and the gift you have in one another every day."

Kyra blinked away a tear. She noticed Mia didn't bother to hold hers back. Two tiny rivulets trickled down her cheeks as everyone clinked bottles and shouted agreement to Jesse's words.

Malt and hops never tasted so good.

Kyra wanted to tell Jesse how much she liked his speech. For a guy who had never believed in commitments, he sure knew how to make "forever" sound pretty appealing. Did he harbor just a little longing in his soul for the same things Kyra did?

She didn't know what the future might hold for her and Jesse or if she'd ever have another chance to find out after tonight.

But Brock was too quick to snag Jesse's attention in the wake of the toast, asking him a few building questions about converting an old storefront into a new moped rental shop Noelle hoped to open within the year.

Noelle scooted across their little circle to hug her daughter and shed a few happy tears of her own. Kyra moved closer to the women to extend her congratulations. Much as she wanted to talk to Jesse alone, ask him how he'd grown so well versed in the rewards of marriage, she wanted to congratulate Mia, too.

Now more than ever, Kyra appreciated that good committed relationships didn't just happen. They required effort, compromise. Friendships were easy. Great sex was simple—at least for her and Jesse.

But love?

She hadn't figured that one out yet. And for the first time, she wanted to crack the mystery for herself.

THE MOON was high by the time Kyra found a few moments to slip away from the party and gaze out at the night sky. Her evening with Seth and Mia, Brock and Noelle had been the closest thing to a family gathering she'd been to in more years than she could count. What would it be like to belong to a family reminiscent of this one? To share your hopes and dreams, to share the workload in making those dreams happen?

Jesse had already signed on to help Brock and Noelle update the old storefront for Noelle's moped rentals. Seth had given Jesse a few tips about managing escrow accounts for his home-building clients.

Mia and Noelle had made a deal with Kyra to trade horseback riding hours at the Crooked Branch for moped riding hours at Noelle's new shop. Kyra enjoyed every minute with the Chandler men and the Quentin women, but she couldn't help but wonder if she'd have a chance to follow through on the bargain they'd made today.

Would she and Jesse have anything left to their

relationship besides a few great memories after to-night?

The idea that tonight might be her last chance sent a swell of panic through her.

Footsteps sounded on the deck behind her, upping the ante on her panic level. She recognized the pace, would know that laid-back, all-the-time-in-the-world step anywhere.

But instead of greeting Jesse at the rail of the yacht, Kyra jumped as she felt something sheer and silky slide over her eyes from behind.

A familiar pink scarf.

The warmth of Jesse's body hovered a few inches from her back. One of his hands slid down the bare expanse of her spine revealed by her navy, backless dress, while his other hand held her thin blindfold in place.

"I've got you now, Kyra." Jesse's voice wafted over her shoulder, a warm rumble across her skin. "What would you do if I kidnapped you tonight the same way you abducted me at Gasparilla?"

She swayed against his skillful touch, longed for more of those expert hands on her bare skin. Even more, she yearned for a deeper relationship with the man who had been captivating her for over a decade. "For starters, I don't think I'd give you any lectures like you gave me."

"You wouldn't?" He leaned closer, his grip on the scarf relaxing just a little. "What if I wanted a whole lot more from you than just one night of fantastic sex? Then would you break out the lecture?"

She smiled beneath the silk. Propping up the fabric with one hand over her eyebrow, she peered back at him. "I'd probably settle for telling you that you're a whole lot smarter than me."

Jesse let go of her scarf, allowing the gauzy material to settle around her shoulders as she turned to face him dead-on. The torches still flickered in the distance on deck, perfectly outlining his incredible body. No wonder one of the world's most renowned beauties had fawned all over him.

Yet Kyra saw the rest of him. She appreciated the sensitivity that made him as smart about animals as he was about people. Recognized the business savvy he'd always possessed but never smothered her with.

Now he skimmed a fingertip over her cheekbone and then down her jaw. "I do want more, Kyra. More than tonight. More than next week."

Her heart skipped. Still, she owed it to him to be honest about her fears. "I want that, too. But Jesse, I don't know that I would make a very good girlfriend. I know I've sucked as a business partner. Anyone else would have pulled their hair out trying to deal with me because I can be so independent. I don't know how you've put up with me. And I'm just afraid I wouldn't live up to your expectations if we became…more than partners."

He opened his mouth as if to speak, but as Kyra reviewed her words to him in her mind she wondered if she'd blown it by reminding him of all her bad qualities. She couldn't stop herself from blurting a last little caveat. "That being said, I would try very hard to be more open-minded if we did try to be together. Have I told you lately that you were so right about the ponies and that it was a great idea to buy them? And have I admitted that I was being really stubborn about selling Sam's Pride?''

Jesse laughed. Brushing a strand of hair behind her ear, he shielded her from the night breeze with the breadth of his body.

"You are independent, I'll grant you that. Maybe a little bossy." His brow furrowed as if starting to remember how much of a slave driver she'd been when he'd been building her barns, stringing her fences or working on their accounting reports. "And I'll be the first to admit you're stubborn as hell."

She felt the overwhelming need to toss a few of her good points out there, too, before he talked himself out of a second date with her. "But—"

"But you're also level-headed. Which is a good thing when I'm wound up because I grounded out to second base or I botched a strip of crown molding." He brushed his fingertips across her chin to tilt her face up to his. "You give me perspective."

She wanted to remind him that perspective was a very good, useful thing, but he covered her lips with the pad of his thumb, clearly ready to talk now.

"Being with you gives me a sense of peace I've never found anywhere else. For years I told myself that I always liked going back to the Crooked Branch because of the ranch environment or the horses, but it's not either of those things. I like to be there because of you." His dark eyes glittered with the reflection of the torches. Or maybe their fierce heat came from within.

Kyra couldn't help the smile that slipped across her face any more than she could staunch the hope growing inside her. Her heart skipped.

But Jesse wasn't through. He slid his hands down her shoulders, to her back. Pulled her closer and molded her body to his, hip to hip. "And all these years that I've been dating—extensively—I think I was just marking time, waiting for the right woman. The same woman I've already been committed to in a lot of ways for half my life."

Oh.

Kyra's heart quit the sissy skipping and hammered her chest with a vengeance. She felt the same happy tears tickle her eyes that Mia had shed only a few hours ago. Kyra plucked at the pink silk scarf that still dangled around her shoulders. "Then I guess I'm all yours to carry off."

"I don't think so." Jesse shook his head. "I haven't even said 'I love you' yet."

Oooohh. Something melted inside her. "Really?"

"Not unless I missed it." He wrapped the ends of the scarf around his finger and started winding the fabric around his skin, effectively reeling her closer.

"No. You didn't miss it. I definitely would have noticed if you'd put that out there." Warmth filled her along with a resounding sense of rightness. Her and Jesse together—it made so much crazy, beautiful, perfect sense.

"Then let me fix that right now. I love you, Kyra.

In a way, I think I always have. I've just been in serious denial. And maybe I was just too scared of messing up what we had to ever take a risk on us.'' He trailed his lips across her forehead, to her temple. ''I'm so glad your practical self took that one calculated, daring chance for both of us.''

She vowed to retrieve her black leather corset from the cleaners with all due haste. The costume deserved a special place in her closet for helping her open Jesse's eyes to new possibilities.

As the moist Gulf air wrapped around them, Kyra thanked the sky full of her lucky stars for putting her in this man's path that day fourteen years ago.

For putting him in her arms tonight.

''I love you, too, Jesse. Not just today, and not just tomorrow. Always. No matter what.'' She arched up on her toes to kiss his mouth, to squeeze him to her in a way she'd never dared before.

In a way she would every day from now on.

Kyra had no choice about controlling her happy tears anymore. They poured freely from her eyes to his shoulders and hers, a watery baptism for her very own happily ever after.

BLAME IT ON THE BLACKOUT

by
Heidi Betts

To Maureen Child and Leanne Banks –

Friends and fellow Desire authors,
you've inspired me more than you can ever
know. Thank you for your wonderful stories
that remind me of why I love this line so much,
and for all the great advice you've offered
this past year.

And to my absolutely fabulous editor,
Melissa Jeglinski – Thank you for taking me
under your wing, teaching me the ins and outs
of the Desire line and making me love what I
am writing even more than I did to begin with.

With many thanks to fellow WRW member
Sandy Rangel for her help with the research for
this book and willingness to share her firsthand
knowledge of the Georgetown area.

And always, for Daddy.

One

Lucy Grainger tapped softly in warning on the front door of Peter Reynolds's town house, then used a key to let herself in. Gathering the morning mail and paper from the foyer floor, she made her way past the den that held her office to the large kitchen at the back of the house. Setting the paper and mail alongside her purse on the island countertop, she started a pot of coffee and began clearing away some of last night's mess.

It wasn't her job to clean up after Peter. He did have a housekeeper, after all, who dropped by once a week to do laundry and dishes and relocate some of the dust that settled on miscellaneous surfaces. But Lucy was so used to taking care of him that it seemed only natural to move a few dirty dishes to the sink or throw away a near-empty carton of milk that had been left out of the refrigerator too long.

From there, she walked back toward the front of the house, up the stairs, and down the short hallway that led to Peter's bedroom. He might have slept in, especially if he'd been up late working on some computer program or another. Or maybe he'd simply forgotten to set his alarm clock—again. But his bed was empty, the sheets tangled and nearly stripped off the mattress.

Only one place left to look. Lucy eased the bedroom door closed and walked across the hallway in the opposite direction to Peter's home office.

Less conservative than the den, Peter liked this room because it was small, private, and casually decorated to his personal tastes. Which basically meant unadorned walls painted periwinkle-blue with white trim, a three-part desk taking up one whole corner, and low tables of sliding file drawers lining the remaining three. Every available surface was filled with assorted computer equipment, ongoing work projects, and Peter's collection of original *Star Trek* action figures.

Inside, the computer tower hummed softly from its home on the floor, telling her she was right about Peter's location. With one arm folded beneath his head, Lucy's boss slept hunched over his cluttered desk. He wore an old gray T-shirt and plaid boxers, his sandy-blond hair ruffled and sticking up in places—probably from all the times he'd run his fingers through it in frustration during the night.

Lucy's own fingers clenched at her sides as she fought the urge to flatten those spiky spots or slide a palm down the strong curve of his spine.

She sighed. This was the problem with working for a man she had half a crush on. The line between employer and potential lover got blurrier by the day.

But only for her. Peter didn't see her as potential lover material. Most of the time, she didn't think he saw her as a woman at all.

As a secretary, an assistant, the person he ran to when he needed just about anything, yes. But as an attractive, interested, flesh-and-blood woman? He'd never glanced up from his computer screen long enough to notice.

Then again, that was one of the things she loved about him—his passion for software design and starting his own company from the ground up. He was brilliant and already had corporations from around the world calling him to help work bugs out of their systems or simply get things running more smoothly. But what he loved most was designing his own games and programs, and that had been his focus for the past two years, ever since she'd started working for him.

Reaching past his sleeping form, she collected several empty cola cans scattered over the desktop and on the floor. He drank too much of this syrupy stuff, especially when he was busy and became nearly obsessed with a particular project.

Two of the aluminum cans slipped from her grasp and rattled as they bounced against each other on the way to the carpeted floor. The noise startled Peter and he shot upright. Blinking sleepily, he looked around as though he wasn't quite sure where he was.

"I'm sorry," Lucy said softly. "I didn't mean to wake you."

He rubbed a hand across his eyes and yawned. "What time is it?"

"A little past nine. How long have you been working?"

"I started after dinner. Around six, I guess."

Pushing back his chair, he got to his feet and stretched. His knuckles nearly grazed the ceiling as he raised his arms high above his head and stood on tiptoe. The posture puffed out his chest and showed the taut, well-defined muscles of his calves and thighs.

A ripple of awareness shot through Lucy, but she pretended not to notice.

"I was working on that GlobalCon glitch. It took me longer than I expected, but I think I took care of the problem."

She moved to the wastebasket near the door and dumped the soda cans in, making a mental note to recycle them later. "So those were billable hours you spent last night. What time did you finish?"

"Damned if I know." He scratched a spot on his chest and yawned again. "The last time I remember looking at the clock, it was about 3:00 a.m."

She nodded, wondering if GlobalCon and all of Peter's other clients realized just what a bargain they usually got with him. Sure, he was expensive, but he was also the best. And since he rarely remembered to log the times he began and ended his work for them, the bills she sent were generally best-guess estimates.

"Why don't you go lie down for a couple of hours. You look exhausted."

The grin he shot her swept right down to her toes and curled them inside her plain navy pumps.

"Nah. Now that I'm up, I might as well get showered and dressed."

Peter in the shower. Now there was an image she needed floating around her brain the rest of the morning. As though he didn't already keep her wide-awake most nights.

"Besides, I want to call GlobalCon and let them know I took care of their problem, then see if I can make any more progress on Soldiers of Misfortune."

Soldiers of Misfortune was Peter's latest obsession, a virtual guerilla warfare game with enough blood and guts to keep adolescent boys entranced for hours. Lucy tried to work up a modicum of outrage for his perpetuation of teen violence, but she played the games herself from time to time and had to admit they were fun. And so far, she hadn't snapped and committed any acts of mass destruction.

Careful not to touch him, she moved around the office, collecting the rest of the clutter from Peter's long work night. "Don't forget to try on your tux and see if it needs alterations before tomorrow night."

Halfway out the door, he froze. Twisting his neck just far enough to look at her, he asked, "What's tomorrow night?"

"The City Women benefit against domestic violence. You're giving a speech and receiving an award for your support of the organization and donations of refurbished computers to local battered women's shelters."

He'd spent weeks upgrading old systems so women who were trying to escape unbearable situations could train for new jobs to support themselves and their children instead of feeling forced to return to abusive husbands.

His eyes closed, chin dropping to his chest. "Damn, I forgot. I don't suppose there's any way I can get out of it," he said, shooting her a hopeful expression.

She bit down on a smile, not wanting to encourage him. "Not unless you want to disappoint hundreds of grateful women and children."

With a sigh, he rested his hands on his hips. "Fine. But I'm going to need a date."

A stab of pain hit her low in the belly. Followed quickly by envy and regret.

Peter had dated hordes of beautiful, successful ladies. Models, actresses, news anchors, real estate agents… He was handsome, funny, charming, and—though he was still striving to build his software company into one that would rival the best of the best—wealthy enough to catch a single girl's attention.

Lucy told herself it didn't hurt to see him with all those other women. Except when she came to work in the morning and discovered them still in his bed, or just leaving, or found a stray pair of panties while cleaning up between the housekeeper's visits.

"I'll go through your Rolodex and see who might be available."

A minute ticked by while Peter stood in the doorway and she lifted the now-full plastic bag from the metal trash can.

"No," he said, startling her. "I don't feel like putting on a show for someone who just wants to be seen with the great Peter Reynolds."

"That's all right. I'm sure the City Women will understand if you attend alone."

"I have a better idea," he announced, turning around to face her. "You can come with me instead."

He said it as though he'd decided to have chicken for dinner over steak, and Lucy couldn't help but feel like the feathered creature unfortunate enough to be dragged to the chopping block.

If he'd meant it as a real invitation, if he'd even once looked at her as though he wanted her on his arm for the evening because he was attracted to her, she might have considered it.

Oh, who was she kidding? She'd have jumped at the chance and prayed he didn't lose interest before the main course.

Shaking her head, she gathered the edges of the garbage bag together to keep the items from falling out and headed for the stairs, brushing past him with barely a millimeter of space to spare. "No, thank you."

"No? What do you mean *no?*"

His voice, raised in surprised indignation, followed her down the steps. As she rounded the newel post and headed for the kitchen, she noticed he was hot on her heels.

"Lucy, you can't possibly mean to leave me to my own devices. I'll drown in a sea of shiny, happy people. You know how much I hate crowds and public speaking."

"You should have thought of that before you agreed to be there." She set the trash from his office on the countertop and began separating it into the plastic recycling bins set in one corner.

"God, that coffee smells good," he murmured, tossing a longing glance at the pot that had just finished dripping. "Look, I can't go alone. I *need* you with me. There are going to be some very important people in attendance. People who could turn into future clients or help get Reyware and Games of PRey off the ground. You're my assistant. You know our software programs and intentions for the company almost as well as I do. And no one works a room like you do. People love you."

When she didn't respond, he continued, sounding more desperate by the second. "Consider it in your job description. I'll pay you overtime. You can take the appointment book and set up a dozen meetings with potential backers for the next month."

Ah, yes. She was, indeed, his assistant. And if he was making this into a work-related affair, then she had no choice but to go with him.

But she didn't have to make it easy for him.

Turning from the recycle bins, she leaned back against the counter and crossed her arms beneath her breasts. "You won't be so impressed when I show up in jeans and a ratty sweatshirt. I don't have anything appropriate to wear to a high-priced charity dinner."

Relief washed over Peter's features and he slapped his hands down flat on the marble island as the corners of his mouth turned up in a grin. "Not a problem. I'll take care of everything. Or rather, you'll take care of everything, but I'll foot the bill. Here…"

He reached back, as though digging into a hip pocket, then realized he was still in his boxers. Shaking his head, he rushed to assure her. "Don't worry, I'll get you a credit card. I'll get you two credit cards. Buy whatever you want."

Then he came around the island, reached her in three long strides, and wrapped her in a hug tight enough to crush her ribcage. "Thank you, thank you, thank you." He punctuated each adulation with a kiss to her temple.

Lucy's knees grew weak and she let her eyes drift shut as the heat of his body seeped through the thin material of her white blouse, short navy skirt and stockings.

Oh, sure. She could spend the evening with this man and remember it was nothing but business. No problem. And maybe after performing that small miracle, she'd practice turning water into wine.

Peter slugged back his sixth cup of coffee since Lucy had awakened him this morning and punched the computer mouse to send the cache of e-mails he'd composed in the last half hour.

He was learning that it wasn't easy taking care of himself. She'd only been gone two and a half hours, but she was usually around during the day to answer the phone and come when he called, so he was finding it difficult to carry out his normal routine.

He'd finally given up answering the telephone when it rang every five minutes, and was now letting all calls go directly to voicemail. Lord knew Lucy would be better able to deal with the messages when she got back. And even though she often went through his electronic mail for him, forwarding only those that required his personal attention, today he'd done it himself. He wasn't completely helpless, after all.

The snail mail, however, was a different matter. No way was he going anywhere near that pile of paper cuts. Lucy would let him know if there was anything he needed to see.

From his office upstairs, he heard the front door open and a wash of relief poured over him. Thank God. Now he could lock himself in his room and concentrate on his real strength—program design—instead of dealing with the other odds and ends of getting through the day.

Crossing his office threshold, he stopped on the second floor landing and watched as Lucy struggled to close the door while balancing assorted shopping bags and boxes in both arms.

Looking up, she spotted him and blew a stray strand of straight black hair out of her face. "You could offer to help, you know."

"Oh. Right." He spent more time with computers than people, and Lucy would be the first to point out that he sometimes lacked social graces. But the minute she called him on it, he rushed into action, bounding down the stairs and grabbing up her entire load.

"Sorry about that. It looks like you had luck shopping, anyway."

She shrugged out of the lightweight jacket that matched her dark blue skirt, tossing it over the banister and leaving her once again in a soft white blouse that showed off her feminine attributes to perfection. It didn't help that he could see the outline of her black lace bra through the gauzy material, either.

Peter's blood thickened and a lump of temptation formed in his throat. But a moment later, he tamped down on both, refusing to let his mind wander a path he had no business exploring.

Lucy was a beauty, no doubt about it. From the moment they'd met, when she'd first interviewed for the job as his personal assistant, he'd been fascinated by the silky fall of her long ebony hair, the smooth complexion of her porcelain skin, the bright, sharp blue of her doe-shaped eyes.

Of course, there was no chance of anything happening between them. Peter had long ago put a mental block on the possibility of building a relationship with any woman, let alone one who worked for him. God forbid he turn out like his father.... He had too much in common with the old man already and had no intention of making a wife or children as miserable as his father had made his mother and him.

But he'd hired Lucy in spite of his attraction to her, simply because she was the best damn applicant on the list. She typed, took dictation, had a phone voice that could make a saint fall to his knees, and knew her way around computers almost as well as he did.

So, if he found himself staring at her ripe red lips most of the time while she spoke, or taking an unnatural number of cold showers after she'd gone home for the day, he had no one to blame but himself.

Dressed now in a clean pair of tan chinos and dark green polo shirt, he noticed the curve of her mouth and wondered what she found so amusing. Lord knew he was in too much physical pain to mimic her contented smile.

"I hope you still think it was a good idea to make me go with you tomorrow night once you see your credit card statement."

That gave him a moment's pause, but then he shrugged. The tissue paper in several of the boutique bags rustled with the movement. "How bad could it be?"

Her brows shot up. Holding a hand out like she expected him to shake it, she quipped, "Hi, let me introduce myself. I'm a woman with *carte blanche* to charge anything I want on a man's account. I also happen to know your net worth. Any questions?"

He chuckled. Her sense of humor had always been machete sharp, but that was just one more reason he enjoyed her company.

"Remind me to have a couple of drinks before I open the bill," he returned. "In the meantime, how about a little fashion show?"

Eyes wide, she shook her head. "I don't think so."

"Come on," he cajoled. "I want to see what I paid for."

Furry, multilegged caterpillars wiggled inside Lucy's stomach as she considered Peter's request. The last thing she wanted to do was attend tomorrow night's charity benefit with him, and the next to the last thing she wanted was to model her new evening gown before she absolutely had to.

But—whether he knew it yet or not—he had spent quite a lot on the fancy ensemble, and if he wanted an advance viewing, she supposed it was only right to give it to him.

He must have read the indecision on her face because

he started up the stairs without her. "You can use my bedroom to change. And this way, I'll know what color corsage to order."

"Corsage?" With a roll of her eyes, she began to follow. "Peter, we aren't going to a high school prom."

He swung around at the balcony railing and flashed her the unwitting, thousand-watt smile that made her teeth sweat. "Too bad. It sure would be more fun than what we have to endure." Then he spun back and walked into the bedroom.

When Lucy arrived, the bags and boxes he'd carried up for her were scattered atop the chest at the foot of his bed. Peter rubbed his hands together and gave her a friendly wink before moving back toward the hallway.

"Give me a yell when you're ready. I'll be in my office."

The door closed with a soft click, leaving her alone beside Peter's bed…and Peter's mattress…and Peter's pillow. The covers were still rumpled from the last time he'd slept there and it took a great deal of effort not to throw herself across the bed and inhale his scent from every fiber of the tan, five hundred thread count Egyptian cotton sheets. She ought to know, she'd bought them for him.

Sad, that's what she was. Pathetic and sad and unworthy of being a member of the female race. What other twenty-nine-year-old woman spent her life mooning over an unattainable boss? A clueless man who never looked twice at her…at least not the way a man should look at a woman.

Other than throwing herself down on his desk and screaming, "Take me, big boy!" she'd done everything she could think of to let Peter know she was interested. From the time she'd started working for him two years ago, she'd tried to drop hints that his advances wouldn't be unwelcome. She'd worn her skirts a little short and her blouses a little low. She'd worn a dozen different perfumes, trying to find one that would pique his interest. She'd worn her hair up and down, short and long, straight, curly, braided...She'd leaned close while they talked and fabricated excuses to interrupt him while he worked.

Finally, when nothing seemed to catch his attention, she'd given up. A girl could only take so much humiliation, and her breaking point came the day she'd arrived at work to find another woman, half-dressed, leaving Peter's room. Her theory that he must be gay had been shot all to hell, and she'd vowed then and there never to make another move on him.

Unfortunately that pledge didn't keep her eyes from wandering over his well-muscled form, or her heart from skipping a beat when he said her name in that low, reverberating voice of his.

Not for the first time, she thought about quitting. She really should. She was talented, good at her job, and could probably find another position anywhere in the city within the week.

But she liked this arrangement. Despite the personal misery she suffered on a daily basis, Peter was a great employer. She believed in what he was doing and enjoyed being a part of it.

Besides, what other boss would spring for a gorgeous new evening gown and accessories that she would probably never have occasion to wear again?

Lifting items from their bags, she began to peel out of her practical skirt and blouse, ignoring the skittering of awareness that skated down her spine when she realized she was standing half-naked in the middle of Peter's bedroom. If only he were here with her, and she was stripping down to her skin for something other than an impromptu fashion show.

Instead of bothering with the fancy undergarments she'd purchased to go with the dress, she remained in her normal bra and panty hose, and simply slipped the gown on overtop. She did trade her plain pumps for the black, glitter-covered velvet stilettos, though.

Sweeping her hair back off her shoulders, she left the bedroom and crossed the short, carpeted hall to Peter's office. She stopped in the doorway, leaned casually against the frame and watched his fingers fly over the keyboard.

"So," she said, catching his attention. "What do you think?"

Two

Peter glanced up from the computer screen, wondering why she hadn't called for him when she was finished. He'd have gone over to the bedroom to see her new dress instead of making her come all the way over here.

And then his brain stopped functioning altogether. Every thought in his head flew out his ears as he stared at the vision before him.

He slid the wire-rim glasses from his nose to get a better look, but she still looked stunningly beautiful. Her hair fell about her face in an ebony curtain and the red satin of her gown, overlaid with black velvet in an intricate flowered pattern, brought out the rosy tint of her alabaster skin.

And that was just from the neck up. From the neck down, she made his eyes sting, his mouth go dry and his nerve endings sizzle.

He'd always known Lucy had a fabulous body. All the straight skirts and tailored jackets in the world couldn't hide that. But this dress, with its spaghetti straps and scallop-edged bodice, high-slit skirt and the three to four inch heels that made her legs go on for eternity, brought out every nuance of her drop-dead figure.

His gaze drifted over the generous swell of her breasts, the slim line of her waist, the gentle curve of her hips, and up again. Her ice-blue eyes met his and for the first time in his life, he found himself at a loss for words. Speechless, when he'd thought that was something only movie stars suffered because a script called for it.

After several long seconds of complete, utter silence, Lucy interrupted his total lack of thought and started blood flowing back to his brain.

"What?" she asked, glancing down at herself as though something was wrong with the awe-inspiring concoction she was wearing. "Don't you like it? Should I take it back?"

"No!" he yelped, too fast and too loud. Taking a breath, he tempered his tone and added, "It's perfect. I was just…" *Admiring the view…thinking sinful thoughts…looking for a way to get you out of it…* "Thinking of all the heads you're going to turn tomorrow night. We may have to beat men off with a stick."

Her cheeks colored prettily and she lowered her eyes for a moment. "Thank you."

"You won't have any trouble stirring up interest for Reyware in that outfit."

He regretted the words as soon as they left his mouth. What was he thinking, effectively equating her attending the charity soiree in that dress to prostitution? *Hey, Luce, how about fixing yourself up and coming to dinner with me so you can give new meaning to "pressing the flesh" and drum up a little financial support for my personal corporation?*

Lord, he felt like a pimp.

And he knew his comment hurt her because she lowered her head and traced invisible designs on the carpet with the toe of her shoe.

Scrubbing a hand over his face, he cursed silently. "That didn't come out right," he tried to apologize.

She raised her eyes to his, dark and shadowed, and offered a weak smile. "I know what you meant."

No, she didn't, but he couldn't think of a way to further explain himself without making matters worse.

"I'd better go change back," she said, letting her gaze slide away from him again. "Before I get stained or torn or wrinkled."

He could think of a couple of things he wouldn't mind doing to tear or wrinkle her gown. And he'd happily pay for another when they were finished.

As quickly as that image entered his mind, he shut it down. Lucy turned, heading back to his bedroom, and there was enough testosterone swimming around in his veins at the moment to watch her walk away and enjoy every elegant, long-legged stride.

But that was as far as it could go—watching. Lucy wasn't one of the women who snuggled up to him at parties and made it clear they were hoping to spend the night in his bed.

As much as he might wish differently, he couldn't use her to scratch this itch that was suddenly driving him crazy. She was his assistant, and he hoped a friend. Those were two things he wasn't willing to risk.

Worse than that, though, Lucy wasn't a woman he could walk away from in the morning. She would always be here, working for him, helping him to market his software designs and computer know-how, and filling the holes in his own personality with her award-winning people skills.

Dropping into his desk chair, he sent it spinning and watched the blue of the walls swirl around him. What a mess. He should have hired a man to answer the phone and open his mail. He sure as hell wouldn't be having this problem then.

But Lucy was the best, and he honestly wouldn't want to work with anyone else, no matter how hard it was to ignore her presence.

If he started something with Lucy, there would be no one-night stand, no casual roll in the hay that could be forgotten and ignored ten minutes later. She wasn't that kind of girl.

And if she wasn't *that* kind of girl, then she was the other. The forever kind, with visions of marriage and children and picket fences dancing in her brain.

That kind scared Peter to death. He'd decided long ago never to let a personal, romantic relationship cloud his acumen for business.

His father had tried to have both and failed miserably. Oh, his company was a smashing success, but his marriage might as well have been a house afire. He'd spent all his time at the office, put all of his energy into deals and negotiations…while Peter and his mother were the ones to suffer.

Peter had seen the anguish in his mother's eyes. The slump of her shoulders, the air of dejection she carried when her husband disappointed her yet again with late nights or canceled plans.

And Peter would be damned if he'd burden another woman with that type of lifestyle, the way his father had burdened his mother. Especially a woman he cared for.

Marriage, family, happily ever after…they weren't for him. His entire focus was on building his business and designing software to rival the competition. Which meant he had little or no time to devote to a relationship.

Even if he did…even if Reyware and Games of PRey were well-established enough to relax a bit, to go out and enjoy a healthy social life…he still wouldn't.

For Peter, it was all or nothing. He could concentrate all of his efforts on business, or he could concentrate all of his efforts on finding a wife and starting a family. He couldn't do both. And for now—probably for the next ten or twenty years—he chose to concentrate on his work.

It was a damn shame, though. Spending a few hours in the sack with Lucy might just have been worth losing time on a project or two.

The night of the charity event, Peter arranged for a limousine to pick Lucy up at seven o'clock. That gave her two and a half hours to get home from work, shower, change clothes, fix her hair and do her makeup.

It probably shouldn't have taken her half that long, but she wasn't used to attending high-priced dinners and fancy fund-raisers. And the thought of going with Peter, perhaps being mistaken for his latest bit of arm candy, had her stomach in knots.

Her apartment, only a few blocks from Peter's town house in downtown Georgetown, was small, but served its purposes. She'd bought several paintings from a local art gallery and framed some pictures of her family and friends to decorate the otherwise sparse white walls. Small area rugs added color to the brown pile carpeting, and the African safari images on her full-size bedspread made her room feel—in her opinion, anyway—wild and exotic.

And, of course, there was Cocoa, her beautiful, long-haired calico cat, who always rushed to the door to greet her, but ran from anyone else.

"Hello, baby," she cooed, heedless of the hairs covering her skirt and jacket as she swept the cat into her arms. Cocoa began to purr and nudge Lucy's chin with the top of her head.

"All right, all right. You're hungry, I know."

As was their habit, she set the feline on the kitchen table while she opened a can of Deluxe Dinner and chopped it up into bite-size pieces on a platter with pastel pawprints and Cocoa's name painted in flowing script.

"Enjoy your liver and chicken," she said with a kiss to the top of the cat's head. "I have a big party tonight and need to get ready."

Every item she intended to wear to the benefit lay strewn across her bed, for fear she might forget something. After a quick shower, she rubbed moisturizer into her steam-warmed skin and dabbed her pulse points with her favorite perfume. Then she blew her hair dry and began the painstaking process of getting dressed.

She started with the matching bra and panty set she'd bought to go with the red satin and black velvet gown before sliding on the black silk thigh-highs the saleslady had talked her into. Thigh-highs or stockings and a garter belt, the woman had assured her, were much sexier than panty hose.

Personally, Lucy questioned the need for sexy lingerie for a nondate with her boss. She could walk out to the limo naked and doubted he would spare her more than a glance before once again burying his nose in his laptop.

With the expensive gown molding to every curve of her body, she swept her hair up and fixed it into a loose French twist at the back of her head. Makeup and jewelry came next, and she pretended not to notice the slight tremor in her fingers as she applied mascara and lipstick.

This was ridiculous. She was a grown woman, attending a charity event to raise money for domestic violence victims and hopefully stir up interest in Peter's company. Not a geeky teenager attending the homecoming dance with the captain of the football team.

Steeling her spine with renewed determination, she slipped into high heels, grabbed the tiny sequined clutch with little more than a compact and lipstick inside and headed for the front door.

A glance at the microwave clock showed she was five minutes early, but if she headed downstairs now, she could meet the limousine when it arrived instead of making the driver buzz up for her.

She gave Cocoa one last stroke as the cat continued to lick her plate clean. "Be a good girl. I'll be home as soon as I can."

To her surprise, the limo pulled up just as she reached the double glass doors of her building. Draping a fringed black shawl around her shoulders, she went out to meet the car.

She half expected the driver to come around and hold

the door for her, but instead the door opened on its own. Her steps faltered as a foot emerged, followed by a leg, an arm and finally a head of sandy-blond hair. She'd thought Peter was simply sending a car for her, that she would meet him at the hotel where the dinner was being held. Now, it looked as though she would have to ride there with him. In the back of the limo. In close proximity.

He stood on the curb, waiting for her, looking like the California version of James Bond in his black tuxedo, and she had to remind herself to breathe, then put one foot in front of the other until she reached his side. He smiled brightly, letting his gaze slide over her as he reached out a hand for hers.

"If possible," he said, giving her fingers a gentle squeeze, "you look even more amazing tonight than you did yesterday."

The compliment washed over her like a warm breeze, causing the corners of her mouth to lift.

And then, from behind his back, he produced a single long-stemmed red rose. "For you. I thought you might appreciate it more than a corsage."

Although a small lump filled her throat at his thoughtfulness, she laughed. Peter could be incredibly charming when he wanted, but until this moment, she'd never been the recipient of that seductiveness.

She knew it wasn't real. He was only being polite for this one night because she was doing him a favor by accompanying him to the fund-raiser.

Still, for her, for now, it *was* real. And there was no reason she shouldn't enjoy it while it lasted. Soon enough—like first thing Monday morning—it would be back to work, back to their usual employer/employee relationship.

She lifted the bloom to her nose and inhaled its rich fragrance. "It's beautiful, thank you."

When their eyes met over the top of the rose, she thought she saw something deep and meaningful flash across his features, but it was just as quickly gone—if it had been there at all.

Clearing his throat, he moved away from the limousine and waved an arm for her to precede him. "Shall we?"

She nodded, stepping into the plush rear of the limo. Peter slid in beside her and the car rolled forward.

"Would you like something to drink?"

A bottle of champagne, already open, sat chilling in an ice bucket on the opposite seat. He poured a few inches of the golden liquid into a cut crystal glass and handed it to her before filling a flute for himself.

Lucy wasn't much of a drinker, and normally she never would have started in the car on the way to an event where she knew she would probably consume even more alcohol. But tonight, her nerves were jumping like kernels of corn over an open fire. Maybe a few sips of champagne would calm them down.

"Thank you again for coming with me," he said as the cool bubbles tickled their way down her throat. "I already feel more relaxed about the evening than if I were going alone or with a practical stranger."

If the majority of Peter's dates were "practical strangers," he certainly cozied up to them enough to invite them in at the end of the night.

She took another gulp of wine to wash away the depressing thought. Peter's love life was none of her business. His personal life was none of her business. Only his professional life, filling the hours from nine to five, were any of her concern. And sometimes a slice of overtime, such as tonight. But other than that, he could do whatever he wished with whomever he wished, and it wouldn't bother her a bit.

"This isn't a favor," she felt the need to clarify. "It's part of my job."

"Yes, but you didn't have to come along. You could have said you were busy, already had a date, or just plain refused."

She could have...if she'd thought of it.

The rest of the drive passed in silence until they pulled up in front of the Four Seasons on M Street, very close to the city limits of Georgetown. Peter set aside their empty glasses as the driver came around to open their door, then stepped out and turned back to offer Lucy his hand.

Arms linked, they walked into the elegant hotel lobby. A large banner and smaller, raised signs announced the City Women benefit and directed guests to the bank of elevators leading upstairs. Several couples were already there, and Peter and Lucy joined them.

The last ones in, they were at the front near the doors. She could feel the heat of Peter's hand at the small of her back, through the sheer material of her shawl. She tipped her head to look at him over her shoulder, noticing the thin line of his mouth, the tightness in his jaw. Her eyes narrowed, and she was about to ask if he was all right when the elevator doors opened with a swish. The pressure at her back increased as he urged her forward, into the plush, paneled hallway and in the direction of the crowded ballroom.

Round tables draped with hunter-green and pink linens to match the City Women's trademark colors filled the room, each seating ten to twelve people. At the front, a raised platform held long, rectangular tables on either side of a tall podium.

As soon as his eyes landed on the microphone he would be using for his acceptance speech, Peter made a choking sound and stuck a finger behind the collar of his shirt, as though the small black tie was cutting off his air supply.

"You'll be fine," she assured him, laying a hand on his elbow and running it down the length of his arm until their fingers twined. "Now we'd better get up there before Mrs. Harper-Whitfield starts 'yoo-hooing' for you over everyone's heads."

He groaned. "Please, no. Not Mrs. Harper-Whitfield."

Laughing, they started through the crowd, nodding and saying hello to acquaintances, stopping to chat only when they weren't given much choice. When they finally reached their seats, the City Women directors and founding members flocked to Peter's side, thanking him for coming, complimenting him on his latest donation or software creation.

Lucy sat beside him, a smile permanently etched on her face for the stream of admirers who paraded past, wanting a moment or two with the esteemed Peter Reynolds.

Finally dinner was served, and they were left mostly to themselves while everyone enjoyed delicious servings of thinly sliced beef, steamed broccoli, lightly seasoned new potatoes, and fruit tartlets for dessert. Hundreds of mingled voices filled the room, making a private conversation difficult.

Lucy realized, too, that Peter was inordinately nervous about getting up in front of such a large group. But no matter how slowly he ate, the meal was soon over and the City Women president was addressing the crowd, describing the organization's accomplishments of the past several months and relaying some very moving success stories.

As soon as the speaker began talking about that one special contributor who had helped to fill their shelters with computer equipment and offer women avenues other than remaining in abusive situations, Lucy felt Peter tense beside her. His entire body went taut, and his knuckles turned white where they tried to squeeze the life out of a poor, defenseless cloth napkin.

Turning unobtrusively in his direction, she leaned close enough to be heard and whispered, "Relax." She covered his clenched fist with the palm of her hand, gently stroking his warm skin until his grip on the linen loosened. Setting the napkin aside, she slipped her free hand beneath the lapel of his tuxedo jacket and retrieved the stack of index cards she knew would be there.

"Take a deep breath," she ordered in a soft, soothing tone. "You've done this a million times before, you'll be fine. And if all else fails, remember to picture everyone naked."

His head whipped around and his gaze, hot, green and intense, drifted over her, lingering a little too long on the area of her waist and breasts.

"Not *me*," she growled with a roll of her eyes, putting three fingers to his cheek and pushing him away.

The City Women president smiled brightly as she finished her introduction and the spotlight swung to Peter. Lucy shoved the note cards into his hand and urged him to his feet before joining in on the applause.

In the end, he had nothing to worry about. His speech was both funny and poignant, delivered with perfect pitch by a man who could flirt a nun out of her habit. Before he finished, Peter promised to continue refurbishing and donating used PCs for the organization's use, earning him a standing ovation and another round of boisterous applause. The City Women then gifted him with a plaque in appreciation of his aid.

From there, everyone moved across the hall to a second ballroom where an orchestra was set up to play for the rest of the night, as well as four cash bars that would split their profits with the hosting charity.

Now that his speech was over, Peter was much more relaxed and willing to mingle with a crowd that obviously adored him. And Lucy knew this was her cue to spring into action. To approach some of D.C.'s wealthiest citizens and talk up Peter's freshman software company, convincing them that any man who would volunteer so much time and money to such a worthy cause certainly deserved a modicum of support for his own interests. She would set up appointments for them to visit Peter at home, see samples of his work and discuss his plans for the future of Reyware.

Two long, exhausting hours later, Lucy had set up twenty-odd meetings for the following weeks and was fighting not to yawn and offend all the people she'd just spent half the night trying to impress.

Coming up behind her, Peter slid an arm around her waist, resting his chin on the slope of her shoulder. "Have we put in our time yet? Can we get the hell out of here?"

"I thought you were enjoying yourself," she said without turning around.

"Making the most of a bad situation…it's not quite the same thing. So how about it—wanna blow this Popsicle stand?"

She checked her watch. Nearly midnight. "I suppose it wouldn't be too terribly rude to leave now. We have been here for almost four hours."

"Feels like six. Besides, I want to get home and find a place to hang my new plaque." He waved the chunk of wood and gold plating in front of her as they made their way to the outskirts of the ballroom and sneaked off—*hopefully*—without being noticed.

The elevators were free, the doors sliding open as soon as Peter punched the down button. They were alone inside the carpeted, glass-walled car, and Lucy once again spotted signs of strain bracketing his mouth, his fingers clenching around the brass handhold that ran along all three sides.

"Do you have a problem with elevators?" she asked, drawing his attention from the glowing red numbers above the door.

"Elevators? No, why?"

"Because you seem awfully uncomfortable. I noticed it on the ride up earlier, too. We could have taken the stairs, you know."

He shook his head. "I'm fine. I just like getting off elevators more than I like getting on them."

That was an understatement, she thought, but didn't say anything more since they were only going from the fourth floor to the lobby. But then the lights flickered and Peter glanced up in alarm. A second later, the entire car went dark, lurching to a stop somewhere between floors as the cables and computerized panels groaned in protest.

"What's going on? Why aren't we moving?" Peter wanted to know, banging on the controls as though hitting all the buttons at once would miraculously send them back into motion.

"I think the power might be out," she told him, waiting for her vision to adjust to the pitch-black.

"Oh, God. How long do you think it will take them to get it back on?"

She shrugged and then realized he couldn't see her. "You know how these things are. Sometimes the electricity only flickers off for a few minutes, other times it takes all night."

"Oh, God," he groaned.

Peter's breathing echoed off the walls, heavy and exaggerated. She reached out, feeling for him, until her fingertips encountered the soft fabric of his tuxedo jacket.

"Take it easy, Peter. The elevator isn't even moving now."

"That's the problem," he gritted out, punctuating each word with a hard rap to the metal doors. "The damn thing isn't moving!"

A shiver of dread skated down her spine. "I thought you didn't like being in elevators because of that weird up-and-down sensation you get in your stomach."

"Ha!" The sound came out strangled and his breathing grew even more ragged. Beneath her hand, the muscles of his arm bunched and released.

"It's not *elevators*," he snapped. "They haven't invented an elevator yet that moves fast enough for me. It's enclosed spaces. I can't stand small, enclosed spaces."

Three

Uh-oh.

"You're claustrophobic?"

How could he be claustrophobic? And how could she not know about it?

She'd been working with him for two years now. She knew his favorite foods, his favorite color, his favorite pair of boxer shorts, for heaven's sake. How could she have missed the fact that he was claustrophobic?

"Just a little."

His response came out on a wheeze and she realized he was seriously downplaying just how upset he was by this sudden set of circumstances.

"All right, let's not panic," she said, as much to herself as to him. She moved closer, rubbing his arm, his shoulder. "The power will probably come right back on. Until then, why don't you tell me how long you've had this little problem."

"Forever. Long as I can remember." A beat passed while he sucked in air like a drowning victim. "Is it hot in here? It's too hot in here."

She felt him struggling to shed his jacket even though she didn't think the temperature had gone up a single degree since the lights went off. His high level of anxiety probably had his internal thermostat going haywire.

"Here, let me help." She took the suitcoat, folding it in half and setting it aside in what she hoped was a safe corner.

"And what do you usually do when you find yourself in an enclosed space?" If she could keep him talking, maybe he wouldn't think so much about where they were. She might even get lucky and figure out a way to keep him calm until the elevator started moving again.

He laughed, a raw, harsh sound. "Go crazy? Throw up? Pass out?"

This was a side of Peter she'd never seen before. Sure, he was slightly scattered, a bit of a computer nerd. More focused on the new program he was designing than whether his hair was combed or there was enough milk in the refrigerator for breakfast.

But, other than the occasional round of public speaking, he was also strong and self-assured. So handsome, he made her teeth hurt. And he was in better physical shape than anyone would expect for a man who spent twenty-three hours of most days staring at a computer screen. He carried himself like a man with a mission; one who knew exactly why he'd been put on this earth and was simply going about the business of carrying out that task.

Little had she known he harbored this secret claustrophobia.

"Oh, God." He was punching buttons again, growing more agitated by the second. "We're going to die in here."

She bit down on her lip to keep from laughing out loud at that outrageous pronouncement. "We are *not* going to die. Come on. Come over here and sit down."

Taking his elbow, she tugged him away from the front of the elevator until they hit the rear wall. It took some doing, but she finally got him to the floor.

Covering his face with his hands, he muttered, "I don't feel very well. I think I might be sick."

"You're fine. Everything's going to be fine." She brushed his cheek with the back of her hand, finding it warm and damp with perspiration. "Close your eyes."

"What?"

"If your eyes are closed, you won't even know the lights are off. We'll talk and pretend we're back at the house, and before you know it, that's exactly where you'll be."

He gave a raspy chuckle. "I don't think that's going to work."

Running two fingers lightly over his eyelids, she whispered, "You never know until you try."

His chest still heaved with the speed of his breathing and she could feel his body shaking against her own.

"You're in your office," she murmured, thinking she sounded an awful lot like a hypnotist. "Working on the latest version of Soldiers of Misfortune, throwing in some extra severed heads and damsels in distress. The kids will love it."

"Too much violence. Should be more socially conscious."

She laughed at that, knowing how much time he spent worrying that his computer games were too mature for their audiences. "You're just socially conscious enough. Now focus. You're at your desk, swigging down your tenth can of soda…I'll be in any minute with your mail, and to chastise you for drinking too much of that sugar water."

"Nectar of the gods."

"The gods of Type-2 Diabetes, maybe." She played with the ends of his silky hair, trying to keep him from hurting himself as he banged his head rhythmically against the back wall of the elevator.

"You worry too much about me."

His comment caught her off guard, and for a minute she didn't respond. She did worry too much about him, but she couldn't help it. She cared about him, too—too much. She cared that he worked long hours and didn't get enough sleep, that he didn't eat right and inhaled cola like it was oxygen. And she cared that he was so upset about being stuck in this elevator in the middle of a blackout.

"Not too much," she said finally. "Just enough."

Was it her imagination, or was he calming down? His breathing didn't seem quite as loud now, and the fidgeting had slowed to a bare minimum.

A minute ticked by in silence while she waited to see if he was all right. If maybe he'd fallen asleep or really believed he was in his office, working on his latest Games of PRey installment.

But suddenly, the trembling started again, worse than before, and he shot to his feet. "This isn't working. We have to get out of here before we run out of air. Why isn't anyone trying to get us out?"

He pounded on the doors with his fists, shouting for help, on the verge of hyperventilating. Lucy made another grab for him, pulling him away, fighting the claustrophobia for his attention.

"Peter. Peter, stop. Listen to me." She framed his face with her hands, able to see the barest outline of his silhouette now that her eyes had adjusted to the darkness. "You're okay. Everything's going to be okay."

"No, no, no…" He shook his head emphatically, not listening or unwilling to believe. "I can't breathe."

She could feel the pulse at his throat beating out of control and knew she was losing him. But what else could she do? How did you calm someone who was on the brink of a breakdown?

The answer came to her in a flash and she didn't give herself time to second guess. Leaning up on tiptoe, she pressed her lips to his, kissing him as she'd always imagined. Her fingers slipped from his cheeks to his nape, tangling in the slightly long hair growing over his collar.

He tasted of scotch and heat and just plain Peter, and she wondered why she'd waited two years to do this. It was crazy, it was wrong, but it was also so darn good, her skin was threatening to melt right off her bones.

And best of all, Peter's panic seemed to have subsided. He wrapped his arms about her waist and dragged her closer, opening his mouth to let their tongues parry and thrust.

Their bodies rubbed together like two pieces of flint, all but shooting sparks. Her breasts, crushed to his chest, grew heavy and sensitive with desire, her nipples beading to nearly painful points. Lower, the hard line of his arousal nudged the area between her legs.

In the back of his mind, Peter knew he was supposed to be thinking about something. The dark, the broken-down elevator, getting out, or dying before anyone discovered them. But damned if he could find it in him to care about anything other than the warm, willing woman in his arms.

Lucy. He shouldn't be kissing Lucy…his assistant, his friend, the one person he didn't want to offend because, as he often joked, she knew where the bodies were buried.

But, God, she felt good. She smelled good, like flowers in springtime, with an overlaying scent of musk that made him think of hot, sweaty sex. And she tasted amazing.

Since puberty, he'd had his share of fantasies about making out with beauty queens and X-rated starlets; sometimes both at the same time. But no dream, no matter how erotic, could ever live up to what was happening right here, right now. She made steam rise from his pores and every drop of blood in his veins rush straight for the equator.

His hands slid from her waist to her buttocks, drawing her up and crushing her against the straining evidence of his enthusiasm. If they didn't stop soon, it would be too late.

But he had no intention of stopping. The ground would have to open up and swallow him whole. This elevator that had trapped them so securely would have to break from its cables and crush them like pancakes. Because unless an act of God pulled them apart, he was going to make love to Lucy Grainger.

Finally.

The lack of light heightened every sensation, the fireworks exploding behind his closed eyelids almost more than he could bear. He'd wanted her far too long to take things slow.

Letting his lips trail from her mouth to her chin, to

the tender flesh of her throat, he found the zipper at the back of her gown and slowly dragged it downward. His knuckles grazed her spine with each click of the zipper's teeth and she moaned, sending shivers of awareness through to his nerve endings.

As the barrier of her dress fell away, he unhooked the clasp of her strapless bra and cupped the two glorious globes of her breasts in the palms of his hands. His thumbs teased the nipples, drawing a gasp of pleasure from her parted lips.

Peter kissed her again, wanting to devour her, absorb her into his every pore. Her hands on his chest felt like iron brands. She fumbled with the buttons of his shirt until the tails came free of his pants. He reached up and yanked the bow tie from his neck before it choked him as she pushed the shirt off over his shoulders.

Her soft, delicate hands explored his body like a blind man exploring a work of art. Her sharp, manicured fingernails left trails of fire along his skin, making him want to growl low in his throat and take her like an animal. Only the knowledge that this was Lucy, a woman he cared about and would never intentionally hurt, kept him from throwing her down and driving into her right that second.

Instead he wrapped an arm around her back and lowered her slowly to the carpeted elevator floor. The shirt caught at his elbows hampered his movements, but he didn't want to waste time removing his cuff links and stripping down completely. Cradled in the hollow of her thighs, the gown bunched now around her hips, he let her thread her fingers into his hair and pull him down for a soul-stealing kiss.

Circling her ankle first, and then the sleek curve of her calf, he ran his hand over the satiny stocking encasing her leg. When he reached the top of her thigh, he found a wide band of elasticized lace and groaned. No panty hose to deal with, just sexy, convenient thigh-highs and a pair of barely there French-cut panties that could be slipped off in one quick motion or simply pushed aside when the time came.

Which would be soon. He couldn't last much longer, being this close to her, feeling her breasts with their pebbled peaks and the dampness of her desire soaking through her panties.

A muscle in his jaw jumped as his hand encountered that moisture and he rested his head against her brow for a moment, praying for the restraint it would take not to lose it then and there. But either God was on a break or Lucy was determined to shatter his self-control because she arched her back, ground her pelvis into his throbbing erection, and panted his name on a whisper of sound.

It was the name that did it. If she had only moaned or muttered nonsensical words, he might have kept it together. Hearing his name on her lips, though, realizing that she knew exactly who was touching her, making love to her, and that she had no intention of coming to her senses and asking him to stop, sent him straight over the edge.

Reaching between their hot, writhing bodies, he undid the front clasp of his slacks, shoving them down just enough to free his rigid length. At the same time, he stripped the flimsy satin triangle from her hips and spread her legs farther apart. With his hands on her bottom, he found the tight, feminine opening that beckoned him like a siren's song and entered her in one long, solid thrust.

Lucy cried out as Peter filled her. Her lungs felt ready to burst, her body burning with rising lust. She lifted her legs, crossing them at the ankles behind his back, and dug her nails into his shoulders, imploring him to move, to put an end to this torture.

"Please," she begged, surprised she could speak at all. Every fiber of her being vibrated with desire, pulsed with need. If he didn't bring her to orgasm soon, she thought, she just might die.

"Yes, please. Now."

His voice rasped like sandpaper as he pressed into her, then slowly began to retreat. In and out, his movements sending delicious shock waves through her system. The faster he thrust, the more rapid her breathing became. The tighter her insides wound. And when he slipped his fingers over the mound of curls, into her pulsating heat, to toy with the tiny nub of pleasure nestled there, she went wild.

Hips bucking, arms clutched around his back, her

inner muscles spasmed, milking him until he gave a low, guttural shout of completion and came inside her.

For long minutes after the most powerful climax of his life, Peter could do little more than lie there, sprawled across Lucy's supple body. Her heart pounded against his chest, keeping time with his own. Her nails clung to his back like talons, much as his dug into the cushiony flesh of her hips and buttocks. Her harsh breaths beat out a staccato rhythm in his ear and the pitch-black confines of the elevator car, echoing his own struggle to suck air into his deprived lungs.

And all he could think was that he'd just had earth-shattering, mind-blowing, rock-my-world sex with the one woman he'd sworn he would never touch.

The walls were beginning to close in on him again, but in a whole different way. Yes, the elevator felt stuffy and too small for his large frame. He wondered if they'd even have enough oxygen to survive until power was restored. But all of that drifted to the far reaches of his mind as he imagined the repercussions of what they'd just done.

He could lose her as his assistant, which would be more than a personal loss—it would be a blow to Reyware and the future of his program designs. She not only often gave him fresh ideas, but made it possible for him to work long hours without interruption.

He could lose her as a friend. He wasn't sure how to feel about that, since he didn't have many women friends and had never worried about forfeiting one of them before. He did know, though, that it would be tough not having her around. To talk to, to joke with, to ask for her opinion about everything from names for his latest games to which socks to wear with which shirt.

On the opposite side of the coin, he could be stuck with her. She might think this spontaneous bout of passion meant more than it did and expect him to feel the same way. She could want a relationship… commitment…marriage…

The very possibility sent fear stabbing through his bones like ice water. Wasn't that exactly what he'd been trying to avoid? He would be a terrible husband, an even worse father. He didn't think he had it in him at this point to be even a decent boyfriend or significant other.

If that's what it took to keep her from running, from leaving him for either another job or another man who could give her what she needed, then he would try. But he already knew he'd fail. It was in his genes.

He'd play the part of attentive lover…and relish every minute of the loving, he was sure. But soon enough, she would get tired of the hours he kept. Of being neglected when a new software program claimed more of his attention than she did. And that's when the resentment would begin, quickly turning into hate, and finally indifference.

Hadn't the exact same thing happened with his mother and father?

Lucy's sigh and the feel of her arms and legs falling from around his sweaty body brought him back to the present. He was probably crushing her. Lord knew he hadn't been as gentle as he could have been.

"I must be suffocating you. I'm sorry." As reluctant as he was to move, to draw away from her, he rolled to the side.

"It's all right," she said in a low voice. "I kind of liked it."

Her comment hit him like a punch to the gut. He wanted so much to be pleased by her words...but at the same time couldn't avoid worrying that it was simply the first step of an attitude that would soon become clinging.

Reaching out, he found her bare arm in the darkness and stroked from elbow to shoulder. "Did I hurt you?"

He heard a gentle tinkle and thought it must be her earrings as she shook her head.

"No," she answered aloud. "Did I hurt you?"

His bark of laughter bounced off the mirrored walls. That was Lucy for you; self-confident enough to believe she was just as capable of rough lovemaking as any man.

"Only in a good way, sweetheart."

As soon as the endearment passed his lips, he cringed. Bad move. What if she took it wrong? What if she thought he was inviting her to a whole new level of their relationship?

When she didn't respond, however, the moment of

alarm passed. Beside him, he heard her moving around and pushed to his feet.

"We should probably get dressed," he said, holding out his hand to help her up, and then leaning down to make contact when he realized she couldn't see the offer. "Never know when the power will come back on and the elevator doors will open."

"Wouldn't want that," she murmured.

Her removed tone reminded Peter that she was probably having second thoughts about their encounter, as well. Regrets.

That didn't sit well with him. As unsure as he was about what they'd done, about what the future might bring because of it, he didn't want Lucy to be sorry she'd let him make love to her. Hell, he wanted her eyes to still be glazed over, wanted to be the best lover she'd ever had.

But he couldn't have it both ways, could he? He had to either curl her toes and be ready for the possibility of building a relationship with her, or chalk it up to hot sex under duress and deal with the blow to his ego when she didn't fall at his feet, begging for more.

Patting their way around the floor of the car, they collected discarded pieces of clothing. It was impossible to identify them all, but they managed to zip up and rearrange their clothes just as the lights and buttons inside the elevator began to flicker.

Peter's stomach turned over in relief. He'd been okay, distracted as he was by this newest turn of events with Lucy. But if they'd been trapped much longer, he honestly couldn't be sure the claustrophobia wouldn't have come back and sent him hyperventilating again.

Eyes slowly adjusting to the return of fluorescent brightness, he stuffed an extra garment—likely his tie—in the pocket of his tuxedo jacket, watching Lucy tug at her gown, run a smoothing hand through her long black hair, and slide her toes back into a high-heeled shoe as the car gave a giant lurch and once again started its descent.

When the doors opened, he was relieved to find the lobby level fairly empty. A few people milled around, looking disoriented by the unexpected blackout, but in the process of going about their business.

As Peter and Lucy stepped out of the elevator, the hotel's manager raced up to them, offering effusive apologies for the inconvenience of being stuck between floors for so long. Peter waved off the man's worries. It wasn't the manager's fault he was claustrophobic, after all. And being trapped, even for such a short time, had given him the chance to finally make love to Lucy, which he couldn't bring himself to fully regret.

Instead Peter asked for the limo to be brought around. As they walked, he helped to arrange the shawl over Lucy's bare shoulders to protect her from the late-night chill.

Inside the limo, the air was warm and he instructed the driver to take them to her apartment first. The silence between them was stifling, growing more uncomfortable by the minute, and he racked his brain for something to say.

Thank you didn't seem quite appropriate. Nor did *I'm sorry.*

He wanted to ask her to come home with him, to stay the night and let him touch her again the way she had in the elevator. Only this time, he would go more slowly…explore those luscious curves in more detail, study every nook and cranny of her beautiful body.

Stealing a glance at her still form out of the corner of his eye, he felt himself grow hard with wanting her again.

So much for scratching an itch or thinking once would ever be enough when it came to Lucy Grainger.

The car pulled to a stop outside her building, and Peter escorted her to her apartment. She didn't speak as they climbed the stairs, and he couldn't think of any way to fill the awkward quiet.

At her door, he touched her arm, tried to take her hand, but she pulled away. "Lucy…" he began.

"Good night, Peter," she said, cutting him off and making it clear she wasn't interested in conversation. "I'll see you on Monday."

And then she turned the key in the lock and disappeared inside.

With a heavy sigh, he slid his hands into the pockets of his jacket and let his forehead fall against the cool grain of her mahogany paneled door. His brows drew together as his fingers burrowed into a strange silkiness.

Pulling his hand back out of the pocket, he found himself staring down at Lucy's lacy black panties. A shudder rocked his tall frame and for a moment he thought his knees might buckle.

If her panties were out here, with him, that meant she had been naked underneath her gown on the ride home. God, he was glad he hadn't known that then or he'd have been hard-pressed not to jump her a second time.

He remembered being inside her. The hot, wet haven of her body, clasping and clenching, driving him insane.

Hot. Wet. Skin to skin.

His eyes fell shut as realization and dread washed over him. He hadn't worn a condom. He wasn't sure he'd had a condom with him to wear, even if the thought *had* occurred to him back in that elevator. Before she'd spun every sane notion from his head with her kisses.

He hadn't worn a condom and didn't know whether or not she was on birth control. Which meant she could be pregnant. With his child.

Oh, this night just kept getting better and better.

Four

When Lucy arrived at work Monday morning, she stood on Peter's front stoop for several long minutes, key in the lock and hand on the knob, trying to convince herself it would be business as usual once she stepped inside.

And why wouldn't it? What happened Friday night in the elevator meant nothing, right? It had been a fluke. An intimate encounter brought on by crisis conditions, and not something that would have ever come about under normal circumstances.

But that didn't explain why Peter had called so many times over the weekend. Thank God she'd let the machine pick up the first time…and every time after that.

With the volume down, she'd almost been able to survive those four rings each time without her heart jumping straight out of her chest.

And then he'd shown up at her door Sunday afternoon. She'd stared through the peephole, bouncing anxiously on the balls of her feet, breathing hard, and biting the inside of her lip to keep from making a sound. He'd looked rumpled and ruffled, and more aggravated the longer he stood outside her apartment, waiting for her to answer.

She felt like a coward, afraid to face her own boss. Which was the only reason she'd come to work today instead of calling in sick. If she didn't, she was afraid she'd never be able to face Peter again.

Taking a deep, fortifying breath, she turned the knob and stepped inside, closing the door silently behind her. On tiptoe, she made her way into the den that housed her work area, quickly but quietly putting away her purse and shrugging out of her linen suit jacket.

With any luck, she wouldn't see Peter for another few hours. Hopefully he'd had another long night and would sleep until noon. And maybe by then she could come up with an excuse to leave early or run some errands outside of the office.

How long do you think you can keep that up? a voice in her head whispered. Sneaking around, avoiding him as much as possible.

If she knew Peter…and after two years, she felt she did…he wouldn't put up with that sort of thing for long. Unless—if she was lucky—he wanted to avoid her, too. Unfortunately, fifteen phone calls and an impromptu trip to her apartment told her that probably wasn't the case.

"Lucy?"

Peter's voice, raised and eager, floated down to her from the second floor. Then she heard his weighted footsteps as he jogged down the carpeted stairs and let her head fall forward over her computer's keyboard. Oh, boy, here it came. The confrontation.

She straightened in her chair a moment before Peter appeared in the doorway, looking even more scattered and unkempt than yesterday when he'd shown up on her doorstep.

He was in his stocking feet and wore a pair of faded jeans that rode low on his narrow hips. The denim was wrinkled, as was the cotton of his plain white T-shirt, making her wonder if he'd slept in his clothes—and for how long.

"Lucy." Her name came out part huff, part sigh. He ran both hands through his hair, leaving sandy-blond spikes sticking up here and there.

"I've been waiting for you all day," he said, apparently unaware that it was only nine in the morning. "I called your apartment a dozen times over the weekend. I even ran over to see you on Sunday. Where the hell have you been?"

She opened her mouth to tell him it was none of his business, but he shook his head, waving a hand in the air to cut her off.

"Never mind, it doesn't matter. We have to talk."

Her stomach fell to her knees as he dragged a chair over and sidled up to her desk, getting right to the point.

"Lucy," he began, elbows balanced on his thighs, hands clasped between his spread legs.

But she couldn't stand to hear him talk about what a lapse in judgment that night in the elevator had been, how they were employer and employee, and he didn't feel that way about her.

"Peter," she cut him off, not quite meeting his gaze. "I know what you're going to say, and I agree one hundred percent. What happened the other night was a mistake. We were caught off guard by the blackout and being unexpectedly trapped in that elevator. Neither of us would have indulged in such behavior otherwise, and I'm sure we never will again. Let's just forget it and go back to business as usual."

Peter sat back, intently studying Lucy's face. The alabaster skin, the sparkling violet shadow shading her black-lined eyes, the red-hot lipstick glossing her full, kissable mouth. She had a small beauty mark to the left and a little above the corner of that mouth, making him want to lean in and swipe his tongue across it for a quick taste.

Speak for yourself, he thought. She might believe their sexual encounter after the charity dinner was brought on solely by the lack of electricity and his unfortunate bout of claustrophobia, but what she didn't realize was that he'd been fantasizing about making love to her for a very long time.

Sure, the city-wide blackout had spurred him into taking actions he probably would have otherwise managed to control, but he wouldn't go so far as to say it never would have happened. And he most certainly wasn't going to forget it anytime soon.

As if that was even possible.

Still, it was a relief to hear she was prepared to brush the incident under the rug rather than turning it into something it wasn't or expecting more from him than he was willing or ready to give. That made one element of the situation easier, but not the portion he'd spent the weekend working up the courage to discuss with her.

"That may be easier said than done." He kept his tone low and serious enough to catch her undivided attention. Finally she raised her head and met his gaze directly.

"What do you mean?"

Instead of blurting out his primary concern, he tried to broach the subject in a more delicate way. "I don't suppose you're on the Pill," he said, and then realized that was about as subtle as a bull in a china shop.

Immediately her hackles went up. She stiffened, leaning away from him and folding her arms beneath her breasts. Those luscious, mouthwatering breasts that he'd kissed and fondled only two days ago. It was enough to bring his body to full, highly aroused attention and force him to shift in his seat for a more comfortable position.

Brow furrowed, Lucy crossed her legs, driving her

skirt up a good two inches and jiggling a high-heeled foot—which didn't help one bit—before snapping, "What business is that of yours?"

"None," he said carefully, "until Friday night. We didn't, um, use any form of protection. Unless…"

He let the word hang, watching realization dawn in her sapphire eyes. Hoping against hope that she'd laugh and slap him on the back and tell him not to worry, she'd been taking birth control for years. Instead, the color washed from her face while at the same time two rosy flags of embarrassment bloomed on her cheeks.

Something cold and ominous settled low in his belly. "I take it that's a no."

The muscles in her throat convulsed as she swallowed. "No," she croaked, giving an almost zombielike shake of her head. "There was no reason to be taking anything. And I always thought that if the situation presented itself, we'd both be smart enough to use a condom."

A wry smile curved his lips. "Yeah, me, too. Guess we both went brain dead there for a while."

Taking a deep breath, he got to his feet and began to pace. "As careless as we were, what's done is done. Now we just have to figure out what to do about it."

Silence filled the room for several long minutes, the only sound the tick-tock of the grandfather clock drifting in from the foyer. And then Lucy seemed to collect herself. She uncrossed her legs, unfolded her arms and stood.

"This is ridiculous, Peter. We're jumping to conclusions, fretting over nothing. What are the chances of my becoming pregnant from that one short encounter?"

"Spoken like any number of single mothers just before the stick turned blue."

She shot him a quelling glance. "All I'm saying is that we shouldn't borrow trouble. I'm sure there's nothing to worry about."

"I hope you're right," he said slowly, "but all the same, when will we know?"

A blank expression washed over her features, and then it donned on her what he was asking. Once again, her cheeks blushed pink.

"I'm not, um…a few weeks, I guess."

Weeks. Great. Peter made a mental note to stock up on antacid. Waiting days, let alone weeks, to find out if she was pregnant with his child was bound to give him the mother of all ulcers.

He wanted to demand an answer now. Drag her to the nearest drugstore for one of those over-the-counter tests and insist she take it. Of course, it probably wouldn't tell them much. He knew next to nothing about women's cycles and symptoms of pregnancy, but thought it took more than a few days to be able to tell about these types of things.

So he would be patient—swig his antacid, watch her like a hawk and wait until they knew for sure.

Lucy stepped out of the downstairs powder room tucked beneath the stairwell and nearly jumped to find

Peter staring at her from the other side of the kitchen island. She rolled her eyes, tamped down on the annoyance that seemed to be brimming too close to the surface these days and headed back to her office.

What did he want from her? she wondered, not for the first time. It had been three days since he'd brought up the topic of an unexpected pregnancy. And since then, he'd followed her around like a shadow. He was always nearby, asking if she needed anything, watching her every movement. It was as though he expected her to sprout feathers or in some other way show outward signs of carrying his child.

If only it were that easy. Truth be told, the waiting was driving her crazy, too.

She'd bought a pregnancy test on her way home from work Monday, after spending the day on eggshells, pretending his pronouncement that they hadn't used protection didn't concern her a bit. The test had come up negative, but that only served to increase her sense of anxiety.

Maybe the test was wrong. Maybe it was too early for an over-the-counter method to show accurate results. Maybe one of these days—since she'd bought out the corner store's supply and taken to running one each morning before she left the apartment—the stick would show a plus sign instead of a minus one and her whole world would come crashing down around her ears.

That thought sent a lead weight of dread straight to the bottom of her stomach.

She should call her doctor and make an appointment so she could get a definitive answer once and for all. But, God help her, she couldn't bring herself to do that. She was too frightened of what he might tell her.

What if she was pregnant?

Her initial response had been elation. Pregnant. With Peter's baby. Wasn't that the twist her overactive imagination often took when she pictured the two of them together? There were dating scenarios, seduction scenarios, marriage scenarios, family scenarios, even retirement scenarios for when their children were grown and they were once again alone in the house as the ripe old age of sixty.

Under the right circumstances, she would be delighted to be having a baby with Peter. The way things stood between them now, however, she couldn't think of a worse development.

If it turned out she was pregnant, Peter would likely offer to marry her, or at least insist on being involved in the child's life. That's the kind of man he was.

But he would resent Lucy for locking him into a situation he wanted no part of. The child would be a constant reminder of the mistake he'd let himself make one night in an elevator in the middle of a blackout, and of the freedom he'd lost because of it.

She didn't want that. It would be better, she thought, to leave. Go somewhere else, raise the child on her own, and never let Peter know he'd been right about their lack of birth control producing a child.

Not that she could ever bring herself to do such a

thing. A child deserved to know its father…and a father deserved to know about his child. Besides, Peter could be like a dog with a bone. He wouldn't rest until he knew for sure, and if she went away, no doubt he would track her down. With his computer skills and contacts all over the world, he would find her, if only to get a final answer to his question.

But she was getting ahead of herself. The smart thing would be to find out whether or not she actually was pregnant before making any drastic plans on how to handle the situation.

Without so much as a creak of the hardwood floor in warning, Peter appeared in the archway of the den, once again startling her out of her reverie. Lucy put a hand to her heart in an effort to slow its erratic pace. If he didn't stop sneaking up on her, she was going to tie a bell around his neck.

"Is everything okay?" he asked.

He was wearing a pair of dove-gray dress slacks today, with a casual, light blue button-down shirt. His feet were bare, as was his habit, and which probably accounted for his ability to move silently through the house. Leaning a shoulder against the carved wood molding of the doorjamb, his green eyes ran over her intently, making her squirm.

Turning back to her computer screen, she did her best to act impervious. "Fine."

"Is there anything I can get you?" he pressed. "Juice, water, a sandwich?"

She'd eaten lunch less than an hour ago, and she noticed he didn't offer to bring her coffee or tea, which might be harmful to a growing fetus. Little did he know she helped herself to a cup or two each morning before leaving her apartment. Of course, she'd switched to naturally decaffeinated, just in case. She honestly didn't believe there was any reason to be concerned, but on the off chance she *was* pregnant, she wasn't willing to risk eating or drinking anything that might hurt her—possibly imaginary—unborn child.

"No, thank you," she answered. And then a beat passed and she changed her mind. "On second thought, I could use a glass of milk. My stomach has been a little upset lately, so maybe that would help."

Peter blanched, the muscles in his face going slack as he pushed himself away from the wall and stood there for a fraction of a second before nodding stiffly and darting toward the kitchen.

She shouldn't have done it. It was cruel to play on Peter's fears about an unplanned pregnancy. But his hovering and endless stream of inquiries about her health and daily well-being were beginning to grate on her nerves.

When he returned with her glass of milk, she would apologize and tell him she was fine—no outward hints of impending motherhood so far. But for now, she leaned back in her chair, let her head fall over the hard cherry wood edging, and laughed until every drop of stress and strain that had built up over the past few days drained out of her body and left her feeling much, much better.

"So, are you coming to the club tonight for a drink?"

Peter shook his head, his breathing labored as he fought to raise the hundred pound barbell over his head.

"Thirty-nine. Forty." Ethan Banks, his best friend and spotter counted off for him. They tried to meet at the gym at least three times a week for a full workout and to catch up on current events…or in Ethan's case, current conquests.

Ethan owned The Hot Spot, a local Georgetown nightclub that drew in a bevy of handsome men and lovely young ladies looking to party. It was the ladies Ethan liked the most, and according to him, he took a different one home with him every night. With his dark good looks and sparkling smile, Peter supposed it could be true.

"Forty-six. Wanna get together Sunday for the baseball game?"

Peter shook his head again. "Huh-uh."

"How about letting me bring a couple girls over later and we'll get a group thing going? Forty-nine. Fifty."

"No." His brows drew together as he sat up and wiped the sweat from his face and neck with a towel. "Wait a minute. What did you say?"

Ethan chuckled. "I thought that might get your attention. You've been distracted all night. Care to tell me what's going on?"

With a sigh, Peter got up and moved to the bank of treadmills along the far wall. Ethan followed, stepping onto the machine next to him and adjusting his speed.

For long minutes, Peter said nothing. His relationship with Lucy was nobody's business and he didn't particularly relish the idea of telling his best friend he was waiting to find out if the rabbit died, so to speak.

But it was clawing at him. Every moment of his time with Lucy in that elevator. Every day since, wondering how that night would change things between them and whether he was about to become a father.

Maybe talking it over with his friend would help. Ethan might be a ladies' man, but he had a good head on his shoulders. If he ribbed Peter too much about his indiscretion with his assistant, though, Ethan would find his teeth at the back of his throat.

"You know Lucy, right?" he said finally, after they'd both jogged at a leisurely pace for about half a mile.

"Of course," Ethan replied with a wicked grin. "I've only been trying to get her to come work for me and eventually come to bed with me since the day you hired her. Has she changed her mind? Is that what you're trying to tell me?"

"Hell, no." Annoyed, Peter snapped his head around to glare at his friend's cocky expression and nearly lost his footing. Regaining his balance, he said, "Lucy isn't interested in you. Let it go."

"Never say die, man. They all fall for my potent charms eventually."

"You wish," Peter answered with a snort. "Look, you wanted to know what was going on, so just shut up and listen, okay?"

"Okay, okay, I'm listening. Spill. What's up with Lucy?"

"You remember the big blackout that hit last Friday night?"

Ethan swore. "How could I forget? The club was a madhouse, trying to find flashlights and keep everyone from panicking and causing a stampede."

"Yeah, well, it wasn't a shining moment for me, either."

"Why, what happened?"

"I attended that City Women benefit with Lucy."

"The one where they were giving you the award? Cool. How'd it go?"

"I'm getting to that." Peter reached out to click the speed dial up another notch, making it harder to talk, but burning off some of the excess energy that had been crawling under his skin since he'd made love to Lucy. "Lucy and I sneaked out around midnight. We were in the elevator, on the way down to the lobby, when the power cut off."

"Oh, man. I'll bet you had fun. Did it get bad?"

Ethan had known about his claustrophobia for years, and since he wasn't speaking loudly enough for anyone else in the room to hear, Peter didn't feel embarrassed at having it brought up.

"It wasn't fun," he admitted. "But that wasn't the worst part."

"There's a worst part?"

Peter shot him another aggravated glance at his continued interruptions. This was difficult enough to get out, both because of the topic and the workout he was getting.

"I slept with her," he blurted.

"What?" Ethan stumbled, grabbing onto the treadmill's sidebars and saving himself at the last minute. "Whoa," he muttered in a low voice. "Are you serious?"

Peter's mouth twisted. "As a snake bite."

"So…was she good?"

The look Peter pierced his friend with this time was hot enough to burn. "None of your damn business. And don't talk about her that way."

Ethan threw his arms up in surrender. "Hey, take it easy. We always share the four-one-one about women and how they were in the sack."

"Yeah, well, this is different. It's Lucy. Don't talk about her that way," he said again.

Peter knew he was acting strangely. He didn't want his friend thinking there was more going on between him and his assistant than a regrettable one-night stand, but defending her honor that way had definitely clued him in. He should have kept his mouth shut or simply shrugged and said she was great. Then maybe Ethan wouldn't be eyeing him like he was afraid Peter's skin was about to peel back to reveal some alien life form.

"Fine. Sorry. So you two did the dirty deed. Is there a problem? Is she getting all clingy and romantic?"

Ha! If this past week was Lucy's idea of clingy and romantic, he'd hate to see her give him the brush-off.

"No, it's not that," he said instead. "We, um…didn't use a condom, and now there's a chance she might be pregnant."

Ethan didn't trip over his own feet at that pronouncement, but he did let loose a string of curses blue enough to turn the heads of other gym patrons. Peter cringed and waited to hear what his friend of ten years would say about his responsibilities and failure to practice safe sex.

"Damn. She's not stringing you along, is she? Buy one of those tester things or take her to the doctor and find out for sure, but don't let her sucker you into anything."

For a moment, Peter let his anger at Ethan's low estimation of Lucy's character simmer through his veins. And then he realized it wasn't really Lucy his friend thought so little of, it was all women.

Ethan met too many frivolous, promiscuous women at his club and was dumb enough to go home with them. He'd probably never met a tasteful, genuine woman like Lucy. To Ethan, women were gold diggers, or party girls, or steel-heeled bitches who would as soon emasculate a man as look at him. So, of course, his first thought would be that Lucy was using a pregnancy angle to trap Peter.

Thankfully, Peter didn't believe it for a minute.

"It's not that. Lucy wouldn't do something like that.

And before you ask—" he lifted a hand to stop his friend's tirade before it began "—I know because it isn't Lucy's style. My problem is a hell of a lot bigger than 'is she or isn't she?' or what her motives might be."

Ethan wiped sweat from his forehead with the back of his arm, his mouth turned down in a frown at Peter's refusal to consider ulterior motives. "Oh, yeah? What's that?"

Peter swallowed, trying to put the thoughts that had been swirling around in his brain for the past week into words. "The problem," he said, "is that I'm kind of hoping she is."

Five

Two Mondays later, Lucy knew what her future held…and it wasn't Peter or a baby. The knowledge hurt more than she'd anticipated, sending a low throb of disappointment through her entire system.

Shaking off the light sprinkling of rain from the short walk to Peter's brick-fronted row house, she stepped inside and braced herself for his immediate appearance. Surprisingly he didn't materialize at the top of the stairs to greet her, but she heard the sounds of movement coming from the kitchen.

After hanging her raincoat in the hall closet and stowing her purse in the bottom drawer of her desk, she headed for the back of the house. Peter stood at the counter, scooping coffee grounds into a filter.

She leaned forward against the island, her fingers clutching the edge of the cool marble. Taking a deep breath, she said, "I'll take a cup of that when it's ready."

He fixed her with a laser-sharp gaze as he finished what he was doing and punched the button to start the coffee brewing. "Are you sure that's a good idea?"

She nodded. It was an odd way to break the news to him, but easier than anything else she'd come up with.

"It's fine. I got my period this morning," she admitted with more than a little embarrassment.

A minute ticked by while he stared in stony silence. It wasn't quite the reaction she'd expected. A sigh of relief or maybe a few handsprings. Instead he seemed almost…reticent.

"I don't know what to say," he finally replied. "'I'm sorry' doesn't seem quite appropriate, but then neither does 'I'm glad.'"

"Are you?" she asked softly. "Glad or sorry?"

He stepped forward, rolling his shoulders as he stuffed his hands into the front pockets of his jeans. "I honestly don't know, Luce. A part of me feels like we dodged a bullet. But another part of me…You know, it might have been nice to be a father."

Lucy felt the same way, but was dismayed to hear Peter say as much. And then her eyes began to mist, surprising her even more. She blinked quickly and cleared her throat, moving to the refrigerator to hide her sudden rush of emotion.

What was wrong with her? For the past two weeks, she'd been worried she might be pregnant from a spontaneous intimate encounter with her boss…a man she'd been attracted to for years, but who had never shown a trace of attraction himself before the night of the charity dinner. And now she was getting weepy because she *wasn't* carrying his child? If that was the case, she seriously needed her head examined.

Grabbing the orange juice jug from the top shelf, she stalked across the kitchen and retrieved a glass from the cupboard, careful to give Peter a wide berth. She poured a few inches of juice and swallowed it.

"At least things can go back to normal now," she said when she thought her voice was steady enough not to shake.

"Yeah." His reply was low and dispassionate. He turned, starting out of the kitchen without the coffee he'd spent so much time preparing. "I'll be upstairs, working."

She watched him go, wondering about his strange behavior. When had he started thinking about family and fatherhood? And had he really been considering having them with her?

It didn't make sense. Peter had never shown the least bit of interest in her before, and she knew for a fact that what had happened in the elevator was merely a result of his claustrophobia. If he hadn't been desperate for an escape from his panic and she hadn't been so readily available, there was no doubt in her mind that matters between them would have continued in the usual pattern. She would have shown up on time for work each morning, trying to ignore the sweet ache of longing that coursed through her every time she looked at Peter, and he would have continued to treat her as nothing more than a valued and competent employee.

Instead he'd caught her at a weak moment, when she'd let her longtime attraction to him merge with her concern over his reaction to the blackout, until she'd convinced herself that he wanted to make love to her as much as she did to him.

A person was entitled to make one mistake in her life, wasn't she? One huge, throbbing, monumental mistake.

The coffeemaker on the counter sputtered and Lucy poured herself a cup, doctoring the dark, fragrant brew with a sprinkle of sugar and dollop of milk.

The funny part was that, despite everything, Lucy thought they probably would have been able to put the weekend's incident behind them and return to their normal routine…if it hadn't been for that little pregnancy scare.

And that's what confused her the most. Peter should be relieved; dropping to his knees, thanking God their one indiscretion hadn't put an end to his carefree bachelor lifestyle. But when she'd told him she wasn't pregnant, he'd acted almost…disappointed.

Could that be right? Could he have *wanted* a baby?

No. She shook her head, carrying the steaming mug back to her office in the den. It was silly to think Peter might have wanted a child. Especially now, especially with her.

If he was beginning to consider settling down, then he would want to find a nice woman to marry and have children with. He wouldn't be hoping a one-night stand with his assistant—a woman he'd never looked at twice before—would result in surprise fatherhood.

She must be reading the situation wrong. For all she knew, he was upstairs right now, dancing a jig and e-mailing his buddies to tell them about his near brush with disaster.

Which is exactly what she should be doing. She didn't want to be a single mother any more than she wanted to be the wife of a man who'd only married her because they forgot to use a condom.

Taking a sip of the still-warm coffee, she pulled her chair closer to the desk and doggedly decided to put this entire fiasco with Peter and their nonexistent baby behind her and get down to business.

But that didn't keep her heart from squeezing or her eyes from growing damp at the thought of what might have been.

Peter sat in front of his blank computer monitor, struggling to wrap his mind around what he was feeling.

Lucy wasn't pregnant. There was no baby. And damned if he didn't think he might be sorry about it.

He probably shouldn't have projected so far into the future, but he'd let himself imagine, let himself plan...Lucy, pregnant from their single encounter the night of the city-wide power outage. Taking responsibility for his actions and asking her to marry him. Watching her grow round as a pumpkin with his baby inside her.

He'd pictured her in his house, living here, belonging here. Making love to her every night. Holding her in his arms in a tangle of sheets while they slept and then waking the same way every morning.

For a man who'd sworn he would never tie himself down with a wife and family, those images had gotten pretty damn specific.

And while he wouldn't mind having Lucy in his bed—just once or twice more to get his fill—he supposed he should be glad things were working out this way.

Having a child at this point in his life just wasn't feasible. He wasn't a man to neglect his responsibilities, and if he'd married Lucy and had a child with her, he would have felt the need to spend time with them. Lord knew he'd want to be a better father to his children than his father had been to him.

And a better husband. He might not have planned it, but he genuinely liked Lucy, and if they'd made a baby together, then he would have done his best to treat her right, too. Which meant he could kiss Reyware and Games of PRey goodbye.

A wave of dread washed over him, followed by the cool, cleansing breeze of relief. Yes, it was definitely better this way.

If Lucy had wound up pregnant, he'd have married her and turned his focus on her and their child…maybe even someday children. But his own lousy childhood had taught him that he couldn't have a family and run a successful business, so he would have had to give up his thriving software company and look for some other, less demanding job. Probably computer repair, which was about all he thought he'd be good at.

He shuddered at the thought. He'd have changed diapers and played horsey and done everything in his power to let his children know he loved them, but he would have been miserable working nine to five for someone else just to keep food on the table.

Maybe someday, after he'd made a few billion dollars and could afford to hire a staff of corporate go-getters to run things for him, then maybe he'd start thinking about finding a woman to settle down with and having a couple kids. If Lucy was still available at that point, he might even consider hooking up with her again.

But for now…For now, this was good. Hell, it was freaking fantastic. He'd really lucked out. Slipped the noose, so to speak.

And it probably wouldn't take long at all for Lucy

and him to get back to their old camaraderie, their old habit of working together like a well-oiled machine. She already looked more recovered from their encounter than he felt, thank goodness. He'd have hated to have her hanging on him, expecting their relationship to change, take on new meaning.

If it took him a while to get the memory of her warm, writhing body out of his head, well, that was nobody's problem but his own. No one needed to know he still felt her beneath him at night while he struggled to fall asleep. Or that just the sight and smell of her sent a shock of awareness through his bloodstream.

Those things would haunt him, *Lucy* would haunt him the rest of the time they worked together. Maybe even forever.

Days turned into weeks as Peter and Lucy functioned around each other like virtual strangers. She came to work every day on time, went through the motions, took care of him as well as she ever had. Anyone looking in at them would think they had the perfect employer/employee relationship.

Only Peter—and Lucy, if she were being honest—knew that was far from the truth. The air between them fairly sizzled with tension and sexual electricity. He expected sparks to shoot from his fingertips every time she sauntered into his office and handed him the morning mail or a fresh cup of coffee, and he couldn't remember the last time he'd had a decent night's sleep.

Lucy might look like a model stepping straight off the runway, more beautiful every time he looked at her, but he was beginning to feel like something the dog dragged in. Exhaustion and hot, ceaseless desire were taking their toll.

He leaned back in his desk chair, rubbing his eyes and running a hand through his hair. The letters, numbers and symbols making up the codes on his computer screen jumbled together as his vision blurred.

Even his work was suffering, he thought with frustration, though he tried hard to not let it show. And Lucy, bless her, was a pro at fielding questions and making excuses for how busy he was.

But William Dawson, a client in New York, was a different story. He'd been badgering Peter to fly up, look over his company's computer system and design a plan to upgrade and get things running more smoothly and cost-effectively. It was a reasonable request, one he'd honored numerous times in the past.

Peter had worked with Dawson before and knew him to be a good guy who would pay Peter's hefty fee on time and use his powerful influence and word-of-mouth to send more business Peter's way.

Darned if he could work up the least bit of enthusiasm about it, though. Getting far away from Lucy would probably be the smart thing to do. Give them both some breathing room, hopefully help to dispel the taut, sensual awareness buzzing around them like a hive of horny little honeybees.

But something in his gut, in the back of his brain warned against it. A niggling sense that if he left town, Lucy might not be here when he got back.

She'd been acting strangely since that night at the Four Seasons. Keeping to herself as much as possible, avoiding his gaze when she couldn't.

Not that he blamed her, but she was a talented, educated woman who could get a job with anyone, doing almost any kind of work in the city. And he was afraid if he went somewhere, left her alone for even a short amount of time, she would decide things between them had grown too strained and would begin looking for a position elsewhere.

He didn't want that, and if he had any say at all, he wouldn't allow it. Which meant he couldn't take off for Manhattan without knowing what Lucy planned to do while he was gone.

Unless...

He blinked and sat up straighter in his chair, halting the swivel motion.

The trip to New York would be business-related, and Lucy was his assistant. He could ask her to go along. No, insist. They could fly up, stay a couple of nights in a nice hotel, then fly home. That way, he'd know where Lucy was at all times and she wouldn't get the chance to do something stupid like leave him.

Now he just had to figure out how to convince Lucy that her presence was required on a job he'd always before accomplished on his own. He sat there, spinning back and forth in slow circles, biting his way through a small stack of pencils while his mind raced.

She was going to balk. She probably would have even before they'd slept together, but now that they had, she'd be less inclined to travel with him in such close confines and possibly share a hotel suite or connected rooms.

At the thought of spending so much time with her, his blood thickened and things began to stir below the equator. Lucy, however, would probably have the exact opposite response. At least, she'd shown no signs so far of being attracted to him or wanting to repeat that night's performance.

He didn't know whether to take that as an insult against his sexual prowess or simply her way of distancing herself from what she considered a lapse in professionalism.

Well, this was getting him nowhere. Slapping his hands on his knees, he stood and headed for the hall. He heard the almost musical tap of Lucy's keyboard drifting upstairs from her office and started down the steps, one hand on the smooth mahogany banister.

Though she didn't stop what she was doing or acknowledge him in any way, he knew she sensed his proximity the minute he crossed the threshold into the den by the slight pause in her frantic typing. She recovered quickly and kept working, eyes on the screen, pretending he wasn't there—which she'd gotten pretty good at over the past few weeks. Her disinterest annoyed him, but he swallowed back the urge to confront her, to make her notice him on a personal, primitive level, and walked forward.

Lucy did her best to ignore Peter as he waltzed into her office and made himself at home by propping a hip on the edge of her desk. The faded plaid boxer shorts he'd been wearing for two days now left his legs bare and put a hairy, well-muscled thigh nearly at eye level and definitely too close for comfort.

He was beginning to look tired and run-down. Not for the first time, she thought about telling him to take a shower and climb into bed for a much-needed nap, just as she had a thousand times before. But that brought to mind images of Peter naked…wet and soapy, on a soft, wide mattress, on top of her, inside of her… It was enough to drive a person mad, so she bit down on her lip and said nothing.

"Are you ever going to look at me?"

"Not if I can help it," she tossed back. And then she did, because there really wasn't any other choice. "What do you want, Peter? I'm very busy, trying to keep your business afloat."

"And I appreciate it," he said cockily, "but this is business-related, too."

That got her attention. Reluctantly she lifted her hands from the keyboard and sat back, meeting his green and hazel gaze for the first time since he'd entered the room.

"All right, I'm listening."

"William Dawson wants me to come to New York, look over his setup and give him some advice."

"I know, I've been telling him your schedule is full for a week now. If you want, I'll—"

"I've decided to go."

Her brows lifted at that. Only days ago, he'd been adamant that he wasn't interested in an out-of-town trip and told her to do whatever she needed to put off Dawson without alienating him as a client.

"All right," she said again, more slowly this time, "I'll make your plane and hotel reservations."

He gave a sharp nod. "Good. Make them for yourself, too. I want you to go along."

A shaft of panic speared her chest. Oh, no, she couldn't go with him. Just the two of them, on the plane, in the hotel when he wasn't meeting with William Dawson? No, that didn't sound like such a smart idea.

Taking a deep breath to reclaim her composure, she cleared her throat and said, "Thank you, but I'd rather not. There's more than enough work to be done here, and you've gone on plenty of these types of trips by yourself before. I'm sure you don't need me."

"Of course I do. Dawson is a big client. I want you there to help me charm him, but also to take notes and keep me in line. You know how distracted I get. I'll probably get up there, see what a mess his system is and offer to update it for free."

She gave a small snort. Peter wasn't quite that bad,

but probably close. When he saw something that needed to be done to a computer to bring it up to speed, he became almost entranced and lost sight of the fact that he was running a business and trying to make a living with his skills.

And he had been more distracted than usual lately. She'd found herself cleaning up after him and reminding him of daily tasks more often than in the past.

Of course, she couldn't blame him. She'd been feeling a little off her game, too, ever since letting her guard down in that elevator. They couldn't seem to find their stride again, regain the easy friendship and comfortable rapport that had made the workplace so peaceful in the past.

Curling her fingers into the palm of her hand, she fought the urge to reach out and stroke the firm line of his sculpted calf and pinned him with a sober glare. "You wouldn't be doing this just to get me alone, would you? Because we both know that night at the charity was a mistake and—"

He threw his head back and laughed loudly enough to startle her. "Are you kidding? That was ages ago," he said, waving a hand in dismissal. "This is business, Luce, and you're my right hand gal. I need you there. Besides, if I had any thoughts along those lines, we're alone now and are just about every day. I haven't tried to jump you yet, have I?"

Not giving her a chance to respond, he hopped off the desk and silently crossed the oriental carpet in his sock-clad feet. At the archway, he stopped and turned his attention back to her. "So what do you say? Do you trust me enough to help me out on this? I'll put you up at a great hotel," he added with a wink.

Tiny ripples of wariness caused her stomach to contract, but he looked and sounded so sincere, she felt almost guilty for thinking he might be trying to trick her into going along.

Darting her tongue out to wet her suddenly dry lips, she tipped her head in acquiescence. "Fine, I'll make the arrangements. But I have to find someone to watch my cat before we can leave."

"That's right, you have a calico, don't you? Chocolate, Mocha…"

"Cocoa," she supplied, surprised he remembered that much about her personal life. And she didn't think he'd ever noticed the tiny framed photo tucked away on the far side of her computer monitor.

"Cocoa," he repeated. A warm smile curled the corners of his mouth. "You'll have to introduce me sometime."

She let that comment pass for a moment. "I can't leave her home alone and I'm not sure any of my friends will be available to check on her."

"How about a kennel or a pet sitter?"

She frowned slightly. "A pet sitter would be okay, as long as she's reliable, but I won't even consider a kennel. Cocoa is much too skittish and set in her ways. She's never been out of my apartment, except to visit the vet."

"So you're a protective pet owner," he teased with a grin. "I don't blame you. How would you feel about a male pet sitter, though? Would that be okay?"

She studied him carefully, wondering what he was getting at to show such interest in Cocoa's well-being. "Of course. Why?"

"I know a guy…" he told her cryptically, shrugging one shoulder. "If you can't find anyone else you'd be satisfied with, let me know and I'll see if he's available."

"All right." She wasn't sure what to think of Peter's helpfulness, but it seemed he was willing to call in a few favors with his friends just to get her to go to New York with him.

He kept his gaze on her for several more seconds, then shot her a last gentle smile before heading upstairs and returning to work. She watched him go, exhaling lung- fuls of stale air and inhaling fresh as she collapsed back- ward in her chair. Life was never going to be simple again, she thought wearily and with more than a hint of sadness.

His assurance that this trip would be devoted to business only made her feel more secure about mak- ing the arrangements and going along, but it still stung to know their heated, impulsive night together meant so little to him.

Not that she'd expected anything less. In truth, it's what she'd hoped for—that a single indiscretion wouldn't put her job or their friendship in jeopardy.

She couldn't be happier, she told herself; she'd got- ten exactly what she wanted.

But for some reason, her father's voice sounded in her head, warning her to *be careful what you wish for, you just might get it.*

Six

"So let me get this straight. You were worried Lucy'd be pregnant from your night of hot sex in a hot elevator, but she isn't. Then you were afraid she'd misinterpret what happened between you and expect more of a relationship than you're ready for, but she didn't. And now you're making her go with you to New York on a so-called business trip with the flimsy excuse that you might need her to take notes, so *I* have to baby-sit her *cat*."

"It's a legitimate business trip," Peter said, doing his best to ignore Ethan's deep, animated scowl from the passenger seat of his sleek silver Infiniti.

"I think you're missing the point," his friend argued. "I've been relegated to a damn cat-sitter."

"What's the big deal? You like animals. And you do owe me for setting up the club's computer system and teaching your employees how to work the software."

A growl worked its way up from Ethan's throat. "I knew you'd make me pay for that, even though at the time, you claimed it was nothing. 'Just a friend helping a friend,'" he mimicked.

"That's right, and now I'm the friend who needs help."

Peter sighed, his fingers tapping nervously against the steering wheel as he drove in the direction of Lucy's apartment from The Hot Spot, where he'd picked up Ethan.

"Look, all you have to do is check in on Cocoa a couple of times a day, stick around for an hour or so to keep her company, if you can. You said yourself it wouldn't be a problem, and that you could get someone to cover for you at the club, if you needed. Lucy would really appreciate it, and I'll owe you one."

Ethan slouched down in his seat, crossing his arms over his chest. "You'll owe me more than one if the thing scratches or pees on me."

"It's a cat, Eth, not a rabid toddler. And you'd better not let Lucy hear you talking like that or make faces in front of her, or she'll call off the whole thing."

"You're that desperate to get into her pants again, huh?"

It was Peter's turn to glower. "I told you to not talk about her like that. I'm just looking for someone responsible and reliable to watch her cat while we're away."

"Just what I've always wanted to be—responsible and reliable." Ethan pouted.

"Oh, come on, you're a decent guy when you're not trying to charm some sweet young thing out of her thong panties."

Ethan grinned, flashing a row of sparkling white teeth. "Can I help it women find me irresistible?"

Peter rolled his eyes, but refrained from commenting, considering he needed Ethan in a good mood so he would do this favor for him. "Remember that when it comes to convincing Lucy you're head over heels about watching her cat, okay?"

"Hey, by the time I'm finished, she'll be asking you to watch the cat and me to whisk her away for a weekend of sweaty monkey sex."

The thought of the two of them together was so ridiculous, Peter nearly laughed out loud. But if there'd been a chance Ethan actually had a shot with Lucy, he'd be smiling around Peter's fist right this second.

He found a spot not far from Lucy's building and parked, then checked his watch. They had plenty of time for Ethan and Cocoa to get acquainted, Lucy to feel comfortable with the arrangements he'd made, and still get to the airport for their scheduled flight.

Lucy answered the door looking slightly flustered. "I'm almost ready," she said, waving them inside.

"Take your time," Peter offered.

She slipped back into the bedroom to finish packing, reappearing several minutes later.

With her bags by the door, she finally stopped moving long enough to take a breath and relax. "Thank you so much for doing this, Ethan. I know it can't be your first choice of ways to spend the better part of the week."

"Nonsense," he replied with his patented, full-points grin. "I'm happy to do it. This might even give me the chance to catch up on my stories. I just hope Cocoa likes soap operas."

Lucy's eyes narrowed cautiously and Peter cleared his throat, trying to warn Ethan that he might be laying it on a little thick.

Taking the hint, Ethan rubbed his hands together and glanced around the small kitchen. "So where is Cocoa, anyway? I'd like to meet her before you take off, see if she minds me staying with her for a while."

"She's afraid of strangers, which means she's probably hiding under the bed."

They moved in the direction of the bedroom, in search of the cat.

"You don't have to stay here the whole time, though," Lucy told Ethan. "She's used to me being gone a lot of the time for work. If you could just stop in once or twice a day to make sure she has enough food and water, that would be okay. I realize you need to be at the club at night, when I'd normally be home with her, but if you could stick around a while when you're here during the day, I'd really appreciate it. That way, she'll get some company and not feel quite so abandoned."

"No problem. Like I said, I'll watch some television, and Cocoa can sit on the couch with me, if she wants. At the very least, I'll keep up a steady stream of conversation so she knows someone is in the apartment with her."

Lucy beamed at that and Peter shook his head. Ethan in action was a sight to behold. No wonder women fell at his feet. Fifteen minutes ago, he'd been turning Peter's ears red with complaints about lowering himself to this task, and now he had Lucy gazing up at him like he was king of the damn universe.

If Peter hadn't known his friend was putting on an act for her benefit, he probably would have been annoyed. At the very least, he thought, he should be taking notes.

At the foot of the bed, made up with a thick safari comforter covered with lions, elephants and giraffes, Lucy got on her hands and knees and crouched down to peer beneath the raised bed frame.

"Cocoa, baby. Don't you want to come out and meet Ethan before Mommy leaves?"

Ethan's head lifted, one dark eyebrow quirked comically as he shot Peter a look that seemed to say, *You're sure this girl is sane, right?*

He nudged Ethan in the side with his elbow, afraid Lucy might look up and see the expression on his

friend's face. And though Ethan might not be one to use
baby talk to converse with another species, Peter knew
his friend liked animals well enough and would take
good care of Lucy's cat while they were away.

It was no less than he'd have expected of Lucy,
though, to be so devoted to her pet. She was a caretaker,
inside and out. Lord knew she took care of him better
than anyone he'd ever known, including his own parents.

He wasn't surprised that she treated her cat like a
child, the same way he wouldn't be at all amazed if she
turned out to be the best mother in the world when she
decided to have children of her own. Those kids and her
family would come first above everything else.

Peter had never known love like that. His mother had
tried, and he knew she loved him, but he'd always felt
like an afterthought growing up. And he'd *never* been
a priority in his father's life. For all the attention the old
man had shown him, he might as well have not even existed.

Peter shook off the maudlin thoughts spiraling and
multiplying in his brain like gnats when Lucy climbed
to her feet, a fluffy ball of multicolored fur in her arms.
The cat looked angry and put-out, her body arched,
ears pressed flat against her head. But she let Ethan pet
her with little more than a low growl from deep in her
belly.

And Ethan, big, bad bully that he'd been in the car,
seemed completely enraptured. He scratched the fe-

line's ears and clicked his tongue. Peter thought he might even have cooed at one point. *Pushover.*

Once introductions were made and it was clear Cocoa and Ethan would get along like peas in a pod, Lucy showed him where everything was, gave him emergency phone numbers, then took a last glance around the small apartment before turning to Peter.

"All right, I think I'm ready."

He inclined his head, collecting her bags from near the door. "If you need anything," he told Ethan, "call us. You know where we're staying and you have my cell and pager numbers."

Ethan nodded, cat cradled under one arm like a football. "Have fun," he said, closing the door behind them.

Peter led Lucy out of the apartment building and across the street to his car, stowing her luggage in the trunk with his own. Once they were on the road, heading for the airport, Peter chanced a glance in her direction, noting the attractive but professional purple suit she'd worn to impress William Dawson, along with sleek high heels and dangling silver earrings.

"I hope Ethan meets your approval as a cat-sitter."

She tipped her head in his direction and gifted him with the ghost of a smile. "I like your friend. He's a bit of a smooth talker, but deep down, I think he's just an old softie. Cocoa will have him rolling around on the floor, dangling a string from his finger in no time."

"You're probably right." Peter chuckled, impressed that she'd pegged Ethan so quickly. Of course, his friend had been coming by the house ever since she started working for Peter, plying her with his good looks and playboy attitude.

Luckily Lucy had so far seemed immune to Ethan's advances. And Peter wasn't exactly the Hunchback of Notre Dame; he could hold his own with a group of pretty women—even up against Ethan. And especially where Lucy was concerned.

Ethan hadn't been completely right about his reasons for wanting Lucy along on this trip, but he hadn't been far off the mark, either. A part of him hoped they might end up making love again. He couldn't get the memory of being inside her out of his head, and if he got half the chance, he thought he would probably do his best to lure her back to his bed.

On the other hand, if she made it clear she wanted nothing more to do with him—at least in that respect—then he would have to take a step back and come to terms with her decision. He might not like it, but he would deal. And in a way, maybe it would be for the best.

But Lucy would have to be the one to throw her hands up and say no, because he honestly didn't think he had the strength to do it himself anymore. He wanted her too damn much.

Lucy turned slightly in her cozy, leather-upholstered business class seat, leaning against the plane's tiny rectangular window to watch Peter as he stowed his briefcase and her laptop computer in the overhead compartment. His broad chest and flat stomach rippled beneath the fine fabric of his shirt, pulling the material taut and making her mouth go dry.

Not for the first time, she wished she'd fought harder not to come along on this trip. It was too much to ask that she be required to work with him on a daily basis *and* travel out of town with him on business.

Sitting so close to him in the car on the drive to the airport, she'd felt like a sardine, stuffed into a tiny steel can next to the only other sardine who sent her pulse throbbing and her blood pressure skyrocketing out of control. And now she would be forced to endure the same type of conditions for the flight to New York.

Her stomach did a pitch and roll at the prospect. And then Peter settled into the seat beside hers, adjusted his seat belt, stretched his legs out in front of him, and Lucy thought she might have to reach for the airsick bag. Her poor nervous system was about to revolt.

Thankfully, the flight attendant came by then, asking if they'd like drinks before the plane took off. The woman smiled, her gaze lingering on Peter as she patted his shoulder and leaned so far over his seat, her breasts just about popped the front of her blue uniform.

Lucy was used to such blatant displays around Peter. Women flocked to him, and he usually flocked right back. The fact that he seemed oblivious to the flight attendant's current flirtations surprised her, but perhaps he was simply preoccupied by his upcoming business meetings.

"Excuse me." She cleared her throat and tried again, speaking more loudly until the blonde dragged her attention away from Peter. "Yes, I'd like a glass of Chardonnay, please." *A large one, and maybe later the bottle.* It was the only thing she could think of to slow her runaway heartbeat to a mere gallop.

It was small consolation, she supposed, that she wasn't alone in having this reaction to him. She was just the only one who'd apparently been driven to drink.

Once her wine and his scotch and soda had been delivered, they settled back in their seats to relax. Lucy noticed again that Peter took his drink and thanked the flight attendant, but otherwise ignored the woman's attempts to gain his masculine attention.

"What's the matter?" she asked, taking a sip from her glass. "Not interested in blondes this month?"

Peter shot her a confused glance. "What?"

"The flight attendant. She did everything but sit on your lap and wiggle."

His brows knit in a frown. "I don't know what you're talking about."

"Didn't you notice?" But to herself, she muttered, "That would be a first."

Over the rim of her glass, she saw Peter studying her intently. She knew she was being irrational and snippy, but she'd spent the past two years watching him parade around with one woman after another, and lately it felt like more than she could handle.

A tiny voice in the back of her head told her he

hadn't been hitting on the flight attendant. Hadn't even reacted to the woman's giggles or bounce. And as far as she knew, he hadn't been out—or in—with a single pretty girl since they'd been together. But that didn't seem to matter when the memory of dozens of other lovely young ladies were traipsing through her brain, getting her dander up.

"Are you angry with me, Lucy?"

"Of course not," she replied with a scoff, even though a part of her was.

"Then what's wrong? I've never seen you like this before. I've never seen you drink during a flight, either, let alone before we've gotten off the ground," he pointed out, flashing a look to the wine in her hand.

With a sigh, she placed the glass on the tray in front of her, then sat back in her seat and turned to face him more fully.

"I'm sorry," she said, the wind going out of her sails. "It's just…Don't you ever think about the future? About having more than the flavor of the month to warm your bed?"

Eyes widening, Peter shifted uncomfortably but didn't break the visual hold he had on her. With a nervous chuckle, he wanted to know, "What brought this on?"

She shook her head, unwilling to answer, since the first thing that flashed across her mind was an image of the two of them, on the floor of a hotel elevator, making love.

"I guess I'd have to say no," Peter murmured, his lips thinning. "I try very hard not to think about the future, except where business is concerned."

"Why not?"

If possible, his mouth compressed more tightly, the sides sliding down into a frown. "It's better not to spend too much time contemplating things that can never be."

A ripple of sadness flowed outward from the region of her heart at such a grim declaration.

"I'm not sure I understand what you mean," she said carefully. "Are you suffering from some dread disease I don't know about and only have a few months left to live? Or maybe you're sterile and can't have children, so there's no point in contemplating marriage."

Peter whipped his head around to see if anyone was listening in on their conversation. "Jeez, Luce, talk a little louder, why don't you. I don't think the people in row twenty-three heard you." Then he grew serious. "I'm not sterile and I'm not dying. At least not that I know of. But let's face it, there's no such thing as happily-ever-after, and I'd be a terrible husband and father even if there were."

Lucy stared at him, incredulous, so many thoughts whirling around in her brain, she could barely make sense of them. *Bad husband, no happily-ever-after, things that can never be. What* was he talking about? And how had he come up with such outlandish notions?

Granted, they'd only known each other for two

years, but if he'd ever been married, she thought she'd have heard about it by now. Some brief mention of an ex-wife or whispered rumors about why the marriage hadn't worked out.

"I'm sorry," she managed once she'd blinked and regained some of the moisture in her suddenly dry mouth, "but you're going to have to elaborate. Why in heaven's name would you think you'd make a bad husband and father?"

"Genetics don't lie."

"Genetics," she repeated, still not understanding. She felt as though he was speaking another language, with none of the words finding definitions in her limited vocabulary.

"I take it you've never heard me talk about my father."

She searched her memory, but couldn't recall a single time he'd spoken to her about his parents, and only now began to think that fact odd.

Not waiting for an answer, he continued. "My father was a real son of a bitch. A shark in the business world, and well respected for it, but as a husband and father, he stank. I don't know why he bothered getting married at all, and I think I must have been conceived either by immaculate conception or in a moment of extreme weakness.

"Throughout my entire childhood, I don't think I ever heard him say a kind word to my mother or saw her smile when he was around. We didn't go on outings or spend quality time together. We didn't even have meals as a family, or if we did, they were eaten in relative silence, with my father hurrying through so he could rush off to another business meeting or lock himself in his study to work."

Peter held himself rigid, as though barring against any hint of emotion that might seep past the bitterness and resentment. Her heart ached for him, for the little boy he'd been, starving for his father's affection and getting none.

"What about your mother?" she inquired softly. "Was she good to you?"

He responded with a careless shrug. "She did her best, tried to compensate for my father's absence. But she was distracted by it herself, always trying to keep him home, give him reasons to spend time with us."

Lucy wanted to wrap her arms around him and offer comfort, hug him tight for all the times in his childhood when he'd been ignored or pushed aside or made to feel like less than the most important thing in the world to the two people who should have loved him above everyone and everything else in their lives.

"And because your father wasn't very good at marriage and family, you've automatically decided you won't be, either. Is that right?"

"Does an apple fall far from the tree?" His mouth twisted, the question dripping with cynicism.

"Peter." She stopped, worrying the inside of her lip, unsure how to go on. There was so much she wanted to say to him, so many fallacies she wanted to lay to rest. But her mind was a jumble of facts and feelings. She knew if she said the wrong thing, Peter would clam up, curling in on himself to once again hide the little boy who had been hurt and disillusioned at such a young age.

"You can't believe that," she whispered. "Not really."

The expression on his face, though, told her he did—unequivocally.

The engines of the plane turned over then, making it harder to be heard over the loud, humming whir. Crossing her legs in his direction, she leaned closer so she wouldn't have to raise her voice, laying a hand on his arm. Beneath her fingers, the muscles bunched and tensed as he clutched the metal armrest.

"Peter, your father was distant and uncaring, and I'm sorry for that. I don't think anyone would argue the fact that neither of your parents did right by you. But you're not a clone of your father, you're your own man. That's the beauty of children; they can grow up wiser than their parents and learn not to make the same mistakes as previous generations."

She squeezed his arm and brushed the back of her hand lovingly along the line of his jaw. She knew she should play it safe and walk away. Accept his reasoning and count herself fortunate not to have gotten too heavily involved with his personal demons.

But she was already emotionally invested in this

man. Her heart had been engaged soon after she started working for him, and she was only more soundly entrenched now that he'd shared a part of his past with her.

"I happen to think you'd make a wonderful husband and father," she told him earnestly. "You're kind and generous and patient, and have a great sense of humor. Any woman would be lucky to have you, and your children—if you ever have them—will think you hung the moon and the stars."

Seven

Lucy's words penetrated deep into his soul, warming a place he'd thought long dead. He only wished he could believe them.

A part of him wanted to…so badly, he felt a burning sensation at the backs of his eyes. He turned his head and blinked quickly, taking a moment to catch his breath and steady his out of control emotions.

But you couldn't rewrite history, and he knew what happened when a man tried to have a wife and family while also trying to build and maintain a thriving business. One would suffer, and if his own upbringing was any indication, it would likely be the family. That was a risk he couldn't—*wouldn't*—take.

"I wish I could believe that," he rasped, turning his arm over and twining her fingers with his own when they slid into his palm. "But I've had too much experience with the other side of the coin. I learned early on that a person can either concentrate on his job, his corporate image, or he can concentrate on his family—he can't have both. And I'm sorry, Lucy, but Reyware is too important to me to let anything interfere. My entire focus right now is on getting the company off the ground and well into the black. Maybe later, when I'm older and Reyware is stable enough to put others in charge…maybe then I'll take a chance on a wife and kids. For now, though, I can't put someone—adult or child—through what my father put my mom and me through."

"You only think that way because it's all you've ever known," Lucy pointed out gently. "If you'd grown up differently, you might have a dozen kids by now."

He wrinkled his nose at her wild supposition. "I'm only thirty-two, Luce. How is that even possible?"

She shot him a cheeky grin. "Well, maybe not a full dozen, but if you'd gotten started early, you could be close."

His expression must have still looked doubtful because she adjusted her weight until her shoulder and the full length of her arm rested firmly against his.

"Let me tell you about my family," she said, a wealth of warmth and affection clear in her affectionate tone.

"My father is a civil engineer. He's been at the same

company for twenty-five years, beginning as a low-level assistant and working his way up to Vice President. My mother has worked as an elementary teacher all her life. They met in college, got married right after graduation, and had my brother, Adam, before their first anniversary. I came next, and then Jessica. Both of my parents worked full-time through all of our childhoods, but I don't ever remember a time when they weren't there for us. We sat at the dining-room table every night for dinner, shared the day's events. We went on picnics and took vacations, played checkers and board games and Frisbee, went to the beach and the community pool. Some of the best times of my life were spent with Mom, Dad, Adam, and Jess. I can't wait to get married and start a family of my own so I can recapture some of that early happiness and show my own children how it feels to be loved and adored, unconditionally."

With the hand he wasn't holding in a near-death grip, she patted his knee. "Now, do you want to tell me again that a man can't be a successful entrepreneur and doting father at the same time? My father certainly managed well enough, and my brother is following firmly in his footsteps."

He understood what she was trying to say and envied her blissful, storybook upbringing. But it still sounded like a fairy tale to him. And in his life, was every bit as fictional.

"I'm glad you have happy memories of your childhood," he told her judiciously, "and that your parents were able to find time for the three of you, given their busy schedules. But your father and brother obviously come from different stock than the men in my family. For me, it's just not possible, the same as it wasn't possible for my father or his father."

When Peter cocked his head and met her gaze, he saw the sadness and sympathy in her eyes, and almost resented it. With a sigh, she loosened her fingers from his grasp and uncrossed her legs, moving back to her own side of the roomy, first-class leather seats.

Retrieving her glass of wine, she took a healthy sip and then said, "I hope you're wrong, Peter. I truly, truly do. Because you deserve to be a husband and father, and to prove yourself wrong."

They arrived at the downtown Manhattan hotel a few hours later, tired and uncomfortable from the tack their conversation had taken on the plane. After that, they'd barely spoken unless necessary.

For her part, Lucy found herself distracted by Peter's confession and the picture he'd painted of his childhood. It explained so much about him.

Why he dated beautiful but vacuous women with no thought past the night they'd spend in his bed. Or the ones obviously interested in little more than his money, whom he seemed to use and discard as easily as yesterday's newspaper.

It suddenly all made perfect sense. He surrounded himself with people who wouldn't expect too much of him, wouldn't pressure him to make promises. Because the idea of committing to anything more permanent than a goldfish scared Peter straight down to his boxer shorts.

Which might also be why, up until that Friday night in the elevator at the Four Seasons, he'd never made a single move on her. Never seemed to notice her feminine existence, let alone the hints she dropped to let him know she wouldn't turn him down if he did.

And now, she wasn't sure how to feel. She'd spent so long being half in love with him, and then getting to experience the long-awaited, earth-shattering sensation of making love with him, that she found it hard to let go of the fantasy she'd built in her mind.

Given his strong aversion to marriage and family, however, she would probably be better off setting her sights on someone a bit more attainable. Like Mel Gibson or Brad Pitt.

Peter desperately wanted to avoid the ties and responsibilities of marriage and children, and though Lucy thought a few stern arguments or hours on a therapist's couch would go a long way toward relieving him of his adolescent burden, the fact was she *did* want those things.

She'd grown up in a happy home, with two loving parents, and someday she hoped to create those same qualities for her own kids. For a time, she'd even let herself imagine she would have that life and those children with Peter. Now she knew she would have better luck teaching Cocoa to bark like a guard dog.

Watching him from the corner of her eye as he checked them in at the front desk, she had the sudden urge to put her head down on the countertop and weep. It was such a waste. Like many women, she'd often joked that all the good men were either gay or married. Now she realized the best of those men was highly allergic to any sign of a serious relationship.

Sliding the key cards into his jacket pocket, Peter picked up both their carry-on bags and started toward the bank of elevators on the far side of the elegant lobby. Lucy followed at a more sedate pace, swallowing the mild nausea that threatened from the day's keen disappointments.

The ride to the tenth floor passed in relative silence, soft instrumental music filling the small space and spurring the start of a headache just behind her eyes. She remembered the last time they'd been alone together in a hotel elevator…

Her inner muscles clenched at the very thought as heat rushed over her, and for a moment she wished for another city-wide power outage. Ten minutes when the rest of the world would disappear and they could once again find complete, satisfied abandon in each other's arms.

But then the doors slid open and reality returned. The lights stayed on, Peter's breathing remained steady, and there was no repeat performance of the wild lovemaking they'd shared before.

Lucy couldn't decide whether to be happy or sad

about that, but she let Peter open the door to her suite and usher her inside. She crossed the room, flipping on lights as she went and opening the heavy drapes to reveal a panoramic view of the city. Tall gray buildings obscured the skyline while cars filled the streets below like ants trailing away from a picnic buffet.

Behind her, Peter set her overnight bag on the bed and moved toward the door that connected their two rooms. "We're meeting Dawson for dinner in the hotel restaurant at seven," he reminded her.

She checked the watch at her wrist, then turned her head a fraction, taking in his sandy blond hair and suit, both slightly rumpled from the trip. It took every ounce of will in her body not to offer to iron his jacket and slacks or otherwise help him get ready for his meeting. But with only half an hour until they were supposed to get together with William Dawson, she needed every spare moment to freshen up.

"I'll be ready," she said.

He stood there a second longer, looking like he might say something. Then he stepped through the connecting door and closed it quietly behind him.

This was good, she thought. Getting back to business, putting their relationship back on a professional footing. It might not be what she'd been hoping for, for the past two years, but now that she knew about his deep-rooted aversion to anything permanent, it was better for her to wrap her mind around the fact that Peter was not the marrying kind.

And since she wasn't in the market for a man to simply warm her bed or fill her life on a temporary basis, she needed to get it through her head that Peter Reynolds was off her short list.

It wasn't the end of the world. There were other men out there, ones who wouldn't be quite as apprehensive of the "M" word or the idea of settling down and starting a family.

Maybe it was time to seek some of them out.

Peter scowled, his brows dipping so low, they almost completely obliterated his vision.

What the hell did she think she was doing? And who the hell had told her to pack a dress like that, anyway?

Lucy sat across the table from him, entirely too close to William Dawson, laughing loudly and hanging on the man's every word. And Dawson, in return, was practically drooling on Lucy.

This was supposed to be a business dinner, but she'd changed from her classy purple suit to a low-cut, high-hemmed cocktail dress. Black, with flowered and filigree lace at the edges, which left much too much of her arms and neck and legs and chest bare for Peter's peace of mind.

She'd come with him in a secretarial capacity, but she acted as though she was on a date—with Dawson, no less. And they had yet to discuss Dawson's company or the plans he had for Peter's involvement. The man seemed content to bask in Lucy's feminine attention, and she, in turn, seemed determined to work Will into a lather.

But if she thought she could send Peter back up to the hotel rooms and take off on Dawson's arm to spend the evening doing God knows what, she had another think coming.

If she spent the night with anyone, it would be Peter. And if she wound up in anyone's bed, it would be his, not Will Dawson's. He didn't care how much she was flirting or how receptive the man obviously was.

Lucy laughed again at something Will said and Peter felt his blood pressure spike. One more suggestive joke or over-the-top giggle and he thought he might snap. He'd shatter the wine glass in his hand or drive the tines of his fork into his former friend's fingers where they covered and wrapped around Lucy's atop the linen tablecloth.

"Don't you think we should get down to business?" he finally said, the words rumbling from his throat in something close to a growl.

Both Lucy and Will cocked their heads, glancing at him for the first time in more than an hour, as though they'd forgotten he was even present at the same table.

Untangling their twined arms and hands, Lucy sat back a bit in her chair, away from Will and gave a small smile.

"Of course," she murmured. "I'm sorry, I didn't mean to distract you from your purpose." She pulled a small legal pad and pen from her handbag, poised to take notes. "Please, go on. I'm ready when you are."

Peter felt a punch to his gut as powerful as any an opponent could have delivered in a title fight. He had used the excuse of needing her along as his assistant to manipulate her into coming, and now she was throwing her notepad down like a gauntlet. Showing him she knew her place, reminding him of their professional arrangement, and all but spelling out that their conversation on the plane meant if he wasn't open to marriage and family, then she wasn't open to him.

He'd known that. Even as he was relating facts from his childhood to her, he'd known that she would take it to mean he wasn't interested in developing anything of a permanent nature with her.

Lucy had grown up very differently than he, and though she may not be on the hunt for a husband right this minute, he knew she had visions of picket fences and two-point-three kids running through her brain. He might be fun to have as a lover for the short term, but he would either have to let her go or turn into a long-term kind of guy right quick. And knowing he never intended to marry or reproduce meant she'd likely knocked him off her list completely the minute he'd admitted as much.

A little voice in the back of his brain cheered. He should be happy, relieved, grateful she'd cut off any chances of an ongoing relationship. That way, he would never have to worry that she'd begin to expect more from him than he was willing to give. He'd never have to prepare a speech for letting her down easy or explain why she might share his bed, but would never share his life. He would never have to see her tears or listen to her wails as she stormed out of his house and cursed him for wasting her time.

Been there, done that.

So why, instead, was his stomach churning, his upper lip sweating? Why was there a sharp pain in the region of his heart?

Because he was a sap, that's why. Ridiculous to think it could be more than a fanciful notion of keeping Lucy with him forever. As anything other than his assistant, at least.

Maybe he'd been watching too many chick flicks lately or leaving the television on the wrong channel while he worked. Whatever the cause of his recent bout of melancholia, he was damn certain he didn't plan to change his lifelong goals and beliefs just because he'd spent one night in an overheated elevator car with Lucy. Best sex of his life or not, no woman was worth running the risk of turning into his father, of irreparably ruining multiple lives.

Refusing to meet Lucy's gaze or the censure written there, he shifted his focus instead to Will and steered the conversation back where it belonged—firmly on the business at hand.

Lucy didn't know what had crawled up Peter's butt and died, but about halfway through dinner, he'd turned surly and cross. He'd discussed William Dawson's company and the software system he thought best for the man's growing business, but he'd been so curt about it that he might have been a rival CEO in the center of a corporate takeover.

And darned if Lucy could figure out why. Before they'd left Georgetown for New York, Peter had given the impression that he and Will were friends, as well as associates. They were roughly the same age, had grown up with similar backgrounds, and were both building personal companies they hoped would be successful.

So why was Peter suddenly acting as if Will had stolen his favorite toy?

Unless Lucy's behavior during the meal had set him off.

Her cheeks flushed as she remembered, and she admitted to herself that she might have gone a touch overboard.

Once she'd made the decision to go in search of an eligible man—or men—her seductive side had come out full-force. Will Dawson was an attractive, unattached man. The minute they'd walked into the hotel restaurant and Peter had introduced them, she'd detected a note of interest in the man's dark eyes and decided to see where it led.

It had led rather quickly to a lot of laughter, a few fluttered eyelashes, and some tentative touching of both hands and legs beneath the table.

Lucy hadn't realized Peter noticed, let alone that her actions would bother him. After all, he'd made it clear immediately following their one night together that it had been a mistake and he didn't intend to let it happen again. Then, on the plane, he'd gone even further by telling her a bit about his childhood and assuring her he never intended to settle down with anyone, not even her.

So why shouldn't she be allowed to date other men? Even those of Peter's acquaintance. Even in his presence. He wasn't her brother or father, with some overblown sense of familial protection that allowed him to tell her who she could see or flirt with. She was a grown woman, looking forward to a happy future that would hopefully someday include a husband and children. And if Peter wasn't willing to give her those things, then he had no right to keep her from them, either.

As she strolled across the hotel room, stripping out of her dress and stockings, Lucy couldn't decide whether to be amused or angry by the entire situation. Peter was the man she wanted, but he didn't want her. And yet, it seemed he also didn't want her to be with anyone else.

Well, he couldn't have it both ways. She'd spent the past two years fawning over him, believing he might one day sit up and take notice of her, and that they might have a future together. Now that she knew that wasn't the case, she wanted to get on with her life.

She thought of Will, with his short black hair, set in glossy spikes along his head with a touch of gel. His chocolate-brown eyes and easy smile. She might have invited him upstairs after dinner if Peter hadn't been all but shooting daggers and chewing glass.

A second later, though, as she reached into the shower to turn on the water, she knew that wasn't true. She might have invited Will up to her room, but she doubted anything would have happened. For one, she wasn't the kind of girl to sleep with a man she barely knew the first night they met. For another, she was afraid she wouldn't be able to banish Peter from her mind long enough to be intimate with somebody else.

Stepping under the warm spray, she let water sluice down her body, wet her hair. It felt wonderful, and for the first time all night, she let herself relax completely, let the tension wash away from her muscles as easily as the shampoo and soap suds slid down the drain.

She stayed in the shower longer than usual, until steam fogged the glass of the bathroom mirror and her skin turned warm and silky. Then she wrapped one towel around her hair and another around her body, tucking the corner between her breasts to hold it fast.

While she was still damp, she squeezed a dollop of sweet-smelling moisturizer into the palm of her hand and smoothed it over her arms and legs, then patted herself dry. With the floral scent of lotion filling the small room, she combed and blow-dried her hair before opening the door and stepping out into the rest of the hotel room.

Letting the towel from around her body drop at the foot of the king size bed, she took the three strides to the dresser in the nude and dug a nightie out of the top drawer. The emerald satin slipped on over her head, settling its spaghetti straps over her shoulders and lace bodice along her breasts with a gentle whoosh.

A throat clearing across the room spun Lucy around with a startled yip. Peter sat in the corner, slouched down in a chair, hidden by shadows.

"Good Lord," she breathed, "you scared me half to death."

It was a testament to how comfortable she felt with him that she didn't even realize she'd just pranced in front of him completely naked for a full minute. When she did, she gave another yelp and grabbed for her earlier discarded bath towel.

"Peter!" she chastised, using the white terry cloth to cover herself from neck to knee, even though she was now more than adequately dressed in the short, slinky nightgown. "What are you doing here? How did you get in?"

He cocked his head in the direction of the connecting door. "It was unlocked. I wanted to talk to you, but I didn't expect you to be walking around naked." Sitting up a bit straighter, he had the decency to look abashed. "Sorry."

For the first time since sending her heart into overdrive with his sudden appearance, she noticed the condition of his suit, wrinkled and disheveled. His tie had been loosened and draped down his chest at an odd angle, and it looked as though he'd run his fingers through his hair a few thousand times.

Her embarrassment faded, replaced by concern, and she moved to sit on the corner of the bed nearest his chair.

"Is something wrong?" she asked.

For a moment, he didn't answer. Then he bent forward, resting his elbows on his thighs, hands clasping and unclasping between his parted knees as he hung his head dejectedly.

"I came to apologize for dinner. I acted like an ass."

Lucy crossed her legs, letting the towel fall to her lap. "You were a little asslike," she agreed softly.

He lifted his head and gave her a small smile. "You noticed that, huh?"

"I noticed. I'm just not sure what came over you. I thought you and Will were friends."

"We are, at least as far as business goes."

"Then why did you treat him so shabbily? And me, too, for that matter."

"Truth?" He slanted an uneasy glance in her direction. "I didn't like the way he was looking at you, touching you. Or the way you reacted to him."

Setting the still-damp towel aside, she scooched another inch toward the edge of the mattress. "Why, Peter? Why do you care what I do or who I do it with? It's not like you're interested, not judging by what you said on the plane."

In one fluid motion, Peter abandoned his chair. Towering above her, he leaned in, fists digging into the bedspread on either side of her hips until their noses nearly touched.

"That's where you're wrong," he whispered, his voice low and rough, running over her like a sheet of sandpaper. "Because I am interested. God help me, but I am."

Eight

Desire stabbed through Peter, and the closer he got to Lucy, the sharper that desire became. Going down on one knee in front of her, he breathed in the clean, shampooed fragrance of her long, black hair, let his gaze roam over the rosy glow of her shower-fresh skin.

"I tried to deny it," he said, the words ripped from his throat as he stared up at her, blood pounding in his veins. "That one night was supposed to be just that—one night. One night when I finally got to experience what I'd been dreaming of since the first time you came to interview for the job as my assistant. One night when things got a bit crazy and my claustrophobia served as the perfect excuse to taste your lips, caress your body, feel you move beneath me while we made love."

He lifted a hand to her face, stroked the back of his fingers over the baby-soft silk of her cheek. "I hoped that would be enough, for both of us. Because I can't give you what you need, what you deserve. You want it all—a wedding, babies, happily ever after. And I want those things for you, but I can't be the one to give them to you. Not now, maybe not ever."

Letting his hand dip lower, he traced the line of her jaw, the slender column of her neck, the gentle slope of her chest. The lacy front of her liquid green gown exposed all but the very tips of her breasts. They drew his eye and then his touch.

"Seeing you tonight, though, flirting with Will... There were a couple of times during dinner when I had to stop myself from leaping across the table and choking him with his napkin."

His hold shifted from below the curve of her breasts to her waist and squeezed. "Tell me to leave, Lucy," he implored, meeting her ocean-blue eyes. "Say you hate me and never want to see me again. Kick me out before I do something really stupid like beg you to go to bed with me."

Lucy raised an arm, feathering her manicured fingers through the hair at his temple. "I don't hate you," she murmured. "And you don't have to beg."

Lowering her head, she pressed her lips to his, her hands spreading across his cheeks and neck. Her mouth felt like molten lava flowing from an active volcano. Heat poured through his veins, all but giving off steam, bringing every hormone in his body to full attention.

Coming up on his knees, he started to stand, only to push her back on the mattress. The satiny fabric of her nightie rode high on her thighs as he hovered over her, mouth devouring, hands exploring.

He'd missed this the first time around. Watching her, seeing her beautiful hair spilled out around her like a halo, her eyes turn dark with passion, her nipples pearl at the tips of her pert breasts. And it was a damn shame, because every inch of her was so beautiful, his teeth ached.

He stroked her shoulders and arms, memorized the shape of her womanly form with its hills and valleys, dips and swells. Electricity sparked at his fingertips as they skimmed across her flesh, sending the sensations straight to his groin.

A moan rolled up from his diaphragm as their tongues tangled and twisted. Her legs wrapped around his like vines, and he could feel the silk of her skin even through the material of his dress slacks.

The nails on one of Lucy's hands dug into his back while the other loosened the knot of his tie. Tossing it aside, she moved to the buttons of his shirt while he rocked his hips into the cradle of her thighs and skimmed a hand beneath the hem of her gown.

With each movement of their bodies, he slid Lucy farther and farther up the length of the mattress, until her head was propped on the pillows. The new position gave them more than enough room to spread out and enjoy themselves.

As soon as she'd finished with the buttons, he shrugged out of both the white shirt and gray suit jacket, letting them fall to the floor. He began inching her gown upwards, over her hips, her torso. Lucy raised her arms so he could slide the slinky material off completely.

She lay beneath him, blessedly naked. Sexier and more lovely, if possible, than when she'd stepped out of the bathroom after her shower and dropped the towel. And this time, he didn't have to just sit back and watch, he could touch and taste and stroke to his heart's content.

Her fingers at his waist succeeded in unhooking his belt, then shifted to the button and zipper of his pants. When both slid free, she tunneled her fingers inside, into the band of his briefs and pushed everything down past his hips.

He groaned as she raked her nails across the sensitive flesh of his buttocks and the backs of his thighs, then quickly kicked off his shoes and shrugged out of his slacks and underwear. Stretching out atop her, their heated bodies molded together. Hard on soft, rough against smooth, they fit like pieces of a puzzle, creating a picture that felt…right. Unbearably perfect, even if it was only temporary.

He used his lips and teeth to graze her collarbone, working his way down to her breasts. With light, butterfly kisses, he circled the pert, plum-colored areolas, then eased closer, blowing lightly on the tight flesh, letting his tongue dart out to lick her pointed nipples.

"You smell delicious," he murmured against her moist skin. "Like strawberries and cream."

She gave a breathy chuckle. "It's flowers. Rose soap and honeysuckle shampoo."

"Whatever it is," he said, "you smell good enough to eat."

He dug his teeth into the cushiony side of her breast, then licked away the sting with this tongue. Continuing the onslaught, he suckled one breast while kneading the other with his palm until Lucy writhed beneath him, arching her back and twisting her hips. Little sounds, like a mewling kitten, rolled past her lips, urging him on.

"Unfair," she whispered. And then she slipped a hand between them, reaching down to stroke the long, hard length of his erection. It pulsed in her hand and sent fireworks bursting behind his closed eyelids.

"That's better," she told him. "Now you know how I feel. How you *make* me feel."

With a growl, he yanked her legs up and over his shoulders, switching his attention from her breasts to her ribcage. He kissed a ring around her belly button, a path across her abdomen, and then lightly nuzzled the springy curls at the vee of her thighs. She moaned in protest, pushing at his shoulders to dislodge him, but he held firm.

"Hush," he ordered against her womanhood. "Let me. I've been dreaming of this longer than you can imagine."

She seemed to relax then, her head sinking into the pillow, her ankles crossing in the middle of his back. He licked her like a cat, tasting the musky sweetness that was her own intimate flavor.

Lucy hummed with pleasure as his tongue lapped and explored. Her pelvis rose and fell, begging for completion. And he gave it to her, deepening his attentions, focusing on the tiny bud of desire that made her squirm. Her breathing began to come in pants, shorter and louder, until her spine bowed and she screamed in ecstasy.

Peter felt the orgasm vibrate through her body and into his own, arousing him even more. He couldn't wait to be inside her again, to feel that heat, that wet, that sense of completeness he'd never experienced before in his life.

Only with Lucy.

Only when he shut off his brain and let himself enjoy the spell she wove around them. Without thinking of all the reasons they wouldn't work, all the ways he could hurt her.

Her legs slid from his shoulders, boneless and limp. He took the opportunity to crawl back up her long, lithe frame to her lips, drawing them into his mouth one at a time.

"Thank you," he whispered against her cheek. "That was amazing."

Her eyes opened to slits, looking droopy and satisfied. She tried to laugh, but it came out as more of an amused wheeze.

"I should be thanking you. It *was* amazing. And you didn't even get to have any fun yet." Her fingers combed through his hair and a soft smile crested her lips.

"Oh, I had fun, believe me. Watching you come, knowing I brought you to that point, is the single most incredible event of my life. Not counting the little escapade in the elevator, since I couldn't see you. Or anything that might come next, which I'm guessing will be equally remarkable."

"I don't know," she said with a teasing grin, still stroking his scalp. "What we've already done was pretty out-of-this-world, at least for me. I'm not sure anything could top it. Maybe we should just quit while we're ahead."

"Oh, no." Peter dug his teeth into the taut flesh between neck and shoulder, branding her with his mark. "We're just getting started. Before the night is over, I intend to make you scream at least six or eight more times."

"Six or eight, hmm? That's quite a bar you're setting for yourself. Are you sure you can handle it?"

He gazed down at her, feigning irritation with what he hoped was a devilishly raised brow. "*I* can handle it. The question is, can you?"

She drew her legs up and encircled his waist, bringing him that much closer to the entrance of her femininity. The damp warmth dusting his throbbing erection made him clench his teeth to keep from popping like a bottle of champagne right then and there.

Her low voice washed over him, full of sensual promises. "I'm certainly willing to try."

He rested his forehead against her brow, then placed a light kiss on the tip of her nose. "This time, we're going to be more careful," he told her.

Rolling slightly away, he reached to the floor for his earlier discarded pants. He dug his wallet out of the back pocket and a condom out of the wallet.

"I've been carrying this with me ever since our encounter in the elevator, just in case."

"Do you only have the one?"

Pulling himself back up on the bed, he shot her a pirate's grin, then ripped the foil-lined packet open with his teeth. "Unfortunately, yes. But I'll run down to the hotel gift shop for another box before we need them."

"Mmm, a man with a plan. What a turn-on."

He chuckled as he took the condom from its wrapper and moved to sheath himself. But her hand stopped him, taking the latex circle from his grasp.

"Let me."

Lowering her feet to the mattress, Lucy shimmied toward the headboard, getting to her knees. Peter did the same, until they were kneeling on the bed, face-to-face. She skimmed a palm down the broad expanse of his chest, marveling at the play of muscles. How they defined his sculpted, mouthwatering form and rippled beneath her touch.

Her own stomach clenched in anticipation as she leaned forward and kissed first one flat male nipple and then the other. He shuddered in response.

His reaction made her bold…not that she hadn't already been more daring than usual with him. But that's what Peter did to her. He made her feel powerful and uninhibited. Womanly and wanton.

"Lie back," she ordered, advancing on him and pushing firmly on his pectorals.

He followed her instructions, going flat on his back across the bunched and slippery hotel-issue bedspread. She straddled him, crawling up his long, rough-haired legs until she could rest her bottom high on his thighs.

He watched her through thick blond lashes, his hands moving to cup her hips. "You're trying to kill me, aren't you?"

Lucy shook her head. Her hair fanned out in a black veil and fell around her shoulders. "Just a little death."

The air left his lungs in a hiss. "Very funny. If you're not careful, it could be a big one, and maybe the real thing."

She bent over, letting her belly come in contact with his pointing erection. It pressed like steel into her flesh, even though the surface felt like crushed velvet.

His chest rose and fell with his heavy breathing. Hovering just above his parted lips, she exhaled, letting her warm breath caress his mouth and cheeks. "You're not afraid of a little pleasure, are you?"

"A little?" he spoke raggedly. "No. But with you,

there's no chance of 'a little.' It's going to be a lot, and it's going to be phenomenal…if I make it that far."

"If you don't make it all the way the first time," she teased wickedly, "we'll just have to try, try again."

Peter groaned, deep in his throat, and his hips arched off the bed almost of their own volition. A shock of awareness shot through her at the action, and suddenly she didn't want to play anymore. She only wanted him inside her, pounding and thrusting until their teeth rattled and their minds turned to mush.

Lifting up again, she took hold of his arousal with one hand at the base while she situated the condom over the tip with the other. She felt his entire body tense under her and wasted no time rolling the protection into place.

His fingers dug into her buttocks as she repositioned herself and began taking his hot length into her body. Inch by inch, she eased down. He pulsed inside her, seeming to grow larger even as she engulfed him.

When she was fully seated, they both released heartfelt sighs.

"That's a pretty good start," he muttered.

"And it's bound to get even better, right?"

"God, I hope so."

Flattening both palms on his ribcage, she rose up on her knees a fraction, letting him slide partially out of her body even as she tightened her internal grip to keep him in place. He bit his bottom lip, stifling a moan, and she moved back down.

Then she arched forward and repeated the motion. Up. Down. Back. Forth. Side to side. She changed direction with each stroke, keeping him on edge. His hands clutched her hips, clenching and unclenching as he lifted off the mattress, thrusting upwards to reach her.

Her fingers curled against his firm abdomen like talons as heat lightning raced through her. Tension spiraled at her center, growing tighter and tighter until every muscle in her body grew tightrope taut and her lungs froze in her chest.

Ecstasy rolled over her in a waterfall of sensation, sharp at first and then warm and comforting. Beneath her, Peter's lips curled back from his gritted teeth as he flexed his hips one last time and climaxed inside her.

They floated back down to earth slowly, hearts pounding, bones the consistency of vanilla pudding. She fell across him, limp and sated. Her hair covered them like a blanket, hiding her eyes and getting in her mouth, but she didn't care.

She'd never felt anything in her life even close to what she'd just experienced. The things Peter did to her, the heights and emotions he wrung from her. He played her like a well-tuned instrument, and she sang in response.

His chest rose and fell as he struggled to draw air into his lungs, and his heart beat erratically under her ear. Both made her feel safe, as though she never needed to move again. She could die right here, right now, and not suffer a single regret.

Her eyelids were too heavy to open when he smoothed a hand over the back of her head. She purred in contentment, but remained wilted.

"Are you okay?" he asked, his mouth moving against her temple.

Her only answer was a noncommittal grunt.

He chuckled, the sound vibrating along both their bodies. "Well, I have to say I'm surprised the bed held up. Halfway through, I expected the springs to give out and the two of us to find ourselves on the floor."

"Halfway through, I'm surprised you could think at all," she muttered lazily. "But the floor might not be a bad idea for the next time around."

"God, I love a woman who plans for the future."

He shifted, sending aftershocks of desire through her lower regions where they were still intimately connected. With a small groan, he rolled to his side, depositing her on her back on the mattress and kissing her brow.

"I just need to take care of this," he said, sitting up on the edge of the bed and removing the used condom. He made his way to the bathroom, closing the door all but a crack behind him.

Lucy lay there as the seconds ticked by, staring up at the ceiling. It was too much effort to move, though she knew she should. And Peter's last words were humming through her brain, sending nerve endings that were previously numb with pleasure into unpleasant awareness.

Love. He'd used the word, but he didn't mean it…not the way she wished he would.

A part of her knew she shouldn't be upset. She should shrug off his comment as the simple turn of phrase it had been. But another part of her was reminded in living color of the problems that still stood between them.

Great sex was one thing…if they handed out awards for outstanding performances in the bedroom, Peter would have a wall full of gold medals. With him, she might even win a few of her own.

She'd let herself pretend nothing else mattered for the chance to be with him again, but the fact remained that he still didn't want a wife or family. And she still did.

They could remain lovers for an unspecified amount of time, enjoy each other's company and the magic they created together between the sheets. But it wouldn't last, and she had to decide whether to delude herself for a couple months, then deal with the pain of his eventual rejection, or take the handful of blissful memories they'd created already and cut her losses.

Peter returned then, breaking into her thoughts as the mattress bowed beneath his weight. She rolled into his bare thigh, finally forcing her eyes open to stare up at him.

"You look like a Greek goddess, replete after an afternoon of being pleasured by her love slaves."

The back of his hand dusted the length of her arm,

sending shivers down her spine. "Just one love slave," she corrected. "But he's very talented."

"Thanks." One corner of his mouth quirked in a sexy half-grin. "I aim to please. Speaking of which, we need more condoms if we hope to repeat the performance on the floor, or in the tub, or anywhere else. I'm going to run down to the gift shop and see what they have. Don't move, okay?"

She didn't move, but neither did she nod in agreement.

He retrieved his slacks and shirt from the pile on the floor, shrugging into them as he headed for the door. Checking for his wallet, he threw her a wink and wave from the hallway just before the door slammed shut.

Lucy lay there for a minute, letting her mind race and trying to decide what to do. Then she slowly got out of bed and began to dress in the same purple business suit she'd worn for the trip up.

Dragging her suitcase from the closet, she threw her belongings inside in no particular order, her movements becoming more and more hurried the longer she took, afraid Peter would return before she'd completed her task.

If he caught her trying to sneak out, there's no telling how he would react, and she wasn't sure she could explain. She just knew she couldn't stay here a minute longer.

She double-checked the drawers and bathroom counter, then quickly used the automatic checkout on the television set to let the hotel know she was leaving. No sense letting them charge him for nights she wasn't even using.

Peter would be crushed when he came back and found the room empty. She knew that, and yet she couldn't spend the rest of the night with him, no matter how much it might hurt his feelings not to. She couldn't finish out their trip as his lover when there was no hope of ever being more.

As she passed the door that connected their two rooms, she stopped and took a deep breath. Pressing a kiss to her fingertips, she then touched them to the cool panel.

"I'm sorry," she whispered, as though he could hear her and might someday understand her decision and the price she paid in making it.

With tears gathering along the rims of her eyes, she hurried out of the room and down the carpeted hall toward the stairwell exit.

Nine

Peter was whistling as he returned to the room and knocked on the faux wood panel. He had his key card, but it wouldn't work on her door. And as lovely as Lucy had looked when he left, stretched across the bed gloriously naked, he knew she wouldn't mind jumping up to answer his summons. After all, he came bearing gifts…the kind that would allow them to make love at least a dozen more times before morning.

The thought brought a wide smile to his face. He continued whistling and waited.

Maybe she'd fallen asleep. He rapped again and then listened for noises that would mean she was moving around inside.

Okay, so maybe she was really, *really* asleep. No problem. He'd go in through his room, crawl into bed with her, and proceed to wake her with long, wet kisses up and down the line of her bare body. The thought turned him hard and caused the blood to rush heatedly through his veins in anticipation.

Or maybe she was taking a bath. In which case, he'd strip down to his birthday suit and join her in the warm, sudsy water. This hotel had nice, roomy tubs with plenty of erotic potential.

Deciding to leave her to whatever she was doing, he took a few steps to the side and opened his own door, the gift shop bag rattling as he juggled it to get the job done. He crossed the room and went through the connecting door, noticing right away that she was no longer in bed.

She must be in the bathroom, then. He didn't hear the water running, but that only meant she wasn't taking a shower. She had probably run a bath as soon as he'd left and was even now luxuriating beneath a layer of fluffy bubbles.

He dug inside the brown paper sack and pried a single condom out of the box. *Always be prepared.* He recited the Boy Scout motto with silent amusement, clasping the protection in his tightened fist.

When he reached the bathroom, though, the door stood wide open. The lights were off and the room was empty.

Peter frowned, turning his head to search the entire

hotel room, even as he realized the effort was futile. The rooms weren't that big, and it wasn't like she'd be hiding in the closet or under the bed.

Still, just to be sure, he checked both places. Then he stalked over to his room, repeating the process. Lucy was nowhere to be found.

Maybe she'd thought of something she needed and run down to the gift shop herself right after he'd left, and they'd simply missed crossing each other's paths.

Figuring that was the most likely scenario, Peter stuffed the loose condom in his pocket and moved to the mini-bar for a drink. She'd be back any minute now, and he didn't want to be dehydrated for their next bout of mind-blowing, teeth-rattling sex.

God, but Lucy turned him on. It wasn't just her long, luxurious black hair or the red-hot come-and-get-me lipstick she normally wore. Not just her body or the way she moved it, which could tempt a saint to sin. It was so much more than that, even if he couldn't quite put it into words.

She made him feel good—aroused as hell nine times out of ten, but also happy, comfortable, safe, accepted. When she was around, he just felt…better, in every way imaginable.

He looked forward to her arrival at his house each morning and knew she'd have everything under control while she was there. But it was more than just his reliance on her as a personal assistant, more than simply her extreme competence in the workplace.

He could have hired anyone to answer the phone, deal with his correspondence, and charm his associates. Lucy was exceptionally talented at those things, he'd be the first to admit, but he doubted any other employee would plague his thoughts the way she did or make him break his own iron-clad rule about not getting seriously involved.

He was involved, all right. Dammit. And he didn't know quite what to do about it, except to go with the flow until a solution came to mind.

Slugging back the last of his bottled water, he raided the small refrigerator for something a little stronger. This time, he grabbed a gin and mixed it with a splash of tonic in one of the glasses that the hotel provided.

He was on his fourth trip back from the mini-bar, drinking scotch straight from a tiny plastic bottle, when he realized Lucy had been gone for over thirty minutes.

Where the hell was she?

The gift shop had been on the verge of closing when he was down there, so she couldn't still be shopping. He racked his brain, but couldn't think of anywhere else she might have gone, especially without leaving a note.

With a curse, Peter stood, smacking a hand to his forehead. A note. He'd checked the rooms for Lucy, but hadn't thought to look for a note. Duh!

Leaving the half-full bottle of scotch on the night-stand with his growing collection of empties, he went back to her room. The scratch pad on the bedside table was blank, as was the hotel letterhead in the desk drawer, and he didn't see a slip of paper anywhere.

The only other place he could think of where she might have left a note was the bathroom mirror or countertop.

The reflective sliding doors of the closet stood open as he passed and what he saw from the corner of his eye froze him in his tracks.

The closet was empty. He hadn't noticed before, or at least it hadn't registered in his otherwise preoccupied brain, but the closet was completely and utterly empty, except for the bare wooden hangers and plastic dry cleaning bag provided by the hotel. No suitcase, no bright, tailored business suits, no sign of Lucy's presence whatsoever.

A sinking, slimy feeling began to uncoil low in Peter's gut. Bleak, heavy footsteps carried him to the dresser, where he discovered the drawers to be as vacant as the rest of the room.

My God, she was gone. Not just off on an errand, but dressed, packed and checked out.

He sat down heavily on the end of the unmade bed, disbelief washing over him.

Why? Why would she leave when things had been going so well between them? His mind couldn't even begin to wrap itself around the concept.

Where could she have gone? To another hotel? The airport? Back to Georgetown? He wasn't even sure how to find out.

And then he had to wonder if he *wanted* to. She'd taken off just when he thought they were closer than ever, which meant his radar was seriously skewed.

What if he located her, only to have her tell him she never wanted to see him again?

A hard fist squeezed around his heart at the very thought.

He wasn't sure he could handle not having Lucy in his life. Holding her at arm's length, sure. Fantasizing about her but not being able touch her, or being allowed to make love to her and then having to stop…well, it wouldn't be fun, but he could deal with it.

But not having her around, not seeing her on a daily basis, not hearing her sexy, throaty voice and watching the sway of her hips as she walked down the hall…

No. He refused to contemplate such a thing.

Lucy's mindset was a mystery to him. He couldn't possibly know what she was thinking or what had driven her to leave him this way, but he could certainly find out and take steps to rectify the situation.

If that meant promising to put their relationship back on a strictly professional keel, so be it. It might turn him into a hollow shell of a man or send him into the arms of a dozen faceless women for some semblance of meaningless intimacy, but if it kept Lucy around and feeling secure, then he would do it. Happily, regardless of his own personal suffering.

Taking a deep breath, he got to his feet, then blew the air out through his nose. Fine. She'd sneaked out five minutes after making love with him, so it was obvious she wanted to be alone. He'd let her. He'd finish up his business here in New York with William Dawson, which should only take another day or so, then he'd head back to Georgetown and see how Lucy acted toward him. Try to feel her out about how she wanted their relationship to progress from there.

That would give them both a little time to cool down and think things over. Then maybe they could decide together what to do. Lord knew he'd bungled the situation enough on his own.

The wheels of Lucy's suitcase rolled over the toe of her shoe as she came to a stop in front of her apartment door and she swore in pain. She was tired and stiff from the sudden trip home, and on the way to being depressed about her decision to leave Peter alone at the hotel.

But it was for the best…or so she kept telling herself.

Fishing the keys out of her purse, she unlocked the door and let herself in, careful to guard the entrance in case Cocoa got it into her head to slip out. The last thing she needed was to spend the night searching the corridors of the building for her runaway cat.

She flipped on the kitchen light and was surprised to find Cocoa nowhere in sight. Usually the kitty met her at the door and couldn't wait to be scratched behind the ears or given a quick snack.

Lord, she hoped Ethan hadn't dropped the ball and let her cat either escape or starve to death.

But Cocoa's food dish sat in the middle of the table, looking freshly licked clean. And the water bowl in the corner was full.

With a frown, she started tiptoeing through the apartment, looking for signs of life. And as she rounded the corner into the living area, she had to bite down on a chuckle to keep from waking both the man and feline asleep on her couch.

Cocoa lay perched on Ethan's gently rising and falling chest while Ethan's hand rested over the calico's mottled back. An infomercial playing on the television in the background, casting blue and yellow shadows over the two forms.

Sensing her presence, Ethan slowly came awake, blinking to bring her into focus. "Hey," he almost croaked. "I didn't expect you back so soon."

"Obviously." She grinned and moved closer to give Cocoa a pat.

"Where's Peter?" he asked, glancing around as though he expected his friend to suddenly appear behind Lucy.

At the mention of Peter's name, her lips thinned. "He's still in New York," she told him, averting her gaze and taking several steps away.

Ethan sat up, careful not to jar the sleeping cat unnecessarily. Unperturbed, Cocoa jumped from Ethan's stomach to the couch cushion, then stopped to yawn and stretch before curling up and going back to her nap.

Getting to his feet, Ethan brushed the stray fur from his shirt front before turning his attention back to her. "Did something happen between the two of you?"

She lifted her head, meeting his eyes once again. His insight stunned her, but then, he was Peter's best friend, so maybe she shouldn't be surprised by how well they knew each other.

"You could say that."

He stuck a thumb into the waistband of his jeans, cocking his hip to the side. "Was it good or bad?"

"First it was good," she said, remembering their lovemaking as not just "good" but spectacular. "And then it was bad."

"I take it Peter did or said something to upset you."

Lucy sighed, rubbing the spot between her brows where a headache was forming. "Actually, he didn't. I just…"

Her throat closed with emotion and she turned away to get hold of herself. Crossing the kitchen, she pulled a container of orange juice from the fridge and poured a glass. She offered to do the same for Ethan, but he shook his head.

"I love him," she admitted, the words going down better with a sip of juice.

A beat of silence passed and then he said simply, "I know."

She glanced up at him, standing on the other side of the kitchen table, jaw slack in astonishment.

"Come on, Lucy, I've seen the two of you together.

I didn't notice anything at first, but lately… Lately, it's become more obvious," he finished.

A flush of heat crept over her features as she realized she hadn't hidden her feelings for Peter all this time as well as she'd thought.

"Don't worry," he told her, practically reading her mind. "I don't think anyone else has noticed, least of all Peter the Oblivious."

Wetting her lips, she turned and made a production of putting her empty glass in the sink and returning the orange juice to the refrigerator. "So the fact that he feels nothing for me is also…obvious."

"I don't know about that."

Ethan came up behind her, placing his hands on her shoulders and giving them a light squeeze.

"Like I said, Peter tends to be oblivious. I think he feels plenty for you, he just won't admit it, even to himself."

She didn't know how to respond to that or where to begin with the questions clamoring in her brain.

"You could still go out with me," he suggested, blowing in her ear. "I've been asking you out for months. So maybe now you'll cut Peter loose and give me a shot."

She spun around, spearing him with an annoyed glance. "You would do that? To your best friend?"

"For a pretty woman?" He gave a snort. "Hell, yes."

"Let me clear this up for you once and for all," she snapped, physically removing his hands from where they rested on her upper arms. "Not on your life. Not even if you were the last man on earth. *Especially* if you were the last man on earth because I would never want to take the chance of letting you breed and spread your reprehensible DNA on to another human being."

Stalking across the tiled kitchen, she put her hand on the doorknob before turning back to him with a scowl on her face. "I think you should leave."

Ethan held his hands up in surrender. "Whoa, there, take it easy. I was testing you." He moved back to the table, straddling one of the spindle-back chairs as he held her gaze. "You gave exactly the right answer, by the way. And I may talk tough, but for your information, I *wouldn't* move in on a friend's girl. At least not one he's genuinely interested in."

Some of the fire went out of her at his admission and she dragged herself over to take the chair opposite him, feeling even more tired and weary than when she'd arrived.

"You say that like you believe it. I just wish I could."

"I don't think Peter does, either. Or he's afraid to. And going out with me would be one sure way of finding out…either he'd let it go and you'd know for certain he had no feelings for you, or he'd go through the roof and you'd know he does."

He gave her a hopeful look, which Lucy now recognized as simply teasing.

"There is one other option," he offered. "Come to work for me at The Hot Spot."

She raised a brow at the unexpected proposal.

"I know I've tried to lure you away from Peter before—only partly in jest, since I'm jealous as hell that he gets such a great assistant and I'm stuck running my business myself. But maybe now is the time to make a change. Get away from him for a while. Give him some time and space to think about what he's lost and how he really feels about you. You can always go back later; you know I won't hold you to anything, and Peter would be stupid not to give you your old job back if you wanted it."

"Do you really think I should?"

"I do. Peter and I have been friends for a lot of years. I know how his mind works and how hard it's going to be for you to face him while things are still up in the air between you. Consider my club part-time work while you figure things out."

The minutes ticked by while she considered his offer from every angle. In the end, though, it came down to only a single point: she didn't think she could bear to see Peter bright and early Monday morning with her heart still raw and bleeding, so soon after leaving him alone in that hotel room.

Taking a deep breath, she looked at Ethan—her new boss, if only for a while—and nodded.

Ten

Well, those had been two of the longest, most excruciating days of his life.

Normally he loved delving into a computer system, finding all its bugs and quirks, and then putting it back together to run even more efficiently. But this time, every moment had felt like an eternity. Every word Will Dawson had uttered, every joke he'd tried to crack to lighten Peter's mood had grated on his nerves.

He'd done the bare minimum to improve Dawson's productivity and then promised to return at a later date to smooth out the edges so he could jump on a plane and head back to Georgetown.

It was two in the afternoon by the time he arrived,

but that was okay because it meant Lucy would be at his house, working, and he would get the chance to talk things through with her instead of waiting another day to hash out their differences.

When he reached his town house, he used his key to unlock the front door and dropped his overnight bag just inside on the foyer floor. Cocking his head, he listened for the telltale sounds of Lucy's fingers at the keyboard of her computer or the soft classical music radio station she sometimes turned on while she worked.

He didn't hear anything, but that didn't mean she wasn't there.

A thread of doubt niggled as he closed the door and noticed the pile of mail spread across the carpet. Strange that Lucy hadn't gathered it up already. She usually did, first thing. But maybe she'd forgotten or gotten busy doing something else.

Yeah, a tiny voice in his head replied sarcastically, *forgot to pick up the mail when she'd done it automatically every day for the past two years.*

But he wasn't giving up yet. Moving through the house, he checked the study that doubled as her office and pretended not to notice that her computer was turned off and the call light on the telephone was blinking uncontrollably.

So she hadn't had a chance to boot up or collect messages yet. That didn't mean anything. There were plenty of days when she went to the kitchen to start a pot of coffee or up to his office to clean up a bit before getting started.

From there, he peeked his head into the den, the kitchen, then climbed the stairs for a quick sweep of his own office and bedroom. Not that he expected to find her in either place.

His heart sank and his mouth grew dry as he realized she wasn't there. From the mail on the hall floor and the number of calls stored up on the phone, it didn't look like she'd been to work at all since returning from New York.

The knowledge worried Peter more than a little, but he tried not to panic. She was probably still upset by whatever had driven her to run out on him after they'd made love and just needed a day or two more to get herself together enough to face him.

Or maybe she was waiting for him to contact her and say he was sorry. He was as clueless about what he needed to apologize for as he was about why she'd abandoned him in Manhattan in the first place, but if there was one thing he knew for sure about women, it was that the man was always wrong, the woman was always right, and it was the man's place to say he was sorry before things got too far out of hand.

That, he could do. Because a part of him was sorry…for whatever had spurred her to take off on him. For not having the self-control to keep from making love to her the first time *and* the second, when he knew nothing could come of it. And for not being the man she wanted him to be, one who could provide her with the future she so desperately needed.

Scrubbing a hand over his face, he ran back downstairs for his luggage, and decided to put the new mail on her desk along the way.

As long as he was there, he might as well check the waiting messages, too. With any luck, Lucy might have called and he would have an idea of what was on her mind. If not, he'd have helped her out a bit and not left quite so much for her to catch up on once she finally returned to work.

He sat down at her desk and grabbed a notepad and pen, then punched the buttons necessary to access voicemail. Business call, business call, phone company calling about Lucy's request to add another line to the house, business call… He wrote everything down, thinking he could probably take care of a few of these on his own, but would leave the important ones for Lucy.

Then her voice drifted out to him through the speakerphone and a hitch of awareness rolled over him, sending his pulse rate stuttering. She sounded stiff and unhappy, but he chalked that up to the mechanics of the electronic technology.

And then her words began to sink in. She hadn't phoned to explain why she'd left New York without him or to ask for a couple days off while she got her thoughts and feelings in order. She was blowing him off.

Peter, this is Lucy. I'm just calling to let you know

*that I've accepted another position and won't be back
to work. I'll be by within the next couple of weeks to
collect my things, unless you'd rather send them to me.
I'm sorry I couldn't give you more notice, but my new
job begins immediately. I'm sure you'll find someone
to take my place in no time.*

He sat, stunned, for several long minutes while the
rest of the messages played through unheard. Her words
echoed over and over again in his ears, making him feel
light-headed and more confused than ever.

Why? Why would she take another job? Nothing
that had happened between them was so awful that she
needed to *quit.*

And *take her place?*

How was he ever supposed to find someone to re-
place her? Someone competent, reliable, and willing
enough to do all the things he needed taken care of on
a daily basis. It had been miraculous enough to find
Lucy to begin with, he couldn't even begin to be lucky
enough to find a second decent assistant.

But was that really the part that was bothering him
so much? The fact that he was losing his favorite secretary?

Hell, no. He was on the verge of a breakdown because this was *Lucy* and she'd just left him. Left his em-
ploy, left his house, left *him.*

He wasn't going to get the chance to find out why
she'd sneaked out while he was off buying condoms.

He wouldn't be able to apologize for whatever had upset her and promise to make things right.

It seemed Lucy wasn't interested in repairing their relationship—not even their professional one.

The hollow sensation at the base of his gut began to fill…but not with acceptance, with anger.

She didn't want anything more to do with him? Fine. He didn't want anything more to do with her, either.

His feelings for her had been nothing more than lust, anyway. And maybe a fraction of dependence, for the way she took such good care of everything for him.

But all that was over now. She'd quit, taken another job. From now on, she wouldn't be around for him to fantasize about or desire or rely on.

A part of him wanted to mourn that fact, but then the logical side of his brain kicked in and reminded him that this was probably all for the best. Just because they'd spent a few very memorable moments in each other's company didn't mean they had a future together. He'd known that all along and had never wanted Lucy to be hurt. So maybe having her leave now was better than having to push her away later.

It sounded good, and in a few days, Peter thought he might even start to believe it.

"Set 'em up again."

"Are you sure?" Ethan asked. "You've already had quite a bit."

Peter scowled at his so-called friend and tapped the

bar in front of him where three empty shot glasses and three empty beer bottles sat. "Don't lecture me on the evils of alcohol, just keep them coming."

Ethan held his tongue, pouring another finger of whiskey with a beer chaser, just as Peter had ordered when he'd first walked into The Hot Spot.

At this time of day, the club was officially closed, but Ethan and some of the other staff came in early to set up and check supplies for the evening crush. A Top Forty ballad played softly in the background, but by eight o'clock tonight, the speakers would be blaring with rock, disco, rap…whatever the party crowd liked best.

The idea of people drinking, dancing, having fun made Peter scowl even harder. He was miserable and the rest of the world should be, too, dammit!

"So…" Ethan ventured while Peter nursed his beer, "are you going to tell me what's bothering you, or do I have to wait until you drink me out of all my profits?"

He thought about making a smart remark, telling Ethan to mind his own business, but he'd come here with the sole intention of getting a little advice from his best friend. Or at the very least, spilling his guts and hoping the sour taste in his mouth would finally go away.

"Lucy," he said simply, noticing the way her name caught in his throat. He had to swallow hard before he could even take another sip of his beer.

"What about her?" his friend asked, filling a segmented tray with bits of fruit and olives for mixed drinks.

"She left me."

"For another job, you mean?"

A beat passed before he answered. "Yeah." Among other things. "She quit and went to work for somebody else."

"Lucky bastard. She's a real treasure, that one. So what did you do to run her off?"

At that, Peter's brows lifted, then turned down in annoyance. "What makes you think I ran her off?"

"For one thing, you slept with her. And I know you, buddy. You're not big on commitment. The women you date and take to bed may all look different—tall, short; stacked, petite; blonde, brunette, redhead—but they have one thing in common: they're easy to pry yourself away from. You don't promise them anything more than a couple of good rolls in the hay and maybe a photo op or two when you take them along to social events, and they don't expect it."

"What's your point?" Peter asked, wondering why he stayed friends with this guy when he was turning into such a colossal pain in the ass.

"My point, Mr. Grumpy Pants, is that Lucy isn't like those other women, and you damn well know it. You knew it before the two of you ever got stuck in that elevator together. She's not the kind of girl you can just have sex with and then not call in the morning. The kind who's good for a thrill, but who won't expect more.

Lucy isn't clingy or demanding, but she's also not looking for a fling."

With a huff of frustration, Ethan slammed down a jar of maraschino cherries, then braced his hands on the edge of the bar. "Holy heck, Peter, when did you get so damn dense? She's in love with you, for God's sake. Probably has been since the day she started working for you."

Peter felt as though his friend had just dropped a ton of bricks on his head. He couldn't have been more stunned if Lucy had materialized at that very moment in a G-string and pasties and started dancing on the countertop for dollar bills.

"What are you talking about? Lucy doesn't have those sorts of feelings for me. She's a great gal, don't get me wrong, but her problem with our sleeping together wasn't that she was in love with me, it's that I was also her boss. The conflict of interest made her uncomfortable."

Ethan rolled his eyes and muttered some truly creative curses beneath his breath. "'Great gal,'" he repeated. "'Conflict of interest.' Man, I'm surprised you can dress yourself in the morning. Did all that booze I served you kill off your last functioning brain cells?"

He leaned across the bar, so close Peter's eyes nearly crossed trying to keep him in focus.

"Haven't you ever noticed the way she looks at you? Or the way she cleans your house and takes care of you?"

His head ached and his memory was becoming suddenly fuzzy. "She doesn't look at me any differently than she does anyone else. And as for cleaning up…that's part of her job."

"Blind as well as dumb," Ethan mumbled with a toss of his head. "She looks at you like the stars in the night sky were your idea, Peter. She's certainly never looked at me that way. She also thinks you're the smartest, most talented man ever to design a computer game. Now, granted, you're good at what you do, but to hear Lucy tell it, you might as well be Bill Gates, Mahatma Gandhi, and the president of the United States all rolled into one.

Ethan pulled the towel from his shoulder and wiped cherry juice off the bar. "And she cleans up after you and makes sure you have everything you need or want because she *cares* about you, not because she thinks she's being a good little assistant. She's *in love* with you, you big blockhead."

Peter's chest tightened. His heart was pounding a thousand beats per second and his lungs refused to draw in oxygen. Ethan was wrong. He had to be.

Peter had met women like that before, diamond rings dancing in their eyes. He identified the look immediately and always managed to keep them at bay.

If Lucy had harbored feelings for him all this time, he would have noticed. His force fields would have gone up, and he damn sure wouldn't have let himself get involved with her, no matter how badly he might have wanted to sample her luscious body.

"No," he said, shaking his head in acute denial. "No, I think you're wrong."

He knew Lucy wanted the big picture from whatever man she eventually ended up with, but he hadn't gone so far as to assume *love* was involved.

"Oh, yeah?" Ethan seemed amused now. He pushed away from the bar and leaned back against the low shelf of colorful liquor bottles. "Maybe this will get through to you, then. I'm Lucy's new boss. She came home from New York alone and upset, and I offered her a job here because she said she couldn't stand the thought of working with you every day for the rest of her life. She's upstairs right now, in the office."

"What?" Peter leapt to his feet, the bar stool teetering at the speed with which he left it.

Ethan took a menacing step forward. "Don't even think about it," he warned in a low voice. "She doesn't want to see you, and I promised her I wouldn't tell you she was here, so if you move so much as an inch in that direction, I'll have to ask Archie to take you out back and pummel you a while."

Archie was Ethan's head bouncer, built like an eighteen-wheeler, and Peter searched for a glimpse of him as he turned his attention to the glass-fronted office on the second floor of the nightclub. He didn't see any signs of Lucy because the blinds were drawn, but the urge to climb the curved staircase at the back of the room and find her was strong.

Ethan came out from behind the bar and laid a hand

on Peter's shoulder. "You've screwed this up royally, buddy, and I'm not real sure it can be fixed. But before you do anything, you need to go home and sleep off your little drinking binge. I already called a cab. When you wake up, take a long, hard look at this thing and how you feel about Lucy, then maybe you can talk to her."

Feeling like he was walking through a thick fog, Peter nodded. His friend's words didn't make complete sense at this very moment, but he knew Ethan was looking out for his best interests. Even if he had hired Lucy behind his back, he wouldn't give Peter bad advice. They'd been friends too long for that.

With a nod, he let Ethan lead him outside and put him in a bright yellow taxi.

"Get some rest," Ethan told him in an understanding tone. "We'll talk later, and I'll take good care of Lucy until you decide what you're going to do."

Even as exhaustion swept him and his eyes fell closed, Peter realized that's exactly what he was afraid of—someone else taking care of Lucy because he was too screwed up to do it himself.

Lucy peered through a slit in the vertical window blinds of Ethan's office, careful not to let Peter see her. She suspected Ethan had already told him she was up here, otherwise he wouldn't have been staring so intently in her direction. But he didn't start forward, didn't storm up the stairs to confront her about quitting her job with so little advance warning. If he had, she'd have probably gone running, escaping through the emergency fire exit at her back.

Instead, Ethan laid an arm across Peter's shoulders and steered him toward the entrance of the club, presumably to send him home. She hoped Ethan had called him a cab, considering the amount of alcohol Peter had consumed since arriving only a few short hours ago.

A frown marred her brow as she considered that. Peter wasn't a big drinker. He might have a glass of wine with dinner or the occasional scotch and soda at the end of the day, but other than that, his main vice seemed to be gallons upon gallons of sugary-sweet cola. Today, she hadn't seen him order so much as a ginger ale.

That bothered her, probably more than it should have. She didn't work for Peter any longer, which meant his eating and drinking habits were none of her concern.

But she still loved him, despite her best efforts to lock him out of her heart, so she supposed it was only natural to wonder about him and worry that he wasn't taking good enough care of himself.

Ethan came back inside alone and headed directly for the polished onyx stairs that led to his office. Lucy let the blinds fall from her hands and darted back to the desk, managing to take a seat and look busy just as the door opened.

She glanced up and smiled, pretending she'd been working on his books all along. "Hi."

He didn't return her greeting. "Peter just left," he reported flatly.

Her eyes widened as she feigned a sense of startlement. "He was here?"

One corner of his mouth curved in mock amusement. "Peter may have been too drunk to notice you peeking through the blinds, but I sure wasn't." He shook his head. "You two are really something. Both so desperate to pretend you don't feel anything for the other that you're sort of missing the point."

Lucy bristled slightly at his chastising tone. He'd been so supportive up until now, she'd hate for him to suddenly turn critical of her feelings for his friend. "What point would that be?"

"That you love each other. You should be together, celebrating that love, not working this hard to come up with ways to hide it."

"And you're such an expert on the subject?" She made it a question because she knew all about Ethan's reputation as a ladies' man and his track record with women.

"No. That's just it. I haven't had much luck in the romance department myself, but it's always easier to see the truth of a situation when you're not personally involved. And it's pretty darn clear from where I'm standing that you and Peter feel the same about each other, you're just too damn stubborn to admit it or take a chance on being shot down."

Her eyes welled with sudden tears at Ethan's words. Was he right? Was she being a coward? If she walked up to Peter and told him exactly how she felt, would he surprise her by admitting he loved her, too?

Her gut told her no, that he would stick to his long-held beliefs that he couldn't open himself to a relationship and still be a successful entrepreneur. But a tiny voice in her head asked *what if?*

What if she was wrong?

What if he did feel something for her?

What if she held her tongue out of fear when all it would take was one well-placed question to possibly make all her dreams come true?

But was she brave enough to risk it? She didn't know. Ethan had given her something to think about, though, and she promised herself that she would.

Blinking to disperse the dampness fringing her lashes, she inclined her head to let him know she heard what he was saying.

"Do you know why Peter won't let himself get involved?" she asked, wondering if they were close enough for Peter to have shared his past with his friend.

"Yeah, I know," Ethan said with a derisive curl of his lip. "And if you ask me, he doesn't give himself enough credit. But I have a feeling that when he finally stops worrying about turning into his father, he'll discover he's not half bad at juggling his software company and a family."

Lucy swallowed hard, trying to dislodge the lump in her throat. "I've always thought the same thing."

"So tell him," Ethan said simply. "And then make him believe it."

Eleven

Three days. Three days without Lucy and he had yet to sleep, eat, or change his clothes. He hadn't showered or shaved, and had barely touched the case of soda she always made sure to keep in the refrigerator for him.

As soon as he'd gotten home from The Hot Spot, instead of taking Ethan's advice and sleeping it off, he'd stripped down to his boxers and undershirt and gone straight to work on a new computer program.

He'd worked for hours, days, but nothing seemed to go the way it was supposed to. Ideas were slower to come, codes harder to write, and solutions more difficult to find. His mind kept wandering—always to Lucy and how much he missed her. To what might have been.

Without her here, his house was a just a big, empty building, with cold walls and even colder rooms. The entire place was dark because she wasn't around to flip on the lights.

The phone rang, but he didn't pick up. There was no one in the world he wanted to talk to right now except Lucy, and he doubted she would be calling anytime soon.

Ethan had told him he needed to think things over, decide what he really wanted. Since then, all he'd done was *think,* but he still didn't know what to do.

He knew what he wanted, but only in general terms: Lucy. He wanted her to come back to work, be in his life—and his bed—again. But he was smart enough to realize that as far as going back to the way things were, that ship had sailed. He couldn't go to her and say, *Hey, how about being my lover and my assistant again, but without all that pesky emotional baggage?* He suspected that would go over about as well as a Yankee fan at a Red Sox home game.

And to be honest, he wasn't positive that's what he wanted any longer, either. He still didn't think it was a good idea to mix business with pleasure.

His father had been an abysmal failure when he'd tried to handle the jobs of both father and businessman, but Peter was beginning to wonder if trying and possibly failing in the long run still wasn't a better alternative than never trying at all. Especially if it meant the difference between having Lucy in his life or not having Lucy in his life.

Because *not* having her was becoming unbearable.

He pictured his life ten years from now, without Lucy being a part of it, and all he saw was darkness, sadness, misery.

Oh, he might be sinfully rich and famous for his games and software designs, but most likely he would also be a lonely hermit.

His assistants would be pimply-faced college interns from the local university who didn't stick around long enough for him to learn their names.

Women would flirt with him at social events or drop by with baked goods to try to lure him out, but none of them would be as attractive or interesting as Lucy. And he already knew with complete conviction that no other woman would ever touch him the way she had, emotionally or physically.

So what are you going to do about it, smart guy? a voice in his head whispered none too subtly.

Good question. He didn't have an answer just yet, but since it didn't look like he'd be going to bed anytime soon, he certainly had time to figure it out.

Lucy stood on the stoop outside Peter's front door, breathing deeply, concentrating on not hyperventilating. She didn't want to be here, had half hoped he would ship the last of her things so she would never have to see him again.

No, that wasn't quite true. She wished on a daily

basis that she could see him…not to mention touch him, smell him, hear his low, rumbling voice.

God, she missed him, and they hadn't even been apart a week yet.

Her stomach took a tumble and she locked her teeth together to keep from throwing up. Lord, she was nervous. She'd come to collect her things, but only if Plan A didn't work out.

Ethan's way was Plan A because she hadn't been able to get his comments out of her head since he'd told her to go down fighting, instead of feeling sorry for herself and giving up like she had when she'd flown home from New York.

So here she was, preparing to confront Peter and lay all her cards out on the table, regardless of how he might react. Her heart would shatter like glass if he rejected her or told her again that he couldn't get seriously involved because it might influence his work. But she was willing to risk it on the off chance that Ethan was right. Even if the odds were a zillion to one, she had to know for sure.

Swallowing the knot of dread lodged in her throat, she lifted her hand and rang the doorbell. She still had a key, but didn't feel right using it when she no longer worked for him.

She waited for Peter to answer the door and braced herself for the sight of him, but he never came. Seconds ticked by and she pressed the bell again.

This time, she heard the thump of footsteps on the staircase and mumbled curses. The door swung open before she was fully prepared, stealing the air from her lungs.

Peter stood on the other side of the threshold, fully dressed in a light blue suit and pale yellow tie. His shoes were polished to a high shine, his hair neatly combed. It was enough to stun her into speechlessness.

"Lucy."

Her name burst from his lips in a rush, breathless from more than just the race downstairs, she suspected.

"Peter. I, um…came for my things."

Coward! she chastised herself. *Wimp. You weren't going to say that.*

But he took a step back, motioning her inside. "Come in. I'm glad to see you," he said as he closed the door behind them. "I was actually planning to come by The Hot Spot soon to talk to you. I guess you've saved me the trouble."

She gave a weak smile, not sure how to respond to that. She suppose she should be grateful she'd decided to come over, somewhat prepared, before he could catch her off guard at the club.

At the look on her face, he stumbled. "Jeez, I didn't mean it that way. Going to see you wouldn't have been an inconvenience at all. I just meant…we must be on the same wavelength for you to show up here at about the same time I was getting ready to come see you."

Her grin grew a little then, becoming more sincere as he rushed to correct himself and reassure her. This was the Peter she knew, always aware and courteous of her feelings. The suit had thrown her off at first, but the hair, the eyes, the lips, the shape of his well-shaven, chiseled face were all familiar and dear to her heart.

She curled her fingers into her palm, resisting the urge to reach up and smooth a stray lock away from his forehead.

"Your things are all where you left them," he said, walking backwards ahead of her as he gestured toward the den. A slight blush tinged his cheeks. "I was sort of hoping you'd come back to work so I wouldn't have to gather them up at all."

She held his gaze for a split second, then looked away, studying the oriental design on the red and beige runner that covered the hardwood floor.

"Actually," she ventured, steeling her spine and forcing her chin up, "I didn't come only to collect my belongings. I also wanted to talk. About us."

She saw his chest hitch as he sucked in a breath, and her hopes flagged. Oh, God, this wasn't going well at all. He hadn't changed his mind. He didn't want her back—at least not as anything more than his assistant. Her pulse pounded in her ears and she wanted to turn and run, except her feet wouldn't seem to move.

And then Peter reached out and wrapped his warm, strong fingers around her wrist, sending a shock of electricity skittering along her nerve endings.

"Wait here," he told her. "I'll be right back."

Part of her wondered why she was just standing

there, rooted to the spot. She should leave, or at least begin clearing her desk.

But Peter bounded up the stairs, returning less than a minute later carrying his brown leather briefcase. He grabbed her hand on the way past and dragged her into the study.

"Sit," he ordered, taking the chair beside her desk and setting the briefcase down on top to open.

Lucy bristled slightly at his perfunctory tone and she locked her knees rather than doing as he'd instructed.

"I don't need to sit," she said, finding a bit of her courage in the annoyance he'd stirred up. Funny how she could still love him and be ready to spill her guts about it even after he'd rubbed her the wrong way. "But there is something I need to say to you."

He raised his head, green eyes washing over her like a cool breeze over a meadow. A muscle ticked in his jaw. "I need to say something to you, too," he said softly, though his voice was strained.

He probably wanted to beg her to come back to work, but she couldn't do that, given the way things stood at the moment.

"Please," she murmured. "Let me go first." She had to get this out before she exploded, and hearing Peter ask her to resume her position as his assistant would only weaken her resolve.

The sinews of his neck contracted and released as he swallowed, but he inclined his head for her to continue. Inhaling deeply, she tried to get her thoughts in order and figure out where to begin. She took a seat, finally, before her legs gave out and she ended up on the floor.

"I'm sorry about running off that night at the hotel," she admitted. "I didn't mean to worry or upset you, but I just couldn't handle what was happening between us and had to get out of there."

She laid her hand atop his where it rested on the edge of the briefcase. The heat from his skin soaked through to her bones, comforting her more than she'd expected.

"The fact is, Peter, I have feelings for you. You've probably figured that out already," she added with a touch of a smile, "but what you don't know is that I've felt this way for the past two years, ever since I started working for you."

Panic raced through Peter's veins, causing his eyes to go wide and fear to clog his windpipe. "Wait, wait, wait!" he all but shouted. "Don't say anything else."

He leapt to his feet, shaking his head and digging frantically through the papers in his briefcase. She was about to say she loved him, he could sense it. And while he wanted to hear those three little words from her mouth almost more than he wanted to draw his next breath, *he* needed to be the one to say them first. He'd fought this for so long, put her through so much, he wanted her to know how he felt about her before she said any more.

Finding what he was searching for, he dropped back onto the seat of his chair and turned to face Lucy once again. She looked startled and confused by his sudden outburst, and he didn't blame her one bit.

Pulling his chair a few inches closer, he braced his knees on either side of her closed legs, lifting her hands from her lap and cradling them in his own. The paper rattled in his tight hold, but he ignored it.

"I'm the one who should be apologizing to you, Lucy," he said solemnly. "You're so good to me…you always have been. And as hard as it may be for you to believe, you've meant more to me from the very beginning, too. You're a great assistant, and I'd do just about anything to have you back on the payroll, but there's something I want from you even more than your exceptional secretarial skills."

He brushed long strands of ebony hair over her shoulder, caressing her cool cheek with his fingertips on the return trip. "I want you to be with me, Lucy. Stay with me, live with me, marry me…love me."

A flood of emotions flashed across her face, not the least of which were incredulity and wariness. Fear squeezed him low in the solar plexus. He'd known this wouldn't be easy, known she would doubt him after all his talk about never tying himself to a wife and family, never letting his personal life interfere with his business plans.

"Hear me out. Please," he said, his hand clutching hers even more tightly. "When I got back to the hotel room and found you gone, I didn't know what to do or think or feel. I'd gotten it into my head that everything was great. We could be lovers without strings, have a good time together without it ever meaning anything more. But when I realized you'd left and weren't coming back, I was faced with the fact that you *needed* more."

He lowered his gaze for a brief second, still somewhat unsure of the narrow path he was traversing. "It was one of those life-altering moments," he admitted. "I knew I had to make some serious decisions or risk losing you forever. I don't want to lose you, Luce. I love you."

The admission passed his lips quickly, and then he realized they hadn't been as difficult or as painful to utter as he'd anticipated.

"I love you," he said again, louder this time, with more conviction, even as he watched her mouth turn down with skepticism.

"I know that has to be hard for you to believe, given everything I've said in the past, but I swear on my life and the future of Reyware that it's the absolute truth. You're a part of me, Lucy, permeating every cell of my being.

"I love your hair and your eyes and the full swell of your bottom lip. I love the way you laugh and smile and take such good care of me. I love that you know what I'm thinking almost before I know myself and are as familiar with the inner workings of Reyware and Games of PRey as I am."

Licking his dry lips, he went on, willing her to trust him. "You're my inspiration, Lucy. When I got home from New York, I told myself you had been just a fling, that I could always find another assistant and certainly other lovers, and I tried to get back to work."

He chuckled shortly. "I might as well have been building a space shuttle in my basement. I couldn't think, couldn't concentrate, couldn't remember codes I'd learned as a teenager. Without you here, in my life, I'm helpless. Hopeless."

She opened her mouth to speak, but he stopped her with an index finger pressed to her lips. He was afraid she would shoot him down before he'd told her every-thing he needed her to hear.

"No, don't say anything. Not yet. I know I'm mak-ing it sound like I want you back just so I can work again, but that's not true. Don't you see? *You're* what makes my world go 'round. You're the one person who makes me want to get out of bed each morning to face the day…to see you and be with you. But actions speak louder than words, so I have a proposition for you."

Peter sat up straighter, smoothing the paper he'd been clutching and shoving it into her hands.

Lucy's fingers closed around the page automatically, but her head was swimming, her eyesight blurry with unshed tears. She wanted so badly for Peter to mean what he was saying, wanted so badly to believe he ac-tually loved her even a fraction as much as she loved him. But he'd been so determined to distance himself, keep himself separate from any woman who might re-quire a commitment, that she was afraid he was only saying what he thought she wanted to hear.

"I want you to come back to work for me," he continued before she could begin to make sense of things. "Whatever Ethan is paying you, I'll double it. Whatever perks he's giving you, I'll beat them. And this…" He tapped the paper she was holding. "I'm making you a full partner in the company. We'll share everything, fifty-fifty—the designs, the profits, the decision-making process, everything. There's only one catch."

His voice dropped to a near hush and he pushed his chair back, falling to one knee in front of her. His palm cupped the curve of her knee while the other covered the hand that held the business agreement. His gaze locked with hers, the sincerity in his dark eyes turning her resolve to mush, even as her vision swam and she had trouble making out the details of his beautiful face.

"Marry me, Lucy. Put me out of this misery of being without you. Give me a chance to show you that I can be a good husband and father and still keep my company above water."

His lips tipped up with wry humor. "I know I said it couldn't be done, but I'm willing to give it a shot. And even if I fail, even if Reyware goes under and we end up living in a cardboard box down by the river, I'd rather be in that cardboard box with you than in the most lavish mansion in the world without you."

She swallowed hard, struggling to regain her voice as her heart pounded furiously enough to burst from her chest. Twin streaks of dampness trailed down her cheeks and she blinked several times to bring Peter back into focus.

"I don't care about the money or the company. I never did," she told him quietly, tracing smooth line of his jaw and running her thumb around the alluring shape of his mouth.

"I didn't come here today just to collect my things, either. I came because Ethan warned me that if I didn't lay myself on the line and let you know how much I love you, and give you the chance to share your feelings in return, that I'd regret it for the rest of my life.

"But you do love me," she whispered, still awed by his confession and the depth of her own reciprocal feelings. "And I love you, too. So much. But, Peter, are you sure? You were so dead-set against all of this…are you sure you're really ready to get married and start a family?"

"I am totally ready," he swore with conviction. "I want to be with you for the rest of my life, Lucy Grainger. I want to watch you walk down the aisle and slip a ring on your finger that marks you as mine for all time. I want to have babies with you. I'm especially looking forward to the 'making babies' part," he said with a Groucho-like wiggle of his arched brows that made her laugh.

"I want to do my very best to be the father I never had, to be the best damn father this country has ever seen. But I'll admit, I may need your help. I need you to keep me on track, Lucy. Tell me when I'm working too hard or missing out on precious time with you or our kids. Smack me around, if you need to, but know that you come first and I really do want to make this work."

She leaned closer, until their noses almost touched. "Then we will," she told him. "We'll make it work."

And then she ran her fingers through his hair, messing up the neat style he'd probably struggled half the morning to achieve. "Just think. If I hadn't come here today, I might never have known you felt this way."

"Oh, you'd have known. Ethan told me pretty much the same thing he told you—that I needed to figure out what I wanted before it was too late. And once I knew, I'd have tracked you down to the ends of the earth to tell you what you mean to me."

Fresh tears flooded her eyes again as his words seeped through her, filling every nook and cranny of her spirit with pure contentment.

"Thank God for Ethan," she confided. "Your friend is a very smart man."

"Tell me about it," Peter said on a heartfelt sigh, drawing her down to the floor with him and into his arms. "Because *his* friend hasn't been acting very bright lately."

"Oh, I don't know." She toyed with the fringe of hair at the nape of his neck, pressing a firm kiss to his warm lips. "It seems like you came to your senses in time."

"Just in the nick of time. I don't know what I'd have

done if my stubbornness and stupidity had caused me to lose you."

"You'll never need to find out," she promised. "Now that I've got you, I'm not letting you go."

"Does that mean you'll marry me? You never did answer me before."

"Of course I will. It's all I've ever wanted."

A grin as wide as the Potomac split his face. "Me, too, although it took me a while longer to figure it out. Good thing you're a patient woman."

"Very patient."

He was loath to let go of her, now that he had her wrapped safely in the circle of his arms again, but there was one last thing he needed to do. Pulling back a little, he reached into the pocket of his suit jacket and removed a small, black velvet box. "This is for you."

He tipped open the lid and held it out to her, absorbing the look of startlement and happiness that filled her eyes as she took in the huge, marquis-cut diamond and fancy gold setting. Once he'd realized how much he loved her and decided to propose, he'd gone all out, buying the biggest, shiniest, most expensive engagement ring he thought she would accept without a fuss.

"Oh, my lord," she breathed. "It's beautiful."

Taking the ring from its satin bed, he set the box aside and slipped the band on her finger. She admired it for several moments, turning her hand this way and that so the diamond could catch the light from the window at her back. And then she turned that blazingly joyful expression on him, zapping him right down to his toes.

"What do you think?" she asked. "Should we go show Ethan and let him know his advice worked?"

Curling his hands around her waist, he waggled his brows and nuzzled the sensitive flesh just beneath her ear. "Actually, I thought maybe we could go upstairs and celebrate, make up for lost time."

"Mmm, that sounds like fun, too." Her blue eyes flashed with amusement as her arms slipped up to wind around his neck. "But afterward, we really should thank Ethan and let him know I won't be coming in to work anymore."

"We will." Peter scooped Lucy into his arms and got to his feet, heading for the stairs. "And I want to ask him to be my best man at the wedding."

"That's nice," she said, her fingers already loosening the buttons at the front of his starched white shirt. "He's your best friend, after all, and he did play the part of an unlikely matchmaker there toward the end, didn't he?"

"Yeah," he answered, taking the stairs two at a time. "But we have the blackout to thank for our start."

Epilogue

Peter scrubbed a hand over his dry, tired eyes as the last of his latest program processed across the computer screen. Stifling a yawn, he turned just as his wife tiptoed into the room.

God, he loved that word: *wife*. But he loved her even more.

She wore the same long, sapphire blue satin negligee as when they'd gone to bed several hours ago. Of course, he'd systematically stripped the gown from her body so he could make soft, sweet love to her for about an hour and a half. She must have put it back on sometime after he'd slipped away to his office.

He still worked best in the wee hours of the night,

but Lucy didn't seem to mind a bit. She simply drifted over when she thought he'd been gone too long or started to miss him, and lured him back to the bedroom.

Now, she crossed the carpeted floor in her bare feet and came to stand behind his chair, running her hands over his shoulders and across the worn cotton T-shirt covering his chest.

"How's it coming along?" she asked, her voice raspy with sleep.

He caught her fingers and folded them inside his own, holding them close above his heart. "All done. I'm just waiting for these sequences to run before I shut down."

"Think this one will be as popular as Soldiers of Misfortune?"

"It's hard to tell, but I hope so."

She sighed, resting her face against his temple where her warm breath stirred through his hair. "I'll bet it will. And then I can say 'I told you so' because you managed to design a brand new game and still be a wonderful husband, all at the same time. Amazing."

He grinned at her teasing tone and tipped his head back to meet her loving gaze. "Hey, when you're right, you're right. And this happens to be one of the few times I'm pleased to admit I was wrong, wrong, wrong."

"Me, too," she said softly, punctuating the response with a kiss.

And then she straightened, pulling him to his feet as

she tapped a few keys on his keyboard to turn off the system. Walking backward, she tugged him in the direction of their bedroom.

"I'm also pleased you have this penchant for being up at all hours. It will make things much easier on me down the road."

His brows knit in confusion at her cryptic statement and the sly smile curving her lips. "What are you talking about?"

"You know. Midnight feedings and 2:00 a.m. diaper changes. I'll leave those to you so I can sleep through the night."

He blinked, his bare feet dragging along the carpet. "Midnight feedings? Diaper…?"

Her meaning registered in his sluggish brain and he froze in his tracks. "You mean…Are you…?" He couldn't seem to form a complete sentence. But then, with Lucy, he didn't need to.

Her grin widened and she nodded her head. "We're going to have a baby," she confirmed.

With a loud whoop, he wrapped his arms around her waist, lifted her off the ground and spun her in circles. Before they could get too dizzy, he set her back down, but didn't let go.

Through her laughter, she said, "I take it you're happy about this."

"Are you kidding? I'm ecstatic. I can't wait." He took a minute to catch his breath and then asked, "When?"

"Seven months. The doctor says early June."

"June. I'm gonna be a daddy in June," he breathed in wonder. And then he looked deep into her blue eyes. "I'll be a good one. I swear it."

"I know you will." Raising up on her toes, she held his cheeks in her cupped hands and kissed the corner of his mouth. "I've always known. You're a better man than you give yourself credit for, Peter Reynolds."

He swallowed past the lump of emotion clogging his throat. "I love you, Lucy Reynolds."

Leaning back in his arms, she smiled softly. "I know that, too."

* * * * *

TEMPTING TROUBLE

by

Dorien Kelly

My thanks to Patti Denison of the
Village Grounds and Chris Shiparski of the
Nickerson Inn for permission to draw two of my
favourite "real world" places into the fictional
realm of Sandy Bend.

This book is dedicated with much affection
to Jennifer Green – a goddess among editors.
Thank you for your insight, enthusiasm and
boundless patience!

1

KIRA WHITMAN WAS SURE that if the concept of karma had any teeth to it, she'd now be a cockroach instead of one of South Florida's top-selling real estate agents. And as for those cynics who considered real estate agents on a par with cockroaches, Kira had no time for their negativity. She was too busy making hot bundles of cash.

Today was yet another perfect day in paradise. Kira and Roxanne, her partner in Whitman-Pierce Realty, had taken a long, top-down, music-cranking drive in Roxanne's beloved red Porsche. The nearly three-hour trip to Big Pine Key to check out a potential listing had been worth it. Casa Pura Vida was five bedrooms and six bathrooms of waterfront perfection.

The heels of Kira's sandals clicked against the flagstone terrace surrounding the swimming pool and guesthouse. She drew in a deep breath and smiled at the salty note in the tropical air. A humid breeze—nearly cool compared to Florida's customary June weather—eddied around her, flirting with the sheer silk of her skirt. Yes, she was one lucky girl. Far luckier than she deserved.

Kira turned back toward the house.

"Let's do one more walk-through," she said to her partner.

Roxanne's cell phone rang. She slipped it from the small designer bag slung over her shoulder. Kira watched as Roxanne checked the caller's number, muttered something blunt, then tucked the phone away without answering it. Hopefully the caller hadn't been a client, but Kira knew if she asked, she'd only be setting herself up for another of the in-your-face exchanges that she and Roxanne had been having recently.

By the time they reached the house, Roxanne's phone had stopped its hot Latin salsa ring tones, then started once again. She ignored it—something Kira was finding impossible to do.

"Don't you think you should get that?" she finally blurted.

"It'll keep," Roxanne said with a shrug that came off more like a nervous twitch. "So, what do you think we should ask for this place—five and a half?"

"No, six-four at least," Kira replied as she swung open the French doors leading into the great room.

She glanced over her shoulder. Roxanne had stopped in her tracks and was scrolling through the missed calls on her cell phone. Whoever was listed made her partner wince.

Focusing on something more positive than Roxanne, Kira moved on to scope out the gourmet kitchen, with its one-way glass wall facing the lush landscaping around the circular drive in front of the house. She had just enough imagination to know why the homeowners wanted to make sure they could see out while no one could see in. The secluded waterfall nook off the dining area brought to mind activities with more sensual sizzle than cooking a hot meal.

Kira returned to the middle of the kitchen and rested her hip against the central island where she and Roxanne had left their briefcases when they'd come in. She stood straighter as her partner finally made her way into the room.

"Six-four? Are you sure?" Roxanne asked, picking up the conversation as though it had never been interrupted.

"Positive."

Kira's ability to sniff out the last cent of value was a family gift. Her father, who she hadn't spoken to in three years, was a major real estate mogul in Chicago. He collected office buildings the same way some men his age did classic cars.

All those teenage years Kira spent half listening to dinnertime business talk had paid off. She was a natural at real estate and loved being paid to snoop around other people's houses. Even if she'd had to drastically downscale her lifestyle, earning her own income was proving to be far easier than dealing with the killer strings attached to her father's money.

Roxanne scrounged through her disaster zone of a briefcase and pulled out her PDA—her one concession to organization, and that only because she thought it made her look important. She distractedly tapped some numbers into it, then shook her head. "I say we list lower. We're talking less than a million dollars' difference, anyway. We're better off turning the place quickly."

Roxanne had been Kira's "in" to the moneyed set when she'd moved south and settled in Coconut Grove three years ago. Their partnership had made good sense when they'd first joined forces. Roxanne had kept the books and the office operating smoothly, while Kira had concentrated on sales. Both of them had loved the wild escape of the South Beach nightlife.

Then Roxanne had changed. And, to be fair, maybe Kira had, too. Still, Kira managed to have her share of fun. She enjoyed fast boats and good champagne as much as the next ex-heiress. But for the past several months Roxanne had been partying as though it was an extreme sport. She'd dropped the set of friends that she and Kira had in common, saying they'd begun to bore her. She was showing up at the office later, working less and still expecting more cash to magically come her way. Kira's tolerance was wearing thin.

"This isn't about us," Kira said. "I ran the comps, and for this area six-four is right in the market." For emphasis, she nudged the file jutting out of her own better organized portfolio. "The client deserves to get the full value. You told me that this is a second home, so there's no rush to sell, right?"

"He, uh—" Roxanne broke off from whatever she'd been about to say.

Kira followed her line of vision. An enormous black SUV had pulled up behind Roxanne's car.

Roxanne stilled. They watched a man get out of the passenger side of the vehicle and circle Roxanne's Porsche. Another guy got out of the SUV and joined him.

"Is one of them the homeowner?" Kira asked, though she already had her doubts. Roxanne wouldn't be acting this uptight if it were.

Roxanne shook her head. "Not exactly."

"Friends of yours?"

It had taken all of Kira's willpower not to pour on

the sarcasm when saying *friends*. Back in Kira's wild days, she might have dabbled in low places but never quite the depths that Roxanne was currently plumbing. These guys were so slick looking that they could trigger a run on the sanitizer market. Kira wrinkled her nose at the imagined scent of their cologne—one of those kinds with a hypermacho name like Spike or Thrust, and applied with an industrial sprayer, too.

"They're more acquaintances," Roxanne said quickly, pocketing her cell phone. "Hang on for a second and I'll get rid of them." She left before Kira could respond.

Kira watched though the front window as Roxanne talked to the men. Her arms were crossed and her stance had enough bulldog to it that Kira knew this was no friendly chat.

After a few moments, Kira was distracted from her efforts at long-distance lipreading by her phone's ring. She checked the number and fought the urge to ignore the call, figuring it wouldn't be fair when she'd just zapped Roxanne for the same behavior.

On the other end was Kira's most demanding client. Kira greeted Madeline and tried to answer her questions about the exact number of electrical outlets and light switches in an old Coral Gables mansion while she kept an eye on whatever the hell was happening outside.

Kira finished humoring Madeline, but the argument on the other side of the glass wall raged on. Just as Kira debated the wisdom of going out there to play peacemaker, Roxanne subtly raised a finger toward Kira and mouthed something that looked like *Be right back.*

Kira shot to the window wall and smacked her palm against the cool, thick glass. "Hey! What are you doing?"

Roxanne, of course, could neither see nor hear her. Kira watched in disbelief as her partner climbed into the back of the SUV.

"Dammit!"

She made a mad grab for her cell phone and autodialed Roxanne's number as the SUV backed down the drive then disappeared. Roxanne's message kicked in after one ring.

"Hi, you've reached the voice mail of Roxanne Pierce. Please leave your name, number and a detailed message after the tone. I'll get back to you as soon as possible."

Yeah, like *now* would be good. "Roxanne, it's Kira. Give me a call and tell me what's going on."

Kira snapped her phone shut and glared at Roxanne's car, since that was as close as she could get to its absent owner. She checked her watch—one-twenty—then called the office.

"Hey, Susan," she said once their receptionist answered. "Do me a favor and call my cell if Roxanne checks in…. Yes, she's supposed to be with me, but it looks like she got sidetracked." After fielding a few questions about new listings from a sales associate who had floor duty for the afternoon, Kira hung up and returned to waiting.

Fifteen minutes passed. Then twenty grew into forty. Two more calls to Roxanne's phone had produced only the same message. Kira supposed she should be worried, except this was Roxanne. The combined fingers, toes and sundry other appendages of the Miami Dolphins wouldn't be sufficient to count the number of times in recent memory that she'd forgotten an appointment, taken an unannounced vacation or otherwise left Kira to twist slowly in the wind. The only thing that stopped Kira from being totally fed up was the knowledge that just a few years ago she'd been as irresponsible as Roxanne.

For lack of anything else to do, Kira walked to the waterfall nook and touched her fingertips to the cool spray tumbling down the slate wall into the pool beneath. A bit of the tension eased from her muscles as she stood there. Kira smiled. This was definitely a house to be shared with a man. Someone sexy, tall and muscled, with slow, sure hands and a fast sense of humor...

Someone like Mitch Brewer...

Yow! Where had that come from?

Totally rattled, Kira backed from the water. Maybe Casa Pura Vida had a Fountain of Truth instead of a Fountain of Youth. Wouldn't that look great on the features sheet if she ended up listing the place?

She hadn't consciously thought of Mitch Brewer in years. Okay, months. And never mind the recurring dreams; she was willing to admit that her subconscious was beyond her control. It wasn't easy to forget a man who ticked her off as easily as he turned her on. But Mitch and the town of Sandy Bend, Michigan, were in her past. She'd been another girl, and not one she—or much anyone else—wanted to revisit.

A full hour inched by. To mark the event, Kira searched Roxanne's briefcase—a zero-guilt activity. She turned up the keys to both Casa Pura Vida and Roxanne's Porsche. At least she wasn't going to have to call someone from the office to come get her. So far she'd managed to hide Roxanne's increasingly erratic behavior from the staff.

Kira snooped around and found the command center for the house's built-in stereo system. Music made better company than the silence shredding her nerves. She wished she had something to sit on, but the homeowner hadn't left any furniture behind. Even a hard folding chair would have done. She'd hurt her right hip and leg as a teenager, and too much standing flat-out hurt.

The hour crept all the way to two-thirty and twenty seconds, enough time to play three games of solitaire on her PDA—the twin to Roxanne's and a Christmas gift from her partner.

Kira wasn't one hundred percent clear on what the correct amount of time to wait when given a be-right-back-message might be. Her mother and sisters would know; they could give Miss Manners a run for her money. Even her older brother Steve, who was far more laid-back, seemed to have a rule for every situation. If Kira had been on speaking terms with any of them, including Miss Manners, that tidbit might have been helpful. Since she wasn't, she decided to give Roxanne another half hour.

By three o'clock Kira was running on the pure steam of anger over being victim of yet another stupid Roxanne trick. She gathered her belongings and Roxanne's, locked up Casa Pura Vida and began the long trip back to the Coconut Grove office.

Whitman-Pierce's parking lot was empty and the sun was beginning to flirt with the cityscape by the time Kira pulled in next to her car. She felt fried, both physically and mentally. She quickly sorted through the jumble of stuff on the front seat, pulling out what was hers and leaving Roxanne the rest. She stopped in the empty office just long enough to check her voice mail for a message from Roxanne—there was none, naturally—and to toss Roxanne's car keys on her desk.

As she headed for home, Kira debated whether to pour herself a well-earned cocktail before or after she called her father at his summerhouse in Michigan.

"Definitely before," she murmured to herself.

She was already well aware that her company's short track record didn't make her a favorite with banks. It was going to take some world-class boot-licking to get her father to lend her the money to buy out Roxanne. A shot of vodka would temporarily numb her hard-earned pride.

Kira turned onto Jacaranda Drive, to the one-story same-as-all-the-others rental house where she'd been living for the past three years. Relatively cheap rent meant that she had a decent sum saved to buy a place she really wanted. Unfortunately that amount was nothing compared to what she'd have to pay for a life away from Roxanne.

As Kira neared her driveway, she saw two men standing on her front stoop. They didn't look familiar from behind, at least. She slowed her car to a near crawl. An older man dressed in a black golf shirt and pants hideously too tight for his gut walked around the side of her house to join the men at her front door.

On a day less weird, she would have considered the possibility that she was being paid a fund-raising visit by a door-to-door advocacy group—Polyester Addicts Anonymous or something. Not today, though.

Kira hauled butt past her driveway, turned the corner, and then proceeded at a less breakneck pace. A blue minivan was parked on the opposite side of the street about halfway down the block. As Kira neared, her gaze briefly locked with the occupant's. There was nothing special about the woman in the driver's seat. She looked like any brown-haired, conservative, suit-wearing, middle-management something-or-another pulled over to use her cell phone. Nothing in her bland expression that should have caused a jolt to Kira's nervous system. But jolted she was. Since she believed in trusting her instincts, Kira settled her foot harder on the accelerator and shot toward the main road.

A muttered litany—"Man, oh, man, oh, man"—didn't do much to calm her. Among the problems that came with being the currently celibate, overworked type was a lack of guys to call when the air-conditioning quit or goons lurked at her door. Kira had found a good AC man but remained fresh out of goonbusters. The only person she could think to call was Susan, the office receptionist. Susan's brother was a private investigator. Maybe Kira could just casually ask for his number for a friend of a friend or some other such semitransparent lie. It wasn't much of a plan but she was out of better ideas.

Watching the traffic, she sent her hand searching across the car's console for her cell phone. She'd retrieved it and was ready to dial when it rang, sending another blast of adrenaline through her veins.

Once she'd retrieved her heart from her throat, she answered. "H-hello?"

"We know you have them."

"Have what?" she managed to say to the unfamiliar male caller as she hit her right-turn signal and pulled into a dry cleaner's parking lot. No way could she drive and deal with a mystery caller all at once.

"Don't play stupid."

Sad to say but this was no act. "I really don't know what you're talking about. Scout's honor."

"Roxanne said you do. You know who Roxanne is, right?"

"Yes."

"Then you're not too stupid. She said she gave them to you yesterday. Now all you gotta do is deliver."

Kira briefly rested her forehead against the center of the steering wheel. Roxanne gave her *what*, besides enough stress that she'd taken up teeth grinding as a hobby? "Did it ever occur to you that Roxanne's lying?"

The caller laughed, but somehow Kira didn't feel charmed.

"Not this time, babe," he said. "Stick them in an envelope and leave 'em tonight at the front desk of the Hotel Coco for Suarez. And do it alone. Got it?"

Kira rolled her eyes. She wasn't going anywhere alone, and especially not to the Hotel Coco, which had some sort of cokehead-Miami-Vice-retro-sleaze attractant in its air. Roxanne loved the place as much as Kira hated it. "Yeah. Alone. Sure."

"Good."

The jerk clearly didn't grasp the finer nuances of sarcasm. Kira tried again. "Look, buddy, you're wasting our time. Talk to Roxanne again. I don't know what 'they' are and no way am I going to the—"

She drew to a stop as she realized from the absolute silence on the other end that her caller had hung up. Kira flipped shut her phone, then checked her caller log.

"Great."

According to her phone, Out of Area had just been harassing her. She dialed Roxanne one more time, since there was no one better to clear up this mess— a stinging indictment of her life.

"Hi, this is Roxanne Pierce," a new, cheery Roxanne voice-mail greeting announced. "I'm on vacation, and you're not. Leave a message and I'll get back to you."

On vacation? Kira gripped the phone tighter, fantasizing that it was Roxanne's throat.

"Roxanne, this is Kira. I don't know what kind of mess you've dragged me into this time, but I'm not playing, okay? Call me, and do it now."

Kira closed her phone and considered her limited options. She could take Roxanne at her perky vacation words and go with a no-worries attitude, but she figured she wasn't delusional enough to pull off that act.

The police were out. If Roxanne was missing—and that was an enormous *if*—she hadn't been gone long enough for them to even bother preparing a report. Kira knew she needed an outsider, though. Someone objective. Someone experienced. Someone who wasn't functioning on shot nerves and the paranoia born of spotting polyester goons on her doorstep.

She rearmed herself with her phone, called Susan the receptionist and prepared to do some private-investigator-type wheedling. As she waited for Susan to answer, the blue minivan Kira had earlier spotted illegally parked drove slowly by.

A chill chased across her skin.

Paradise had grown very ugly around the edges.

2

LIE LOW, THE PRIVATE investigator had told her. Go someplace out of the norm.

"You've got that one covered," Kira muttered to herself.

A day and a half after the visitation of the goons, she had reached her destination. Gritty-eyed from endless driving and one failed sleep attempt in a not-quite-chain motel outside Knoxville, Tennessee, she could safely say she'd sunk about as low in matters of personal hygiene as she ever wanted to.

Welcome to Sandy Bend read the sign on the southern edge of the approaching town.

"Welcome? Fat chance," Kira replied as she drove past.

It had been three years and oceans of bad blood since she'd last visited. Back in her bad old days, a stay in the quaint Lake Michigan resort town had seemed nearly as appealing as being dropped bikini-clad into Siberia.

Except for the Mitch Brewer factor.

No matter how boring she had found Sandy Bend's lack of designer-label amenities, the knowledge that he was around had always been worth a thrill. They were dead opposites and had clashed whenever in the same place. In fact, Kira had made sure of it, verbally pushing him until he'd pushed back. He'd been a tough adversary, unwilling to back down just because she was very female and very rich. Back then one of those two factors had been enough to turn nearly everyone else around her into doormats.

Out of habit, Kira slowed her car and noted the speeding of her heart as she passed the police station. Feeling that old tingle of excitement, she searched for Mitch's aged black Mustang—more salvage project than classic—in the lot. Nope, not a Mustang to be seen. Of course, she had no idea if Mitch still drove the same car.

She did know that he remained a Sandy Bend cop. She'd managed to pry that much loose in a nearly civil Christmas phone call she had exchanged with her brother, Steve. Steve was married to Mitch's sister, Hallie. Once upon a time, many screwups ago, Hallie had been Kira's friend. There was no clear definition of what Mitch had been to Kira—not friend, not lover, but definitely memorable.

But she wasn't here to see Mitch, Hallie or anyone else in town. She was here because nobody in their right mind would expect it. Including herself.

Also unexpected were the changes in town. As Kira drove down Main Street, she noted a day spa, several clothing boutiques, a jeweler and more new restaurants than she could take in. If the place had been this interesting when she was younger, she might not have spent so many bored hours trying to annoy the locals. Then again, maybe not. After a few years with a shrink and a lot of growing up, she knew now that she would have been hell to deal with no matter where she was.

Kira turned left off the main route and headed for the beach road to her parents' cottage, which bore no more resemblance to a small, homey retreat than she did to a saint. Theirs was the sort of place that made editors of glossy architectural magazines pant and drool. Kira also recognized that it was a spectacular investment, even if it was as stark and empty as a gallery of modern art. Matters of personal taste aside, since her parents were seldom in town, it remained the ideal spot to settle until matters in Florida could be sorted out.

Kira pulled into the mouth of the driveway, put her car in park, stepped out and punched the security code into the gate's lockbox. The number hadn't changed—062671, commemorating the day her father closed his first deal on a piece of Chicago's Miracle Mile real estate.

"Very touching, Dad," she said as the gate drew open. With a soft whirring hum, the security camera turned its cyclops eye her way. She waggled her fingers at whoever was watching on the other end.

Once up the winding drive, Kira parked, exited the car again and tried to smooth the worst of the wrinkles from her formerly gorgeous skirt. She knew she looked as if she'd crawled semievolved from the laundry pile, and her right hip ached more than usual.

By the time she'd trudged up the countless bluestone steps to the house's entrance, someone was waiting at the door. Not family, but nearly so. Rose Higgins had taken care of the Whitman family's Sandy Bend home for as far back as Kira could remember.

Rose took in Kira's less-than-perfect appearance and looked pleased at the flaws. "Well, if it isn't Miss Kira."

Despite the sting to her ego, Kira forgave the housekeeper the slight smirk lingering at the corners of her mouth. She'd done a great job of earning that expression through a childhood of snotty behavior. Though to fairly allocate blame, the British-born Rose hadn't exactly been Mary Poppins when Kira was little.

"Hi, Rose. It's nice to see you. And do you think we could drop the 'Miss' in front of my name?"

One efficient arch of Rose's silver brows was enough to convey the message that she had words other than *Miss* that she'd be willing to substitute.

Kira pressed on, since she wasn't ready for the death march back to her car. "Are my mom or dad home?"

"They're in London with your brother and sister-in-law and won't be back till late August."

Perfect!

Kira was now the recipient of seven thousand square feet of gated, luxurious solitude. She took a step closer to the door, nearly salivating at the thought of the steam shower in her bedroom suite.

"I don't think they'd mind if I stayed a few days, do you?" Kira asked, though she considered the question a mere formality.

Rose barred the door, one hand on its frame. "Perhaps not, but I suspect your bed will be a bit tight, what with the renters in residence."

"Renters? Come on, Rose. Dad never rents out this house."

"Until now. New business associates of your father's, you know." The housekeeper stepped back from the door and readied to close it. "Should your parents call, I'll mention that you dropped in for a visit."

Visions of steam showers began to fade into the mist, leaving Kira with the solid knowledge that she was tired, ripe and stuck in a town where she was only slightly more welcome than the tax assessor.

"Don't bother," Kira said.

Rose's smirk blossomed into a full evil grin.

"'Bye, then." The door closed with a convincing thud.

Kira squared her shoulders and ignored her stomach's grumbling that it was past lunchtime and no lunch had been delivered. She'd never been this exhausted. Or desperate, either. She was out of cash and unwilling to use her ATM card or credit cards for fear of being traced. Maybe she was overreacting, but she preferred being conservative to being goon-stalked.

"Okay, so next?" she asked herself as she wound down the hillside toward her car.

Either hunger or desperation had sharpened her mind, because she quickly settled on a plan. If Steve and Hallie were in London, their house might at least be vacant. And since their house just happened to be the old Whitman cottage, left to languish after the monument to glass and steel now behind Kira had been built, she knew its flaws—right down to the bedroom window with the broken latch that she'd slipped out nearly every summer night as a teenager.

Kira smiled. Sometimes being a bad girl was a very good thing.

THE WORST THING ABOUT LIFE in Sandy Bend was that everyone knew everyone else's business. That, Mitch Brewer felt compelled to add, could also sometimes be the best thing about life in Sandy Bend.

Thanks to a highly concerned citizen—one usually the source of complaints about misaligned garbage cans and unsightly gardens—whoever had broken into his sister's house hadn't been there very long. Since Mitch was keeping an eye on the place for Steve and Hallie while they were gone, he damn well knew that no visitors were expected.

Mitch walked a circle around the sleek blue car parked in front of the large, rambling log home. He'd been a cop for nearly ten years. In all that time he couldn't say that he'd run across many members of the local breaking-and-entering set who drove a Mercedes. He checked the car's rear plate—Florida—and called in the numbers.

A few moments later, a high-tech office worker called the search results to his low-tech squad car.

"No sh—" managed to escape before Mitch got a grip on his mouth.

"None at all," answered Barb over at the county sheriff's office.

Mitch gave his thanks to Barb, then a silent one to whatever power had just delivered him Kira Freakin' Royal Princess Whitman. He knew she'd been in Florida and he never expected her to return to Sandy Bend. Finally he had a chance to return about one one-thousandth of the crap she'd shoveled his way over the years.

His smile grew as he walked to the house.

"Police," he called as he pounded on its door. "Anyone in there?"

Of course there was. And damn, what he'd give to see her I'm-dead-now expression.

Mitch counted to three, pounded and called again. When no one answered, he fished a key ring from his pants pocket and unlocked the house.

"Police," he repeated as the ancient oak door creaked open.

Mitch entered, then pocketed his keys. Somewhere upstairs a radio blared. Following the sound, he climbed the broad staircase. The station that Her Royal Highness had chosen was only partially tuned in, static competing with music. As he neared the source, he picked up two new noises: a shower running and a woman wailing. Not girlie sniffing, crying or weeping, but the full-out howl that he usually got from little kids who had misplaced their parents.

Mitch ventured a step closer. "Police?"

He scowled at the way the statement had come out as a question. Not that it mattered. Kira Whitman had begun to drown out even the radio.

Mitch settled his palm against the bathroom door, debating the wisdom of knocking. He'd barely begun to consider the pros when the door moved away from his hand, swinging inward. As it did, time slowed and he forgot how to swallow...and breathe.

Mitch kept a mental tally of never-to-be-repeated errors he called his Big Mistake List.

Not going immediately from college to law school? Big Mistake number one.

Not moving out of the family farmhouse the second that his older brother—and boss—Cal had gotten married and moved his bride in? Big Mistake number two.

Forgetting that Kira Whitman had a body that had kept him hard and aching for most of his formative youth? Big Mistake number three and rising fast. Very fast.

Her back was to him as she stood in the claw-foot

tub, head tipped back and water pouring down as she wailed. If he were a responsible citizen, he might warn her of the dangers of drowning, standing with her mouth open so close to that stream of water. Of course, if he were a responsible citizen, he might also turn away, since the clear plastic shower curtain painted with the occasional dragonfly wasn't doing much to hide her.

Mitch wasn't feeling at all responsible. He looked long enough to confirm that she was still sleek, blond and possessed of the finest butt that Sandy Bend would ever see.

Then he remembered how she'd swung between taunting him and being nearly tender for too many summers. How she'd gotten herself arrested during a Chicago bar brawl and never managed to make it to Steve and Hallie's wedding, diminishing his sister's joy that day. And how she'd coldly ditched her own fiancé at the altar less than a year later. Yeah, looking elsewhere got a whole lot easier with all of that to balance the action going on below his belt.

Mitch made his way downstairs to the living room, then settled in for a wait. He could afford to be a patient man...especially now that he'd seen Kira Whitman bare-ass naked.

A GIRL COULD CRY FOR ONLY SO long, and Kira for less than most. She lasted until the radio began to blare an old disco song about tough girls surviving. Even the most well-deserved bout of exhausted self-pity couldn't survive the feel-good power of Gloria Gaynor.

Kira ignored the sharp stinging of her skinned knees and elbows—victims of the fact that she couldn't climb trees and negotiate roofs quite as well as she had at age fifteen. She slicked back her hair and joined in for the song's last chorus. Then, after giving herself one last scrub with Hallie's marvelous lavender-scented soap, she turned off the tub's taps.

She dried her hair with a fluffy white towel after wrapping another around her body. Kira sighed at the soft comfort.

"Egyptian organic cotton…nothing better," she said.

And she should know, since she'd sent Steve and Hallie a dozen of these buggers as a wedding gift. That she'd done it on her dad's store account no longer sat very well. She shook off the guilt twinge. If something as simple as a mooched wedding gift was making her feel bad, she'd be flogging herself on Sandy Bend's village green before her little visit was over.

Now that she was clean enough that she could tolerate being in her own skin, food was the next order of business. Her stomach's grumbling had risen to an angry growl. She wasn't sure what she'd find in the kitchen, but unless Hallie's tastes had changed, Kira knew that survival was a good bet.

When they were teenagers, Hallie had scarfed down all the stuff Kira wouldn't permit herself to eat—French fries, chocolate, ice cream and soda with a full load of calories and sugar. And the girl had stayed downright skinny, which Kira had viewed as both unfair and unnatural. Today, though, she was thankful.

Mouth watering, she tightened her towel and made a beeline downstairs. She'd just crossed the hallway past the living room when a male voice said, "All cried out, huh?"

Kira screeched. The sound carried all the shrill

terror of an ingenue in her first slasher film. No faceless bad guy approached, though. That might have
been preferable as she had six feet four worth of
Mitch Brewer ambling her way. At the sight, her intellect turned tail, leaving only instinct to do battle.

"But you're not all screamed out, I guess," he added.

Fight-or-flight response had kicked in, and Kira
was coming down on the side of fight. "Are you out
of your mind, creeping around and scaring me to
death? I should call the police on you." Which
sounded very good until she realized that a man in
blue already stood in front of her, and yes, he was in
uniform. "Okay, forget the police, but you'd better
give me a really good reason for being here."

He smiled, and as always she was a sucker for it.
What female wouldn't be when looking up at tanned
skin, white teeth and matching dimples?

"Funny, Your Highness," he said. "I was going to
ask you for the exact same thing."

The real estate business had given Kira a certain
relaxed glibness, but any talent she'd ever had at
bald lies was damn rusty. Still, she gave it a try. "Not
that you need to know, but Steve and Hallie said I
could use the house while they're gone."

Mitch settled the knuckles of one hand against his
lean hip and scratched at the back of his neck with
the other hand. Kira could have recited in alphabetic
order the names of her favorite designers—and there
were many—in the interval before he spoke.

"Huh. Really?" he asked.

The Mitch Brewer she recalled was as sharp as
they came, and Kira was in no mood for his clueless-
country-cop gambit.

"Yes, they really said that."

"Interesting. How about the use of Hallie's clothes? Any offers there?"

She frowned, trying to get a sense of where he was heading, since Hallie was inches taller and probably still a clothing size smaller. "Why?"

"You're a little underdressed," he said, gesturing her way with a casual flick of his hand. "Now, don't get me wrong, Highness. I don't mind at all, but I thought you might."

Kira's hands tightened over plush terry cloth. Why was it that the most humiliating moments in life seemed to take the longest? Pleasure danced and flew, but the realization that you were wearing only a towel in front of the guy you'd least like to lose your dignity around—again!—took for-stinking-ever.

She glanced down in a last futile hope that he was jerking with her. But the nearly naked truth remained: she was wearing one lovely and expensive towel.

She looked back at Mitch. His blue-eyed gaze traveled a leisurely route from her head to the tips of her toes and then up again. She knew she should be angry, but more than anything she was *aware*.

Aware of the blood rushing just beneath skin growing more sensitive by the second.

Aware of the appreciation—and something more dangerous—in Mitch's expression.

Then that damned smile of his returned, playing slowly across his face. Something about it—as though he held a secret that he had no intention of sharing—really frosted her.

"I'm going upstairs," she said, letting a chill settle in her voice. "Unless you're not through staring."

"Oh, I've seen enough."

Kira turned heel. "Then you can let yourself out."

She had reached the lower landing when she heard him say, "Actually, I'll be right here when you're done dressing, Highness. We're going to give Hallie and Steve a call."

Kira stopped, shaken at the thought.

A call to Steve risked too much: her safety, her pride and most of all the potential deep pain of having her brother pitch her into the street. Considering all the grief she'd thrown his way, she could hardly blame him if he did.

She figured she had one shot left. She could derail Mitch Brewer. For the hardwired-to-flirt Kira of summers past that would have been a no-brainer. After drawing a steadying breath, she turned to face the guy who'd always seen the worst of her and offered up some more.

"How about if I just take off this towel, instead?"

3

MITCH WAS A REASONABLY perceptive guy. Good thing, since both his present and future careers demanded a nose for the truth. He moved closer to Kira. Not too close, because he was also a sane guy, which was a miracle considering his life recently. He'd survived four years of attending law school on and off while still working endless shifts on the force. Still, he knew his limits, and the sight of Kira Whitman wearing only a white towel was outside the bounds. But even from his circumspect three feet away, beneath the flowery scent that clung to her damp skin, he smelled fear.

Sure, she had a sexy purr down to an art, and the hot promise in her brown eyes seemed almost real. A more gullible guy—or even one with less conscience—would snap up her offer.

Kira's fingers toyed with the upper edge of her towel, venturing into the valley between her breasts. Until that moment, he'd been sure that she was bluffing. Now he had his doubts. Since Kira had always been mostly talk, she must be damn scared.

"Hang on, there, Highness," he said, regretting that back when he was a kid, he'd listened to and absorbed his father's speeches about duty and moral fiber. "Whether you're naked or not, we're calling Steve."

"But—but…" Her gaze skittered around the entry hall, then settled on the grandfather clock that was just outside an archway leading to the dining room. "It's after midnight in London."

It was tough not to grin at her triumphant expression, but Mitch was up for the job.

"Hallie's a night owl," he replied. "I'll bet they're still awake."

"There's no point in bothering them. Do you really think I'd move in here without my brother's permission?"

Mitch snorted. "Given your track record, I don't think you want me to answer that one." He walked to the kitchen, knowing that she would follow. He lifted the phone from its base and began to punch in the number that Hallie had left for him on the message pad.

Kira made a grab for him. "Wait! Don't call!"

He was less than impressed at the way he was rousing from something as simple as the touch of her hands on his arm. Mitch resettled the phone, and Kira backed off, fear still shadowing her expression. He was curious to see what would happen next. From the time she'd first noticed guys, Kira Whitman had been a class-A ballbuster, in a stealthy sort of way. She lulled males with her looks and then messed with their minds—himself included. He'd seen her blow hot and cold, but he'd never seen her this vulnerable.

"So?" he prompted.

"Really, I didn't break in," she said. "Maybe I came inside, but technically I didn't break in. I just—"

"Let's skip the semantics." He got enough of that stuff at school. "You're in here without permission, right?"

Her nod was almost imperceptible.

"Want to tell me why?"

"I decided to come for a visit."

This definitely placed in the top ten of total BS tales. "Unannounced? After three years?"

She didn't even hesitate. "Why not? Maybe I haven't been the best of Whitmans, but better late than never."

"So you're telling me that you drove all the way from Florida on the spur of the moment?"

She frowned. "How did you know that I've been in Florida?"

Luckily he had an easy answer to fall back on, since there was no way he'd confess that he'd known for a couple of years that she'd taken her party act south. Her ego was already plenty healthy without evidence of his continuing curiosity.

"Your car's plates," he said.

"Oh."

"Time to come clean, Highness." Saying the words only reminded him that she *was* clean and girlie-fragrant…and nearly naked. Mitch swallowed hard. "What's really up?"

Other than his hard-on.

She nibbled at her lower lip and then asked, "Haven't you ever acted on impulse?"

Bad question. Between the way his brother Cal drove him at work and the hours he spent studying, he had no room for impulse—a fact that ground at him.

"No," he said.

"Well, I have. It just so happened that I fell on a week or so that I could be away from work. I was thinking that I had relatives and old friends up here that I haven't seen…plus, uh, I just broke up with my boyfriend and I really, really needed to get away. You know, escape the places we'd been together and all that? So here I am, Brewer, and it shouldn't make any difference at all to you if I stay here."

Mitch started with the most obvious point. "Your family's not coming back until late August." He could have added that she was also seriously low on friends to visit in Sandy Bend, but that seemed too cruel—even when talking about Kira. "I can't let you stay here. I promised Hallie that I'd keep an eye on the place. If you'd let me call her, then maybe…"

He let the offer hang out there, half hoping she'd take it just so he could get the hell out of the house and not have to wonder why Kira Whitman was lying to him and why he was beginning to feel the need to help her.

"I can't."

"Then you're going to need to get your stuff and cruise on out of here with me."

She turned away from him, gripping her towel with both hands. "I can't do that, either."

Mitch hesitated—something he seldom did. He looked at the delicate curve of her shoulders, which appeared kissed gold against the white of the terry cloth. And he reminded himself once again that she was the laziest, most manipulative female he'd ever met. He almost had his hard-assed attitude back in place when he noticed that those perfect shoulders were shaking.

"Are you crying?" he asked.

"No. I never cry."

Which was another lie, but not one he could call her on, since that would clue her in that he'd been upstairs while she'd been showering. Mitch settled his hands on her shoulders and turned her to face him again, taking care not to let his grip linger longer than it had to.

"Go get dressed," he said. "I'll call one of the B and Bs in town and see if I can snag you a room."

"No!"

"What now?"

"I...um..." She brushed away the tear trailing down one cheek, and Mitch pretended that he didn't notice. He wasn't sure why he was trying to protect her dignity when she'd spent a youth jacking with others', but just because he didn't understand himself didn't mean he was in the mood to play tough with her, either.

She stood taller. Even then, the top of her head wasn't much above his chin. "I...just can't," she said.

Now, there was an explanation for the ages. Mitch did a gut check and knew he couldn't live with himself unless he said what had jumped into his brain. Of course, he wouldn't be able to live with himself once he had, either.

"You can stay with me, Highness, but just for the night. Got it?"

Her brown eyes widened. She was quiet for so long that he almost thought he was going to escape the payback for his insane impulse.

Yeah, *impulse.*

He guessed he had room for it in his life, after all.

"Okay," Kira said.

And now he had room for nothing else.

IF SOMEONE HAD ASKED KIRA where in Sandy Bend she'd least expect to find Mitch Brewer living, this would be the spot.

"Amazing," she said to herself as she pulled in behind Mitch, just in front of the Dollhouse Cottage.

She couldn't think of any image more incongruous than muscled, macho Mitch in this miniature white confection of a house. And she couldn't think of anything that would distract her from the sting of her battered sense of self-reliance better than finally seeing the inside of a place she'd secretly adored since childhood. It almost made up for crying in front of Mitch, who was definitely the last damn person she ever wanted to appear weak before again.

Kira felt a sense of peace come over her as she looked at the cottage. According to local lore, the house had been built back in the 1800s as a wedding gift from one of the town fathers for his youngest daughter. Just one story tall and dwarfed by the larger houses on the quiet residential street, it was far from the most elegant house in town, but Kira had always found its Victorian embellishments and two rose-hued stained-glass windows perfect.

Mitch climbed out of his car and walked to the white-spindled front porch. Kira trailed after him, appreciating the view...and not just of the house. As she did, she felt a waking of the awareness that had gripped her—and tripped her up—back at Steve and Hallie's house.

Mitch glanced back over his shoulder. "You coming?" he asked.

Since her mouth had gone dry, Kira simply nodded.

It seemed she could think of one activity that would distract her better than a tour of the Dollhouse. Too bad she wasn't an advocate of meaningless sex.

"I can't believe you live here," she said as Mitch unlocked the front door.

"What does that mean?"

He sounded irked, so she took a conciliatory tone. "Nothing, really. It's just this house is so feminine that it doesn't seem like your kind of place."

He stepped inside, then ushered her in. "I can afford it, which makes it my kind of place. Life's not cheap here, you know? The more the town changes, the more rent rises. But I guess that's not the kind of thing you Whitmans have to worry about, is it?"

She gave him her best socialite's smile. "We never discuss finances. Mother considers it crass." Which was true, as far as it went.

More nagging was the sense that Mitch was talking to a female long gone. He seemed to view her as some museum piece, frozen forever at age twenty. She wished she could shake him from that, but she'd learned ages ago that trying to change a guy was more painful than a Brazilian bikini wax.

Kira checked out her surroundings. The furnishings were most generously described as seventies curbside retro, but the bones of the house were spectacular. The ceilings were surprisingly high, which had to be a bonus to someone of Mitch's height. The living room floor was oak with an inlaid border of what appeared to be rosewood, and the old plaster walls were in amazing shape. She walked to the fireplace and rested one hand on the intricately carved mantel.

"Very nice," she said.

"I've been renting the place since Cal got married last year. Life on the farm got kind of crowded."

"Cal's married?" Mitch's older brother had always seemed too happy being the hot guy in town to ever marry.

Mitch nodded. "To Dana Devine. Remember her?"

"Sure." Dana was the same age as Kira and one of the few townies who'd awed her enough that Kira hadn't once harassed her. Dana was tough, smart and never backed down. All of which Kira supposed were essential qualities to have if one was, God forbid, married to a bullheaded Brewer.

"Don't you have a suitcase?" Mitch asked.

"I have a couple of things in the car. I can get them later." She always kept a change of clothes and a toiletry bag in her trunk, just in case. Still, one spare skirt and silk tank top weren't going to get her too far.

"A couple of things, huh? We're talking really spur of the moment. The sidewalk still rolls up at six around here, but tomorrow you should be able to pick up pretty much whatever you want at the shops."

True, except for that lack-of-cash problem...

"So," Kira said, "give me a tour."

"You're standing in the living room. Kitchen is that way. Bedrooms and the bath are on the other side," he said, pointing to his left. "You'll be sleeping there." He hitched a thumb toward a couch that looked like a fraternity-house castoff.

"There?"

A slow smile spread across his face. "Not quite the Four Seasons, is it, Highness?"

"I thought you said you have more than one bedroom?"

"Two. One's mine, and I guess you can have the other if you want to sleep on my weight bench."

"Oh." Kira walked to the orange, yellow and brown plaid couch and ran a hand across it. The thing was clean, even if it had the texture of a scouring pad. "This will be perfect."

The look he gave her was skeptical, but he didn't say anything. Instead he left the room and then reappeared half a minute later with an armful of blankets, folded sheets and pillows.

He tossed them onto the couch, saying, "You're going to want a little padding. The springs are shot."

Kira couldn't quite decide if she'd ever encountered a couch with springs but figured it had to be more comfortable than sleeping in her car.

Mitch glanced at his watch. "I have to get back to the station. I'll be coming in late tonight, so don't wait up for me, huh?"

"Trust me, it wasn't an option," she said. Then impulsively added, "And, Mitch...thanks."

"Sure."

He looked as though he planned to take a step toward her. She settled one hand on the back of the terminally ugly couch, bracing herself for whatever might come. For all that she'd tried to repress her memories of one particular summer afternoon with this guy, she still knew the way his muscles felt beneath the palms of her hands, still remembered the taste of his kisses and still wanted more. She wondered what he remembered, what he wanted.

As they gauged each other, Mitch's relaxed expression honed itself to something harder.

"Don't get too comfortable," he said, then left her alone, her heart pounding, her knees uncharacteristically weak.

`Comfortable?

While suffering from the Brewer effect, there was little chance of that.

HALF AN HOUR LATER, WHEN IT was nearly nine o'clock, Kira had recovered enough to cushion her "bed" with sufficient padding that she thought she might sleep, but found she was still too wired on emotion and unfamiliarity.

Seeking distraction, she perused the music collection in the corner of the living room by Mitch's stereo and found only one artist who didn't sit squarely in the headbanger camp. She'd bet anything that the Sheryl Crow CD had been a gift from a girlfriend, but she set aside the niggling and inappropriate bit of jealousy long enough to put the music on.

Songs passed. As Sheryl began to sing about her favorite mistake, Kira again felt bold enough to raid the kitchen. She smiled as she padded across the linoleum floor. This was the real deal—decades old and with a patina to its black-and-white pattern that the new stuff just couldn't ape.

Next to the back door sat an apartment-size stacked washer and dryer with a basket of neatly folded laundry in front of it. On top of the pile was a white T-shirt with the Sandy Bend Police Department emblem. Kira picked it up and unfolded it. The shirt came to her knees.

"Looks like jammies to me," she said, then quickly changed out of her dead-by-travel skirt and top and into Mitch's shirt. She tucked her undies into his dirty-laundry basket, planning to wash a load tomorrow as some minimal compensation for the lumpy couch he'd offered her.

Figuring that if she had the nerve to wear his clothes, she might as well also eat his food, she opened the fridge and peeked inside. The bagged prewashed lettuce and a package of cooked chicken-breast strips would make for a tolerable dinner. After snagging a bottle of Italian dressing from the door, Kira removed her haul and put together a salad in a big red plastic bowl that she found in a dish drainer next to the sink.

Bowl in one hand and fork in the other, she wandered from the kitchen, through the living room and toward the uncharted territory of the bedrooms. Door number one was ajar, so she nudged it with her elbow and strolled in the three steps she could.

Mitch had clearly saved up his decor dollars for the piece of furniture he thought most mattered. Kira stuck her fork into the salad bowl, then tested Mitch's king-size mattress with her free hand. It felt like paradise. Part of her—the tired and whiny part, to be exact—wanted to curl up on that bed, safe in the belief that it was so big, he'd never know she was there. The rest of her pathetically rational soul knew that wasn't true. Even if the bed were the size of the entire cottage, they'd sense each other's presence. They'd been tuned to each other for too many years to have it otherwise.

Kira turned her back on the bed, with its rumpled dark green paisley comforter and distinctively male scent of wood smoke and outdoors. Some territory best remained uncharted.

Room number two proved less unsettling. In the glow from the hallway's small light fixture she saw Mitch's weight bench with some free weights next to it. In one corner sat what appeared to be a desk, complete with computer.

Kira ran her hand along the wall to a light switch. She flipped it on, then walked toward the desk with no particular plan in mind.

Mitch had left his computer on, its soft hum blending with the louder sound of the ceiling fan turning overhead. Kira balanced her salad bowl on the edge of the desk and then nudged aside a massive book to make more room for herself. As she did, she noticed the title on the book's spine: *Federal Jurisdiction*. She'd have figured him for a guy fond of lighter reading.

Once she'd settled in the desk chair, she picked up her salad and munched for a while. Computers weren't her thing. She knew exactly enough to get her job done and no more. Roxanne had always been the one to play with the accounting and e-mail programs and to keep the firm's Web site current.

Still, Kira was computer conversant enough to see that Mitch's Internet connection was enabled.

"DSL in the backwoods. Who'd have imagined?"

She went to Whitman-Pierce's Web site and used her password to get in the back door to her e-mail. She held a deletefest with the bigger-faster-longer spam, then picked through the real items. While she hadn't expected an e-mail from Roxanne, it still ticked her off that there was none.

Time slipped by as she answered e-mails and sent some reminders to Susan back at the office about clients she'd need to find an associate to cover. Kira wondered how long she'd be able to act as an absentee boss. For better or worse she was a self-professed control freak, and not forty-eight hours into her "vacation," she was losing it.

She wished she hadn't trusted Roxanne to the degree that she had. If she'd been smart enough to get her partner's computer password, she'd be fifty percent more in control than she was at this moment.

Kira speared her last bit of bland salad, returned to the Web site's entry screen and began guessing at Roxanne's password. She worked her way through dead pets, parents and Roxanne's favorite cocktail but came up blank. It was time to move on to a new category.

"Boyfriends, crushes and flings," she muttered to herself.

"Alex, is the answer 'What are Kira's fondest memories?'" sounded a male voice from behind her.

Kira gave herself credit for not screeching this time, though sending the empty salad bowl flying when she jumped wasn't much better. She quickly exited out of the Web site password screen, then turned the swivel office chair to face Mitch. He'd shed his uniform in favor of a pair of jeans and a Michigan State football T-shirt that fit all too well.

"You've got a great future as a sneak," she said.

He raised the beer bottle in his right hand and toasted her. "So do you."

"Do you always creep around?"

"My house," he said. "I'll move any way I want to. That's also my cereal bowl and my shirt," he added.

Kira stood and smoothed out her pilfered T-shirt, perilously aware that she was lacking any form of underwear.

"So, what had you so busy that you didn't hear me come in?"

"Just cruising my favorite sites."

"Right. I've been watching you from the doorway

and you've been typing, not cruising." He took a swig of his beer and said, "I'm going to be straight up with you. I don't have patience for subterfuge and the other garden varieties of BS that you deal in. And for reasons I don't plan to spend a whole lot of time thinking about, I want to help you with whatever you've got going on."

She'd done nothing to improve his opinion of her tonight. And for reasons that *she* didn't plan to think about, Mitch's opinion mattered—very much so. The old Kira he'd known had used everyone else to make her life work. Need money? Suck up to Dad. Need dinner out? Manipulate some poor fool into thinking you were hot for him. Need a place to crash? Impose on a friend.

That last one hit way too close to home.

She'd fought so hard to change, to learn to stand alone. Now even Mitch's grudging hospitality made her ready to pull up the emotional drawbridge and put alligators in the moat. Her current situation was a snag, nothing more. She could handle it without him and maybe even redeem herself a little in his eyes. Spoiled rotten user of a princess just didn't cut it anymore.

Though it was tough to appear innocent when going commando, Kira tried. "Mitch, I don't have anything 'going on.' I'm here on vacation."

"With either no clothes or a T-shirt fetish."

"I'll plead guilty to the fetish."

He lifted one lazy fingertip and traced the top of the police-department emblem where it rested above her left breast. "I'll bet you will."

She could feel her nipples grow achingly sensitive and her heart nearly jump from her chest, but she kept her bluffer's face intact, not letting her gaze waver from his.

Then he leaned down and murmured low into her ear, "You're a good liar, Highness, but not that good. I'm gonna go get some rest. But if you feel the need to confess, come wake me. I've got a feeling your story would be worth the missed sleep."

For the second time that night, he left her. And for the second time that night, Kira Whitman wondered exactly what it took to get a step ahead of Mitch Brewer.

4

DAWN CAME EARLY ON THE WEST side of Michigan's lower peninsula—especially in mid-June. It wasn't much past six in the morning and already the sky had lightened to a watery blue. Mitch stood in his kitchen, full coffee mug in hand. He'd just finished his first round of breakfast—a meal that was usually a multi-course event for him.

He knew he should go to his desk and get some studying in before he was due at the station, but the lure of the woman sleeping so restlessly on his living room sofa was too strong. More than once last night he'd awakened to the sound of Kira's sleep-talking. Or more accurately, sleep-panicking. He'd wanted to check on her but couldn't allow himself that weakness.

Addiction was a word Mitch didn't use casually. As a cop, he'd come across too many people who'd had their lives shot to hell by the real thing. Still, whatever he felt for Kira had messed with him in one way or another since he was seventeen years old. Now he was over thirty and still not free of this…hell, he didn't know what it was.

On some subliminal level he'd always measured the women he'd dated against Kira Whitman. What made it even more miserable was that many of those girls had come out on the favorable end of the comparison. Some had been smarter and sexier, and damn near all of them had been more honest and good natured. But not one woman had lingered in his mind the way she did. She had the whole package—brains, beauty and attitude.

A few summers ago, when his sister had fallen in love with Kira's brother, Mitch had learned exactly how hooked he was. In a miserable mood that summer, Kira had launched a small-scale sabotage campaign against the couple. It seemed as though she'd decided that if she couldn't be happy, no one else could. The morning of the town's annual Summer Fun parade, Mitch had finally seen enough. He'd hauled her away from the throng gathered at the starting point of the parade, ready to deliver some pretty unattractive truths.

Hot words had given way to an even hotter kiss. And then after that, hell, his hands had been everywhere—on top of her clothes, under her clothes, touching places he'd fantasized about forever. She hadn't been exactly pushing him away, either. She'd been slammed by an orgasm, and her cry of pleasure—which he'd swallowed with a kiss—had reminded him that there was a crowd yards away, just around the corner of the high school.

Mitch had felt like garbage for taking advantage of a situation. Before he could pull his act together to apologize, she'd shoved him and sent him reeling backward. While she had straightened her clothes, he'd tried to make some verbal sense of what had happened, but she'd told him to shut up. A little while later he'd returned to his family's parade float and acted as if he'd gotten the best of Kira Whitman. In truth, she'd always had the best of him.

Nearly three years older but not one hell of a lot wiser, Mitch stuck the strawberry jam back in the refrigerator. As he settled his tub of marshmallow fluff into its easy-access place of honor next to the sink, he heard Kira on the couch, stirring and muttering something edged with stress.

What could be going on in a trust-fund princess's life that money couldn't cure?

"Focus," he reminded himself as his curiosity began to stir.

His summer session at school ended in less than a month. Assuming he passed this last course, he'd have enough credits to graduate and begin to study for the February bar exam. Though he was near the top of what had been his class, he hadn't graduated with them two weeks ago. Last November, the night before deer season opened, one drunken hunter with a bad attitude and worse aim had taken care of that.

Mitch knew that he was lucky his injuries hadn't been any worse, but that didn't mean he still wasn't pissed off. From his hospital bed, he'd worked a deal with the law school administration and withdrawn from two classes. He'd made up one class this past semester, but it hadn't been enough.

What really killed was that Betsy, his study partner, had been offered a clerkship with a federal judge in Grand Rapids. Mitch had interned with the same judge the year before. If he'd graduated on time, the position would have been his.

A federal clerkship was the sort of short-term opportunity that made a résumé hit the top of the stack. Since Betsy had also been one of those women who couldn't compete with Mitch's memories of Kira, he'd ultimately decided he was happy for her—in a green-tinged sort of way. But he was equally hungry for his own bite at success. Now he damn well needed to keep his eyes on the books and not on her sleeping Highness's tempting curves.

Averting his gaze, Mitch cut through the living room, went to his desk and grabbed the hornbook for his Federal Jurisdiction course. Maybe if he studied out on the back deck, he could find some measure of peace, if not solitude. Just then, Kira was murmuring something that sounded strangely like *polyester.*

So fashion nightmares were what plagued her?

On his return trip to the kitchen and its back door, he hazarded a quick glimpse to be sure she was still asleep. He doubted she'd be pleased to know that he'd seen her with her hair looking like Medusa's and her face bearing crease marks from the rumpled sheets she slept on. He also doubted she'd believe that he liked this look on her—but he did.

Her usual practiced perfection—and he did mean *practiced,* because each summer he'd watched her facade evolve—kept him on edge. He wanted her accessible. He wanted to get her messy and real to see if she'd taste of salty sweat when she lay beneath him. He wanted to hear her cry his name as she had that one incomplete encounter three summers ago.

Bottom line: he wanted her.

Mitch shook off the image of what she'd look like and uttered a brief but heartfelt profanity as he shot out the back door to the peace beyond.

There was a boundless difference between wanting and getting. He could want all day long, but he'd never allow himself to get.

WHEN SHE WAS FIFTEEN, KIRA had starred in her school's production of *The Princess and the Pea*. That earlier affair with the stage hadn't prepared her for the reality of sleeping on Mitch's spring-shot sofa.

Unable to swing her aching legs around and gracefully sit up, she settled for wriggling her way from the couch to the floor, taking her blanket cocoon with her.

It totally stank to move like a sixty-year-old ex-pro hockey player, when the most strenuous sport she indulged in was avoiding her Pilates class. Kira squinted. A rosy pink glow bathed her from the room's east-facing stained-glass window. If she were her usual optimistic self, she'd consider this a cheery omen. Since, however, she'd had bloodstained nightmares involving Roxanne and oily henchmen, she just viewed the morning sunshine as a sign that she had no further hope of calm sleep. A check of her watch confirmed that it was nearly eight o'clock.

Kira untangled her blanket, sat up and rearranged it for walking, then strolled into the kitchen. Mitch was sitting at an antique enamel-topped table she'd vaguely noted in last night's wanderings. He seemed to be taking notes from the book she'd definitely seen. Next to the book was a plate of toast remnants smeared with gooey white and red stuff.

"Good morning," she said.

"Morning," he answered without looking up from the notebook he wrote in.

Kira wasn't fond of being ignored. "What's that?" she asked, nudging the plate.

"Toast with marshmallow fluff and strawberry jam."

"Eww. Sugar overdose."

He looked up from the notebook. "I take it I shouldn't offer that as a meal for the road?"

In yet another case of attitude overcoming better judgment, she said the first smart thing that popped into her mind. "Why? Are you going someplace?"

"No, you are," he said.

Dressed in his dark blue uniform, he was pretty sexy-looking for a cranky guy. His hand nearly engulfed the coffee mug he held. Some sex-deprived imp residing in Kira's brain whispered, *Big hands... big—*

—*deal*, she mentally finished for the imp, then tried to concentrate on Mitch.

He scowled at her. "Hey, are you listening to me? Remember, I told you yesterday—one night only."

"I heard the deal. Come sundown, I won't darken your doorway." She lifted her right hand. "Cross my heart," she said, action following words.

Of course, even with a blanket over the spot, her touch brought to mind Mitch's finger right there last night. It seemed that the sight spurred the same memory in him, because he now looked even crankier.

He pushed away from the table. "Have a good life, Highness. I'm going someplace with fewer distractions."

A distraction?

She'd been called worse.

Kira stepped aside and let him go.

While he banged around in his bedroom, then closed the front door so loudly that it bordered on a slam, Kira stuck a load of laundry in the washer. Despite her promise to Mitch, she didn't consider it a foregone conclusion that she'd leave his house today.

It depended on her options, and she wasn't accustomed to having them so narrow. But no matter where she went, it wouldn't be in unwashed panties.

While she waited for the laundry, Kira checked her cell phone messages. It was early, but there was nothing from the private investigator she'd hired. Don, the P.I., had told her to expect little for the next forty-eight hours unless Roxanne decided to reappear on her own. A not-necessarily-missing adult wasn't the easiest of people to track. Kira could only hope that the same held true for her, here in her Sandy Bend hideout.

It was just before ten when she slipped into clean underwear and the backup work outfit she kept in her trunk. While she stood in front of the bathroom mirror, Kira dug through the meager selection of cosmetics in her purse seeking something to cover the raccoon rings under her eyes.

Sure, she admitted to a certain measure of female vanity, but more than that, she knew how important illusion could be. By the time she left this house, it was imperative that she look like a Whitman heiress—the queen of all she surveyed. Desperation and empty pockets wouldn't get her a new wardrobe and some food other than bagged salad and marshmallow fluff.

Makeup as good as it was getting, Kira left the Dollhouse Cottage. Since Mitch's house was only five town-size blocks from Sandy Bend's limited shopping district, she decided to walk. With luck the exercise would loosen her tight muscles and clear her mind of last night's ugly dreams.

It was a perfect Michigan summer morning, with

a cornflower-blue sky and the scent of lilacs on the breeze. Kira inhaled deeply. Sandy Bend might not be as lush and exotic as her current home, but it had its compensations.

Leaving the quiet street of clapboard-sided houses with their well-tended cottage gardens, she turned onto Main Street and stopped dead. Tourists already thronged the sidewalks.

"One foot in front of the other," she told herself, then winced at her choice of words.

The last time she'd used that exact phrase was when she had fled from the almost husband her father had picked for her. Her feet—and a cab—had taken her from Chicago's Fourth Presbyterian Church straight to O'Hare Airport. It had been the right choice, even if her timing had been socially and personally disastrous. And today the right choice would be to show some of the same backbone she'd found when she'd rebuilt her life. Crowds shouldn't rattle her. They never had before.

Sandy Bend was far from the town it had been three years ago. Even then a childhood of summers had meant that most of the faces were known to her. Not so today. Other than the local market owner, old Mrs. Hawkins, no one looked familiar. And while it usually didn't bother Kira when men gave her a second glance, today she wanted them to keep their eyes to themselves. She wasn't up for the attention.

As she wove through the clusters of window-shoppers, it occurred to her that she'd fooled herself into believing that she was over the events of the past few days. Being with Mitch in the close confines of the Dollhouse Cottage had seemed somehow safe and normal. Out in the open, though, she felt like a target. Just to look busy, she dug in her purse for money. When she'd managed to mine about three dollars in change, she spotted a coffee-house called, fittingly enough, the Village Grounds. Kira headed inside.

The woman behind the counter smiled a greeting.

Kira ordered on autopilot. "A small iced mocha skim latte with a shot of hazelnut, please."

The worker's smile faded just a little. "Kira, you don't recognize me, do you?"

Brown hair…brown eyes…her age or maybe a lit-tle younger… Kira could find nothing that sparked recognition, though she did feel a twinge of envy at the woman's expression. It was one of total content-ment with life.

"I, uh…" Kira hedged.

"I'm Lisa Cantrell. We took sailing lessons to-gether for about four summers?"

"Lisa?" Kira blinked. They hadn't exactly trav-eled in the same pack of friends. She couldn't recall ever actually speaking to Lisa and suspected that if she had, the words had been some of her old snob-bery. "You look wonderful."

"Thanks. I lost a few pounds," Lisa replied as she packed freshly ground espresso into the small metal mesh funnels of the machine behind the counter. "I haven't seen you around town in a while."

Kira relaxed a little, figuring that if Lisa were out to seek revenge for whatever petty, teenage Kira might have done, the moment would have already come. "I moved south and haven't had much of a chance to make it up this way."

Lisa nodded. "This is the kind of town that you either stay in forever or forget entirely. I guess I've fallen into the stay-in-forever camp. Jim, my fiancé, and I lived outside of Detroit for a few years while he finished his orthopedics residency. It was just too big for both of us. We moved back here and I opened this place last summer."

"Congratulations," Kira replied. "It looks like Sandy Bend is booming."

"Summers are great," Lisa said. "Winters are a little quieter. Not like now."

Kira surveyed the seating area in the small space. Every table was taken, as was nearly every stool at the counter overlooking Main Street. Young moms laughed and chatted. Men sat at the window paging through newspapers.

"Are you in town long?" Lisa asked over the hiss of the espresso machine.

"I'm kind of loose on my plans," Kira replied.

"Jim and I are getting married Saturday on the town green. Why don't you come?"

The generous gesture warmed Kira and embarrassed her a little, too. "Thanks, but I couldn't. It's such short notice for you."

"Really, it's nothing fancy. We're having the reception right on the green, too. It's just a big, early afternoon picnic—no seating charts to worry about, or anything like that. Come join us."

The joy of a wedding between two people who really wanted to get married sounded appealing—and in Kira's recent experience, rare. She nodded. "If I'm still here, definitely."

"Great!" Lisa paused and settled two miniature silver pitchers of brewed espresso into a small tub of ice, then filled a plastic cup with the same. "So where south did you move?"

"I'm in the Miami area. I've got a real estate business in Coconut Grove."

"Wow, that's big time."

Kira smiled. "In a small sort of way. I—"

She broke off. One of the men seated at the window had suddenly caught her attention. He wore what was left of his dark hair in a comb-over that defied both good taste and whatever he'd sprayed it into place with. His nose was crooked, as though it had been well-broken a couple of times. Kira wouldn't have noticed these details if he hadn't lowered the newspaper he was reading to stare at her. It wasn't a friendly look, either.

Kira made herself turn away.

Lisa set Kira's drink on the counter and gave her a quizzical smile. "You okay?"

"Fine," Kira said, then repeated it with more conviction. "Just fine." She put her handful of change on the counter and took the drink. "I'll see you later, okay?"

"Sure," Lisa called as Kira bolted.

She was a stronger person than this, Kira told herself as she exited the coffeehouse. She could leave the nervous imaginings of henchmen behind and have a wonderful day.

Or at least one she could survive.

5

Just when Mitch was beginning to get a grip on his attitude, his boss and brother, Cal, walked into the police station. Since Mitch wasn't in the mood to talk—or even work up a fake smile—he tried to act interested in the paperless paperwork occupying his computer screen.

Apparently Cal didn't buy into the busy act, because he sat in the chair opposite Mitch instead of going to his own. "So, why is Kira Whitman staying at your house?"

Mitch attempted to deflect. "Aren't you supposed to be at the town council meeting? I thought the department budget was on the agenda."

Cal glanced at his watch. "The meeting doesn't start for another half hour. Now, what's the word on your guest?"

"What makes you think I have one?"

"Early this morning—and I mean very early—the ladies who walk saw a car with Florida plates parked out front of your house. Of course they shared this with me while I was buying my morning coffee."

Mitch rolled his eyes. These were the same ladies who also lunched daily. And gossiped daily. Once they knew something, soon so did most of Sandy Bend. "And what—you ran the plates' numbers?"

"No, I just saw Kira walking down the street and did the mental math. One hot Mercedes plus one blonde equals…"

Trouble. Mitch wished that Kira had quietly disappeared instead of swinging her little butt through town. Life was complicated enough.

"It's no big deal. She should be gone soon, anyway." He'd meant to sound matter-of-fact but knew that he must have come off as depressed, because Cal was giving him a speculative look that really fried his ass.

"Don't start," he ordered even though he knew Cal wouldn't listen.

"So, she just showed up on your doorstep for a night?"

Mitch shrugged. "Something like that."

"Huh. Interesting."

"Look, I've got paperwork to get through before lunch, okay?"

Cal grinned. "Far be it from me to stop you from doing your job." He stood. "And with such enthusiasm, too." When he was seated behind his desk he added, "If you wanna talk, you know I'm here."

And Mitch wished that he was far, far away.

Cal loved being a cop. Mitch had no doubt that his older brother would be Sandy Bend's police chief right up until retirement, as their father had been before him. And unlike Dad, who'd moved to Sedona, Arizona, and remarried after decades as a widower, Mitch was also one hundred percent certain that Cal would never leave Sandy Bend.

Mitch was positive, on the other hand, that he would. Maybe it was part of the middle-kid syndrome, but he'd never felt noticed here. Never felt totally connected. Back when he was a teenager, he'd secretly vented his Sandy Bend hostility by removing the carved *n* in *Bend* from the old-fashioned welcome sign at the town's southern limits.

Each time they'd replaced it, he'd stolen another and left an adolescent tribute to "Sandy Be d" in his wake. It was a dumb stunt that had gained him nothing more than a false rebel's thrill and a bunch of *n*s, which he'd ceremonially burned when he'd gotten out of the hospital last November.

His past vandalism hardly rose to the level of a felony, but he wanted a clean break from anything that might even remotely deny him admission to the bar. And he didn't mean Truro's Tavern down the street. He didn't care what it took, how many more months he went without a life to speak of, he would land a job as a federal prosecutor. End of story.

"So, did you finally get to kiss her? You know you've always wanted to," Cal called from his side of the open office.

What big bro didn't know wouldn't hurt him. "Not as much as I want to tell you to kiss my—"

Cal's laughter cut him short. "Hit a soft spot, huh?"

"I can think of a few of my own," he calmly replied while imagining how damn fine it would feel to pop Cal one on his glass jaw.

"Don't let her get to you this time, okay?" Cal said, now using his all-knowing tone instead of his push-you-until-you-snap one.

"Too late," Mitch muttered, not intending the words to carry across the room.

"Damn," his brother said. "I really hope she's gone."

Just as much as Mitch hoped in some bizarre, masochistic way that she wasn't. Then it struck him. Crime wouldn't keep him from that prosecutor's position, craziness would.

KIRA HAD BEGUN TO ENVISION her adventures as a movie: *Down and Out in Sandy Bend*. Once she'd finished her coffee and vanquished her goon hallucinations, she'd cruised the chichi boutiques that had pushed out the town's hardware store, grain supply and general mercantile. Apparently not a single local merchant believed in antiquated house accounts when the miracles of Visa and MasterCard had become commonplace.

If she didn't find a freethinker soon, she was going to be reduced to buying a packet of safety pins and altering Mitch's wardrobe to fit. Two places remained to be cased: Devine Secrets Day Spa and Marleigh's Boutique. The day spa appeared to be carrying a line of locally designed clothes, but the place's name was a strong tip-off that she'd find Dana Devine Brewer inside. Kira simply wasn't prepared to go there.

Marleigh's seemed to cater to the golf-and-tennis set, of which Kira had never been a willing member. Too much sweat was involved, and too many women with bunny names like Muffy and Fluffy. Still, it beat the safety-pin-and-duct-tape set. Kira turned a pained eye from the fuchsia-and-green color palette in the window and stepped inside.

Good thing she did, too, because she finally hit pay dirt. Marleigh was a distant acquaintance of Kira's oldest sister, Caroline, which meant that she bought into the Whitman aura but wasn't privy to the family dirt. It was easy for Kira to persuade the shopkeeper that she'd be in town indefinitely and would like the convenience of a store account.

For once in the past twenty-four hours, complete honesty was Kira's. She fully intended to pay her bills, just not until she was free of worry about being traced through her credit card activity.

While she answered Marleigh's questions about Caroline's life—fudging a little, since she hadn't talked to Caro in ages—Kira flipped her way through the racks of resort wear. Thankfully not all of it was in the 1980s preppy-throwback style she'd seen in the window. As she shopped, she was careful to select some items expensive enough to earn her unquestionable favored-customer status.

Once she'd tried those on and put them at the register, it was time for the nitty-gritty—some undies, skirts and shirts to get her through the next however many days until she could safely return home. On a whim she also selected a golden-taupe silk nightgown that was suggestive in a subtle sort of way, plus a more obvious red bikini and hip-hugging filmy sarong that showed off her curves and yet still hid her flaws.

The purchases showed just how ambivalent she was. Much as she wanted to find Roxanne and stick bamboo slivers coated with hot-pepper oil under her fingernails, she also craved more time around Mitch.

The bell on the boutique's door chimed again. When Kira spotted who'd come in, she was tempted to crawl beneath the dress rack.

"Hi, Marleigh," Dana Devine Brewer said. "I thought I'd stop by and remind you about your massage with Stacy at seven tonight."

If nothing else, Dana was direct. She hadn't managed to keep her gaze off Kira the whole time she'd been speaking to Marleigh. Kira knew when she was being hunted. With the tawny auburn streaks in Dana's dark blond hair and the predatory glint in her eyes, Mitch's sister-in-law made a fine lioness in search of prey.

"My, a personal reminder to follow your phone call an hour ago. You do believe in service," Marleigh replied in a teasing tone of voice.

Dana feigned surprise. "I called earlier? I'm slipping. It must be all the details involved in opening my new Crystal Mountain location." She pinned Kira with another sharply questioning look.

Kira wasn't comfortable with the curious glances being sent her way by the shop's patrons. The last thing she wanted was to be the daily topic on the town's gossip hotline. Marleigh, she had to be nice to. The other watchers got her don't-mess-with-the-heiress glacial glare, though the look was just frosty instead of downright cold since she hadn't used it in so very long.

"So, Kira, what brings you to town?" Dana asked.

"Just a friendly visit."

"Funny, since you're the only Whitman here."

"I didn't say who I was visiting, now did I?"

"I can think of only one possibility outside your family, and—"

"Why don't you show me your spa?" Kira cut in. "We can talk on the way." Before Dana could object, Kira turned to Marleigh. "If you could just hold my purchases for me? I'll be right back."

The boutique owner was clearly disappointed to have the action go elsewhere, but she didn't object.

Once outside Dana started up again. "So, really, why are you here? Steve and Hallie are gone until August, which I know for a fact since I'm helping cover Hallie's shifts at her art co-op."

Kira began to walk toward Devine Secrets. "I'm not sure I understand how any of this is your business."

"You stayed in Mitch's house last night, which makes it my business."

There was no outrunning gossip, was there?

Dana led Kira around the corner and to the back of the spa.

"What—no tour?" Kira asked.

Dana held open the door and ushered her in. "We'll start with my office. First door on your left."

"Great."

Kira entered but didn't take the seat in front of Dana's cluttered desk.

Dana wasted no time in starting her questioning. "This is going to sound pushy, but I'd really appreciate it if you'd tell me what's going on between you and Mitch."

"You're right. It sounds pushy."

"Look, he's been in kind of a fragile state for the past six months."

Kira grinned. "Mitch? Fragile? Forgive me if I can't picture it."

"Trust me on this."

She was so serious that it set Kira aback. She was as guilty as Mitch had been in assuming that she hadn't changed in three years. He was no more immune to life than she.

"Mitch bailed me out of a bit of a situation and I stayed with him, but nothing's going on. Really."

"So, you're not here specifically to see him?"

Kira went with the truth, as personally embarrassing as she found it. "I didn't plan to see him at all. He found me when I had, uh, slipped into Steve and Hallie's house. He wouldn't let me stay there, and for a variety of reasons I had no one else in my family I could turn to."

Frowning, Dana scrutinized her. If there had been a clock in the room, Kira could have counted its ticks as the silence stretched out.

"So, you're being honest," Dana finally said. "Good move."

"I remember you well enough to know that there's no margin in playing you."

"True again." Dana sighed, then said, "Bad family dynamics, I understand. My mom and I could be a case study in what not to do. But now I also understand good family dynamics."

Kira was about to agree that the Brewers were indeed wonderful, since sucking up seemed advisable, but Dana held up a hand and stopped her.

"I don't stick myself in the middle of Mitch's business lightly. And I wouldn't do it if I didn't know that he already has issues where you're concerned."

"Issues?" To Kira, that sounded nearly good.

"Don't look so pleased."

Dana picked up a framed snapshot from her desk and turned it toward Kira. In it Steve, Hallie, Mitch, Dana and Cal were standing on the beach, laughing as though they shared a joke. Kira suddenly felt very alone.

"This is my family," Dana said. "I don't want to be dramatic, but you should know that if you mess with Mitch's well being, you also mess with mine. And you really don't want to do that."

Yes, Dana remained dead-on direct.

Kira took the same approach. "Even if I had the power to—which I don't—the last thing I'd ever do is try to hurt Mitch, okay?"

Dana set down the photo. "The problem is, you've always been able to injure people without trying."

Kira had anticipated some tough moments when she returned to Sandy Bend, but sometimes the truth really did hurt. She let the sting subside before saying, "People change."

"Agreed, but are you one of them?"

She'd had enough. "Consider me warned, okay? I won't be here long enough to even accidentally do damage. Now, if you don't mind…"

Totally ticked, she opened the office door and walked straight into Mitch. He closed his hands on her upper arms and moved her back a step.

"Saved by the cop," she said in a lame attempt to cut some of the tension in the air. It didn't work.

Mitch checked her expression, which she assumed was hardly sunshine and rainbows, then said, "Are you okay?"

"Perfect as always."

He looked beyond her to his sister-in-law. "I had a feeling I was going to find something like this. What do you and Cal do—communicate by telepathy?"

"Cell phone," Dana corrected. "And I'm not going to apologize for butting in."

Mitch actually smiled. "Somehow I didn't expect you to. It's not your style."

"I'm family. I'm allowed to worry."

"Hey, I'm better now, okay? I can survive a few screwups."

Kira wasn't totally following whatever was going on between these two, though she did know that she wasn't very fond of being referred to as a *screwup*. She watched as Dana shook her head and gave Mitch an unwilling smile in return.

"You've got the same look you wore right before you signed up for skydiving lessons last year. What is it with you and risk?" Dana asked.

Mitch was still holding Kira by her arms. He glanced down at her. When their eyes met, it seemed to her that what had been a matter of restraint now almost felt like an embrace.

"The challenge," he said to Dana. "The biggest risks can bring the best rewards."

Kira couldn't have agreed more. If Mitch Brewer was any part of the reward, she was definitely up for the gamble.

WHEN MITCH CAME HOME THAT evening, he knew for form's sake he should hassle Kira because she was still camped out in his living room. He didn't, though. It didn't seem sporting to harass her when she'd filled the house with the scents of some sort of spicy chicken and the chocolate cake he'd just spied sitting on the kitchen counter. If she was manipulating him, she was doing a damn fine job of it.

Besides, she'd taken enough from Dana today. He knew that his sister-in-law meant well. She'd been fiercely protective of him ever since she'd seen him laid up in the ICU, fighting a secondary infection he'd picked up after he'd been dumb enough to get himself shot.

But as he'd told her, he was better now. He'd healed physically and emotionally and was tough enough to do battle with Kira…just not this minute. Not when she was wearing a movie-star halter dress that made her look as though she was channeling Marilyn Monroe.

Recalling his vow not to touch her and thus avoid becoming forever obsessed with her, he nodded a greeting and said, "So, did you kidnap a cook?"

"No," she said. "I cooked."

"Amazing." And he wasn't kidding. With her posh upbringing, he'd have bet that she couldn't run a microwave.

"It's nothing much. I spent two months at a culinary institute in France. I dropped out after my second burn. Some people aren't meant to be around open flames as a career, you know?"

She handed him a cold beer, which at least gave him something to do with his hands. Left to their own devices, they'd be untying that dress.

"Dinner's just about ready," she said, then went to the counter, where she began to toss a salad that was too colorful to be any of his bland bagged stuff.

As she worked, Mitch realized the full benefit of a halter dress. Not only did he get to fantasize about the ease of getting it off her, he also got to see a sleek stretch of her back. Her skin wasn't as deeply tanned as he'd imagined a Florida girl's being, but she definitely looked tasty.

"Where'd you get the dress?" he asked, then took a swallow of beer to see if that would wash some of the roughness out of his voice, though he doubted it.

"Marleigh's," she answered, then turned to face him, salad bowl in her hands. When she bent forward to place it on the kitchen table, he was afforded a brief view of breasts plump and perfect for his touch.

"Ready?" she asked.

For more than he would ever let her know.

6

AFTER DINNER, MITCH, WHO'D been appreciative but oddly distant, retreated to his office. Kira closed herself in the tiny bathroom and slipped into her new nightgown. A cursory glance in the silver-rimmed medicine-cabinet mirror confirmed that there was nothing freakishly wrong with her.

No green bits of cilantro clung to her front teeth.

No smear of chocolate frosting ringed her mouth.

So why the weird behavior? She knew they had a mutual attraction going. And they were both consenting adults—not that he'd asked her any questions in that regard.

As she brushed her teeth and readied for sleep, she decided that she should simply be satisfied that through cooking a decent meal she'd bought herself another night's lodging. She'd felt almost giddy with the possibilities this afternoon when Mrs. Hawkins at the market had automatically put the cost of Kira's apple-and-yogurt lunch on Kira's dad's tab. Seizing the opportunity, Kira had gone back and filled a cart with foods that might tempt a less-than-gracious host. The strategy had worked. Mitch hadn't even asked her why she was still in Sandy Bend. Any guilt over sticking her father with the tab would be alleviated by a donation to a food bank as soon as she had access to her checkbook.

Unfortunately she wasn't sure what she could summon as a follow-up act to the meal, and she needed one. Don, the P.I., had finally left a message on her cell phone, and it hadn't been good. There was no sign of activity at Roxanne's house, none of her friends had heard from her and her car still sat in the lot at work.

At this rate Kira would need a regular legion of distractions. Outside of her real estate skills she'd been pretty much a dabbler in life. A few cooking classes, a miserable month as an assistant to a party planner, a whopping week working with a decorator. All in all, not a very extensive skill set.

Kira stuck her toothbrush in the holder on the sink top and smiled at her small act of dominion. As she returned to the living room, she couldn't help but think of the legend of Scheherazade, who'd bought herself a day of life with a new tale for the sultan each night. Maybe her stakes weren't as high, but somehow they had begun to feel that way.

She had never denied her sexual attraction to Mitch, but now that she'd matured—a word that generally freaked her out—she had begun to suspect that something more than hormones was coming into play. Perhaps something as fragile as the heart she'd guarded all these years.

Putting aside that thought as both absurd and dangerous, she switched on the table lamp next to the sofa and hauled her briefcase onto her lap. She began to dig though it, craving order somewhere in her life.

She sifted through the papers she'd crammed in

the middle pocket days before and ignored ever since, finding her notes on Casa Pura Vida, a listing she now had no intention of pursuing. Too much bad had sprung from a house that had seemed so wonderful. Beneath her notes were all the comparable sales listings she'd pulled in preparation for that day. She set aside the stack of papers and dredged the front pocket in search of a binder clip. Instead she came upon her PDA in its brushed stainless-steel case.

Kira frowned. The case had a new scratch running diagonally across it.

"How did this happen?" she murmured, then flipped open the PDA's cover and pressed the on button to be sure the damage was only superficial. The opening screen no longer had the picture of a shirtless Heath Ledger that she'd loaded in there for a little daily eye candy.

"Weird," she said.

But it got even weirder when she checked her address book. The data wasn't hers. As she hit the toggle button and shot through the entries *A* to *Z*, it became clear that somehow she'd ended up with Roxanne's PDA. As she recalled the angry state she'd been in when she'd returned to the office to dump Roxanne's stuff, she supposed the mix-up should be no shock.

And now it might be a blessing.

Kira walked a circle of the room, turning the PDA over in her hands. In a pure and simple world, the ethical thing to do would be to put the PDA away and snoop no more. But Kira's world was getting poached on by a partner potentially up to no good and goons who were definitely bottom-feeders. She'd have to save the ethical purity for someone with a less hacked-up existence.

Within fifteen minutes Kira was an expert on Roxanne trivia. She knew her dry cleaner, her plastic surgeon and her gynecologist. She'd read her ratings on former boyfriends, her most recent liquor purchases and what she'd bought her father for Father's Day.

But most important of all, Kira was pretty sure that she had Roxanne's password for the Whitman-Pierce Web site. Kira had found it in a memo file, set up like an office-supply shopping list. It wasn't as though Kira felt that the universe owed her a break. Overall she'd been one lucky girl. But if she were to get a break, she hoped that it would be found with this password. She hadn't felt this sort of urgency since she'd made her first house sale. She had to get to a computer and see what more she could unearth. And she had to do it *now*.

Kira padded barefoot toward the doorway leading to both Mitch's bedroom and his office. A bluish light shone into the hallway from the office. She took another step forward, then nearly groaned with disappointment. Mitch was seated at his computer.

"You want something?" he called without turning his head from the screen.

He heard all too well, just as he did most everything else all too well.

"No, nothing. Just wandering a little."

She received a distracted "Yeah, okay" in response.

Kira had never had her fingertips literally itch before, but that was how anxious she was to get her hands on a keyboard. She was totally out of luck, too. Even the new-and-improved Sandy Bend wouldn't have anything as urban as an all-night Internet café.

She tiptoed back toward Mitch, hoping to see if he

looked as if he was there for just a few minutes or if he'd settled in for the long haul.

"If you're bored, read a book," he said, again without looking her way. "There's one in the end table's drawer."

"Thanks." She lingered in the doorway.

"I can hear you back there, you know."

How? It wasn't as though she was a mouth breather, stuffy with a cold.

"Sorry."

"If you're trolling for the computer, forget it. I've got work to finish. Besides, I'm not hot on the idea of you snooping though my files."

She was hardly in a position to claim moral indignation. "Thanks for the vote of confidence," she said.

He chuckled. "Hey, I'm a realist."

As was she. Tomorrow she'd visit the library. She was pretty sure the town had one of those, though she couldn't say that she'd visited it back in her debutante days. And if they did, odds were good she'd find a computer at which she could stomp all over Roxanne's privacy rights.

Until then all she could do was burn time. She'd like to believe that she could curl up on her lumpy sofa, close her eyes and awake refreshed in the morning, but again, she was a realist. To wind down, Kira organized and refolded her new clothes. Then, to make some room to store them, she moved aside a few dusty old trophies on the shelf unit that held Mitch's stereo. One gold-dipped football player clanked against the other, and she uttered a small "Oops."

"What are you doing out there?" Mitch called from the chair she'd still do nearly anything to get him out of.

"Just a little cleaning."

"You mean you kidnapped a maid as well as a cook?"

"Funny," she called back in a tone that added a vehement *not* to her comment. Still, she was glad to hear a little of the Mitch she knew back in his voice.

Kira realigned the statues one shelf up. She remembered when he'd played football while at Michigan State. She'd still been in high school back in Chicago and had thought about inviting him to her homecoming dance. Funny, now that she considered it, she'd spent a great many years thinking of Mitch. Funny, too, that she'd had the ego to imagine that a college guy would want to come to a high school dance. Life sure had a way of knocking teenage arrogance out of a girl.

By ten-thirty, Kira had tidied her belongings, read fifty pages of the paperback thriller Mitch had mentioned and nearly wrestled the sofa's cushions into a comfortable arrangement.

Just when she'd begun to settle, music blasted through the house. She winced at the pickax-to-guitar, death through aural torture making the stained-glass windows rattle in their frames.

"I'm a guest," she reminded herself. "A squatter. An interloper."

She was running out of synonyms for house crasher, and her brain cells were dissolving in the noise.

She shouldn't get up.

She shouldn't go goad him.

Except she suspected that he was as hungry for the diversion as she was. Why else would he do this?

She rose from the sofa and homed in on the source of the noise. Mitch was still at his desk. Instead of gaining his attention through something as bland as calling his name, she used her best hail-a-cab whistle.

Mitch turned down the volume, and the band silently wailed on from the computer screen. He swiveled his desk chair to face her.

"Something wrong?" His expression was bland enough, except for a certain you-took-the-bait glint she detected in his eyes.

"I was kind of hoping to sleep tonight," she said. Never mind that knowing he was yards away had already decimated her chances on that front.

"Sorry. I study better with music when I'm getting tired. It helps my concentration."

She noted that at present he was concentrating on her chest area. Was it possible that the fabric of the nightgown she'd picked up at Marleigh's was thinner than she thought? Kira quelled the urge to look down and find out. She'd already learned that the first rule in dealing with Mitch was to show no weakness.

"You're studying?" she asked as she strolled closer.

"I'm finishing off my last law school course," he replied without ever quite getting his eyes back to hers. "I took a year's leave from the force when I could afford it, but other than that I've been attending classes in East Lansing at night."

The drive alone—over two hundred miles, round-trip—would have killed her. "That's impressive. I didn't know."

One side of his mouth quirked upward. "Should you have?"

She somehow felt as though she should, as though she'd cheated herself by avoiding this town and this man.

"Probably not," she said anyway, then gestured at the dudes on his computer monitor. "I don't suppose classical music or even techno or something would do the job?"

"Not a chance," he said.

Kira spied a set of headphones stowed on the top right corner of Mitch's desk. It wasn't so much the thought of silence but the fact that she'd get to wriggle her body into the small gap between Mitch and those headphones that prompted the next question.

"Okay, then how about if I find a way for both of us to win?" she asked.

"What do you have to offer?"

"This."

Taking her time to savor the moment and breathe in the summer-hay-and-leather scent that would always remind her of Mitch, Kira moved around him and reached for the headphones. His gaze followed her body, feeling nearly as intimate as a caress. She didn't want to think what his touch might do to her.

He moved the office chair forward, bringing his knees within inches of where she stood. Her heart picked up a rhythm more jagged than the music he had muted. She could almost swear she heard Mitch's heart pounding, too.

He reached out one hand and rubbed the silk of her nightgown between his fingers and thumb.

"Nice," he said. "You look good in gold."

If this were any man but Mitch, Kira suspected she'd have a flip comment at the ready. Because he had a way of stealing her words, the best she could offer was a reedy-voiced thanks.

He released the fabric and ran the tip of his index finger across the thin panel of lace that banded the gown just beneath her breasts. His blue eyes grew darker, more intent. She could tell that he wanted more. And she did, too.

Big risks…big rewards.

Then he dropped his hand. His smile was as regretful as it was self-aware.

"I think I've pushed my luck as far as I should. You might want to take a step back, Highness."

Stepping back was the very last thing she wanted. Kira clutched the headphones and took stock of her options.

Strong women didn't beg.

Tough women didn't melt like sweet butter simply because a man smiled at them.

And independent women took control.

She returned the headphones to his desk, then braced a hand on each arm of his chair.

He opened his legs and she stepped into the gap, resettling her hands on his shoulders. His hands closed over her hips, pulling her even closer.

"Want to know why I can't concentrate?" he asked.

For the second time she answered, "Probably not."

Again it was a lie. She did want to know, especially if it involved any part of his body against hers. And really, she wasn't going to be choosy, though mouth against mouth would be a move in the right direction.

He slowly stroked his thumbs over the curves of her hip bones. "You've always made me crazy. Did you know that?"

Ditto to that.

"You'd think that after all these years I'd have

gotten over it," he said. "That I could be near you without wanting to—"

In business, timing was everything, and Kira meant serious business. She settled her mouth over his and took in his low murmur of surprise.

Yes, he made her crazy, but he also made her feel alive down to the soles of her feet—no small accomplishment when those feet were owned by a jaded former jet-setter. And being in this moment was what she'd think of. No worries. No tomorrow. Just now.

Kira sighed with pleasure. Ah, how she remembered this mouth. It wasn't the sort of thing a girl forgot. In one of the universe's small ironies, teasing, unromantic Mitch had a romantic's mouth. His lower lip was full, just perfect to draw between her teeth and caress with her tongue.

His hands moved up, now gripping her waist and pulling her closer. She rested one knee on the edge of the chair and leaned in, at the same time opening to him. Their tongues tangled, and her heart sped. He tasted slightly of the whiskey she'd seen him pour after dinner.

The kiss lengthened. Kira could feel her skin grow warm, then warmer yet, until she was damp and craving more.

She hadn't felt this sort of fire in…

In…

Three years—*the last time he'd last kissed her*.

If she were more athletic, or the chair bigger, she'd have found a way to wrap her legs around him, to feel the contact of her body against his where she needed it most.

He murmured her name, sliding one hand up to her breast. Startled by the new feeling, she broke off the kiss and stood on both feet, straightening a little and looking down at him.

Their gazes locked. He briefly slipped his fingers beneath the silky fabric. She shivered with excitement.

"Let me touch you," he said.

She gave her assent by taking her right hand and sliding the opposite strap of the gown off her shoulder.

Mitch's hand felt hot against her skin as he cupped her breast. He ran his thumb over her nipple, and she let her eyes fall closed and head dip back as he gently played with the peak.

Far before she would have willed it—which was, like, never—his hand was gone.

"I need to see you." He gave her no time to agree or disagree. He merely worked the silky fabric out of the way.

"Beautiful," he said.

She slid her hands into his thick, dark hair and brought his mouth to her breast. He made a wordless sound of pleasure before drawing his tongue across her nipple, then sucking her into the heat of his mouth.

Kira's knees began to buckle. He must have sensed her control slipping away, because he moved his hands to her bottom, supporting her. His fingers flexed in the same slow rhythm that his tongue drew on her sensitive flesh.

She moaned, and he rubbed the curve of her butt almost comfortingly. She pushed her hips against his hands in a nearly involuntary reflex.

He took his mouth from her breast and said, "Open your legs a little for me."

She braced her hands on his shoulders again and hesitated—not because she didn't want to cooperate but because she was too lost in a haze of feelings to immediately grasp his intent.

He blew a gentle stream of air at her wet nipple. She shivered, and he made a sound she'd describe as nearly a chuckle.

"C'mon, Highness," he urged.

Kira widened her stance just a little. Through the silky fabric he traced a path between the globes of her bottom. She began to breathe even faster, trembling.

"Closer," he murmured, and she scooted in.

His hand was broad and his fingers long. She squeezed his shoulders and gasped as he began to explore his way forward, moving the nightgown with him.

Unbelievably, after three sure strokes of his fingers, she was at the precipice of an orgasm.

She wanted to get his attention, to tell him to slow down—or maybe speed up. But all she could form was "Mitch?"

He made a soft sound of comfort but didn't slow his hand. "Shh."

One hard, slamming heartbeat echoed after another. Kira felt her body tighten, then finally totally let go. She cried his name and collapsed forward. As she shuddered, he leaned his forehead against her stomach. He was saying something—she had no idea what. Words couldn't compete with the rush of sheer pleasure still making her heart pound.

Slowly passion subsided. In its place came embarrassment. Twice—once three summers ago and again now—in mere moments he'd made her come apart at his touch. She didn't like what it said about her, the way she lost control with him.

Kira came to her feet, tugging the top to her nightgown into place at the same time. Then she made sense of the bottom half, brushing the back of it from the wet folds to which it still clung.

"I—" She stopped, realizing she had no idea what she'd been about to say.

Mitch was sprawled in the office chair, his head tipped to the ceiling. His erection rode hard against his jeans, and Kira was mesmerized by the sight of him, more at a loss for words than ever. She figured that thanking him was both insincere and dangerous right now.

Mitch looked back at her, his jaw set tight and a dark flush coloring his cheeks. "Like I said, you might have wanted to take a step back."

This time Kira listened.

7

THE SUN HAD RISEN AND MITCH was gone when Kira finally gave up any pretense of sleep. Last night, after she'd pulled on the police department T-shirt and curled up on her couch, she'd heard Mitch in the shower, then back at his desk with his tribute to headbangers playing again, though more quietly. She wouldn't have cared if he'd blasted it. She was too emotionally fried to work up more than an apathetic dislike of his tunes.

This morning, even after another shower and the pleasure of putting on fresh new clothes, she still felt numb, as though she hadn't slept at all. She knew she'd grabbed a restless hour here and there, but nothing that took the edge off her tension.

"Gotta get a grip," she muttered to herself as she made her way into the kitchen. There she found a note from Mitch with a key settled on top of it. Kira read his broad, angular scrawl:

Would you water Hallie's houseplants? Here's the key, which as a point of law you might want to use this time.

She looked at the note an instant longer, absorbing the fact that he hadn't even made reference to last night. It wasn't as though she'd expected a love note, but since he had put pen to paper, she'd have expected some mention.

She wished she were the sort of person who could just cruise on through the rough emotional ruts in life, but she wasn't. Not talking about last night meant that she'd internalize her feelings until they became a knotted mess. She'd been there before and had the checks paid to her therapist to prove it. However, talking it out with Mitch would make for another uptight event in a day that already featured finding out exactly how much business trouble she was in. Maybe for today only she'd take the talk-free route.

Kira folded the note in half and dropped it in the trash, then pocketed the key, which she'd use later. *After* she'd made use of Roxanne's PDA.

Hungry, she grabbed some strawberries from the fridge, rinsed them and ate the sweet berries one by one, leaving only their green, crownlike stems. Then she raided Mitch's office for a pad of paper and packed her briefcase. As an afterthought, she also grabbed a towel and her new beachwear. If she was going to her former cottage to water plants, she might as well take the extra steps to Lake Michigan's sleek sand dunes.

After a quick stop at the Village Grounds for a latte fix and a hello to Lisa, Kira arrived at Sandy Bend's small library. As she pulled into the lot, she saw a police cruiser parked nearby, in the adjoining school complex where a group of kids were playing summertime shirts-versus-skins basketball. Mitch was standing on the edge of the court, joking with some of the players.

She could sense the moment he noticed her. Her heart sped and a tingle she couldn't quell reached her skin. Still, she managed to park her car and get into the building without waving a hankie or otherwise making a spectacle of herself.

Once inside she checked in with the librarian, offering her driver's license in lieu of a library card. The computer room was empty, for which Kira was most grateful. She logged on to the Whitman-Pierce Web site, then pulled Roxanne's PDA from the briefcase's outside pocket.

Seconds later she was smack in the middle of Roxanne's e-mail. Like a good snoop, she was careful to follow the prompts so the mail wouldn't disappear after being read. She wanted to leave no trace of her activities as she worked her way into the layers of her partner's life.

Kira started with the old mail that Roxanne hadn't bothered to delete from the server. Most of the items had headers like Fisher Island Home? or Closing Date—exactly what one would expect to see in a real estate agent's virtual files. Kira started through them in chronological order. At first nothing seemed unusual, and she began to wonder if all the nerves and suspicion were for nothing. Maybe Roxanne was really on vacation…with some ugly, ugly playmates.

Then Kira read an e-mail that struck her wrong. The communication was simple enough, referring to a closing date. But she was almost certain that they had never done business with the client mentioned. Whitman-Pierce's niche was small and elegant. A firm that specialized in multimillion-dollar tropical hideaways didn't do a high-volume business, and Kira recognized most of their former clients' names.

She pulled out the legal pad she'd filched from Mitch and began listing names, dates and any dollar amounts referred to. Out of the thirty remaining old messages, seven others referred to deals and clients that she couldn't recall. While it was conceivable that one or two might have slipped her memory, eight couldn't have. What really made goose bumps rise on her arms was an unread message confirming a "loan document delivery appointment" set for the day before they had visited Casa Pura Vida.

Not only didn't Kira recognize the sender's name, Kira and Roxanne *never* touched mortgage loan documents, which fell into the title companies' domain. Title company representatives coordinated the loan documents with the lender and ensured that the deed to the property was valid and that the funds were good. At that point, all Kira and Roxanne did was a last bit of client hand-holding, followed by acceptance of a hefty commission check. No deliveries, ever.

This was bad, just wrong. And yet subtle enough that Kira was convinced Roxanne had implicated their business in whatever scheme she was running. Kira pushed aside the notes she'd taken, rubbed at the ache forming in the back of her neck and refocused on the computer screen. She needed to somehow double-check the mystery clients before forwarding the names on to her investigator. There was no point in sending Don off track if her business was simply outgrowing her brain.

Still, she didn't want to start talk by giving a find-the-mystery-client request to Susan. Kira was sure that the office antennae were already sensitive to weirdness, since both owners had never been gone at the same time before. That left her with her least best friend—the computer—as her only source of info.

About a year ago she'd sat through a meeting with Roxanne and the software designer she'd hired to put all the company's accounting information in a database that would be retrievable on line by their accountants. Because this stuff bored Kira comatose, she'd paid attention to only about every tenth word. If she were a contortionist, she'd be kicking herself in the rear about now. Since she wasn't, being forced to muddle through the program alone would be punishment enough.

Time crawled as Kira searched. Just when she came up with the monthly reports she was seeking, Sandy Bend's mothers must have made a mass decision to get some time away from their children, because about two zillion kids poured into the computer room and clustered around the open computers.

A few came to stand behind her, sending brain waves urging her to leave. This she didn't need. Bowing to strength in preteen numbers, Kira exited the Web site, packed her briefcase and departed. In a way she was relieved to be done for the day. She needed time to absorb what was going on, time to combat the stress sawing at her nerves. And she had just the place to do it.

Fifteen minutes later she was back in her childhood summer home. Kira doubted that she'd ever be able to fully distance herself from this house, to see it as Steve and Hallie's and in no way hers. Which went a long way toward explaining why she'd broken in without a second thought.

She had to admit that using a key to get inside was certainly easier on a girl's elbows and knees than climbing a tree and crawling across a roof. Kira closed the front door and then set her briefcase and swim gear by a low cocktail table in the living room. While the room bore the stamp of an artist in residence, with walls in new, vivid hues and whimsical bits of art here and there, it still evoked a nostalgic sort of peace. Even with all the changes it smelled the same: old pinewood, lake breezes and damp forest. It was easy to forget that a hectic and sometimes dangerous world waited not too far off.

Once she'd finished watering the plants, Kira changed into her bathing suit to ready for some beach time. First, though, she reached into her briefcase and pulled the list she had compiled at the library, thinking maybe she should give the names one more look. Avoidance got the better of her. Before she even started, a wedding photo album on an end table caught her attention.

Weddings…

She had seriously bad karma when it came to weddings. Missing the one under the embossed white leather cover in front of her had gotten her the role of bride in another.

Kira picked up the album and settled on the sofa. She flipped past the shots of Steve and Hallie on the beach, then slowed when she came to the photos of the wedding party—one which had one more groomsman than it did bridesmaids. That hadn't been the original plan.

Kira knew that she'd been asked to be in the wedding only because Hallie was far nicer than Kira had ever been. In Hallie's shoes, Kira wouldn't have tolerated a female who out of spite and insecurity had tried to tank her romance. But that was forgive-and-forget Hallie.

Because at the time Kira could think of no way out that would fly in the face of her prior behavior, she'd gotten fitted for her bridesmaid's dress. She'd told herself right up until the weekend of the wedding that she could pull it off, too. She could walk down the aisle with Mitch Brewer.

When that moment came, she'd refuse to recall how she'd made a fool of herself in town all that previous summer. She'd forget how angry words with Mitch over one particularly rotten act toward Hallie had led to that hot interlude very much like last night's.

That Mitch was involved at all had made for the ultimate in humiliation. It seemed that ever since he'd been first on the scene for the car accident that had shattered her hip and leg when she was sixteen, he'd also been first on the scene for all the other awful events in her life.

The Friday of the rehearsal dinner Kira had meant to drive from her home in Chicago to Sandy Bend. Instead panic had seized her. She couldn't face Mitch…couldn't face Sandy Bend.

She'd ended up at a Rush Street bar, drinking whatever fruity mixed drink looked most interesting. Whether it was the alcohol or the sugar that did her in, details became blurry. Right up until the fight. With no way out and no one who appeared to have any interest in rescuing her, Kira had used the tools at hand, smashing glasses on the floor and screaming for help at the top of her lungs.

Who'd have ever thought that a bar manager would take the breakage of about twelve bucks' worth of glassware so seriously?

She'd been hauled to jail. By the time she'd been

allowed to call her father and get herself bailed out, it had been too late to make Steve and Hallie's wedding. Needless to say, the consequences had been massive.

Weeks later Kira's father had offered her one hope of familial redemption. She would settle down with a mature man, one who would be a stabilizing influence. The man her father proposed was Winston Evers, his second in command over the Whitman empire.

Yes, in retrospect it was an archaic suggestion. But two things had driven Kira. First, she was well accustomed to having others prop up her lifestyle, and a husband would suit as well as the next guy. Beyond that, she'd been conditioned for years to try to please her father, partially so that the money would keep flowing but most of all because she craved his approval.

Kira didn't think her father was inherently evil or anything. Still, his choice of Winston was far from stellar. Sure, Win was brilliant and had a sharp sense of humor. But he was over twenty years older than Kira. He'd been divorced once years ago, had no children and dated for no reason other than social necessity. He was quite possibly the only person Kira knew who was more personally adrift than she.

They had spent time together, avoided anything more intimate than a dry peck on the lips and set a date for their wedding. Between wedding showers, dress fittings and pamper-me days at the spa, she'd managed to distract herself from the end event: marriage to a man she respected but could never love.

Winston had rescued her, though. She'd been at the church, ready to do the deed, when he'd asked for a minute alone with her. He'd taken her to a window that overlooked the jewel of a courtyard in the middle of the complex, had tipped her face up to the light, then had shaken his head.

"When did you last sleep?" he'd asked.

"I'm not sure." She'd been dreaming a lot. Most had been sexually explicit and all had involved Mitch.

"You can leave, you know."

Panic—or maybe excitement—had seized her. She'd frantically shaken her head. "I couldn't. Never."

"You can, and you probably should. I'm not going to be much of a husband, you know." He'd given her that world-weary smile she'd come to appreciate. "If you leave, my reputation will survive it. Now, *yours*, darling..." He'd chuckled, then kissed her cheek.

What others thought had suddenly seemed unimportant. For the first time in months Kira had felt a sense of freedom, and it was dizzying, intoxicating. "This is crazy. Everyone's arriving for a wedding. How do I do this?"

"One foot in front of the other."

She'd nodded. "One foot in front of the other."

And so she had.

And now here she was, sorry for so much. As part of her growing-up process, she'd written letters to virtually everyone in the family, apologizing for the miserable way she'd behaved for years. Some she'd heard back from, some she hadn't. All she could do anymore was prove that she could stand alone, that she wasn't a perpetual user. And the person she most had to prove it to was herself.

Kira closed Steve and Hallie's wedding album, then returned it to the spot where she'd found it. She walked through the living room's French doors and onto the deck. If a swim in Lake Michigan's chilly waters didn't shock the past out of her, nothing would.

MITCH PULLED HIS CRUISER IN next to Kira's car. It struck him that less than forty-eight hours had passed since he'd last done this very same thing. That was pretty short timing for what they had cooking between them. Of course, it was easy to pack a lot in considering how much else in the way of work he'd let drop. Good thing that crime was minimal and his boss knew he'd soon be resigning.

Before heading up the steps cut into the forested hillside to the house, Mitch grabbed the sack holding a lunch he'd picked up for Kira and himself. Food wasn't the best peace offering for the way he'd let temptation get the better of him last night, but along with an apology, it was all he had to offer.

He knew he'd be way out of his league if he tried to pick her up a piece of jewelry. And there was a good chance she wouldn't be around long enough for flowers to be more than a throwaway—a thought he hated, because now he knew exactly why she'd stuck in his mind all these years and why she would long after she was gone this time, too.

Mitch walked into the house, which was still and silent. He checked the kitchen, where Hallie had lined up her plants—probably because she knew he'd lose track and kill half of them if they weren't clumped together. After setting down the sack of food he touched the first pot's soil and found it freshly watered.

"Kira?" he called. "Are you in here?"

Out of a newly minted sense of nostalgia, he even checked the shower where he'd found her last time, but it was bone-dry. Back downstairs in the living room he picked up her trail. Her black leather briefcase sat next to the couch and some papers were spread on the cocktail table.

Mitch glanced at them, then walked to the room's French doors. He tested the handles and found them unlocked. Since Kira wasn't in sight, she must be down the dunes at the lake. Even though his conscience—one SOB of a drill sergeant—snarled at him, he walked back toward the papers she'd left.

Last night's encounter might have been damn hot, but it hadn't totally scorched his memory. He knew that earlier Kira had wanted to get to his computer for something, just as well as he knew that she wasn't in town for a friendly visit. Exactly what she was doing…that, he didn't know.

Without picking up the papers, Mitch read the jottings a couple of times. The names meant nothing to him, which was no surprise. However, the dollar amounts in the millions with question marks by them and Kira's heading entitled Mystery Clients were more than enough to raise a few questions in him, too.

He regretted never asking Steve for specifics on what Kira had been doing these past few years. He'd been afraid that what he'd hear would fall under the category of more of the same, and he'd wanted to think better of her. Now that he'd spent some time with her—and despite the evidence in front of him to the contrary—he couldn't imagine that she was still flitting party to party, crisis to crisis. In fact, he'd almost call Kira mellow.

He grinned as memories of last night's heat and excitement came to him. Yeah. Almost mellow.

So what was she doing that involved "mystery clients" and the amounts of money she'd noted? No fan of subterfuge, Mitch figured the best thing to do was ask. Of course, he'd have to do it in a way that didn't begin with *I was reading papers I shouldn't have been....* And since nothing was immediately coming to mind, he figured he'd improvise once he was closer to her—a place he was really growing to like.

Mitch grabbed the lunch offering from the kitchen, then made his way down the steps to a sweep of the dunes. As sand sank into his uniform shoes and socks, it occurred to him that he'd have been better off ditching the footwear back at the house.

He crested the last dune and spotted Kira closer to the water, where the sand was hard packed. Her hair was slicked back as though she'd been swimming, and she was wearing a red bikini that was hot enough to rouse him past the semi-turned-on state he'd been in since he'd decided to track her down.

He laughed when he noticed that she lay on a towel he'd last seen in his own linen closet this morning. The woman did have a way of making herself ruler of her surroundings.

As he approached, she spotted him. She shielded her eyes from the sun with her hand, then after checking him out, quickly grabbed a red piece of fabric he supposed was some sort of skirt or something, scooted it under her bottom and tied it low on her hips. He watched her sit up and smooth the fabric over the scars they both knew she'd had for years. She carefully settled her right hand over the old injury before waving with her left.

Mitch's heart tightened at this show of vulnerability. She'd always made an effort to appear impervious to others' opinions. And he'd always been a little sad that she felt she had to be so perfect.

"Hey," she said as he grew close. "Overdressed for the beach, aren't you?"

He held out his purchases from a deli in town. "I'm on lunch break. I saw you leave the library and figured you had to be out here, so I brought us food."

She patted the towel next to her. "Have a seat."

As he pulled out a container of fruit salad he thought she'd like and the pasta salad he knew he'd like, Mitch tried to think of some way to launch the what-the-hell-is-going-on-with-you? topic.

While he hesitated, Kira grabbed the pasta salad. "Carbs! Wonderful carbs!"

He was torn between asking for them back and smiling at her excitement over pasta and a bunch of purportedly Greek vegetables.

She took the plastic fork he offered and dug in. "There's nothing like carbs for stress eating," she said over a mouthful of pasta shells in a very nonsocialitelike way.

Since he was a guy, he considered carbs good for everything, including curing the common cold. That and apparently giving him a hook into the conversation he wanted to have.

"So, you're stressed?" he asked.

She nodded. "Maxed out."

"What's up?"

She hesitated before speaking. "I didn't think I was ready to talk about this, but I guess I am. Last night scared me, Mitch."

Last night? He definitely needed more practice in

crafting leading questions. It was time to redirect the witness.

"So it's just last night that's bothering you? There's nothing else?"

She reloaded her fork and pushed on as though she hadn't heard him. "We've kissed each other twice in three years, and both times I ended up acting like some sort of…I dunno…porno queen. You have to have one of two opinions of me—that I'm easy or nuts."

Clearly she was acquainted with no porno queens. "I, uh…"

She shook her head. "Don't tell me which one applies. I'm better off not knowing."

Good thing, since he had no clear-cut answer for what he thought of her, except that it didn't involve porno queens.

"I don't react like that to all men, okay? Just you, and I don't know why. I mean, you're attractive and everything, but it's not as though we have the friendliest of pasts."

Mitch frowned. "I've always felt friendly toward you." Which was like saying that the beach they sat on had a couple of grains of sand.

She shrugged in an embarrassed way, then speared some more pasta. "Quite an ego boost having me fall all over you, huh?"

He smiled. It would do.

"So, do you think you could share that with me?" he asked, pointing the spare plastic fork toward the pasta.

"Sure," she said, centering the container between them. Actually a little closer to her than him. Mitch got in a few bites before she became too territorial.

Eventually she balanced her fork on the edge of

the pasta container's discarded lid. Mitch watched as she looked out at the endless blue of the lake and sky, then back to him.

"I'm not sure how much longer I'm going to be in town," she said. "It could be as little as a few days if things heat up for me. But for however long—if you'd let me—I'd like to stay at your place."

"I'd like that," he said. He'd also like the chance to figure out what was going on with her—a task more easily accomplished when she was under his roof. "Stay as long as you want."

She smiled. "Thanks."

"So, what sort of things might heat up?" he asked in a casual tone.

"Just work stuff," she said. He didn't bother trying to measure the degree of honesty in her statement. He knew it held enough that she'd spoken with confidence.

"So, you have a job other than kidnapping maids and cooks?" he asked.

"Of course I do. Being the black-sheep Whitman doesn't pay too well. Or at all, actually."

Mitch scratched another assumption from his list.

"After working as real estate agents for someone else, a friend and I got our brokers' licenses and struck out on our own a couple of years ago," Kira said. "We have a small business in the Miami area that specializes in higher-end properties."

He saluted her with his fork. "It suits you, Highness."

She smiled. "It does. It took me a while to find my niche, but I'm there."

"So tell me more about what you do."

She shifted restlessly, still careful to cover that

scar. "It's boring, unless you're a real estate geek like me."

"It can't be worse than some of the dry stuff I've dealt with in law school," he offered.

"I'd just really rather leave my Florida life in Florida."

A sudden awful thought struck Mitch. It was improbable, considering the line she'd spun when she'd arrived in town, but he had to ask. "You're not married or anything, are you?"

She rolled her eyes. "I'm lucky if I have a date every three months."

Selfish as it was, Mitch liked the sound of that. He wasn't quite as thrilled to have the same statistic apply to him lately.

Kira reached her free hand into the sand just past the edge of the towel and ran her fingers though it, leaving a wavelike pattern in her wake.

"Can't we just take these next few days for what they're worth? Not too many questions, just some fun?" she asked.

That was a man's evasion—one he'd used to defend himself from expectations more times than he could count. He'd never figured on being on the receiving end of the play. He didn't much like it, either.

"Sure," he said, just as those women had said to him before. He'd known then that it was a glossing over of the emotions involved, but he'd also been a willing recipient of the lie. Now he wanted to give her the truth and let her deal with it. Maybe she'd have more success at making sense of it than he was.

She'd never believe him, though. She'd never accept that the few days they had were worth more than hot and hungry sex.

That *she* was worth more.

But if this was what she wanted, he'd at least deliver that. And it wasn't as though it would pain him too much in the process.

Kira met his eyes with a direct gaze. "It's pretty clear to me that we're going to end up finishing what we started last night. And since that's the case, let's get the basic stuff out of the way while we're still able to think straight. I'm not on the pill or anything, so you're going to need to use protection. Which I'd expect you to anyway. And I'd also expect you to tell me that you and your doctor are recent acquaintances and that you're the picture of health...if you get my point."

Mitch nodded. He had to respect her pragmatic approach, even if it was rubbing his nose in the fact that she wanted this to be all about sex. "Yes to all of the above."

She relaxed a little. "Same here."

Mitch took her hand and brought it to his mouth for a brief kiss. "Now that we've got that squared away, I should tell you that I have class tonight in East Lansing. I'm going to be leaving at three and probably won't be back until after midnight." He grinned, figuring at least he could get in one last tease. "So, unless you'd like to..."

Mitch trailed off, gesturing at the towel beneath them.

Kira laughed. "Let me see.... I could make love with a police officer under the noonday sun on a beach that has its share of people trooping by or I could just finish scarfing carbs and look forward to being in a real bed with you."

She leaned forward and brushed a kiss against

his mouth. "Hate to tell you, Mr. Officer, but the carbs and a real bed win. Think you can wait?"

Yeah, but it was going to hurt like hell doing it.

Mitch glanced at his watch and then stood. "My lunch break's over, Highness. I'll leave you to your carbs. And stay out of trouble, okay?"

"Hey, my bad-girl days are behind me," she replied with admirable sincerity.

For his sake as well as hers, Mitch hoped that was true.

8

EYES GLAZED FROM READING ONE too many financial reports, Kira shut down Mitch's computer. She glanced at the nearby desk clock. It was not quite nine-thirty, leaving hours yet before he'd be home. Kira stood and stretched, easing tense muscles.

She felt mildly guilty for using his computer for her research. Still, she'd decided to live by the theory that what Mitch didn't know wouldn't hurt him. And the corollary to the theory also would prove true: what he didn't know couldn't hurt *her*, either. As joking as his stay-out-of-trouble request this afternoon had been, it wouldn't have sprung to mind if he didn't have doubts about her ability to handle life.

She was sure she could keep herself together while her private investigator did his thing. Mitch didn't need to be involved, and she didn't need him witnessing yet another Kira catastrophe. Tomorrow she'd call Don, tell him her concerns and give him the list of unfamiliar client names. She wished that she had something more concrete than suspicions, but the monthly reports she'd reviewed tonight showed nothing that matched the names or sums on her mystery client e-mails.

And now she'd finished up with business, it was

time to prepare for pleasure.... She peeked into Mitch's bedroom and shook her head at the clutter of books and magazines. It wasn't a disaster zone, yet it also wasn't the seduction setting she wanted, either.

She laughed at the thought of the word *seduction*. Definitely no seduction would be required on Mitch's part. She'd wanted him since he'd trapped her two days earlier.

Kira gathered the books and magazines into her arms. Mitch certainly was a guy with broad interests. There were sportsman's magazines, almost obligatory for men who lived near both a big lake for fishing and miles of forest for hunting. But there were also current-events magazines and quarterly law reviews from different schools. She felt a little like a voyeur learning about him this way, but she'd take what she could get.

Kira stowed the magazines and papers on top of the jumble of shoes on the floor of Mitch's closet. She barely got the door shut before the mess started to slide her way. As she walked to the living room and gathered the goodies she'd bought in preparation for tonight, she admitted to herself that the wanting hadn't started two days ago. She'd wanted him *forever.* As a teenager, her first sparks of sexual curiosity had always been centered on Mitch. As a woman, she could act on those feelings and planned to do so thoroughly.

Back in his bedroom she dug into the bag and unearthed one of the purchases on which she'd spent the rest of her cash. She unscrewed the top of the bottle of massage oil and sniffed.

"Perfect."

She set it on the nightstand, along with some little sweet-smelling candles in their glass votive holders. Her stint with a party planner might have been brief, but it had given her an appreciation for the importance of a theme in all events. Tonight's was Mitch's Favorite Foods.

Kira had put the box of condoms she'd found in the linen closet on the nightstand and was folding back the comforter and plumping the pillows when the phone on the far nightstand began to ring. Her first thought was to leave it except that the phone in the kitchen had no answering machine. Neither did this one.

What if it was Mitch calling? What if he was running late or out of gas or otherwise unacceptably delayed? She'd gladly drive to the middle of the state to haul him home.

As ring number four chimed out, she made her decision.

"Brewer residence," she answered.

After a short silence a woman's voice said, "This is the *Mitch* Brewer residence?" She sounded confused or maybe shocked.

"It is."

"Then, is, uh, Mitch home?"

Kira stepped into the role of crisp and official personal assistant, trying to distance herself from her own curiosity. "No, I'm sorry, he's not available. Would you like to leave a message?"

"Who is this?" asked the caller.

Kira didn't feel inclined to share. "A friend of Mitch's. And your name?"

"Betsy."

"Betsy," Kira confirmed. "Will he know what this is regarding?"

"I'm... Wait, this is class night, isn't it? I can't believe I forgot."

Okay, so she knew Mitch's schedule. That didn't mean they had any intimate connection. "Should I have him call you?"

"Definitely. Tell him it's something he's been wanting to hear."

"Does he have your phone number?" Kira asked.

The Betsy person laughed, and Kira felt her lip begin to curl, which she feared was step one in a territorial growl.

"Don't worry, he has my number," Betsy said.

After they'd exchanged goodbyes, Kira hung up, wondering who this Betsy was. It wasn't jealousy driving her, exactly. She knew that Mitch didn't have a serious girlfriend. He was straight-up honest and wouldn't have had her overnight in his house if he did—let alone touch her the way he had last night.

Still, Kira felt unsettled. Mitch had an entire existence that she knew little about. And she couldn't ask him—not so long as she was unwilling to share the details of hers.

She'd fully intended to greet him from his bed. Now she couldn't quite get herself to do that. Kira went to the kitchen and riffled through the laundry basket until she found the taupe nightgown. She'd washed it and a load of Mitch's laundry this afternoon—one more bit of playacting that she really was part of his life.

She shed her clothes, leaving them in a pile next to the washer, then slipped into the nightgown. She'd wait for him on the couch. That place was at least clearly hers.

AT ELEVEN FORTY-FIVE MITCH pulled up in front of his house. He'd set what he'd bet was a new land-speed record from East Lansing to Sandy Bend. If he were a good cop, he'd write himself a ticket. But right now he wasn't a cop or a law student. No, he was one lucky and extremely thankful bugger about to have eleven years' worth of fantasies become real. Whatever the ultimate price in continuing this obsession, he decided he'd be willing to pay it.

He opened the front door, stepped inside and dropped his backpack full of books by the coat closet. Quietly he closed the door and walked into the living room.

She was asleep on the plaid beast. The sofa had come with the house. He'd kept it because it was so damn ugly that it deserved a home. He had to say it looked one hell of a lot better with Kira on it, especially when she was wearing the gold-colored nightgown that had brought him to the brink last night.

His foot nudged something—her briefcase maybe—and he took a quick sidestep to avoid ending up on his butt. The noise awakened Kira. In the meager wash of light from the front hall, Mitch saw her sit up.

"Who's there?" she asked, at the same time awkwardly scrambling up from the sofa.

He was quickly telling her it was okay when she clutched at her leg and stumbled to the floor.

"Dammit," she gasped. "Stupid hip."

Mitch strode over and bent down next to her. "Let me help you up."

"I can do it myself," she said, then clambered to her feet, leaving him there with his hand held out. He let it drop to his side.

She limped a slow circle around the room while he stood by the couch feeling useless.

"Maybe you should sit down?" he asked.

"No, I have to walk it off or I'll be stiff all night."

"I'm sorry. This isn't how I wanted tonight to begin." He switched on the lamp beside the couch, leaving the three-way bulb at its lowest setting.

She stopped by the rocking chair that had been his mother's and rested one hand on the back of it. "It's not your fault. I've always been an edgy sleeper and I guess you startled me."

Mitch walked to her and briefly touched his fingertips to her cheek. "Can I get you anything? Some aspirin maybe?"

She nodded. "That might be a good idea."

"I'll be right back," he said before heading to the kitchen for the aspirin and some water. He hadn't quite cleared the room when he heard her hiss of pain as she walked again. Funny how guilt was more effective than jumping into Lake Michigan in January when it came to calming a guy's libido.

He took his time in the kitchen, giving Kira a chance to get a grasp on the poise that he knew was so important to her. When he returned, she was seated on the sofa, her hands settled on her knees.

"Here," he said. She held out her palm and he dropped the aspirin into it. After she'd popped them into her mouth, he gave her the water. When she was through, he took the glass from her, set it on the end table, then leaned back on the sofa.

He draped one arm across the back of the old dinosaur of a couch. Kira moved closer to him, relaxing with her head pillowed on his chest. The emotion that shot through him had a whole lot more to do with the utter rightness of having her there than it did with lust.

"This feels good," she murmured.

"A far better way to start the night," he agreed.

He ran his fingers through her hair, oddly riveted by the way it still managed to shine in the dim lamp-light.

"How was class?" she asked.

"Too long. Then again, so was the rest of the day." She sighed and burrowed closer. "Agreed."

They sat in silence a while. Mitch let Kira set the pace. She would know best when the aspirin had kicked in. While they waited, he took the time to re-member the details of this moment—how she smelled faintly of strawberries and how her skin felt soft and resilient under his touch.

He brought his arm from the back of the couch down so he could trace the line of the gown where it plunged into a vee, exposing the cleft between her breasts. Her nipples rose as he touched her. Soon she leaned her head back for a kiss.

Damn, but he needed her in a bed.

She must have felt the same way, because she un-twined herself from his arms and stood. "You prom-ised me a real bed."

And as he'd promised himself, he would deliver. They walked to the bedroom together. When they were there, matters didn't proceed as he'd expected.

"Hang on," Kira said, closing his bedroom door in his face. Mitch waited, figured he might as well give his self-control its final workout. He could hear her rustling about, then the door swung open.

"Okay, now," she said.

She'd been one busy camper. He took in the white

candles burning in votives on his dresser, the top of which she'd cleared of its usual clutter of books and papers. Both nightstands had received equal treatment. Each held candles, and on one the lamp shone, too.

"Just to keep us safe, don't open your closet door," she warned.

He smiled, imagining the avalanche, and then walked over to the nightstand on his side of the bed. She'd put out a box of condoms and a bottle of... something.

He picked it up, and excitement shot through him. Flavored massage oil. "Strawberry flavored? Do I want to know where you got this?"

"Definitely not," she said after giving him a broad grin.

"Try me."

"Devine Secrets," she said. "It's under-the-counter stuff, special request only. I went in for the scented variety. Cross my heart."

Hot thoughts of using the oil on Kira warred with the sure knowledge that his sister-in-law was going to give him a boatload of grief. "Yeah, like scented-only would have made it any better. You bought it from Dana?"

"It was our lucky day. She's up at the new Crystal Mountain spa. Otherwise I would have retreated with a bottle of nail polish."

"Wise. Very wise," he said as he unscrewed the top to the oil. He put his index finger over the opening and tipped it enough to coat the pad of his finger, then brought the oil to his mouth. "Not bad. How'd you know to choose strawberry?"

"Because I've witnessed your food tastes, and

they didn't have any marshmallow fluff," she replied, then came to take the bottle from his hand as he laughed.

Mitch wouldn't call what he was feeling *love*, but he would admit to his heart expanding to make room for the smart and altogether too sexy woman in front of him.

"Uh-uh. Hand the bottle back," he ordered.

For once she did as he asked. He coated a fingertip again, then ran it over the curve of her shoulder.

"Nice," he said after sucking on the spot just hard enough to draw a shiver from her.

He repeated the process, this time touching the top of one plump breast.

"Very nice," she said.

Mitch knew he could do even better. He went down on one knee and began sliding up the hem of her gown. Skipping the oil for now, he dusted kisses on the smooth bone of her right shin, pushing the silk fabric higher.

Kira stepped away.

"What are you doing?" he asked.

"Turning out the light."

He stood. "Don't. I want to see you."

She shifted uneasily. "Some things are better left to the imagination."

He'd been concerned that this moment would come. "This is about the scars, isn't it?"

Gaze fixed on the carpet at her feet, she nodded.

Mitch scrubbed his hand over his face, trying to decide how to handle this.

"Kira, they don't matter. They're in your past."

"A less-than-attractive part of it." She sat on the edge of the bed. "Look, I know this seems irrational to you, and that's because it probably is, but I don't want you to see them."

He'd seen worse, though. He'd seen her before the wounds had healed. Alerted by Hallie that Kira had taken off in a car filled with wasted college guys, he'd been the first person to arrive at the accident scene. Since she hadn't been wearing a seat belt, Kira had been thrown from the packed car.

He'd just turned twenty and had been pretty damn sure he was a true hard-ass. That was, until he'd seen that jagged white shard of bone sticking through the ripped flesh of her thigh. He'd held himself together, administering first aid as he'd been trained in the paramedics' courses he'd been taking that summer.

When the paramedic crew had arrived and he'd been sure that Kira was in good hands, he'd gone into the woods and had puked until his stomach was empty. Then he'd tried to go after the drunken—and injury-free—moron who'd been driving. Luckily by then Cal had been there to hold him off, because Mitch would have killed the guy. And would have been glad to do it.

Over ten years had passed and he could still feel that anger boiling in him. At sixteen, Kira had meant something to him. At twenty-seven, she meant even more.

"Come on, it's no big deal," he wheedled.

"That's easy for you to say."

He had her now. He smiled, and her brown eyes narrowed.

"Don't laugh," she said.

"I'm not laughing." He unbuckled his belt, then unbuttoned his jeans and worked down his fly.

"I'm not in the mood anymore," she said from her perch on the bed.

This time he did laugh because she sounded damn near like the sulky socialite he used to know. "I'm just playing some show-and-tell, Highness."

"You're assuming I want to see."

"You will." He toed out of his shoes, took off his socks, shucked his jeans, then moved closer. "Think you can beat this?" he asked, settling his left index finger on the knotted and angry red scar that ran a good five inches down his thigh. "I'm betting you can't."

She stood and traced the damaged flesh with one fingertip. He could tell by the line between her brows, by the way she worried at her lower lip with her teeth that her touch was light and careful. She needn't have bothered. His nerves hadn't fully regenerated yet, and he still couldn't feel much there. Now, a hand's length in and up…there, he could feel just fine. And he couldn't recall ever being this hard and aching.

"What happened?" she asked.

"Gunshot wound," he said, doing his damn best to sound casual.

"When?"

"Last fall. Some guys on their way up to deer camp stopped and drank Truro's Tavern dry. There was a fight in the back parking lot and my leg got in the way."

"I'm sorry." Her fingers glided upward, closer to where he wanted them. "All this from one bullet?"

Mitch closed his eyes, figuring he could hold on to some vestige of control if he couldn't see her. "No, the rest is from an infection that followed."

"Wow. I'm *really* sorry."

He shrugged. "I wasn't much to look at to begin with."

He nearly lost it when he felt her mouth settle, warm and wet, just below the edge of his short jersey boxers. Giving himself up for a goner, he looked down and caught her smiling at what had to be one tortured expression on his face.

"We'll leave the looks assessment with the beholder, okay?" she said. "Take off your shirt."

Mitch was happy to comply.

After he'd dropped the shirt to the ground, she hooked her fingertips into the elastic of the boxers riding below his waist. "Not much? I've got a feeling you're a whole big lot to look at."

Mitch started to laugh, but ended up gasping when she followed the contour of his erection with one sure hand. He settled his palm over hers, meaning to stop her, but he lacked the self-discipline to do it.

She squeezed him through the fabric, and he could feel sweat begin to pop out on his forehead. Or maybe it was blood. He'd been too aroused for too long.

But he also planned to follow through with the purpose of this whole show.

"No distracting me," he said. "I've shown you my scar, now you show me yours."

She let go of him, then nudged him back a step. For a moment he thought that it was going to be this simple to get her past the scar hang-up. But he'd forgotten that nothing with Kira was ever straightforward.

Instead she sat on the bed and shimmied up her

nightgown so that it still covered her legs, but was free from beneath her bottom. She held out her hand.

"We're going to go by feel."

And she was going to be the death of him.

He put his hand in hers, and she worked it under the raised hem of her gown. She directed his fingers until they were settled over a broad indentation that was about three inches long. "This is the leg."

"Doesn't feel too bad," he said.

She took his hand higher, over her right hip. "And these are from the socket and pelvis repair."

He had a man's hands, rough from years of football and work. He could maybe feel a small ridge or two, but nothing much.

"I think I'm going to have to look, Highness." His voice had come out kind of husky, but that's because he was having one hell of a time not letting his hand venture elsewhere, to be skin to skin with the places that last night he'd touched through her gown. "Just lie back, sweetheart. Let me…"

She acquiesced with a small sigh, her lower legs dangling off the bed. Mitch reached to his right, grabbed a pillow and tucked it beneath her head.

"It's going to be okay," he said.

She nodded, but he could still see the shadow of self-consciousness in her eyes. Using both hands, he began pushing her nightgown upward, exposing slender thighs, the right one showing the mark of the injury he recalled.

Mitch reached for the oil, poured a little into his palm and rubbed it slowly over the spot. Her muscle tightened beneath his hand.

"Relax," he murmured.

After a few moments he could feel the tension

ease from her. Slowly he moved the nightgown higher, exposing not only the thinner scars on her hip but the soft golden hair on her mons.

Mitch's erection pressed harder against his boxers until he couldn't stand it anymore. He reached down and rid himself of the last of his clothes.

When he returned his attention to Kira, a smile curved the corners of her mouth upward. "You're definitely a lot to look at," she said.

So was she. Mitch's hand trembled as he poured more oil. He gave the marks on her hip the same slow treatment that he had the one on her thigh. Then, unable to deprive himself any longer, he reached for the oil a final time, rubbing it between his fingertips.

"It's time to lose the nightgown," he said to Kira.

She sat up and pulled it over her head, then let it drop on the bed next to her. Mitch's heart slammed. God, she was beautiful. A wash of pink had risen from her chest to her face, and he knew that she was as turned-on as he was. Clearly knowing his intent for the oil on his fingertips, she opened her legs to him. This act of trust made him want her all the more.

He stroked her with oil, dipping his fingers into her tight wetness and using his thumb to work gasps from her. And when he thought she was ready, he bent forward and kissed the insides of her thighs, moving upward bit by bit until he parted her with both thumbs and tasted sweet, slick strawberry heaven.

If a guy had to die, this was the way to go.

KIRA COULDN'T BEAR ANY MORE pleasure. Knowing she was less than a touch away from completion, she tugged at Mitch's hair. When he looked up at her, she said, "I don't want to come without you inside me. Please…"

His hands slid down from where he'd been touching her, to her knees. "Any way you want it, sweetheart."

She scooted up on the bed and felt almost weak limbed with anticipation when he joined her, kneeling between her open legs.

He reached for the condoms she'd left on the nightstand. "I'd like to go slowly, to savor you," he said. "But that's going to have to be next time, okay?"

She nodded, but she still needed to touch him, to feel his heat in her hand.

"Let me," she said, taking the flat plastic packet from him.

Mitch rolled and lay back on the bed, and now Kira knelt above him. She was to the point where even the sound of the condom packet coming open was arousing. Hands trembling, she unrolled the condom down his thick shaft.

Mitch's eyes were half closed, and his hiss of pleasure resonated inside her. She leaned forward and kissed him once deeply, using her tongue to tell him what she needed. When she moved slightly away, he cupped the back of her head with his hand.

"I don't want to hurt you," he said. "Would it be more comfortable if you were on top?"

She ran her palm down the side of his face, tingling with pleasure over the feel of his day's growth of beard. "How about we try it both ways? Just for comparison's sake, of course."

She barely had the words out before he had flipped her onto her back. He entered her slowly, which was a very good thing. It had been so long that she'd forgotten this sense of stretching, the near pain that presaged the pleasure to come. Or maybe she'd never felt everything so acutely as she was now with Mitch.

He stopped. "Are you okay?"

"Better than okay." She tipped her hips upward, urging him on. He received the message, because he pushed the rest of the way in. Holding still within her, he dipped his forehead down to briefly rest against hers.

"Finally," he said, then kissed her.

Kira collected enough scattered brain cells to crack a joke. "What—it's been a long two days?"

"More like eleven years," he said, bracing his weight on his strong arms and looking down at her.

She knew her shock must have shown on her face, but Mitch was too wrapped up in the moment to notice. His jaw muscles flexed as though he were gritting his teeth and his face shone with perspiration.

She wriggled her hips a little, then ran the sole of her left foot over the back of his tight calf. It was rough with hair, and she shivered at the feel.

"With eleven years of buildup, I guess I'd better make this good," she said.

He kissed her hard and then said, "Just hold on, Highness. I've got a feeling that this time's going to be mostly fast."

Mitch picked up a rhythm that had them both soon tumbling over a blissful edge. He'd been half-right, Kira thought, once thought was again a possibility. It had been fast, but, my, it had been good.

He was collapsed facedown on the pillows next to

her. She sent one hand over to settle on his muscled buttocks.

"Don't get too comfortable, lawman. This time I'm on top…."

9

For better or worse, Mitch was an analytical guy. He always began examining a situation—be it a case in law school or a real-life event—by standing on the bedrock of a single fact that he knew to be true. When it came to the woman sleeping so peacefully next to him, he couldn't find that starting point.

All he knew was this: it was possible to have sex without any deeper emotional commitment. Hell, he used to do it all the time. Something had happened, though. With Kira there was no switching off his brain. The stakes had changed for him, and sex alone wasn't enough. He wanted into her life, dammit.

His assumptions about Kira had been shot down one by one. She was smart and ambitious, not the spoiled princess he recalled—and had still lusted after. She was generous, thinking of more than just her own pleasure, as she'd shown him time and again throughout the night.

Yet, she was holding back both emotionally and with the details of her life. He had enough ego and powers of observation to know that it wasn't a lack of feelings for him that drove her. Before it became a habit, he needed to cut out the sex as a crutch. It was too simple for Kira—and for him—to equate that physical intimacy with communication.

Mitch realized that almost any other male would tell him that he was out of his freaking head to even think of giving up what he'd experienced last night. Really, it was that damn risk/reward thing. He was willing to risk *now* for the reward of maybe having a *later*.

Mitch rolled onto his side and looked at the alarm clock on his dresser. It was nearly seven o'clock and soon he'd have to leave for work. He rustled the covers with just enough force to be sure to wake Kira. She stretched and yawned.

"Good morning," she said, then smiled.

Mitch wouldn't be opposed to starting a whole lot of mornings with that smile. He realized that at this moment the odds on that happening were pretty skinny.

Kira pushed back her hair from her face and frowned. "Hey, I forgot to tell you that you had a call last night. Someone named Betsy?"

She'd end-loaded an info-seeking question of her own in the way she'd said Betsy's name. Mitch didn't plan on delivering the particulars. It would do Kira some good to have a taste of unsatisfied curiosity.

She pulled the covers over her breasts, then said, "She wants you to call her. She said it's about something you've been waiting to hear."

Mitch smiled at the thought of Bets. She'd started clerking for Judge Kilwin yesterday. Knowing Bets, she'd probably already reorganized the judge's files, not that they needed it. Bets couldn't help herself.

Kira prodded him in the side. "So, are you going to tell me who this Betsy is?"

Mitch laughed while rubbing at the sting from her pointy fingernails. Her Highness was no better than Bets when it came to control issues.

"I think I'm just going to let your imagination run wild," he said.

"It's a pretty vivid imagination."

"I figured that out last night."

She blushed, which he found an amazing contrast to her inherent boldness. In one evening and on to the dawn, they'd touched just about every square inch of one another's skin and made love in nearly all the ways a creative couple could. Of course, he held out hope for variations on those themes…once she was willing to give over more than her body.

"So, no scoop on Betsy, huh?" she asked.

"Nope."

"I do hope you plan to offer me some sort of compensation," she said primly.

"What did you have in mind?"

She reached over and stroked him. "Oh, I don't know…a little mutual gratification, maybe?"

He would have thought it impossible after last night's excesses, but already he was growing hard. Not that he planned to do anything about it.

"Actually I wanted to talk to you about that mutual gratification issue this morning," he said.

"What do you mean?"

"I can't believe I'm saying this, but we're going to have to go without. I thought I could shut down my brain and live for the moment like you'd asked, but I was wrong. You can't have just part of me, Highness."

She rose over him and stroked him. "Not even this part?"

Yeah, he was certifiably crazy. "Especially not that part. I'm not going to be inside you until you really let me in."

She dipped down and brushed a kiss against his mouth. "Maybe we could save the teasing for later?"

"Kira, I'm not teasing."

Her smile faded. "You're kidding."

"No, I'm serious." Painfully so.

She flopped back on the bed, arms spread wide in a posture of defeat. "What is it that you want?"

"Your words. All of them."

"I don't get it."

He moved closer to her, swept a stray lock of hair off her cheek, then kissed her forehead. "You've been generous with your body, and don't doubt for a minute that I haven't been appreciative. But we've experienced kind of a disconnect here. We know how to please each other physically, but otherwise we're striking out. I want words from you. Real communication."

"Words?" she echoed. "Clearly we're not talking *oh, baby* or *you're so good.*"

He smiled in spite of himself. "I was hoping for something with more depth. You know, something that would let me into your life a little."

"Okay, how's this? When I was eleven, I stole an ice cream from Mrs. Hawkins's market. Every time she looks at me, I swear she knows."

"Ancient history."

She gave an exasperated sigh. "Fine. In college my first boyfriend looked just like you, except he was a lot nicer to me, so I gave him my virginity."

He moved over her long enough to plant a kiss on the base of her throat. "Flattering in a sick sort of way, but no," he said. "I want to know why you're in Sandy Bend."

"To be driven into insanity through sexual frustration?"

"That'll make two of us, Highness."

She rolled on top of him again and braced her hands on his chest. "Come on, Mitch. Play nice."

Nice? He'd thrown nice out the window somewhere around dawn. He flipped her beneath him. "I'm not playing nice, I'm playing to win. Until you're ready to tell me what's going on with you, I'm not ready to repeat last night. So what's it going to be?"

She planted both hands on his chest and pushed hard. Mitch could have stayed put, but he didn't want to antagonize her any more than he already had. She crawled from the bed, then dug through the covers until she found her nightgown, which had migrated between the comforter and the top sheet. After she'd pulled the wrinkled garment over her head, she fixed him with a very angry glare.

"Let me get this straight," she said. "You're going to withhold sex until I tell you whatever this big, dark secret is that you think I've been hiding? How damn manipulative is that?" She grabbed a pillow that had fallen to the floor at some point last night and flung it at him. "Jerk."

She marched out of the room and into the bathroom. Mitch followed. She swung around and said, "Can't I have some privacy?"

He settled his hand on the door. "You can have all kinds of it—once we've worked our way though this."

She stalked out of the bathroom and again he followed. In the kitchen she opened the refrigerator door. Mitch watched as she retrieved some strawberry jam, then set it down with serious force on the counter next to the marshmallow fluff. When she grabbed for the bread, he worried that she was going to smash it flat, but she didn't. Instead, she dropped two slices in the toaster.

She was making his breakfast? He didn't know why the act was slamming straight into his heart, but it was.

"Did it ever occur to you that I have no big secret? That I'm here for exactly the reasons that I gave you?"

"Not for a second," he replied. "And what were those reasons again?"

It was a dirty trick, but it worked. Kira stopped dead in her tracks. "I— I—"

"See? If you can't keep 'em straight, don't expect me to. Rule one—when trying to fool someone, keep it simple. Don't keep piling on stories."

She walked back to the refrigerator and pulled out some grapes. As she washed them, she said, "Why can't you just leave this alone?"

"Believe me, parts of me would like to. And if I didn't care a whole lot about you, I would. I don't mean this as manipulation, but here's the thing. In two, three, however many days, you're going to be gone. If this were going to be all about sex, we'd just have our fun and move on. But for me at least, it's not just about the sex—which, to remind you, was outstanding."

"Really?" The toast popped up, and she dropped it onto a plate, then retrieved a butter knife from the silverware drawer.

"Definitely worth repeating, but don't get caught up in the compliment, okay? The point is we could have more. I want it and I'm pretty sure you do, too."

"Hah. What makes you say that?" Tough words

for sure, but he was reading more than her speech, and even the way her lower lip was beginning to quiver.

He pointed to the toast she was busy spreading with fluff. "You're ticked as hell at me and you're still making my breakfast."

She looked at the hand holding the fluff-covered knife as though it didn't belong to her.

"Reflex," she said firmly before setting the knife aside.

"If the thought comforts you."

She smacked the toast plate onto the kitchen table, set the jam next to it, then picked up her grapes and began eating. Mitch frowned at the toast. He always went jam first, fluff second. He wasn't even sure he could get the jam to stick to the fluff. He was far too smart to point out the inconsistency to Kira, though. While he rose and got a spoon to glob on some jam, she pulled out a seat and sat opposite his customary spot.

"What I'm asking is pretty simple. I want to be included," he said when he'd returned, spoon in hand. "I don't want to be on the outside wondering what's going on. Once we handle that, the geography issues we're going to have to deal with will be nothing."

She set aside the grapes and laid her palms flat on the table. "Okay, here's the scoop. It's just a glitch with my business. It seemed a little overwhelming a few days ago, so I took off. Now that I have some distance and perspective, I promise it's nothing that I can't handle. It's just going to take some time to figure out."

At least she was no longer trying to pretend that nothing was happening, but he still didn't like the way she'd clammed up.

"Why don't you tell me about it?" he asked. "Sometimes another set of eyes on the facts can help."

"It's handled. Really."

"This is what I meant. It's like you're looking for two bodies colliding in the night—and the morning—but nothing more. That's not what I want."

"Mitch, that's all I can give right now. I haven't asked you for every little detail of your life. I don't know how many girlfriends you've had or who you've slept with in town. I don't want to know any of that. I want us to start from here, to enjoy our time together."

"And then what? We get together if you happen to be around? Then after that maybe send a Christmas card for a couple of years before we lose touch altogether?"

"I don't know, okay? I just don't see why you have to take away something that gives us both such pleasure."

"Because the price is too high for me. It's coming at the expense of my pride. I need you to want me as much as I want you."

"Mitch, I—"

Regret and rejection were clear on her face. He'd heard *no* too many times already in this discussion not to recognize it. Mitch pushed his chair away from the table and left his disaster zone of a breakfast.

Good idea, bad delivery.

"DAMNED IF YOU DO, DAMNED IF you don't," Kira said to herself—or maybe to the closest lilac bush—before turning the corner onto Main Street, where the liberty to talk to oneself was severely limited by the number of passersby to listen.

She needed to hang tough for a couple of days, but it was miserably hard to do when she knew that she was hurting someone who mattered so much to her. Last night Mitch had left her loose limbed, relaxed and without even the smallest measure of her usual reserve in place. She'd considered blurting all to him. How—like her stupid, scarred leg—nothing in her life was nearly as pretty as it appeared on first glance. How after all her effort to grow as a sharp, savvy soul, she'd been fooled for over two years by a woman she thought she'd known as well as any of her siblings. Of course, she wasn't all that close to her siblings, either.

Kira had kept her mouth firmly shut, though. In the light of day, she was relieved that she had. Mitch was as stubborn about control as she was, though for very different reasons. If—and this was a *huge* if— they found a way to pursue a relationship once she was back in Florida, she didn't want to fall back into her old needy, wait-on-me ways. She wanted to continue to stand on her own. As a second-generation cop, Mitch was genetically coded to run the show. Once she'd proved that she could deal with this crisis, she'd tell him whatever he wanted to know. And not a moment before.

In need of caffeine and companionship, Kira stopped at the Village Grounds. Maybe some of Lisa's calm pleasure in life would rub off. As she walked by the window, Kira was relieved to see that it was slow in the coffeehouse just then.

She pushed through the shop's door. The cheery chime of the bells was drowned out by a distressed "I can't believe it!" from behind the counter.

Kira blinked as Lisa dipped below counter height.

"Hiding out?" she asked as she approached.

Lisa popped back up, a sopping rag in one hand. "Cleaning a milk bomb. I spilled a gallon of skim milk this time. An hour ago I sent half a tray of blueberry muffins to the ground. I'm a menace." She turned and wrung the rag into a small utility sink, then bent to mop more milk.

Kira came around to Lisa's side of the counter, grabbed a wad of paper towels and pitched in. "So you've got a case of the drops. What brought it on?"

Lisa's brief laugh flirted with hysteria. She cleaned as she spoke. "My wedding's three days off and I haven't had my final dress-fitting. My mother is still trying to hijack my reception and turn it into a cooing-lovebirds and fluffy, huggy hearts disaster. *And* one of the girls I had hired to help me for the summer left me a note this morning telling me that she's decided she needs to see Alaska...now! So much for two weeks' notice."

"All of which definitely stinks," Kira commiserated. "Why don't you close for a few days, until you can get a grip?"

Lisa sighed. "It's tempting, but if I do, I'll tick off my regulars." She rinsed the rag, then washed her hands as Kira threw her sodden mass of paper towels in the trash. "People around here are creatures of habit. If you throw them off schedule, you hear about it forever—assuming they forgive you enough to come back. I fought so hard to actually have regulars that I don't want to lose them."

"Understandable. Word of mouth is everything."

This was a concept that Kira knew all too well from her business. Word of mouth was what had made her. It would also kill her income if the Roxanne mess didn't get straightened out. Because she was beginning to believe that old "What goes around, comes around" adage and because she was overdue to send some good stuff around, Kira made an offer that would have been unthinkable the last time she'd been in Sandy Bend.

"So, what do you need me to do?" she asked, figuring this was penance of sorts.

"Do?"

Kira stepped in front of the sink and washed the spilled milk from her hands. As she did, she said, "As in, how can I help bail you out? If I came in a few hours every day this week, would that be a step in the right direction?"

"You'd do that?"

"Why not?" she replied, drying her hands.

Lisa's expression was best described as shocked. "This isn't an easy job, you know," she said. "We alternate between too quiet and crazy busy. You'd be all by yourself, and…" She trailed off, then laughed again. This time at least the sound didn't have that teetering-on-the-brink edge to it. "You're offering me help and I'm busy talking you out of it. Just shoot me now."

Kira laughed. "Thanks, but my reputation's already bad enough in town."

"Forget 'em," Lisa said with a dismissive wave of her hand. "If you're serious about this, I have to ask…. Have you ever made espresso or run a cash register?"

"No, but I'm trainable. And I'd really like to help." Any positive step, even one not directly related to her problems, had to be a good thing.

"Okay, if you're game, do you have a few minutes right now?"

"Sure," Kira said. All she had in the works was another session at Mitch's computer, and she wasn't ready to return to the scene of the morning's emotional carnage just yet.

Lisa tossed a tan Village Grounds apron her way. "Put this on and I'll teach you coffee, Sandy Bendstyle."

Kira bit back a sigh. If only someone could teach her persuasive seduction, Mitch Brewer-style.

AFTER A MORNING SPENT FEELING as if he'd been sucking the bottom of a manure hauler, Mitch came to a decision. If Kira wasn't going to put to rest his worries about her current situation, he'd have to do it for himself. Concerns calmed, maybe he could show a little more finesse and persuade her to open up to him, instead of trying to coerce her into it.

He pulled out the business card that Kira had left as a bookmark in the thriller she was reading. This wasn't really theft. He'd return the card as soon as he was back home.

"Whitman-Pierce Realty," he read aloud from the posh-looking script. "Figures you'd have first billing, Highness."

Mitch noted the Web site address at the bottom of the card. Couldn't hurt to have a look-see. He glanced over at Cathy, the only other officer in the station. She had her nose stuck in a file, so Mitch felt safe in indulging in a little extracurricular activity, at least until Cal got back in twenty minutes. Mitch typed the Web site address into his computer's Internet browser and waited for the information to download.

The Web site was smart and elegant, much like

Kira. Mitch suppressed a low whistle as he flipped through the gallery of homes currently for sale. If Kira had been telling the truth last night, her "little glitch" at work probably had a whole lot of zeros hanging off its cost. He couldn't find a property for under three mil.

He cruised to the About Us page and read the brief bios for Kira and Roxanne, the woman who was apparently her partner. Based on the glam shot of the two of them in half-flirty, half-business dresses at the ocean's edge, looks sold—both the looks of the property and of the women doing the selling. Kira had found the only environment where her bone-deep blond glamour would come off as understated. Kira was…Kira, and he'd never found any woman more attractive. Roxanne was a total knockout, probably surgically enhanced and far too high-maintenance looking for Mitch's taste. Plus, there was something uncomfortably brittle about her expression. He'd take Kira any day…if only Kira would have him.

The more Mitch looked at the two of them—Roxanne, especially—the more his curiosity grew. Kira came from money, and even though she'd said she was off the family dole, she sure knew how to still look rich. What about this Roxanne? Was she another heiress?

He plugged her name and *Miami* into his favorite search engine, then weeded through the results. Mostly he found blurbs from local magazines and newspapers—name-dropping in the gossip columns and chat about club hopping.

The phone rang, and Cathy fielded the call. Mitch barely looked up from his computer screen when she said she was going to walk down to one of the gift shops to deal with a potential shoplifter. Mitch's mind had traveled elsewhere—over fifteen hundred miles south, to be exact. And the heat had to be affecting his brain, considering the idea that had come to him.

Over the years he'd made some connections. It just so happened that Bart, one of his law school buddies, had moved down to Miami to go into practice with his older brother who had a flashy, high-roller kind of firm. Attorney to the local celebs and all that. Mitch had met Glenn, the big brother, a couple of times when he'd come to Sandy Bend with Bart for some rustic weekends of salmon fishing and rum drinking.

Glenn was the sort of guy who'd do a favor, no questions asked, which had certain benefits since Mitch didn't want to answer any.

Not even the *What the hell are you doing?* that was shooting through his brain as he pulled Glenn's card from the personal file he kept in his lower right-hand drawer. Mitch started dialing.

From the moment he touched the phone, Mitch floated into something he could only call an out-of-body experience. He'd swear he was somewhere around the ceiling while watching this Mitch clone on the phone, pretty much trashing his hard-earned integrity. Good Mitch watched from some far, ethically pure place as bad Mitch cleared a receptionist and a secretary, summoned some small talk, then secured his target.

"Glenn, I was wondering if you could do me a favor? Could you check out two women, Kira Whitman and Roxanne Pierce?... Yeah, Whitman-Pierce

Realty. You've heard of them? I'm looking for word of mouth—if anyone you know has had dealings with them, what kind of friends they hang with, that kind of stuff.... No, no crisis. Tomorrow would be great to hear back from you.... Yeah, next summer we'll get together for sure. Thanks, Glenn. Talk to you soon."

After he hung up, Mitch zoned out into space for a while. He knew that when his conscience rejoined his body, he'd be sucking major manure once again.

10

"ONE TALL NO-WHIP MOCHA LATTE," Kira confirmed as she placed a coffee in front of a customer, then rang up the sale. The reward for doing it right was the jingle of change into a jar with a tag reading Honeymoon Fund that Lisa kept by the register.

"Thank you," Kira called to the teenage girl as she left.

After an hour under Lisa's watchful eyes, Kira had been declared ready to fly on her own. Other than a couple of muffed orders and a twenty-seven-thousand-dollar overring on the cash register, she'd done fairly well. She'd even survived a visit from comb-over man, who'd scared her with his nasty stare days earlier. It turned out he looked at pretty much the whole world that way. Kira would take cranky over inherently evil any day of the week. Today was a short-term gig, anyway. Lisa had promised she'd be back once she'd stopped home to pick up any stray wedding RSVPs, then visited her caterer to tell her to forget her mother's suggestion of heart-shaped butter pats.

In the lull between breakfast and lunch, traffic into the shop slowed. Kira took advantage of the interval by checking her cell phone for messages. She found one from Don, who she'd been meaning to call with the information from last night's research.

Kira hit the autodial and reached him immediately. He had no news on Roxanne's whereabouts but was expecting some leads to solidify early tomorrow. Kira wiped down tables and listened as Don gave her a brief recap of what else he'd found.

"Then I checked with a contact in St. Louis," Don was saying, "and—"

Kira interrupted. "St. Louis? Why St. Louis?"

"That's where she's from."

"No, she told me that she grew up in California— St. Helena in the Napa Valley. Her father's a big land-owner. He even has a hotel and spa." She headed back behind the counter, as if the smaller space could give her a measure of security.

"Not even close. Her father works in a meatpacking plant."

This was bad in so many ways that Kira couldn't begin to grasp them. And what she really wanted to grasp was Roxanne's throat between her own bare hands. She might be a kinder, more rational Kira these days, but Retribution Girl still lurked right under her skin.

Kira looked up when the shop bells chimed, alerting her to a customer. She was about to raise her finger in a just-a-second gesture when she realized that the customer was Mitch. Feeling oddly criminal, she turned her back on him and moved as far from his earshot as she could.

"So, it would be safe to say that she's not independently wealthy?" she asked Don in a low voice.

"It would be safer to say that she's up to her nose job in debt."

Kira assumed that also sent her partner's tales of life in a French boarding school into the land of fiction. Probably the closest Roxanne had ever come was reading *Madeline* books in her childhood.

"I need to cut this call short," she said to Don, "but I have something I need you to check out. I read Roxanne's e-mail and found some client names that didn't make sense. Could I give them to you later?"

"No problem. And, Kira, if you spot any unusual activity, you might think about freezing your business's cash accounts."

"I can't. Roxanne usually…" If Mitch hadn't been watching her, Kira would have smacked her forehead against the counter and chanted, "Dumb, dumb, *dumb*."

"I'll look into them this afternoon," she said to Don. "Talk to you later."

Call ended, she tucked her cell phone back in her purse and turned to face Mitch. There was an uncomfortable pause before he spoke. At least, it seemed uncomfortable to Kira—as though he was waiting for her to tell him who she'd been talking to. But it could have all been in her head, too. She didn't respond well to guilt.

"So I wasn't hallucinating when I walked by," Mitch said. "Where's Lisa?"

"She had a little staffing problem, and I volunteered to cover for her so she can get married on Saturday without losing her mind."

"That's right—Saturday," Mitch said. "Will you go with me?"

She hadn't been expecting that. In fact, when he'd come in the door, she'd anticipated hearing that he wanted her to move out.

"If you want me to," she said, hating the way she felt so tentative.

He gave her a level look. "I wouldn't have asked otherwise."

Seeking to focus his attention on something other than her, Kira gestured at the large coffee menu posted on the wall behind her. "Can I get you something?"

"How about a cup of regular, black? And one of Lisa's chocolate-chip cookies, too. I'm celebrating."

"Celebrating what?" Kira automatically asked as she poured the coffee.

"I've been told to expect a kick-ass letter of recommendation from a federal judge I interned for last summer."

"Really? That's great!" She handed him the coffee, then pulled the cookie from the glass-front case where they were kept. She put it on a plate and slid it across the counter to him.

He took a swallow of coffee, then said, "The letter's a start. There's a glut of lawyers out there. Anything you can do to stand out helps."

Kira couldn't believe he was even worried. Mitch had a law-enforcement background and the cachet of having been a college football player, which she knew gained notice in the good-old-boys' network. Most important, in a few short days she'd learned that there was endless grit and determination behind his lazy smile. Which of course made him all the sexier.

"Trust me, you're a standout," she said as she rang up his order. "What kind of law do you want to practice?"

"I want to be a federal prosecutor, but it might take a couple of years in private practice before I can latch on to a job like that."

Their hands brushed as he handed her a few dollar bills. She tried to show no outer sign of the tingle that went through her from a simple touch.

"Is it a tough job to get?" she asked in a voice a little huskier than usual.

He nodded. "It can be. There's background checks and security clearances and usually a lot of people vying for just a few open slots. But I feel like I can really make a difference in a job like that, so I'm willing to stick it out."

Two customers came in, and after greeting the women by name, Mitch moved to a table while Kira took care of them. When she was done, he returned to his spot at the counter.

"How about you? Do you see yourself selling real estate the rest of your life?" he asked.

"For a long time, at least. I feel like I've wasted so many years just trying to grow up."

Kira's pulse jumped. She couldn't believe she'd said that to Mitch. Whether out of reserve or some need to maintain the Whitman image, she'd never willingly admitted flaws to anyone. Half the trick of dealing with a therapist had been developing the trust to open up. Maybe admitting this shortcoming to Mitch was a reasonable step, but she didn't want to take it any further with a guy who'd seen so much of her bad side.

He laughed. "You're not even thirty yet. How many years can you have wasted?"

There was something freeing even in this small measure of honesty. "Some days it feels like half my life."

He took her hand. "Don't be so hard on yourself, Highness. I know people well into their seventies who haven't grown up."

She smiled. "That gives me another fifty years to work on it."

Mitch was still holding her hand. She knew she should draw it back across the counter, especially since the two customers weren't being too subtle in the way they were watching. At that moment she didn't care. She felt as though she was at least gaining back some of what Mitch and she had lost earlier in the morning.

"See, Highness?" Mitch said. "We've had a full conversation and we've both survived. Don't give up hope for us yet." He moved his grip on her hand so that he was cupping it. Then he brought it to his mouth and kissed the tender skin on the inside of her wrist. "Might as well give 'em something to talk about," he said low enough for just her to hear.

His gaze was intimate, and Kira leaned closer as warmth began to curl through her. "Then let's do it right."

It was a heartbreakingly tender kiss, tasting to Kira of all the things she wasn't yet able to have— love, commitment and a future big enough to hold more than one. When the bell to the shop chimed again, she drew away, regretful to lose the moment.

"Good morning," Mitch said to his sister-in-law, Dana, who'd just come in the door.

"An interesting one," Dana replied, taking in both of them with an arch smile. "How about a tall white-chocolate raspberry latte?" she said to Kira, who was more than happy to have something to do at that moment.

Mitch was saying something to Dana but kept it low enough that Kira couldn't eavesdrop successfully. Once the espresso machine began hissing, she gave up the battle.

When she was done making the drink, Mitch was readying to leave.

"Tonight I cook," he said to her on his way out.

Kira kept her comments to a generic "'bye." The two women who had been watching the kiss also trailed out, figuring the show was over. Kira took a quick glance at Dana and gauged her mood. At least Monday's fighting glint was gone from her eyes.

"You saved me some work, being here," Dana said.

"How's that?"

"I was going to track you down today anyway. I wanted to ask if we could have a fresh start."

"Any reason in particular?"

Dana took a sip of her coffee, then nodded with satisfaction. Kira was pleased to see she could do at least one thing right in this woman's estimation.

"You and Mitch are going to do whatever you're going to do," Dana said. "I could stand in your way, but I think I'll just end up getting steamrollered. So what do you say—can we try again?"

Kira weighed the request and then said, "I vote for a truce."

"It's that easy?"

"When you have my kind of past, you can't be stingy with fresh starts."

Dana laughed. "That's my philosophy, too." She took another sip of her drink, then said, "I owe you an explanation for my pit-bull act when I first saw you the other day."

"I'm used to that kind of response," Kira said, thinking of pit-bull Rose who'd been her *un*welcoming committee to Sandy Bend.

"Has Mitch told you about his accident last November?"

"I've seen the scar."

Dana's brows rose a fraction, but she didn't push the topic. "Did he also tell you that we almost lost him?"

Kira's heart lurched. "No. All he mentioned was a secondary infection."

"It was antibiotic resistant, and he started developing pneumonia on top of that. He really scared us, and I ended up going all maternal on him. There was no one else to take the job, you know? I think he's tired of having a mommy younger than he is, but I can't seem to stop."

"But he's okay now," Kira said, just to hear the comforting statement aloud.

"He is, but he's also changed. Mitch used to be more relaxed about life. I don't know if it was the brush with death or just because he's getting older, but he's almost driven now. He goes for what he wants," Dana said.

"I'd noticed."

"It was surprising seeing him kiss you," she said. "You're the only one I've seen him look at that way."

Kira's heart sped with something that was either excitement or alarm. She couldn't quite peg it. "What way?"

"Like he's playing for keeps," Dana said, then glanced at the clock on the wall. "Hey, I have to get back to work. Tell Mitch that I said to bring you to dinner on Saturday. You'll still be here, right?"

"I will," she replied. Then she added after Dana had left, "Right here, smack in the middle of purgatory."

THE TABLE WAS SET, DINNER was cooking and Mitch was feeling marginally less screwed. He wasn't sure whether he should be appalled or amazed at how he'd managed to cordon off the section of his brain that had spurred the phone call to Glenn in Miami. What little guilt had managed to sneak through, he was drowning in the vintage music of Guns N' Roses, full blast. At least as full as a guy could get with retirees living on both sides of him.

He'd decided to deal with the Glenn incident as a near miss, similar to stealing all the Sandy Bend *n*s when he was a kid. He'd never been caught, and in this instance Kira didn't have to know. Whatever he learned from Glenn he'd keep to himself. And he'd dig no deeper.

Mitch stepped out back to see if for the first time ever he'd managed to cook salmon on the grill without charring it or turning it to jerky. He made a better fisherman than he did chef. When he'd just come back in, Axl and his band fell silent. A moment later Kira appeared in the kitchen doorway.

He didn't like what he saw. There was something in her expression that made him feel as though she was working doubly hard to keep that mask of cool competency in place.

"Hard day at work?" he asked, figuring a little teasing might lighten matters. In the past it had worked like a charm.

She pulled out a chair and sat. "I don't suppose you have any wine?"

"Funny you should mention it." Mitch went to the fridge and pulled out the bottle of sauvignon blanc he'd picked up at the market after getting off work.

While he uncorked it and poured her a glass, Kira was silent. She took the offered drink, closed her eyes and sighed as the first swallow went down.

Mitch wanted to ask her what was wrong but knew better. "Are you okay with salmon?" he asked instead.

Even her smile looked tired. "It sounds great. Is there anything I can do to help?"

"Just kick back and relax."

The meal was quiet. Mitch talked a little about people they'd known in common and what they were up to these days. Kira tried to act interested, but Mitch could tell that she had something entirely different going on in her head.

Over her objections, he insisted on clearing the table and doing the dishes himself. When he was done, he took her by the hand and led her to his bedroom.

At the questioning look she gave him, he said, "Nope, I'm sticking to my word and keeping my clothes on. Stretch out, Highness. It's time for a back rub."

Kira slipped off her sandals and climbed onto the bed. "No way am I turning this down," she said before centering a pillow along the headboard and stretching out, her arms looped above her head.

Mitch kicked off his shoes and joined her, kneeling near her hips. He swept her hair to one side and began with a gentle pressure on the nape of her neck. As he did, he looked at the smooth sweep of her back down to the rich curves of her bottom. She looked so right to him, as though having her here was natural. Maybe even a product of fate.

"I like the way you always wear skirts instead of shorts," he said. "It's sexy."

"Hides the scar better. Most shorts I like are cut too high," she murmured, then shifted her face the other way on the pillow.

He hadn't thought of that and sure as hell hadn't meant to bring it up. Still, as Mitch worked his way up the back of her left leg, deeply kneading Kira's tense muscles, he considered what injury could do.

Some people recovered better than others. On the whole, he was lucky. A few days into his hospital stay, when fairly doped from whatever had been flowing through his IV line, he'd overheard his dad and Cal talking with the doctors about the odds of him kicking his complications. That anyone would be putting odds on his death had scared the crap out of him. He'd sworn that as soon as he left that hospital bed, he'd grab hold of life and do it right. Thus far he had.

"This feels wonderful," Kira said, sounding drowsy.

He slipped his hand under her top and unhooked her bra. She didn't complain. In fact, she gave a blissful sigh as he rubbed his palm down her back. Mitch could feel himself begin to stir. He knew he couldn't fight physical response, but he damn well wouldn't do anything about it.

He began sliding up her shirt, and she briefly raised herself to help him along. He loved the feel of her warm skin beneath his hands, loved the way she entrusted herself to him.

Right up until her accident, Kira had been one of those kids who'd reveled in life. Sure, she'd been spoiled. And sure, her sophistication had intimidated him a little. But Mitch had always been intrigued by her. She'd had an intellect that not much anyone gave her credit for. For Mitch, her looks had been hot, but her intelligence had made it a done deal.

After the accident, when she'd come home acting like another girl entirely, he'd tried once to talk to her about the change, but she'd put him off. She'd been good at those stone-cold dismissals, but he'd always known that the act was coming from fear. Now that she'd grown, the act had changed from superiority to silence. And how he wanted the woman beneath.

It took little time for Kira's muscles to go lax and her breathing take on the relaxed pattern of sleep. Mitch let his hands travel over her back a few more times, as much for his pleasure as for her continued rest. When he was certain that she wasn't going to wake, he went to the kitchen and grabbed a glass and the last of the wine they'd had at dinner. He sat on the back deck looking up at the clear sky with its blanket of stars.

Kira was distracted, distressed—all of those *dis* things that ate at him. What could she have fallen into? As Mitch imagined the possibilities, the air grew chilly with a breeze pushing its way though town from Lake Michigan.

Conjecture was pointless, and he was beat. Mitch left his wineglass by the kitchen sink and walked to his bedroom. Kira was still sound asleep. If he were at all sane, he'd go sleep on the beast of a couch in the living room. But it seemed that sanity wasn't his strong suit these days.

Mitch stripped out of his clothes and pulled on an old pair of flannel sleep pants. Taking care not to wake Kira, he crawled onto the bed next to her. He could smell the faint floral scent of whatever shampoo she used. Her warmth was too tempting. Mitch got as close to her as he could without actually touching her, because if he did that, he wouldn't be able to stop. He'd take the warmth and comfort of her presence for tonight. As he dozed off, his final thought was, *This is what I've been missing all these years.*

HE WAS ASLEEP. KIRA TIPTOED into the second bedroom and closed the door. She switched on Mitch's computer but left the speakers off, not wanting to wake him.

Kira logged on to her bank's Web site for the second time that day. After she'd finished up at the Village Grounds, she'd gone straight to the library and stayed until the five-o'clock closing time. They had not been pleasant hours. Even now, as she again pulled up Whitman-Pierce's client escrow account, the sight of what awaited her sent fury coursing through her.

On some level this was her fault. She should have watched Roxanne more carefully, asked more questions. It was no excuse for inattention that the account had always balanced.

The escrow account was specially set up to hold client funds, keeping them separate from the firm's operating account. Lately about all that should have been going through it were a few good-faith deposits and the rentals on some properties that they'd agreed to handle as an accommodation to a repeat client. But more was funneling through there.

Much more.

Kira looked at the prior month's activity. There alone, when she added up the suspect daily transactions—none over five thousand dollars—more than ninety thousand dollars had passed through the account. Kira had once taken a large cash down payment from an eccentric client who didn't trust banks. She knew from making that deposit that the government had to be notified on cash deposits above a certain amount. Looking at the escrow account's statement, she'd bet that amount was currently five thousand dollars and she'd bet these deposits had been cash.

Someone was trying to run below federal radar. And that someone was still missing. She didn't wish Roxanne physical harm, but the thought of her in an orange prison jumpsuit was highly appealing.

Kira had seen all she could stomach. She clicked on the print button, wincing when Mitch's printer began to squeal as the paper went through the machine. Short of throwing her body over the printer, there was nothing she could do.

"Hurry up," she whispered to it.

When it was finally done, she switched off the computer and tucked the pages into her briefcase in the living room. Documents hidden, Kira sat on the edge of the couch looking at the neatly folded sheet and comforter she hadn't used the night before. She wouldn't use it tonight, either. Her life was unraveling, and she was becoming frightened. She needed comfort, even if it was illusory.

If she stayed in her clothes, in the morning Mitch would assume that she'd slept through the night. She'd have no neediness to confess to, no difficult questions to face. Kira crept back into Mitch's bed and tucked her body snugly behind his. Her racing heartbeat, harried with stress, slowed to match his. In time she felt safe. In time she felt love.

MITCH WATCHED THE MINUTES pass on his digital alarm clock. He'd heard Kira at the computer and felt her crawl into bed. God, he was angry. And hurt, too. But he couldn't make her give what she chose to withhold. All he could do was protect her.

And it would be one hell of a lot easier if he knew what he was protecting her from. Mitch willed his eyes shut and sleep to come.

Love was a definite bitch.

11

IF PATIENCE WAS A VIRTUE, Kira required redemption.
It was impolitic to boot a guy from his own house,
but she feared that's what it was coming down to.
When she'd awakened on Thursday morning, she'd
found Mitch in the kitchen eating his way through
toast topped with his favorite gunk. By the time
she'd emerged from the shower and dressed, he'd
moved on to coffee and cereal. He was in uniform,
which meant that sooner or later he'd go to work.
Much as she loved the sight of him, she was rooting
for sooner. She needed to call Don from the quiet of
the Dollhouse Cottage before she was due at the Village Grounds to cover for Lisa.

Kira hovered by the stove. "So, you're working
today?"

Mitch glanced down at his uniform, then served
up a yes accompanied by a dry smile.

She gestured at the coffeemaker on the counter.
"Mind if I have some?" It was kind of a coals-to-
Newcastle question, considering where she would
be in fifteen minutes.

"Help yourself." As she pulled a mug from the
cupboard, he asked, "Sleep okay?"

"Fine," she replied.

"You talk in your sleep, you know."

The coffeepot rattled against the side of the mug, splashing hot liquid onto the counter.

"So I've heard," Kira said as she set down the pot and mopped up her spill. "Usually it's just nonsense."

She hoped.

Mitch didn't comment.

Short of asking *Just what did I say?* she didn't know how to mine for more information. She sat opposite him. "I hope I didn't keep you awake."

"Not for too long."

"Good," she said, though the word came out sounding as tense as she was feeling. She took some comfort from the fact that he was reaching the bottom of his cereal bowl and would soon be gone.

"No breakfast other than coffee?" he asked.

"I'm not a breakfast person."

"Too bad. You know what they say—it's the most important meal."

She tried to hide her frustration as he reached for the cereal box and refilled. A quick spark in his blue eyes let her know she'd done a poor job of cloaking her emotions.

"You sure you don't want to get a bowl?" he asked.

"Thanks, but no."

He was definitely playing her. Kira stood and dumped her coffee into the sink, then put her mug in the dishwasher. "Time for me to get to work."

Between bites Mitch said, "I've got school tonight. Think you can keep yourself occupied?"

"I'll find something."

She was in the living room readying to leave when she could have sworn she heard a muttered, "I'll bet."

After a glance over her shoulder, Kira tucked the

escrow account information into her purse. Time was running out—for her and for them.

"WHAT'S UP WITH YOU? DID somebody spit in your marshmallow fluff?"

Mitch glared at Cal, who'd just walked into the police station, bottle of water in hand. Some things in life were sacrosanct, and marshmallow fluff was among them. Which Cal should know, since most of their childhood brawls had resulted from Cal thieving Mitch's fluff stock.

Mitch pushed aside the case he needed to read before tonight's class. "You might want to give me some space this morning, huh? I didn't sleep much."

Cal pulled up a chair and unscrewed the top to his bottle. "And it doesn't look like it's for a good reason. What's wrong?"

Mitch had never viewed his brother as much of a confessor, but he couldn't afford to be choosy.

"I've been checking up on Kira," he said.

Cal took a swallow of water and then asked with a deadpan expression, "Any reason in particular or just a desire to kill your best shot at love?"

Mitch looked down at his desk. "It's not love... exactly."

Cal gave a "yeah, right" snort in response.

All things considered, Mitch decided to leave the topic of love alone. Cal had witnessed enough of Mitch's relationship with Kira over the years that he'd be a tough sell to believe it wasn't love.

"Something's going on with her, but she doesn't want to talk about it," he said.

"She's never been much for sharing, if you'll recall. Maybe you should just give her some space."

"I've been trying to do that, but just before you came in I talked to a friend's brother down in Miami."

"You do have a death wish, don't you?"

"Could be. Here's the problem—I don't like what's come back. Kira's clean. She's hardworking. In fact, her whole life appears to be built around her business. Roxanne, her partner, is another story. She doesn't have the best of friends—unless you've got a real fondness for felons and dealers."

"Definitely ugly," Cal agreed. "But why'd you start snooping?"

"Kira's not sleeping. She's sneaking on to my computer in the middle of the night and generally feeding me a bunch of bull. She finally told me that she has a little 'glitch' in her business, whatever the hell that means."

Cal sat up straighter, his cop's radar for trouble no doubt now as attuned to the situation as Mitch's.

"Do you think she's up to something criminal?" Cal asked.

Mitch shook his head. "No way. Other than that bar brawl when she missed Hallie's wedding, she doesn't have a record of any kind. Not so much as a traffic violation."

"Checking out her record, too? You get a kick out of living dangerously, don't you?"

"Someone has to watch out for her."

Cal stood. "I'd give you some advice about minding your own business, but since you're one stubborn SOB, I know you wouldn't take it. Instead I'll scrape you from the pavement when Kira's through stomping holes in you, okay?"

That kind of brotherly love Mitch could do without.

THE VILLAGE GROUNDS WAS hopping, and Kira was developing a limp.

"Torture by latte," she muttered as she steamed yet another pitcher of milk.

When Kira was about ten years old, Rose, then her seminanny, had caught her stealing a corner off the block of Belgian chocolate that Chef kept for making desserts. Rose had made Kira finish the rest of the block. Kira had been all for the punishment until the last three bites. Those had been agony, and many months had passed before Kira had been able to face chocolate again. She still could do entirely without Rose and she was beginning to think she might have also killed off her latte habit.

Calm finally came at about eleven. She retrieved her cell phone from her purse, then put in a call to Don. His tone worried her from the word *hello*, and it sounded even worse after she gave him the bank account news.

"First, there's nothing I've found that makes me think your partner is anywhere against her will, okay?" he said.

"Why do I sense a *but* coming?"

"Here it is.... *But* I've also picked up a rumor that a real bad boy's bearer bonds have gone missing. Granted, the source isn't the most reliable guy you'll ever meet, but based on what you've told me about your account, he just went up on the credibility scale."

Kira frowned. "Bearer bonds? I've heard of them, but I'm not sure I really know what they are."

"They're the ultimate in untraceable funds. They've been illegal in the United States for about twenty years, but you can get them from any number of offshore sources."

"Offshore…like some of Roxanne's favorite vacation spots," Kira said.

"You've got it. Bearer bonds are owned by whoever holds them. No record of ownership is kept. You pick it up, you turn it in and the cash is yours. A lot of drug money gets cleaned by that route. Now, I'm not saying there's absolutely a connection—"

"But with the unaccountable deposits and matching withdrawals, it would make sense, wouldn't it?"

"It would," Don agreed.

Kira closed her eyes in an attempt to quell her simmering fear—and fury, too. "So, do I panic now?"

"No. Let me do some more checking. In the meantime, freeze that escrow account. You might want to give your attorney a heads-up, too."

She doubted that her starchy business lawyer dabbled in this sort of practice.

"I'll give you a call tonight…tomorrow at the latest," Don said.

"Thanks."

"Sorry this hasn't worked out better for you, Kira. I wish she'd just run off with a married guy or something."

"If all of this turns out to be true, when I'm through with her, she'll wish she'd been sucked into the Bermuda Triangle."

Don laughed. "Remind me not to mess with you," he said before hanging up.

Right. She was a regular amazon.

Gutsy talk was an easy emotional release. Real solutions were going to be far more painful. Kira worked her face into a sufficiently cheerful expression to greet a group of sunburned tourists who had just meandered in. As she poured raspberry iced teas, her mind reeled. She wanted to believe that Roxanne wouldn't throw everything away for an easy buck, but in her heart she suspected that's exactly the sort of person her partner had turned into.

At the next brief lull in business Kira pulled the escrow account information and phoned the bank. It turned out that she couldn't freeze the account without either a court order or Roxanne's permission, neither of which were going to happen today. Kira could, however, transfer all of the funds to her personal account, which Roxanne couldn't get to. She figured when stuff was through hitting the fan, a technical violation of client ethics in order to secure their money wouldn't be frowned on. At least, not as much as Roxanne's apparent detour from the straight and narrow. No matter what happened from this point on, though, life would never be the same.

Kira served the lunchtime coffee drinkers with perhaps a tenth of her attention, her thoughts centered squarely on Mitch. Drugs and money laundering. Those had to be the top two on the list of activities guaranteed to tank a romance with a future federal prosecutor.

MITCH GOT OFF WORK AT THREE, then stopped home to mow the lawn and shower up before the long haul to East Lansing. Weary, he stripped out of his uniform and pulled on shorts and an old T-shirt. As he sat on the edge of the bed to tie his shoes, he caught a faint whiff of Kira's fragrance on the pillow next to him. It was a lame-ass thing to pick up the pillow and sniff it. He was damn lucky he was alone with no one to witness the act.

If this was love, he was better off without it. It had

to be a Brewer genetic quirk that was inspiring him to try to protect a woman who had made it perfectly clear that she wanted to be left to suffer alone. He hoped future generations of Brewers would avoid that particular serving of DNA stew. But he was stuck with it and he was tired of fighting its pull.

He was by definition a doomed man. Very soon he'd have to talk to Kira about Roxanne. He couldn't keep quiet when Kira's future—and his—was at stake. And since he was already one piece of very dead meat...

Mitch walked at a gallows-steps pace to his computer. Once it was awake and awaiting his commands, he used his favorite search engine to find a keystroke-logging program, a type of spyware he'd first heard of when attending a forum on electronic privacy rights at school. The results were virtually instantaneous.

His conscience told him that he could stop now. But his compulsion to protect gave him a hard shove. Soon he was on a popular spyware site. The basic program was freeware, so it wouldn't cost him anything—except for some stabbing guilt pains.

Mitch stared at the screen.

It was his computer.

He could download any program he chose.

He just never thought he'd be installing KeySpy. Feeling a little sick, he began his download.

It was done in a matter of minutes, far less time than it was going to take him to cope with the potential consequences of this particular act. From this moment on he'd have a hidden log of every word Kira typed and every site she visited.

Mitch turned away from the computer. He'd protect Kira in spite of herself. Now if he just thought there was any way she'd ever love him in spite of *him*self.

KIRA WALKED BACK TO THE Dollhouse Cottage on aching feet. She was not made of stern enough stuff to stand behind a counter all day. Good thing she still had a day job, assuming that Roxanne didn't manage to drag down the whole company.

Once she turned the corner, the sight of the little white house nestled between its larger neighbors eased her stress. As she neared, she could hear the sound of a mower in the backyard. She glimpsed Mitch as he and the mower made a pass by the white-picket gate that led to the rear of the house. The scent of freshly cut grass wafted toward her. He had yet to mow the postage-stamp-sized front lawn.

She stepped onto the front porch and, instead of going straight inside, breathed in the moment and began a game of pretend. She pretended that she was here with Mitch because that was where she belonged, not because circumstances had thrown them together. She pretended that her future was charged with promise. She pretended that they had loved each other forever.

Just then, the sound of the mower cut out. She heard the creak of the back gate as it opened and the rattle of the mower against the drive as Mitch brought it around to the front yard. Most of all she heard the pounding of her heart as she realized that her love, at least, was very real.

The mower started again, a slow chug growing to a hungry growl. Mitch didn't notice her as he first came out, giving her the wonderful luxury of watching unobserved. If he'd been wearing a shirt, he'd discarded it, leaving his skin bare to the strong afternoon sun. He had the body of an athlete and sportsman, honed fit through activity. She also knew that he had an honorable heart, fiercely loyal to those he cared for. Including her.

Intuition and a growing sense of dread told Kira there would be no sidestepping the mess Roxanne had created. If she asked Mitch to, he would stand by her, no matter the cost to his career. But because she loved him and because she had to learn to stand on her own, she would never do that.

Mitch glanced her way once quickly, then again with more intensity as the mower's path came toward the house. Something incredible, exciting and terrifying jolted through her as their gazes locked. That instant—and it couldn't have been more than that—would live with Kira forever. It was the first time she'd let her love show. Then, in a real display of courage, she turned heel and bolted into the house.

Fifteen minutes later she heard Mitch come in the back door. He went from the kitchen to the bathroom without spending more than a second in the living room. If he'd noticed her curled up on the couch, he'd been kind enough to let her have some time to pull herself together.

Soon she heard the sound of running water in the bathroom. Kira went to the closed door and rested her forehead against it.

She couldn't bear it anymore, not being able to touch him. And she needed to be held as much as she needed to hold. He couldn't refuse her, but if he did, she feared she'd beg.

She slipped out of her clothes, then opened the bathroom door. Its hinges protested a little.

"Is someone out there?" Mitch asked.

Kira didn't bother answering with words. She pulled open the shower curtain and stepped over the edge of the tub, figuring that she might as well take advantage of his state of surprise.

He was potently male, not pretty in the way of those cold nude sculptures she'd seen in museums, but in a rugged way that stole her breath. She took the soap from his hands and turned it over in her own, creating a frothy white lather.

The showerhead was set high, as one would expect for a man of his height. Water pelted Kira— there was no escaping it. She shivered as it hit her oversensitive skin. Mitch just watched her.

"It's been the longest two days of my life. Let me touch you, Mitch. Please."

The house had been built a long time ago, when tubs were tubs only. A window still sat in the back wall of the tiled tub enclosure. Turning from her, Mitch braced his hands on the sill. Kira took the act as tacit permission.

Hands slick, she set the soap on the sill. She started with his shoulders. How she loved the breadth of them, the way hard bone and tensile muscle sat just beneath his skin.

She kneaded her fingers into his strength, closing her eyes and sighing at the sound of his low moan of approval. She took the soap again. As her hands skated over him, committing the feel of rough hair and smooth skin to memory, slowly this emotion— this *love*—became so great that she stilled.

Mitch turned to face her, settling his broad hands on her hips. "Don't stop. Ever."

They kissed as the water rained down on them,

until Kira pulled away laughing. "I'm going to drown."

Mitch switched off the taps and pulled back the shower curtain. When he stepped from the tub, Kira shivered—not because the air was especially cool in the air-conditioning-free house on this hot summer day but because she needed his touch. She needed to feel that everything was going to be okay.

He returned with two towels. One he slung low around his hips. The other he dried her with, letting his mouth precede the area he was next to touch. Kira let him lavish her with attention, though she burned to touch him, too. When he was done—and her knees were so weak that he had to help her from the tub—he led her to the bedroom.

"This isn't about need. This time," he said, "we make love."

Kira opened her arms to him. If she could keep her hands on him forever, she would, for that's how long she wanted him. But she'd take this afternoon.

Before he came to her, he stood and looked at her long enough that she began to feel restless and a little too exposed.

"Mitch…"

"Just remembering." He dropped his towel and joined her.

Kira didn't know that skin could be so hot. His… Hers… Theirs where it met.

He took his time with her, touching, nipping, caressing, until the need to give him the same kind of pleasure was too strong to quell. Kira pushed him back into the pillows and started with that wonderful romantic's mouth. She would have kissed him for hours if she'd had the patience, but there was so much else to love. His cheekbones—high, he told her, from a Sioux great-great-great-grandmother. The strong column of his throat, salty beneath her mouth. His chest, with his heart drumming strong and true.

She moved lower, grasping his erection at its base and then slowly drawing her hand upward. She rubbed her thumb over the head of his shaft, feeling the bit of moisture collected there. A yearning so fundamental and emotionally dangerous came over her that she shook.

Kira wanted to feel him inside her without the barrier of a condom. She wanted to be with him forever and maybe one day have his children. She'd grown up spoiled and willful, with true maturity only recently gained. And even now she wasn't very graceful about not getting what she wanted.

This time she would be. She'd settle for what she could have and what she could give him.

When she drew him into her mouth, his hips arched from the bed. Then he relaxed on a slow breath of pleasure. With his words and his fingertips caressing her face, he let her know how much what she was doing turned him on. He wasn't alone in that. She would have stayed there until he peaked, fully willing to accept that new intimacy.

Mitch had other ideas.

"No more," he said. "I'm not going to last."

Reluctantly she left him and kissed a path upward until she settled her head against his chest. He wrapped her in his arms and rolled so that she lay beneath him.

He kissed her once deeply before moving aside. Kira waited, heart pounding, as he reached into the nightstand for protection. He sheathed himself in quick, sure motions, then positioned himself above her.

"I need inside you now." Action followed words and he surged deep within. "Are you ready, sweetheart?" His expression was so tender that she felt her throat tighten with emotion.

"Forever," she said, running her hands over the strong angles of his shoulders.

He began to move. Kira met his slow, thorough strokes, wanting him to never leave and this moment to never end. Mitch must have felt the same way, too, because he drew out their pleasure. But his touch was too compelling, his taste too addictive for her to be satisfied by his easy pace for very long.

She urged him to move faster, harder, but he gave her a fierce smile and told her not yet. She wrapped her legs above his hips and drove her body up to meet his, trying to push him to the brink.

Mitch laughed. "We're savoring this, remember?"

Easy for him to say. Dizzying sensations shot through her, leaving her breathless. She was poised on a precipice of something amazing, and he wouldn't give her that last push over the edge. She nipped at his collarbone—the first ready bit of flesh she could get her teeth to.

"You're playing with fire," he warned, the harshness of his words softened by his smile.

"What are you going to do—tie me up and spank me?" she teased.

"Not this time. Maybe later, if you're very, very bad."

Kira laughed and then nibbled at him again. She couldn't recall ever being so aroused and full of laughter at the same time. Sex had always been a serious matter, something to do right, as though she was being judged. It seemed that with Mitch joy was the purpose of the act. And she found that the most wonderful turn-on of all.

"Tell me how this punishment is," Mitch said.

He changed his angle ever so slightly, adding delicious pressure where she needed it most. Kira was fairly sure that her eyes were crossing with pleasure.

"It's awful," she said. "Horrible. The worst."

Once, twice, three times more he surged into her. That final time he stayed.

"Tell me the truth," he whispered into her ear, "or you'll get more of the same."

The truth she gave him wasn't what he'd expected—or what she'd planned, for that matter. The words slipped out on a tide of pure joy.

"I love you."

He hesitated a moment, and their gazes locked. She watched the shock register in his eyes, making them seem almost a darker blue.

Finally he moved as she'd wanted him to before, quickly and with enough force that she braced one hand against the headboard as they were impelled toward it. Suddenly her orgasm rippled through her, starting small and finally taking her whole body. She held on to Mitch as her world changed around her. A second later Mitch cried her name and came fully, totally apart in her arms.

She had never felt so utterly, perfectly alive.

Later, when her heartbeat had slowed and passion had left drowsy contentment in its wake, Kira sorted through her feelings. She'd never before told a man that she loved him—a fairly scary admission for someone creeping up on thirty.

Maybe before she'd never been ready. Or maybe before her heart had known that those mad flashes of infatuation which marked her prior relationships had nothing to do with love.

She turned onto her side and watched Mitch sleep. Whatever the reason, she was glad that she'd waited until now.

And for this man.

12

Kira woke after the sun had set. She reached over, switched on the bedside lamp and looked at the clock. Nearly ten—she had two hours and more before Mitch returned home.

She stood and stretched, enjoying the slight ache in her muscles that lingered after their lovemaking. And Mitch had been true to his promise—the afternoon had been about love.

Tonight, though, appeared to be about fright wigs. She made a face at herself in the dresser mirror, where her reflection looked back at her, victim of the worst case of bedhead she'd ever seen. That would be the downside of passionate love with wet hair.

Kira showered again, combed out her hair and slipped into one of Mitch's T-shirts in lieu of pajamas. In the kitchen she scavenged a late dinner. Sheer curiosity made her sample Mitch's marshmallow fluff. One tiny dot to the tip of her tongue was sufficient to let her know that she'd missed nothing in these past twenty-seven years. She opted for the last of the vanilla yogurt she'd bought earlier in the week at Mrs. Hawkins's market, along with some of Mitch's cereal, which at least wasn't sugar fortified.

When she was through eating, Kira remained too restless to sleep. She considered reading a few more pages of the thriller she'd paged through earlier in the week, but when she found the business card she'd used as a bookmark was missing, she decided she didn't have enough interest to find her page.

Television was a poor distraction. The little set in Mitch's second bedroom was aimed toward the weight bench. She rolled the office chair over, sat and channel surfed but could find nothing that entertained her. Nothing that would push away the worries. Alone, she couldn't pretend that life was idyllic in the Dollhouse Cottage.

Kira was drawn to the computer. She had to let the outside world in, at least enough to take care of her responsibilities at work. After much hesitation she gave in, logged on to her Web site mail and began to weed through the crop. Tapping her delete key in an old fashioned Morse-code rhythm, she consigned the spam to cyberhell.

She was ready to tap again when her heart jolted. The sender of the next message was identified as HotRox. There were some pervy meanings for that phrase, but there was also a marginally less suspect one: Roxanne. On her desk in Coconut Grove, Roxanne had a small, wild looking, feathered and sequined character doll a friend had made her. The doll's name was Hot Rox.

Kira aimed the mouse over the message and opened it. Half hoping for yet another erectile-dysfunction cure or a link to an X-rated Web site, she found instead a real message.

Come back home. You'll be safer once I have what I need from you. They know where you are anyway.

Kira minimized the message to the bottom of the computer screen, but its impact remained the same. She felt as though someone were holding a knife to her throat.

She left Mitch's office and began walking circles through the small house, drawing deep breaths and making a mental list of things she was thankful for in order to calm herself. *I'm thankful I'm still alive* seemed to be lodged at number one.

Seeking another route, she went to the kitchen and got a glass of ice water. The way her hands were shaking, she could hardly get the cubes in the glass. Leaving the mess at the sink, she pulled out a chair from the kitchen table and sat.

No one had overtly threatened her, she reminded herself. She was reading the worst into the note, which was probably what the sender had intended her to do.

What could she possibly have that Roxanne needed—assuming the sender was really Roxanne? Kira didn't know all the technical terms, but she wasn't clueless. It was an easy thing to fake another person's identity over the Internet. And Roxanne would be the least of all the potential evils out there. Somehow Kira needed to sift through the possibilities. For now she'd assume the sender was really her partner.

She went to the living room and switched on the lamp next to the couch. Somewhere in her briefcase was the contact information that Don had given her when they'd first spoken. She was pretty sure he'd included an e-mail address. She found the slip of paper in the front pocket and knew a moment's relief that she could reach him now, when it was far too late to call. That he probably wouldn't read the message until morning didn't matter. All that did was that she'd feel better.

Kira hurried back to the computer. Once she'd forwarded the e-mail to Don, she deleted it from the system. She'd done all she could to exorcise that particular demon. She wasn't feeling one heck of a lot calmer, though.

What could Roxanne be demanding in that infuriatingly vague e-mail?

Kira returned to her briefcase, where she dug through the papers checking for anything she might have missed when she'd gone through them earlier in the week. Maybe it was something as simple as a note or number that Roxanne had written on the back of the Casa Pura Vida research. Kira found nothing.

Or maybe Roxanne had returned to the office and discovered the PDA mix-up, and that's what she wanted. If so, there should be some entry in there that would stand out. Kira pulled Roxanne's PDA and leaned back on the couch.

First Kira opened the date book. Luckily the entries only went back as far as December of the prior year. It was painstaking work reading every entry for every day, since Roxanne had been nearly obsessive about detailing the unimportant stuff in her life. It was after eleven when Kira finally finished checking out all of the PDA's files. Nothing stood out.

Frustrated, upset and out of bright ideas, she returned to the kitchen, put fresh ice into the water glass she'd earlier abandoned and rummaged through the cupboards for the whiskey she'd seen Mitch sip the night they'd first kissed.

She pulled out the bottle and read the label. She had no idea whether "single-malt scotch" was good or bad. All she cared was that it might numb her. Kira tried a tentative sip and decided it would serve its purpose. Glass in hand, she returned to the office, where she searched the Internet for articles on bearer bonds.

The ice in the glass had melted and her eyes were heavy with sleep by the time she decided she'd seen enough. At least now she understood what she faced. Exhausted, Kira pushed back from the computer and made her way to Mitch's bed, where she let sleep claim her.

MITCH CLIMBED FROM HIS CAR, then stretched cramped muscles. He was nearly at the end of his long-haul driving days, which was a good thing, since his tolerance for it was gone. As he pocketed his keys and walked toward his house, he noticed that virtually every light inside was turned on. He appreciated a warm welcome, but could do without the hit to his electric bill.

"Kira?" he called as he came in the front door. But no one answered. He switched off the living room light and the kitchen, too. When he reached his computer/exercise room, he halted in the doorway. His computer was on, and he was far too attached to his flat-panel monitor to have left it glowing all night. If that hadn't been tip-off enough that Kira had been there, the half-finished whiskey glass on the desk would have done the job.

He looked into the bedroom. She was curled up on her side, asleep in the center of the bed. He knew a moment's bitterness that she could look so peaceful when his gut was knotted with tension. Then she turned restlessly in her sleep, murmuring the half words, half nonsense he'd heard the other night. No, she had no more peace than he did.

Mitch returned to the computer room, closing the door behind him. After a swallow of the lukewarm diluted whiskey that Kira had left, he opened the KeySpy program and called up the log. He clicked on yesterday's date, since midnight had arrived almost an hour earlier.

Mitch scrolled down the screen and checked the first entry. She'd logged on at the Whitman-Pierce site, but her keystrokes other than her password had been minimal…until five minutes later. Feeling lower than a thief, Mitch read the message she'd typed.

Don,
Do you think the attached is authentic? I'm worried.
Call me when you can.
Kira

She wasn't alone in her worry.

"*What* was authentic, dammit?" Mitch asked.

He downed more of the tepid drink and then went to the Web site's back-door address Kira had used. He began reading through the mail she'd left on the server. It didn't take long to accept that after she'd forwarded whatever this alarming something was, she'd wiped it from the server. He couldn't find it in her sent-mail folder either.

If he'd ever had any real computer training, Mitch was sure he'd have been able to somehow retrieve the message from the guts of his computer. But really he was nothing more than a devious amateur.

Accepting that he'd hit a dead end, Mitch returned to the keystroke log.

What he saw next nearly rocked his faith in her honesty. Kira had been searching the phrase *bearer bonds*.

A couple of years had passed since his Commercial Transactions class, and bearer bonds had been touched on only briefly. Still, Mitch knew one thing for sure—in the United States at least, there was no legal and justifiable reason to be dealing in them. He also couldn't imagine that she'd searched the words out of random curiosity. Not after eleven at night, when he'd earlier made love to her until she'd cried exhaustion.

"What a total goddamn mess," he said, then drained the rest of the whiskey.

He might be an analytical man, but he was also out of avenues. She loved him. She'd said so, even if it was in the act, so to speak. He wouldn't let her take it back and he wouldn't lose her by showing himself for the sneaky bastard he'd proven to be over the last twenty-four hours.

He'd wait until morning. He'd stick with her all day. Whatever it took until she worked up the courage to give him the truth.

Mitch printed the log pages and tucked them into a desk drawer. Once he'd shut down the computer and settled the whiskey glass into the kitchen sink, he got ready for bed.

In his absence Kira had moved diagonally across the mattress, leaving him only a wedge of his usual sleeping space. It amused him in a bleak sort of way that a woman so small could take up so much space in his bed...his mind...and his heart.

"Move it over, Highness," he murmured, trying to get her perpendicular to the headboard.

Mitch folded his body into the territory he'd won. Still restless, she rolled toward him and then came more fully awake.

"I've missed you," she whispered.

Three simple words—not even as intimate as the ones she'd given him earlier—and he ached to be inside her. Mitch made love to her hard, hungry and without the words he wanted to give her in return. First he needed the truth.

THE NEXT MORNING, WHILE KIRA was brushing her teeth, Mitch popped his head into the bathroom and said, "See you soon." Since he was dressed for work and she was off to brew coffee, she wasn't sure what that meant, but she nodded anyway.

Fifteen minutes later she arrived at the Village Grounds. Lisa stuck around after opening the shop long enough to give a few wedding updates. The heart-shaped butter pats were no more. Her dress had been fitted to perfection. And in a true stroke of weirdness, her great-aunt had given them a massive concrete gargoyle as a wedding gift.

Kira asked Lisa if she could stay long enough for Kira to make a couple of calls. She had weirdness of her own to deal with, and nothing so benign as a concrete gargoyle. While Lisa tended the coffee bar, Kira slipped outside and walked across the street to the village green. A woman—and Kira would bet it was Lisa's mother—was on her knees at the edge of the gazebo replacing flower beds of red impatiens with flats of the pale pink variety. Pink was more romantic, no doubt. Kira tactfully pretended not to see her.

She pulled out her phone and dialed the office. Susan answered on the second ring.

"Hey, Susan, it's Kira."

After answering some questions other agents had left with the receptionist, Kira got down to the business that most concerned her.

"Has Roxanne picked up her car yet?" she asked.

"No, it's still in the lot. I thought you said she was gone for the whole week."

"I did, but you know how she likes to change things up. I though she might be back by now."

"Not a sign of her," Susan said. "No calls, no nothing."

Kira frowned. "Do me a favor. Check her office and see if her briefcase is still there."

"Hang on while I put you on hold."

"Okay." While she waited, Kira watched Lisa's mother tuck uprooted red impatiens into the empty plastic packs from the pink.

Susan returned. "It's gone. But, then again, I don't remember seeing it there all week."

Okay, so Roxanne probably knew that she had the wrong PDA. The question was why she cared.

"Kira, is everything okay?" Susan asked. "I've been worried all week...since you asked me for Don's number. It didn't help that Don called and asked me stuff about Roxanne."

Kira worked up the most reassuring voice she could. "Things are a little sticky right now between Roxanne and me, that's all. It should clear up in the next couple of weeks. I promise."

Someone was walking from the back side of the gazebo toward Lisa's mother. It was Mitch.

"I know that you and Roxanne haven't been getting along too well lately," Susan was saying into her ear at the same time Kira was trying to pick up snatches of conversation between Mitch and the flower swapper.

"No, we haven't," Kira said. "And, Susan, if you see anything outside the norm at the office, call Don right away, okay?" Mitch had apparently left Lisa's mom to her gardening, because he was headed her way. "I have to run. I'll talk to you later."

Kira didn't even wait for Susan's goodbye, tucking the cell phone into her purse with the hope of avoiding any Mitch-type questions. The call to Don would have to wait a couple of minutes.

Mitch leaned down and kissed her after he'd arrived.

"This is a pretty conservative town. Isn't there an ordinance against that?" she teased.

He smiled. "Only if we're naked."

She looped her arm through his. "So, do you want to walk me back to work?"

"Absolutely." While they walked, he said, "How would you feel about going out for a nice dinner tonight?"

"Like a date?"

"A date," he agreed. "I'd like to take you to the Nickerson Inn."

The Nickerson was a quaint old place high on a hillside overlooking Lake Michigan. As Kira recalled, it served the most elegant meals in Sandy Bend. She knew that Mitch—the fluff lover—was stretching far to please her in offering this meal.

"I'd love to go," she said, smiling up at him.

When they got to the door, Mitch opened it and ushered her in, then followed. She had assumed he'd be going back to work.

"I'm in the mood for a coffee," he said at her curious look.

He lingered even after he'd been given his coffee, making Lisa laugh and blush with talk about what a beautiful bride she was going to be tomorrow. When he jokingly mentioned that her mom was across the street uprooting the park in favor of a pink theme, she shot out the door. Kira imagined that if Lisa were drawn as a cartoon character, she'd have more steam coming out of her ears than the espresso machine she'd abandoned hissing into a pitcher of milk.

Kira took over behind the counter.

Mitch went to the window and gave a low whistle as both of them watched Lisa lecture her mom.

"Nice job," Kira said. "Get the mother of the bride killed the day before the wedding."

Mitch laughed. "Hey, it's not as though I arrested her. That would have really ticked Lisa off."

Mind on her cell phone, Kira said, "Why don't you go across the street and mediate?"

"No way. I'd rather step into a prison riot than deal with a day-before-the-wedding family spat." To make it clear he wasn't moving, Mitch grabbed a stool from the front counter, carried it back to the coffee bar and tucked it where he wouldn't interfere with the customers—or give her a moment of privacy.

"Is that today's paper?" he asked, pointing to a stack of newsprint Lisa must have left by the bakery case.

Kira tossed the newspaper to him with technically a little more force than what was required. "Read away."

After making a couple of fruit smoothies and ringing up the orders, Kira tried again.

"Don't you have to go walk a beat or do whatever it is you do all day?" she asked.

He looked at her from over the top of the paper. "Nope. I'm done."

She glanced at the clock on the back wall. "You worked for—what—an hour?"

"I got a call from another officer who needed to switch shifts for next Tuesday. I'm sprung. And I was already off until Sunday night, too."

Which was all wonderful, but she still needed to call Don. It was time to get down and dirty.

"As long as you've decided to make yourself a fixture, would you mind watching the store for a few minutes?" she asked.

Mitch set aside the paper, then shook his head. "I don't know how to make lattes."

Kira grabbed her purse and came around the counter. "Fake it."

"Where are you going?" There was an edge of panic to his voice. She would have thought that, as a male, he'd get a kick out of the new toys he could play with.

She came close and spoke in a low, confiding tone. "I'm going to the ladies' room. I think it might be that time of the month. I'm feeling a little crampy," she said, laying one hand low on her belly for added effect.

That shut him up. She figured he was considering himself lucky that she hadn't sent him to the market to buy tampons.

The shop had one small unisex bathroom at the very back. After glancing over her shoulder to make sure that Mitch had parked himself behind the counter, she shut herself in. And just in case he didn't fully buy her story and decided to come eavesdrop, she turned on the sink taps full blast before calling Don.

His secretary quickly connected him.

"Is that water running?" he asked.

"Yup."

"I don't think I want to know where you're calling from."

"You don't," she said. "Did you get my e-mail from last night? Do you think it's really Roxanne?"

"Yes, but the Internet service provider won't just hand over customer information, so it's a tough one to prove very quickly. What do you have that she could need?"

Kira told Don about the PDA mix-up and how last night she'd gone through every file.

"Just because you can't see a file doesn't mean it isn't there. It's simple enough to hide one and password protect it."

When it came to that sort of technical stuff, she'd take him at his word. Still, she had her doubts about Roxanne's level of attention.

"I don't know," Kira said. "We're talking about someone who stuck her business passwords in a shopping list."

"Maybe she's more careful with things that mean more to her." Don paused a second. "I've corroborated the bearer-bond rumor, so if there's a hidden file, it could be worth millions. Literally."

He had a point.

"Did you talk to your attorney yesterday?" Don asked.

At her continuing silence, he said, "This is serious stuff. Do it, Kira."

She looked at her reflection, pale and pinched, in the bathroom mirror. It was as though she'd aged five years in less than five minutes. "I will."

After their call ended, Kira shut off the water and gave herself a moment to work up a calm facade. It was already Friday afternoon. Would it be so horrible to steal a day or two of happiness before everything came tumbling down?

She would call her father on Sunday. He was well connected, far better suited for the job of finding her an attorney than she was. And it wasn't as though too much more could go wrong in less than forty-eight hours.

She'd spend what time she had left with Mitch, then give him an easy out of their relationship. He deserved that much, at least.

After sticking her cell phone back in her purse, Kira left the bathroom. Mitch was at the register.

"False alarm," she said in a cheerful voice as she nudged him aside.

If only she could say the same thing about Don's call.

13

FINE DINING AND TORTURE could be found under the same entry in Mitch's thesaurus. He and Kira weren't even dressed to leave for the restaurant and already he was uptight.

Scowling at his reflection in the dresser mirror, Mitch reknotted his tie for the third damn time. Tie finally neither too long nor too short, he picked up the small red velvet box he'd retrieved from his safe-deposit box at the bank in the early afternoon.

His mom had died when he was just a little kid. As time had passed, a lot of his memories of specific events had faded. He still remembered her laugh and the way she'd always smelled sweet to him, as if she'd just been baking cupcakes. And he remembered this....

Mitch opened the box and touched the delicate necklace that lay on its white silk lining. His mother's family had been farm people and had had little money for luxuries, so this was a simple piece. Once, he'd shown the necklace to Dana, who had a better eye for jewelry than he did. She'd said that the pinkish gold was called rose gold and that the cut of the small diamond it held was old.

The necklace was one of the few keepsakes he had from his mother. She'd always worn it, and his dad had later told him that it had been handed down from her grandmother. Now Mitch wanted Kira to have it. He wanted her to see that he meant the necklace as a symbol of the trust they should have in each other. He was damn sure that the subterfuge and avoidance she'd thrown his way was rooted in panic and he was positive that once they got past this garbage he wanted her in his life.

He couldn't believe he was moving to the level of metaphor, but words hadn't exactly worked between the two of them. Worse, shadowing her today had only put her more on edge. He knew that she'd called someone from the bathroom of the Village Grounds this morning and he knew that she'd seemed sad and subdued the rest of the day.

Mitch snapped shut the box and stuck it in his blazer pocket. He was asking a lot from a simple piece of jewelry, but he didn't know what else to do. He'd never failed at much. To do it the first time in such a colossal way would be a killer.

Kira had closed herself in the bathroom. After fifteen minutes of cooling his heels in the living room, Mitch wondered whether she'd ever come out.

He came closer to the door. The scent of a warm and spicy perfume lingered in the air, but he couldn't hear a thing.

"Are you still alive in there?" he asked.

"Stop hovering. I'll be out in a few minutes," she said.

Duly chastised, Mitch returned to the living room. True to her word, Kira appeared not long after. He stood, but it was pretty much an involuntary reflex, not a show of manners.

"Wow," he finally managed to say.

While he'd been in the bank, Kira must have been shopping. He knew that she deserved more expansive praise for the way she looked in her short, sleek and low-cut black dress, but his tongue seemed to have grown uncooperative.

She twirled once and then said, "So, you like it?"

He nodded. Even with their troubles, he'd have to say that he was one lucky, lucky man.

As IT TURNED OUT, MITCH GOT lucky on a number of counts. First, they were seated on the screened porch off the dining room, a comfortable place where he could look past the green treetops to the blue of Lake Michigan stretching to the horizon. Second, along with the fine food and fancy sauces that a woman like Kira had probably cut her teeth on, the menu also had stuff a guy could eat—cow and everything.

During dinner they talked about the old days and old friends. For a while it didn't feel to Mitch as though whatever she was embroiled in today hung over his head like an anvil, ready to flatten him. He could almost imagine what life would be like once they were past it.

He waited until after the meal had been cleared to give her the necklace.

"I have something for you," he said, pulling the box from his pocket and setting it in front of her.

A pretty tinge of pink climbed her cheeks. "It's really for me?"

He nodded. She seemed so floored that he wondered if all the guys she'd dated had been faced with the same problem he'd had—not knowing what to get a girl who had everything.

Kira slowly opened the box, then touched one finger to the necklace. Her obvious delight was gratifying. "It's beautiful and so delicate."

"It was my mother's." His throat felt thick when he spoke.

"Your mother's?" she echoed. Something he'd peg as dismay flashed across her face. "Mitch, I can't take this."

"Why not?"

She looked down at the tablecloth, then back at him. "It should stay in your family. It wouldn't be right for me to accept it."

"But you're the woman I want to have it."

"I'm—I'm leaving on Sunday," she said in a rush. "Remember how I'd told you that I had a little glitch in my business?"

He nodded.

"I need to fix it now. Life's going to be crazy for a while. I don't know how long it will be until I can come back to Michigan again and I totally understand how busy you are finishing off school and with your work. This is just…bad timing. For both of us."

She closed the box and handed it back to him. Mitch left it on the table, a marker of all that was screwed up between them. If he didn't know about her concerned e-mail and the computer research she'd been doing, he'd have thought that she was dumping him. But he did know and recognized her talk as an attempt to let him extricate himself.

Problem was, he had no intention of doing that. His time in the hospital had taught him that he was tough enough to wait out almost anything.

Curiosity and a sense that they were playing some sort of game of brinksmanship drove him to ask, "And if I want to come to Florida?"

She looked as though she wanted to cry. Hell, he nearly did. Or at least go punch a wall.

"I don't know, Mitch. As I said, there's a lot I have to do. Let's just wait and see."

Mitch knew there was a moral to this evening and he wasn't crazy about being on the ugly end of it. Devious guys didn't deserve to be happy. He took the necklace and returned it to his pocket.

DINNER WAS FINISHED, AND IT felt to Kira as though her brief fantasy of an idyllic Dollhouse Cottage life was, too. Mitch was a generous man, kind enough to try to keep conversation flowing when they both had run out of words.

"Let's take a walk toward the water," he said. "The sun will be setting soon."

Because she wasn't ready to go back to the cottage, Kira agreed. She hadn't planned on telling Mitch so soon that she'd be leaving, but when he'd tried to give her his mother's necklace, she'd had no choice. Accepting it would have been wrong, as would dragging him into the middle of her problems.

They headed to a broad stretch of beach with a boardwalk that lay west of the Nickerson Inn. As she and Mitch walked, she wanted to hold his hand or his arm—anything to try to regain the connection she felt fading. When he led her out onto the pier, at least she had an excuse to do just that.

"Would you mind?" she asked, taking his hand. "High heels and I get along for only so long."

He squeezed her hand once, then wrapped it into the crook of his elbow. They walked past fishermen and other couples strolling. People greeted Mitch. He gave them a restrained greeting in return.

At the end of the pier they stood just apart from a small group waiting for the orange-red globe of the sun to finally touch the water. This time of year it was a long wait. Kira would guess that it was nearing nine and the sun yet had a distance to travel.

She was feeling weary, and it wasn't from the hour. Doing the right thing was very tiring exercise.

"What time Sunday had you planned to leave?" Mitch asked in a low voice.

She didn't want to talk about this. She'd done enough to spoil her last hours in town already. "I don't know…afternoon maybe."

More people gathered on the pier. The sunset was taking on almost a Key West-type festive atmosphere. Kira began to feel out of place, and apparently Mitch did, too.

"Let's head to land," he said.

As they walked past the edge of the picnic area that was adjacent to the state park's beach, Kira hesitated. At a table just ahead sat a man and woman. He was paging through a magazine and she was chatting on her cell phone. Kira was sure she'd never seen the man before, but the woman looked vaguely familiar. As they walked past, Kira scrutinized her. Middle-aged, brown hair, bland expression…

She shrugged off the moment, thinking the woman must look like someone she'd once shown a house to. When they were five or so yards past, Kira paused and looked back. Recognition hit her like a punch. Kira's bad leg gave a little, and she felt her ankle wobble.

Mitch steadied her. "Are you okay?"

"Sorry. Stupid shoes," she murmured, trying to sound unaffected as her mind raced. It had been only days but over fifteen hundred miles since she'd seen that unremarkable woman…in Coconut Grove. Kira was almost certain that she was the same woman she'd seen parked in the blue minivan the night Roxanne had disappeared.

Suddenly dinner wasn't sitting too well. Not with trouble hot on her heels…

MITCH WOKE AT SEVEN ON Saturday. His bed was far too empty for comfort, since Kira had decided she wanted to sleep on the couch. She'd thought it would be better that way. Better for whom, he wasn't exactly sure.

He was about to head out the front door for a lengthy, mind-clearing run when he stopped long enough to watch her struggle to roll to her side, her legs tangled in the sheet she'd put over herself. He didn't like witnessing her discomfort.

Mitch walked to the couch, bent down and kissed her forehead. When her eyes opened, he said, "You're moving." Without giving her time to protest, he scooped her up, carried her to his bedroom and settled her on the bed.

"I'll be back later. Sleep, since I'm betting you didn't all night."

After stretching he began to run his standard loop through the downtown area and out to the beach. Preparations were in full swing for Lisa and Jim's wedding, which was at eleven. Mitch crossed the street to check out the action. A large white tent was being erected on a portion of the green. Tables and chairs were being delivered, and other workers were there, too. Mitch jogged by a white-panel florist's van parked about a block down from the green, no doubt waiting its turn. He smiled at the woman in the driver's seat, and she gave him a quick smile back.

As he continued his run, the florist lingered in his mind. He'd seen her somewhere before, and it wasn't in a flower shop. Mitch knew the best way to make the connection was to stop thinking about it and let his subconscious simmer. Sooner or later it would come to him. It always did.

KIRA WOKE TO FIND MITCH sitting on the edge of the bed. In his hand was a mug of coffee.

Once she'd sat upright, he handed it to her, saying, "You'll have to risk homemade, since the Village Grounds is closed today."

"Thanks. I'm sure it's wonderful." She took a sip, then worked on waking more. "So, what time is it?"

"Ten," he said with a casual nod toward the clock.

"Ten?" Kira pushed the mug back at him. "The wedding's in an hour." She scrambled from beneath the covers. "I don't know what I'm wearing and all I have is a card for them."

"Relax. It's casual, so you don't need to barricade yourself in the bathroom for hours. And the gift I bought can be from both of us. I forgot to buy a card, so we'll use yours."

Kira felt as though she was living on two levels. There was the outward, blissfully normal Sandy Bend Saturday full of social events. Then there was the deeper, upsetting knowledge that nothing was as it seemed.

"Thanks," she said, then accepted the mug again.

"When I ran this morning, I did some thinking, and here's what I'd like. I'd like today to be special…memorable. I accept that you plan to leave to-morrow, but let's not have that carry over into today, okay?"

She nodded. "I'd like that, too."

"We have Jim and Lisa's wedding, then dinner out at Cal's place. After that I plan to bring you back here and make love to you until maybe you change your mind about tomorrow."

"Mitch, I can't—"

He raised his hand, palm outward. "Nope. No negativity."

"Okay."

Mitch stood. "I'll be out on the back deck. Come get me when you're ready."

Kira showered, then fussed with her hair, ending up with it pinned into a knot. She pulled on one of her sleeveless silk tops and a flowing floral skirt perfect for a wedding on a green. Then she joined Mitch and they walked downtown together.

After the disastrous near wedding in Chicago, Kira had decided that if she were ever actually to do the deed, she'd want something more casual. Something like what Lisa had. The white gingerbread of the green's gazebo had been draped with a fat white organza ribbon that shone iridescent in the sun. The folding chairs set up for the guests to watch the ceremony were covered in white fabric with a bow at the back of each. The aisle was marked by baskets of flowers, with white roses, purple Japanese iris and whimsical daisies in the mix. At the back of the gazebo a harpist was playing.

It was perfection, Kira decided. Mitch took her hand and led her down the gentle slope to the seating area. Others Kira knew from town were gathering. She saw Mrs. Hawkins from the market on the arm of a tall, older man, which Kira found surprising, since the market owner had been widowed for years.

"Who's with Mrs. Hawkins?" Kira quietly asked Mitch.

"That's Len Vandervoort, her husband. She remarried last year but kept Hawkins as her last name not to confuse folks at her market."

Kira was pleased for Mrs. Hawkins. The sight of the couple gave her hope, too. Maybe by the time she and Mitch were in their eighties they'd have managed to get this love thing right.

Cal and Dana were seated a few rows from the back. Dana spotted them and waved them over. When the usher came to take Kira's arm, she told him they'd like to sit by the other couple. Dana and Cal stood as they arrived.

In what was one of the shocks of Kira's life, Cal leaned forward and gave her a kiss on the cheek.

"It's good to see you," he said.

Kira managed a polite thank-you to Cal as she sat. So this was what it felt like to belong…. Pity she was learning when it was too late.

"Dinner's at seven," Dana said to them.

"Can I bring anything?" Kira asked, recovering her poise.

"Just yourselves. And don't let Mitch make you late. I'm baking walleye in parchment paper, and the fish will turn to leather if it's in the oven too long."

They chatted until a violinist came forward and stood beside the gazebo. Silence fell as the minister, the groom and his ushers lined up. The violinist began to play. A trio of bridesmaids came down the aisle before the traditional wedding march started.

Everyone rose and turned. Lisa was, as Mitch had predicted, beautiful.

Kira didn't usually cry at weddings, but she began to tear up. She knew it was a reaction from the emotions that had buffeted her the past few days, but understanding the source didn't help. She did her best to stop the tears from escaping and ruining her makeup, but it was a losing battle.

As Lisa joined Jim at the altar, Kira felt a square of fabric being pressed into her hand. Mitch had handed her a handkerchief. He followed up with a quick kiss to her temple. It was going to be so very hard to leave this man.

After the ceremony they joined everyone in a tent at the far end of the green. She tried to be cheerful. She met Lisa's Jim and thanked them both for having her to the wedding. She ate more than she should have and avoided alcohol altogether. She was weepy enough already. Once the band had set up in the gazebo, she danced with both Mitch and Cal. Still, she felt overwhelmed.

While Mitch was dancing with Dana, Kira walked to the edge of the gathering, seeking a little less crowd, a little less noise. Sightseers stood on the sidewalk that bordered the green, a few taking snapshots of the wedding. In all the years she'd visited Sandy Bend Kira had never figured it especially photoworthy. Now her perspective had changed.

As the tourists moved on, Kira glanced across the street at the Village Grounds, where someone had painted *Just Married* in bright red letters on the front window. She smiled at the sight. Then she noticed something that made her smile fade. It was the woman from last night—and maybe last week. This time she was walking past the Village Grounds. Spooked, Kira hurried back to the reception, where she stuck to Mitch's side. After a while she had calmed down enough to let go of his hand.

Afternoon stretched toward evening. Kira saw no sign of the mystery woman again, though that was no surprise, since Kira made sure to keep to the middle of the reception throng. Dana and Cal left around four, clearly intent on reliving some wedding—and honeymoon—memories of their own before dinner.

Over time the reception turned into a town celebration, with more food and more people arriving. Kira expected that it would still be going strong at midnight. It was nearly six-thirty when Mitch suggested that they head back to the house, grab his car and head out to Cal and Dana's.

Fifteen minutes later they were on the road. Cal and Dana lived on the Brewer family farm, several miles into the countryside. Kira was blissfully relieved to have this break from town and from the potential of spotting the mystery woman. She leaned back, closed her eyes and put her fate in Mitch's hands for a few minutes.

Sandy Bend was behind them when Mitch made a sharp right turn onto a dirt road. Kira sat upright and braced her hands on the dashboard.

"Where are you going?"

He glanced her way. "I decided to take the scenic route."

Had he not chosen a road bounded on both sides by asparagus fields and little else, she might have bought in. The harvest was through and the stalks remaining had begun to grow tall, sliver-green and fernlike. The view was pretty enough—for the first half mile or so.

The back roads around Sandy Bend ran fairly straight. Kira soon realized that he was driving in a large square that would take them back to the main, paved road into town. At one point he slowed to let a truck gain on and then pass them.

"You could probably afford to pick it up a few miles an hour," she suggested. She didn't want to be responsible for petrified walleye at dinner.

Mitch barely responded. When they'd returned to the main road, he once again headed east into the countryside. She relaxed until he pulled into the mouth of another road and made a U-turn toward town.

"Where are we going?" she asked.

"Don't talk."

A minute or so later he muttered a blunt expletive. He looked so grim—almost furious—that Kira was actually scared.

"Mitch, what's wrong?"

"I said don't talk."

"But you're heading the wrong way, and Cal's expecting us."

He glared at her in response.

In a matter of minutes they had pulled into the drive at the Dollhouse Cottage. He strode to the door, looking once over his shoulder to tell her to hurry. Once inside he led her to the kitchen, where he looked out the back door before closing it and turning to her.

"Is there any reason someone would want to follow you?"

14

SWEAT BROKE OUT ON KIRA'S palms, but she kept her voice level. "Follow me?"

"Yeah. A dark green Taurus with two occupants."

It was possible, but she far preferred living in denial.

"Are you sure?" she asked.

He turned away from her for a moment, almost as though he couldn't stand the sight of her.

"I want you to come with me," he said when he'd turned back. He wrapped his fingers around her wrist and led her into his office. There he pulled out a sheaf of papers. "I loaded a keystroke-logging program on my computer so I could track you. I don't know what exactly you've been doing, but it has nothing to do with selling houses. I don't like being followed. In fact, it really pisses me off. Now, can you tell me what the hell's going on?"

Horrified, Kira pulled the papers from his hands. "You've been spying on me? How could you?"

"I told you not to use the computer."

"That's no excuse!"

He rubbed between his brows with the fingers of his right hand. "What choice did you leave me?"

"All you had to do was ask me to go."

Mitch walked away to adjust the blind over the

window so that the outdoors was totally obscured. "After a while it wasn't an option."

She tossed the papers into the wastebasket by the desk. "And spying was?"

"No. What I did sucked, okay? But we'll get to my sins later. For now, since I can guarantee that we're going to have visitors of some kind in the near future, I think you'd better tell me what's been going on. And once you're done, I'm getting Cal over here."

Mitch pulled out his desk chair and sat.

Kira was a mess. Anger and fright knotted her stomach. She felt betrayed yet strangely relieved at the same time. Clasping her hands to hide their trembling, she began to speak.

"Roxanne, my partner at work, took off just before I came to Sandy Bend. The circumstances weren't the best. She was with a couple of guys I didn't like the looks of. I got a threatening call, and some more goons were at my house. I wasn't sure what was going on, except it wasn't good."

She paused, looking for some sign of receptiveness in Mitch but finding instead a face devoid of expression.

"Go on," he said.

"I hired an investigator through a friend, and he suggested that leaving town might make some sense. I picked Sandy Bend because no one would expect it." She didn't add that her thoughts of him that afternoon had probably subconsciously urged her north, too.

"And since you've been here? Have you heard from your friend? Learned anything from your investigator?"

"I stumbled on the fact that Roxanne has been

running lots of money through our client escrow account. Things just weren't adding up. I began to worry that she was into something really bad. Roxanne's not exactly an angel."

"I know all about Roxanne."

"How?"

"The usual way," he said flatly. "So, where's Roxanne now?"

Part of Kira didn't want to tell him anything more. But the rest of her knew the time for evasiveness was past. If she didn't give him the truth now—no matter how helpless it made her look—everything they'd shared in the past week would become meaningless.

"I'm not totally sure where Roxanne is," she admitted. "I got an e-mail from her on Thursday night telling me to come home because she needed something from me and her business associates knew where I was anyway. When I received it, I contacted Don right away."

"Don?"

"The P.I."

"You called this guy in Florida instead of looking across your pillow and talking to me?"

"I didn't want to involve you."

"It can't have escaped you that we *are* involved."

Kira knew he was speaking out of hurt, but she was hurting, too. "You know what I mean. And there was no solid evidence that the sender was really Roxanne. It's pretty easy to appear to be whomever you choose in cyberspace."

"It doesn't matter who sent it. Kira, it was a stone-cold threat."

She nodded. "I know, and I thought I could handle it. Then last night at the beach and again today at the wedding I saw a woman who I think was with the guys at my door in Florida."

"Caucasian, short brown hair, about five foot five, maybe forty years old?" he asked.

She nodded.

Mitch swore. "And you didn't share this with me, either?"

She had no doubt now that he was furious and she definitely wasn't going to ask how he knew about the mystery woman.

He stood. "You haven't changed. I can't friggin' believe it. You haven't changed at all. You're still the same selfish and reckless person, aren't you?"

"That's not fair, Mitch."

"But it's true. Let's put the facts together." He began to pace the small, crowded room. "You flee Florida because your missing partner is involved in something that appears to be criminal. You get an e-mail from her saying her associates know where you are. You get followed and you still don't bother to tell me. What were you thinking?"

"This wasn't some sort of plot against you. This wasn't even about you." She was going to be screaming if she didn't calm down, and she'd given up screaming a couple of years ago.

Kira drew a deep breath, then slowly exhaled before continuing. "When I came to town, I didn't know for sure that anything bad was going on. It could have just been Roxanne taking off on a sudden vacation. God knows she's done it before."

"And the men at your door who scared you so much that you took off? Maybe they were bible salesmen, huh?"

"Once I was gone it didn't feel so ominous anymore. They were there, and I was here."

"And when you discovered they were looking for you? Why not then? Why didn't you come to me then? Kira, you've risked your life!"

"I know." She paused to swipe at a tear beneath her right eye. "At least I do now, but I didn't want to drag you into my mess. Here's the last of it—by accident, I ended up with Roxanne's PDA when I left town. Don thinks there's a hidden file that she wants. And he thinks it has something to do with a big amount of bearer bonds that some drug kingpin's missing."

Mitch gave a humorless laugh. "And I'm not being fair in saying that you're still selfish and reckless? Right."

He walked out of the room. Kira stood there, her arms wrapped around her middle as though she could hold in the pain. A few minutes later she heard Mitch in the bedroom talking to Cal on the phone. She went into the bathroom and gathered some tissues. Sooner or later she was bound to snap, and it wasn't going to be pretty.

Ready for the storm to come, she sat in the living room and waited. Cal arrived about fifteen minutes later with an officer he introduced as Cathy.

"Cathy will be staying here tonight," Cal said to Kira. "It's a precaution, really. I've put in some calls to see if the folks who followed you are from any other law-enforcement branch. Usually we get a courtesy visit when they're around, but not always."

Kira nodded, clutching her stack of tissues. "Okay."

Mitch came from the direction of the bedroom, duffel bag in hand.

"Are you going somewhere?" Kira asked.

He wouldn't meet her eyes. "You'll be safe here."

She didn't even care that she had witnesses to her panic. She just wanted him to stay. "Don't leave me tonight. Please."

"I have to. I can't deal with you right now. I'm ticked off and I've said too much already." He scrubbed a hand over his face. "Tomorrow, okay?" he said, then left.

But he'd forgotten...tomorrow, she'd be gone.

Before Cal took off, Kira said, "Tell Dana I'm really sorry about the walleye."

And that, of all things, was what started the tears coming. Overcooked fish.

MITCH HAD WANTED A MEMORABLE day, and damn but he had gotten it. As he drove the last miles to his brother's country place, Mitch tried to calm enough to think rationally. It was a losing battle.

He pulled up to the lodge, which was really an old barn that Cal had converted into a bachelor's weekend retreat. It sat empty more often than not, since Dana understandably wasn't crazy about the place Cal used to take all his women. Now Cal rented it to hunters during hunting season and loaned it to buddies the rest of the year. Since it was summer and Cal's buddies had been there, at least Mitch was guaranteed a full beer fridge—one of the many marvels of the place.

He unlocked the front door and headed across the slate floors and thick wool rugs straight to the small, glass-fronted cooler under the bar counter. Without much regard for what he was choosing, he pulled a bottle of imported German brew and opened it. Then he stalked to the fireplace and scowled into its empty depths.

He'd really blown it, not connecting the woman in the florist's van with the odd tourist he'd seen on the beach. It should have clicked and it hadn't. He hated being taken by surprise, hated missing things. It wouldn't have changed the outcome of the day, but at least he'd feel better.

He was furious with Kira and furious with himself. Oh, he'd figured maybe she was in a little financial hot water. If it were just a money thing—even one of questionable legality—he could have forgiven her for keeping him on the outside. But to be under siege from threats and still not trust him enough to ask for help?

"Unforgivable," Mitch said. And he damn well meant it, too. A guy had his pride, and his had been supremely violated.

The thing that let him know he was a total sucker? He still loved her, dammit.

He just couldn't bear looking at her.

As soon as Kira had conquered the last of her residual sniffles, she got the number for her father in London. She wasn't thrilled with making the call, but there was no one better to find her a top criminal attorney. Clearly, Mitch was out of the question as a resource.

Kira dialed her dad and gave him the lowdown on how she'd managed to mess up her life in less time than it used to take her to choose a nail-polish color. She was calm and factual about it, inviting none of his I'm-in-charge-now behavior.

Really, he was very obliging considering she'd

been forced to wake him in the middle of the night. He'd even offered to fly home immediately. She'd told him not to change his schedule. Now that she had his help on the attorney front, she could handle the situation.

By midnight she'd finished making her plans for the next day. She was going to leave her car at her parents' lake house and have one of Cal's officers drive her to the Grand Rapids airport, where she would fly to Miami. Waiting there would be the attorney her father had retained. They would then deliver Roxanne's PDA to the Miami police, and Kira would give a statement.

She slept restlessly on Mitch's bed until about five in the morning, when she gave up. Cal arrived at seven, saying he'd take her to the airport himself. When she asked about Mitch, all he'd say was, "You're going to have to give him some time."

Kira's suitcase was loaded into Cal's trunk when Mitch pulled into the drive. Her heart leaped, but then dived when she caught the closed expression on his face.

"I'll take her," he said to Cal.

Cal scrutinized his brother. "You sure?"

"Yeah."

Her suitcase was transferred to Mitch's trunk, and Kira began what she was sure was going to be the longest hour-and-a-half drive of her life. They'd been on the road for nearly forty minutes and were heading east on I-96 before she found the courage to speak.

"I don't want to leave things like this between us," she said. "I can't stand feeling as though you hate me."

Mitch was silent for a moment, then said, "Kira, I don't hate you. I just—"

She knew what words were coming next. "Don't say it."

She couldn't bear hearing that he didn't love her.

"Maybe you could let me explain why I behaved the way I did?" she asked.

"Okay." Kira noted the way his knuckles shone white as he gripped the steering wheel. She was fighting a battle she probably couldn't win, but she had to try.

"I know a lot of people think I've had it easy, but there's a price that comes with being a Whitman. When I was growing up, nothing was unconditional—especially not love. You know my accident when I was sixteen?"

He nodded.

"My dad was furious. I felt like I was being convicted for behavior unbecoming a Whitman. After that I tried so hard to earn his love. I involved him in every decision. I'd follow his every rule until I thought I'd go crazy. Then I'd end up committing some act of rebellion."

She glanced at Mitch, who at least looked as though he was listening. "Of course after each grand rebellion I'd step back in with Dad's plans, which is how I almost ended up marrying Winston. When I realized that I was now going to make two people miserable for life instead of just one, I found the nerve to cut my ties. It was drastic, but it was the only way I'd be strong enough to do it."

"I'm glad you figured it out, but I'm not sure what that has to do with this past week."

"Here's the thing…. When I decided that I needed to stand on my own, I guess I did it with the same passion that I used to devote to being my dad's follower. I hadn't really thought about this until last night, after you left, but now I think I get it.

"By pushing you out of my life, all I did was prove that I'd swung too far in the other direction. I didn't want you to think that I was still the same weak person. Add to that my fear that if you were involved with me, I'd somehow wreck your chances for your dream job. And there we have it, another classic Kira disaster. All of which boils down to I'm really, really sorry."

He nodded. "Thank you. And I'm sorry for spying on you. That was wrong. Dead wrong."

"Flawed person that I am, I've already decided there's nothing I can do but forgive you." Kira watched him as she spoke and thought she might have even caught a brief smile. She pulled together the rest of her courage and continued.

"So, I guess what I need to know now is whether there's any way you can love me, horrible flaws and all. Because I love you—headbanger music, marshmallow fluff and all."

"Kira…" He shook his head. "Damn, this is hard. I do love you, but I can't live with you. I've never sunk to spying on anyone in my life, and it scares the hell out of me that I did it. I don't know who I am with you."

He loved her, *but*…

More conditional love.

"I see," Kira said, then turned her attention out the window. The countryside was nothing but a teary blur. She didn't speak again, except to tell Mitch which airline she was flying out on. Mitch offered to come into the terminal with her, but she told him it wouldn't be necessary. He pulled up to the curb, switched off the car and got her belongings from the trunk.

She meant to thank him coolly, then walk away. Love got the better of her, though. "I don't suppose I could have one last hug? I really need it."

He wrapped her in his arms. Her heart turned over when she felt him kiss the top of her head.

"It's been interesting, Highness. With you, it's always interesting."

Ten days later…

KIRA HAD HAD ENOUGH OF "interesting" to last her a dozen lifetimes. When she'd been met at the airport in Miami, her new attorney had informed her that she'd be speaking to the FBI, not the local police. With the international flow of bearer bonds and the activity of the drug cartel involved, the case was under the federal government's jurisdiction.

It seemed that Cal's instincts had been correct. The woman who'd been following Kira wasn't one of Roxanne's associates but a federal employee. And Kira had been followed for months before she'd even noticed. That at least gave her some comfort about the FBI's skill level.

The thugs who she'd seen at her door weeks earlier were just that, at least. And as of this morning all of them were under arrest. It was also the first morning she'd actually had time to go back to work.

She'd spoken to her staff, telling them she'd understand if anyone chose to leave because she was certain that listings were going to die off until the publicity cooled, but it was her intention to continue the business. She knew a few of the more aggressive agents would jump ship quickly, but a few would also stay. Susan had made it clear that she'd be at the front desk as long as Kira would have her. As soon as Kira could afford it, she planned to repay Susan's loyalty by helping with her college expenses.

Kira closed her office door and phoned Mitch, thinking he deserved an update after the hell she'd put him through. She wasn't nervous about calling, since she didn't really expect to catch him. He was seldom home, according to Cal, who'd called yesterday to check on her. Still, after she dialed, Kira took a stupid sort of comfort in knowing that up in Sandy Bend the phone was ringing in the Dollhouse Cottage.

"Hello?" a male answered after the fifth ring.

Kira was tempted to hang up but instead collected herself enough to say, "Mitch?"

There was a brief pause before he said, "Kira, is that you?" His voice sounded almost rusty.

"Yes. I—I thought maybe you'd like to know what's going on down here."

She got another pause, then he said a quiet "Sure."

Kira gripped the phone tighter and closed her eyes. She hadn't thought it would be this hard to hear his voice again. This heartbreaking.

"They arrested Roxanne today. From what my attorney has been able to piece together, I guess Roxanne had been operating a money-laundering business, buying and delivering bearer bonds. On top of that, she was in huge debt. She decided to keep a few of the bearer bonds that she was supposed to deliver, figuring she'd just take the money and flee the country. She wasn't fast enough. When the owner's associates picked her up that day, she told them I had the bonds."

"Nice," Mitch said.

"I get the feeling she wasn't too fond of me," Kira joked, though once she had, she wished she could pull the words back. She wasn't sure Mitch was too fond of her, either. "Anyway, she gave up on that after a few hours and admitted that the bonds were in a safe at a storage facility, except she was so freaked out, she couldn't remember the combination to the safe. It was in the PDA—"

"Which you'd accidentally taken," he filled in.

"So, anyway, Roxanne's in jail, the owner of the bonds and his enforcers have been arrested, and now I get to untangle my life."

"I'm glad you're safe," he said.

That, she supposed, was a start.

"How are you?" she asked.

"Tired. School's a bitch and I haven't been sleeping well."

Her throat grew tight. "Me, either."

"I miss you," he said, "and I don't like missing you."

"Maybe if you came down for a visit…?"

Her tentative offer was met by silence. "I don't think I can do that," Mitch finally said.

"Then, you take care of yourself," Kira replied because there was nothing else left to be said.

"You, too. 'Bye."

And with that, it was over.

Kira looked out her window at the action on the street. People strolled and laughed. Cars drove past, filled with even more souls busy living life. She couldn't be the only one with a broken heart, yet she was letting it conquer her.

She turned from the window. It was time to forget the Dollhouse Cottage and the first man she'd ever loved. It was time to get on with life.

15

Four months later…

GRAY WASN'T ROXANNE'S BEST color. As Kira's ex-partner was led from the courtroom following her sentencing, her suit and skin had taken on the same hue. Kira wasn't surprised. Roxanne had accepted a plea agreement—seven years in exchange for her full cooperation in the cases pending against her associates. According to Kira's attorney, the sentence was far less than what Roxanne could have served. She'd be relatively young when released. But Kira knew that for Roxanne it might as well be a lifetime. She'd be ready for BOTOX and her first tummy job by the time she hit the street and she wouldn't have the money to pay for it.

Roxanne glanced back over her shoulder at the gallery, and her gaze locked with Kira's. It wasn't a friendly or even a regretful look. Again Kira wasn't surprised. Roxanne had decided early on that her legal troubles were Kira's fault. If Kira hadn't mixed up the PDAs, she wouldn't have been caught. The fact that Roxanne had been under surveillance for months prior to the mix-up couldn't shake her from this conviction. Kira didn't care. Roxanne was no longer her problem. And those problems that she did have, she'd never stubbornly insist on bearing alone again. She'd learned *her* lesson, just too late.

Kira walked from the chill of the air conditioned federal building and into the strong Miami sun. She still loved this area and knew that she would continue to build a satisfying and busy life here. She just regretted that it was a life alone.

HOT, SWEATY AND TOTALLY NOT acclimated to the Florida sun, Mitch tugged at the collar of his polo shirt. If he'd had a plan, right now he could be saying that he'd met with an unexpected complication. But he didn't have a plan, other than knowing that he'd had enough.

Enough of finding his bed too big and his life too empty.

Enough of doubting himself.

Enough of wondering nearly every damn minute of the day what Kira was doing.

Now he knew that at least one of the things she was doing was waving at the guard outside her damn gated community.

"This gonna take much longer?" the cabbie asked as Mitch considered yet another approach to wheedle his way past the guard.

"Doesn't matter. The meter's running, isn't it?" Mitch replied.

The cabbie muttered something, then pulled out his cell phone and began to talk to someone in a Spanish so fast that even Mitch, who was fluent, couldn't catch it.

The guard—a middle-aged man with a uniform so starched that it hurt to look at it—wasn't receptive to logic, the sight of Mitch's Sandy Bend Police shield or begging. The best Mitch could figure to do was make the guard feel involved in the situation so he might show some level of empathy.

Mitch gave the guard his best I'm-a-trusted-member-of-the-community smile. "Mind if I step out so we can talk?"

The guard backed into his shack, reminding Mitch of a hermit crab. "Stay in the car, sir."

Mitch took his hand off the door handle. "Look, I appreciate that you're doing your job and that my name's not on the list." He gestured at the guard's clipboard. "But there must be some process for the times when a homeowner forgets to leave word."

"I can call Miss Whitman," the guard offered.

"I already told you, I'm trying to surprise her."

"Sorry, then. You'll have to move along."

"I didn't come here all the way from Michigan just to 'move along.' Is there another contact listed?"

"Her office," the guard said grudgingly.

"Perfect! Now, if you'd just let me borrow your phone?" He opened the car door.

The guard closed the lower half door to his little white shack. "Stay *in* the car, sir!"

"Then you call Susan—she's the receptionist. And—"

"I don't think so, sir."

Mitch was losing patience. Susan knew he was coming. The only rational step he'd taken was calling Kira's office yesterday to confirm that she was in town.

"Fifty bucks to make a call," Mitch said to the cabbie, who was still talking away.

"Seventy-five," the cabbie shot back.

"Done."

After that, it was magic. The guard took the phone, confirmed it was Susan and agreed to let Mitch in. Slowly the gate rolled back. Mitch relaxed. He was almost home.

KIRA HAD NEVER SEEN SUSAN behave so oddly. She'd barely gotten in the door from Roxanne's sentencing and her receptionist/assistant was trying to push her back out. Kira might have to rethink that assistant role if this was the help she'd be getting.

Susan lingered in Kira's office doorway, unwilling to leave. "It's been a really stressful day for you. I think you should go home and relax."

"I've got work to get through," Kira said.

"So take it home and do it by the pool. You've got this wonderful new house and you've barely taken the time to unpack."

"No big deal. I've covered the essentials."

Susan stalked toward Kira's desk, then braced her hands on it. Her threatening stance would have worked a little better if she weren't grinning. "You're not getting this, are you? Let me repeat, you *need* to go home."

"And you *need* to get your blood pressure checked or something. You're not usually this crazed." Kira began tucking papers into her briefcase. "I don't know what's up with you, but I'll go home just to get some peace."

Susan laughed. "I knew you'd see it my way."

As Kira drove home, she considered how far she'd come in rebuilding her life. It had been a miserable few months proving that the company hadn't profited from Roxanne's extracurricular activities, and the stakes had been high. Kira would have had to forfeit the business as Roxanne had her precious Porsche, her home and her freedom.

Kira had been smart enough to know that she couldn't survive those rocky months on her own. She'd gone to her father and worked out the financing arrangements to have Whitman Enterprises invest. It was an arm's-length transaction—no strings, no manipulation, just one businessperson negotiating with another. She was now Whitman Enterprises' southern branch, and so long as her numbers stayed good, life would be golden.

It felt wonderful being back in the family fold—better than she'd thought possible. She'd invited Steve and Hallie down for a visit during Steve's winter break. They had accepted, and Kira was already excited.

Kira pulled her car into the driveway of the house she'd bought as soon as her finances had been in the clear. Rose Cottage was a 1920s guesthouse to a larger property that had been razed years before, making way for a small, gated community.

Her home was little more than eleven hundred square feet, but for one very heartfelt reason, she'd fallen in love with it at first sight. Rose Cottage was Mitch's Dollhouse Cottage done Florida-style. The house's stucco glowed a warm pinkish-white in the afternoon sun. The sight of her one extravagance— a small stained-glass inset above the front door— made her smile grow.

Kira stepped out of the car and was assailed by music. Her first thought was that she was in deep doo-doo, since the noise was decibels and decibels above what the community rules permitted. Her second thought was that she didn't care.

The music blasting from Rose Cottage wasn't hip-hop or techno or even country. It was pure, unadulterated headbanger rock, still popular with only one person she knew: Mitch.

She grabbed her briefcase and headed to the front door. A note had been taped there. Welcome home, it read. Step inside.

Attached to the mirror in the front entryway was another note reading Look down. On the small console table beneath the mirror was a gift. Open me said its tag.

Kira's hands shook as she peeled back the flowery wrapping paper that had been stuck together with about two yards too much tape. Finally inside she found a red velvet box.

She opened it and had to stop herself from getting all weepy. Over the necklace was yet another note. This has been waiting for you.

Kira set aside the note and gently lifted the necklace from its white silk bed. It took a few tries to get it on and the clasp closed, but she eventually managed. When she had it in place, she took a moment to settle her hand over the gold-set diamond and make a silent promise to Mitch's mother that she would take the very best of care both of the necklace and of Mitch.

Speaking of whom…

"Mitch?" she called, but then realized that the music was more muted in the house than it had been outside. She hurried to the patio door, then stopped before opening it, overwhelmed with love and relief and even a good case of nerves.

Dressed in a black bathing suit, he was stretched out in a lounge chair by the pool, sunglasses on, books and papers all around him.

"Don't screw this up," she muttered to herself, then went outside to join him. First stop was to the portable stereo he'd plugged in by the back door. He looked up when she turned down the volume. Mitch pulled off his sunglasses.

As she neared, what she saw in his eyes gave her the courage to be calm. She saw doubt, worry and apology. But most of all she saw love.

"Hey," he said, setting aside the notebook he'd been paging through. "You're home early. Susan said you usually came home around six."

"Let's just say I got hurried along."

When she drew close enough, he pulled her on top of him. He smelled of sunblock and salty skin, and because she couldn't resist, she kissed him. Once their mouths touched, the control they'd both been holding on to so tightly let go. One kiss became a dozen—deep, searing and unending—yet it still wasn't enough. Mitch whispered hot words of desperation, of how much he missed her and burned for her. And then he said the words she wanted most: "I love you."

Kira held her breath, waiting for that *but....* When it didn't come, she rejoiced. "I love you, too. I have since...well, since I figured out *how* to love."

After giving her another kiss, Mitch resettled her so they were facing each other, tucked tightly together in the lounge chair. He brushed a stray lock of hair from her forehead.

"Once I got past acting like a wounded animal, I spent a lot of time thinking over the past few months," he said. "The way I see it, the only thing that messed us up last time was a whole lot of pride. You wanted to prove you could stand alone and I was busy trying to prove I could control the woman who'd spent her teenage years stomping on my heart."

"But—"

He kissed her silent. "I know—we've both changed. You showed me that when I drove you to the airport back in June. You tried to let me in, but I was still too hurt and full of myself to understand what you were doing. I've checked my ego at the door, Kira, and I'd like to stay if you'll have me. I plan to take the Florida bar exam in February, then find myself a job—eventually as a federal prosecutor but until then whatever I can get. I'm going to be underfoot a lot until then. Do you think I'll fit in your life here?"

She smiled, glancing back at her tiny Rose Cottage. "I'll tell you exactly how we're going to fit. Hot..." She kissed him once. "Tight..." This time he kissed her. "And perfect," she finished.

And because Kira Whitman was an independent woman of her word, that's exactly how it worked out.